PENGUIN  CLASS

THE EROTIC POEMS

ADVISORY EDITOR: BETTY RADICE

PUBLIUS OVIDIUS NASO was born in 43 BC at Sulmo (Sulmona) in central Italy. He was sent to Rome to attend the schools of famous rhetoricians but, realizing that his talent lay with poetry rather than politics, he began instead to cultivate the acquaintance of literary Romans and to enjoy the smart witty Roman society of which he soon became a leading member. His first published work was *Amores*, a collection of short love poems; then followed *Heroides*, verse-letters supposedly written by deserted ladies to their former lovers, *Ars Amatoria*, a handbook on love, *Remedia Amoris*, and *Metamorphoses*. Ovid was working on *Fasti*, a poem on the Roman calendar, when in AD 8 the emperor Augustus expelled him for some unknown offence to Tomis on the Black Sea. He continued to write, notably *Trista* and *Epistulae ex Ponto*, and always spoke longingly of Rome. He died, still in exile, in AD 17 or 18.

PETER GREEN, M.A., Ph.D. (Cantab), F.R.S.L., was born in London in 1924, and educated at Charterhouse and Trinity College, Cambridge, where he took first-class honours in both parts of the Classical Tripos (1950), winning the Craven Scholarship and Studentship the same year. After a short spell as a Director of Studies in classics at Cambridge he worked for some years as a freelance writer, translator and literary journalist, and as a publisher. In 1963 he emigrated to Greece with his family. From 1966 until 1971 he lectured in Greek history and literature at Athens; he is now the Dougherty Centennial Professor of Classics in the University of Texas at Austin. His publications include *Essays in Antiquity* (1960), *Alexander the Great* (1970), *Armada from Athens: The Failure of the Sicilian Expedition, 415–413 BC* (1971), *The Year of Salamis, 480–479 BC* (1971), *The Shadow of the Parthenon* (1972), *A Concise History of Ancient Greece* (1973), three historical novels, *Achilles his Armour* (1955), *The Sword of Pleasure* (1957) and *The Laughter of Aphrodite* (1965), a historical biography, *Alexander of Macedon 356–323 BC* (1974), *Classical Bearings: Interpreting Ancient History and Culture* (1989) and, most recently, *Alexander to Actium: The Historical Evolution of the Hellenistic Age* (1990). He has also translated Ovid's *The Poems of Exile* and Juvenal's *The Sixteen Satires* for the Penguin Classics.

OVID

THE EROTIC POEMS

THE AMORES
THE ART OF LOVE
CURES FOR LOVE
ON FACIAL TREATMENT
FOR LADIES

TRANSLATED WITH AN INTRODUCTION
AND NOTES BY PETER GREEN

PENGUIN BOOKS

PENGUIN BOOKS

Published by the Penguin Group
Penguin Books Ltd, 27 Wrights Lane, London W8 5TZ, England
Penguin Books USA Inc., 375 Hudson Street, New York, New York 10014, USA
Penguin Books Australia Ltd, Ringwood, Victoria, Australia
Penguin Books Canada Ltd, 10 Alcorn Avenue, Toronto, Ontario, Canada M4V 3B2
Penguin Books (NZ) Ltd, 182–190 Wairau Road, Auckland 10, New Zealand

Penguin Books Ltd, Registered Offices: Harmondsworth, Middlesex, England

This translation first published 1982
9 10 8

Copyright © Peter Green, 1982
All rights reserved

Printed in England by Clays Ltd, St Ives plc
Set in VIP Plantin

CONTENTS

LIST OF ABBREVIATIONS

Aesch.   Aeschylus (525 or 524–456 BC), Greek tragedian.
Prom.: *Prometheus*

Apollod.   Apollodorus, Greek mythographer (?1st or 2nd cent. AD)

Appian   Appianos of Alexandria: Roman-naturalized Greek historian and *procurator Augusti* (2nd cent. AD)
Bell. Civ.: *Bella Civilia* (= bks 13–17 of his *Romaika*)

Apul.   Apuleius of Madaurus (2nd cent. AD), African-Roman writer and rhetorician
De Mag.:   *Pro se de Magia* (or *Apologia*)
De Orthogr.: *De Orthographia*

Aratus   Aratus of Soli (*c.* 315–240 or 239 BC), Greek Hellenistic poet
Phaen: *Phaenomena*

Cic.   Marcus Tullius Cicero (106–43 BC), Roman writer and statesman
De Div.: *De Divinatione ad M. Brutum*

Dio Cass.   Cassius Dio Cocceianus of Nicaea (2nd–3rd cent. AD), Roman statesman and historian

Diod. Sic.   Diodorus Siculus of Agyrium (*fl* 1st cent. BC), Greek historian

Hes.   Hesiod (*fl.* 8th–7th cent. BC), early Greek didactic poet
Theog.: *The Theogony*

Hom.   Homer (*?fl.* 8th cent. BC), Greek epic poet
Il.:   *The Iliad*
Od.: *The Odyssey*

Hor.   Horace (Quintus Horatius Flaccus) 65–8 BC, Roman poet

Juv.   Decimus Iunius Iuvenalis (AD ?55–?140), Roman satirist

Ovid	Publius Ovidius Naso (43 BC–AD 17 or 18), Roman elegiac and didactic poet (see Introd., *passim*)
	AA, Ars: *Ars Amatoria*
	Am.: *Amores*
	EP: *Epistulae ex Ponto* (*Black Sea Letters*)
	Fast.: *Fasti*
	Her.: *Heroides*
	Met.: *Metamorphoses*
	MF: *Medicamina Faciei Feminae* (*On Facial Treatment for Ladies*)
	RA: *Remedia Amoris* (*Cures for Love*)
	Tr(ist).: *Tristia* (*Poems of Lamentation*)

Ovidiana   N. I. Herescu (ed.), *Ovidiana: Recherches Sur Ovide*, Paris, 1958

Pers.   Aulus (?Aules) Persius Flaccus (AD 34–62), Roman satirist

Plin., *Epp.*   C. Plinius Caecilius Secundus (AD *c.* 61–*c.* 112), Roman lawyer, administrator and writer: the *Epistulae* in nine books form his public and literary correspondence

Plin., *HN*   C. Plinius Secundus (AD 23 or 24–79), uncle of the foregoing: published *inter alia* the *Historia Naturalis* in 37 books

Prop.   Sextus Propertius (between 54 and 47 BC–? before 2 BC), from Assisi in Umbria, Roman elegiac poet

Quint.   M. Fabius Quintilianus (?AD 30–35 to *c.* 100), Roman scholar and rhetorician
    Inst. Orat.: *Institutio Oratoria*

Sen. *Controv.*   L. Annaeus Seneca (the Elder) (*c.* 55 BC–*c.* AD 40), Spanish-born Roman historian and rhetorician, author of *Controversiae* and *Suasoriae*

Sen.   L. Annaeus Seneca (the Younger) (*c.* AD 1–65), son of the above, Roman philosopher and tragedian
    De Benef.: *De Beneficiis*
    De Const.: *De Constantia Sapientis*

Stob.   Joannes Stobaeus (John of Stobi), anthologist (?5th cent. AD)

Suet.   C. Suetonius Tranquillus (AD *c.* 69–*c.* 130), Roman imperial administrator and author of *Lives* of the Caesars from Julius Caesar to Domitian

LIST OF ABBREVIATIONS

	Calig.:	*Caligula*
	De Gramm.:	*De Grammaticis*
	Div. Aug.:	*Divus Augustus*
	Div. Jul.:	*Divus Julius*
Tac.	Cornelius Tacitus (AD *c.* 56–*c.* 120), Roman historian	
	Ann.:	*Annales*
	Dial.:	*Dialogus de Oratoribus*
Tib.	Albius Tibullus (b. *c.* 50 BC), Roman elegiac poet	
Vell. Pat.	Velleius Paterculus (*c.* 19 BC–AD 30–35?), Roman soldier and historian of Campanian descent	
Virg.	P. Vergilius Maro (70–19 BC), Roman pastoral and epic poet	
	Aen.:	*Aeneid*
	Ecl.:	*Eclogues*
	Georg.:	*Georgics*

PREFACE AND ACKNOWLEDGEMENTS

This book has been a long time in the making: so long, indeed, that even the saint-like patience of my editor and mentor, Betty Radice, has at times come dangerously close to breaking-point. Yet in many ways the delay – not that either of us could have foreseen this – proved beneficial. When I was writing about Ovid in the late 1950s his reputation, though on the rise again – Patrick Wilkinson's enthusiastic reappraisal in *Ovid Recalled* (1954) did a lot to help the process of recovery – still remained peripheral and uncertain. Today, twenty years later, his star is triumphantly reestablished in the poetic firmament. Structuralists, symbolists and rhetoricians have combined with more traditional critics to achieve his literary rehabilitation: one more metamorphosis for that eternally Protean creative spirit. The slow progress of my own task meant that I was able to take account of much seminal work (some of it very recent indeed) that has marked the Ovidian revival. Formal thanks to all the scholars whom this book has laid under contribution would require more space than an already over-lengthy text can well spare, and selection would be invidious. In one area, however, I am glad to break my own rule, and to name names. As a translator I owe a quite incalculable debt to the fundamental work done on the text of Ovid's erotic poems by Franco Munari, G. P. Goold and, above all, by my old friend E. J. Kenney, now Kennedy Professor of Latin at Cambridge, on whose Oxford text the present version is based.

For the record, I note here those occasions on which my readings differ from those of the Oxford text: *Am.* 1.2.12, 1.3.24, 1.4.7, 1.6.25, 1.7.33, 1.8.50, 1.9.5, 1.10.5, 30, 57, 1.11.18, 1.13.19, 33–4, 39, 1.14.25, 1.15.25, 2.1.5, 2.5.5, 2.6.27–8, 2.7.25, 2.9.1–2, 2.11.9, 2.15.11–12, 24, 2.17.24,

2.18.26, 2.19.7, 20, 52, 3.1.53, 56, 3.2.5, 3.3.14, 17, 3.7.55, 3.9.29, 37, 40, 3.10.39, 3.12.13, 29; *AA* 1.2.114, 118, 133, 234, 255, 439, 515, 553, 730, 747; 2.196, 300, 307, 317, 356, 589, 590, 611, 612, 647, 689–90, 700; 3.155, 169, 170, 231, 241, 269, 270, 282, 288, 295, 299, 364, 440, 454, 455, 476, 486–90, 594, 629, 742; *RA* 65, 123, 135, 161, 221, 268, 284, 351, 364, [?407], 446, 467, 704, 713, 756; *MF* 27-8, 35, 51, 60, 98. Originally my notes contained full reports on these and other textual problems; but such discussions, together with all specific references to modern scholarship on Ovid, have been, of necessity, excised in order to reduce this book to an economically viable length. It should not be assumed, from either my notes or my Select Reading List (p. 429), that I have not faced the problems, or familiarized myself with the scholarship. I plan to return to such matters elsewhere. Meanwhile, experts will at once recognize my debts, and other readers should remember their existence. To all those whose labours in this field have supported my own work, my profound thanks, and apologies for an apparent lack of academic courtesy as unwelcome as it is involuntary.

Until Professor Barsby edited Bk 1 of the *Amores*, Mr A. S. Hollis Bk 1 of the *Art of Love*, and Mr A. A. R. Henderson, even more recently, the *Remedia Amoris*, there was no commentary whatsoever on these poems available in English, and no full, up-to-date commentary in any language. It is, therefore, my hope that the present volume, besides offering a translation that takes account of recent important scholarship in the field, will also be of some use to students.

Many friends, colleagues and students, in the University of Texas and elsewhere, have contributed materially to my work, often during various courses, lectures and seminars held over the years, from which I invariably learnt at least as much as I imparted, and which at times led me substantially to modify my views. To Mr Joseph Casazza in particular I owe a debt of gratitude for drawing my attention to the possible presence and influence of Ovid's mysterious first wife in the *Amores*. Professor Kenney corresponded with me about various problems of reading and interpretation, and Sir Ronald Syme on the matter of Ovid's exile. The late Professor Gilbert Highet gave the original (and very different) draft of my introductory remarks on Ovid's *persona* a most searching and beneficial scrutiny. From M. Andrej and Mme Halina Pradzynski I obtained invaluable expert advice regarding Ovid's knowledge of cosmetic preparations. The librarians of the American School of Classical Studies in Athens, and the Classics Library and Main (now the Perry-Castañeda) Library in the University of Texas at Austin have given me every possible assistance throughout. My Penguin Classics editor, Betty Radice, deserves special thanks for her resolute patience and faith against odds: I only hope she thinks the waiting was worth it. She must also take full credit for the skilful abridging of what turned out to be a prohibitively lengthy MS.

Serendipity also played its part. A chance meeting in Ottawa, at a crucial late stage in my research, enabled me to read Dr Caroline Callway Preston's long, subtle and infinitely perceptive poem about Ovid, passages from which etched themselves indelibly on my memory, and in many ways illuminated my quest for the poet's elusive personality (besides casting a cold incidental light on the habits of critics). If I now find Ovid 'a single real person' rather than a mere bundle of irreconcilable masks, if I agree that

> contrary
> To what you may read somewhere else, he's so human he tears you
> Apart, he's immensely creative, he's far more complex,
> Far wider in vision and tougher than most people think,

that is, to a very large degree, Dr Preston's doing, and I would like to express my gratitude to her for so generously sharing her vision with me. It is, perhaps, not without interest that she is a research scientist rather than a classical scholar.

But one debt stands out above all the rest, and that is to my wife Carin. Almost every line translated here I have discussed with her over the years till it is hard to remember just where her ideas or insights end and mine begin. Her keen ear for the nuances of the Latin language, her shrewd understanding of political and psychological realities, and her delicate feeling for the poetic *mot juste* have contributed more to this book than I find it easy to express. Above all, she has sustained me throughout the long haul with a blend of encouragement, affection and pungent criticism that offered stimulus and correction, by turns, at the precise moments when each was most needed. What I owe to her is incalculable. This final version, with all its faults – *quidquid hoc libelli, qualecumque* – is hers: a poor return for so much, but at least a labour (appropriately for Ovid) of love.

Austin, Texas   P. M. G.
December 1981

INTRODUCTION

I

We can reconstruct Ovid's life in more detail than that of any other Roman poet: a fortunate accident, since his life and his work are interrelated in a peculiarly complex fashion. Whatever our beliefs concerning the relation of person to *persona* in his poetry (see below, p. 59), it cannot be denied that the work of Ovid's earlier years provided at least the official excuse (p. 49) for his exile from Rome to the Black Sea, while his life as an exile provided the material – and the stimulus – for his two final collections of verse. So intimate a connection between life and art has its hazards, which Ovidian scholars have not always fully appreciated. The famous autobiographical poem (*Tr.* 4.10) is a selective and schematized account of Ovid's familial background and poetic career, remarkable as much for what it omits as for what it includes. While it is true that, because of Ovid's own testimony, we do not have to rely exclusively on later hearsay from such witnesses as Suetonius or St Jerome, this comes as a mixed blessing: the poet's artful self-portrait sets almost as many puzzles as it solves. The line between selective fact and creative fiction is always a narrow one, and never more so than in the case of a poet or novelist who draws his chief material from the details – however transmuted – of his own life. Thus it becomes more than usually important to begin by establishing Ovid's *vita*, since this will then give us some sort of a pattern against which the creative *persona* can be evaluated. The two, as we shall see, are often more nearly identical than modern criticism is disposed to admit.

Like almost every other Roman poet, Ovid was not a native of Rome. Publius Ovidius Naso, to give him his full name – the cognomen Naso means 'Nosy': a relative of Ovid's bore the corresponding title of Ventrio, i.e. 'Pot-belly' – came from

15

Paelignian stock. The Paeligni dwelt on the east side of central Italy, about ninety miles from Rome, occupying a stream-fed upland valley, ringed by mountains, in what is now known as the Abruzzi. The lush fertility of this enclosed plateau contrasts sharply – now as in Ovid's day – with the snow-capped peaks and wild forests that surround it. The Paeligni, tough Italian peasants and (surprisingly for such an area) excellent horsemen, had had generally good relations with Rome under the Republic. However, during the general insurrection of Rome's allies known as the Social War (90–88 BC), the first rebel capital was established at Corfinium, in Paelignian territory, and the Paeligni fought valiantly for the Italic cause; but when they surrendered they were at once granted Roman citizenship. At the outbreak of the Civil War, in February 49 BC, another Paelignian *municipium*, Sulmo, tipped the scales in Caesar's favour by opening its gates to Mark Antony, and bringing over seven Pompeian legions; Corfinium, with fifteen, followed suit. The Julian house thus had good reason to be grateful to Sulmo: and when Augustus was searching the Italian *municipia* for notables fit to serve in what he hoped would be a broader-based, more truly representative Roman Senate, Sulmo was one of the towns to which he naturally turned.

Sulmo, now Sulmona, lies down in the flat, rich plain, as Ovid so well describes it (*Am.* 2.16.1–10, *Tr.* 4.10.3–4). The town has been rebuilt since the great earthquake of 1706, but still vividly cherishes the memory of its most famous son, with a blend of fact and fantasy that would have delighted the poet himself. The acronym SMPE ('*Sulmo mihi patria est*' – 'Sulmo is my homeland') appears at the head of official documents, and on many public buildings, in emulation of the more famous Roman SPQR. In the courtyard of the town's chief school, the Collegio Ovidio, Ovid's (medieval) statue is on display, and the ruins of what is claimed to be his family villa lie on a spur above the valley a few miles away. To judge from his poems, what Ovid liked about Sulmo was its lushness: to the mountain landscape, the local *contadini*, he seems to have had an urban, and urbane, indifference. Local gossip retorted, over the centuries, by inventing legends about him (Highet pp. 191–2). He made love to a fairy beside the Fonte d'Amore, the Spring of Love. He sits guarding his treasure in an underground chamber with an iron mace. On the night before the Annunciation he drives through the town in a four-wheeled carriage, making a fearful din, to scare thieves away. And of course, 'Viddie' dared to seduce the Emperor's daughter, and was sent away to Siberia, and died of cold.

When Augustus was considering senatorial possibilities from Sulmo, at some point after 31 BC, Ovid's family, *prima facie*, merited his serious attention. Its members had held Roman citizenship for generations, and were regularly admitted to the Equestrian Order. Unlike so many new *equites*, they had not been recently ennobled by the fortunes of war or the sudden acquisition of wealth (*Am.* 1.3.8, 3.15.5–6; *Tr.* 4.10.7–8; *EP* 4.8.17–18). They were local landowners, of Paelignian stock, reasonably well-off (no equestrian status otherwise: cf. *Tr.* 2.110ff., 4.10.7–8) but thrifty as well as ambitious. The then head of the family, now in his fifties, had two young sons, born exactly a year apart, on 20 March 44 and 43 BC: the younger of these two was the future poet. Here Augustus found – or thought he found – what he had been looking for. The two boys were granted the rank of *equites* (cf. *Tr.* 2.90), in anticipation of their subsequent admission to the Senate and advancement up that political ladder known as the *cursus honorum*. Despite Ovid's own remarks on the subject, this honour was not hereditary, though the sons of *equites* could, it is clear, obtain admission to the Order more easily than most of those who fulfilled the other requirements (e.g. a minimum capital reserve of 400,000 sesterces). It is important to bear Ovid's early political grooming in mind when considering his subsequent career.

II

Ovid and his brother were born in stirring and troubled times, that had witnessed Julius Caesar's assassination and – as Ovid himself reminds us, in order to fix the date (*Tr.* 4. 10.5–6) –

the death of both consuls (A. Hirtius, C. Vibius Pansa) after defeating Antony at Mutina (43 BC). When the victory of Actium, in 31 BC, finally brought peace to a country too long torn and drained by civil war, Ovid was twelve, and newly arrived in Rome (see below): too young to be swept up in the wave of gratitude, relief and enthusiasm that had fired even so essentially private a poet as Virgil; just young enough, a decade or so later, to take the Pax Augusta for granted, even to find it a little *vieux jeu* and. more than a little vulgar. As Auden (probably with Ovid at the back of his mind) wrote in *Letters From Iceland*:

> We were the tail, a sort of poor relation
> To that debauched, eccentric generation
> That grew up with their fathers at the war
> And made new glosses on the noun Amor.

The. propaganda for imperial destiny and moral regeneration that had been developed, with such skill and enterprise, by Maecenas was to make no impression on him. Self-centred, an intellectual hedonist (though interestingly, no *bon vivant*: he preferred to keep his senses sharp), and *engagé* only in the sense of enjoying sophisticated company, this urbane individualist was perhaps the worst possible choice that Augustus, or his representatives, could have made to promote as a potential future senator.

Ovid never mentions his mother (which may or may not be significant) except as the anonymous half of a parental duo, and, finally, to record her death. Since his father was at least forty, and probably older, at the time of Ovid's birth (*Tr.* 4.10.77–82, 93–8, and below, p. 31), she is unlikely to have been his first wife. The boys received their initial schooling at home (*Tr.* 2.343–4), and if, which seems likely, the family followed upper-class Roman tradition, it would have been their mother (Tac. *Dial.* 28) who supplied it until they reached the age of seven. From that point their education would be taken over either by their father, or in the local school. If we can trust one anecdote in a late *vita* of the poet, the former may have been the case. Ovid's father rebuked him severely for scribbling poetry when he should have been doing homework, whereupon the boy exclaimed: *'Parce mihi! nunquam versificabo, pater!'* ('Forgive me, Dad! I'll never write a verse!'). The words, of course, as we might expect (*Tr.* 4.10.19–20, 25–6), form a neat pentameter, with just one dubious quantity to make the impromptu line look more plausible.

At the age of twelve (cf. *Met.* 8.241–3) Roman schoolboys underwent two or more years of secondary education, in grammar, syntax and literature, at the establishment of the *grammaticus*. We do not know whether, in 31 BC, such facilities existed at Sulmo: they had not done so at Arpinum half a century earlier, when Cicero was a boy, nor at Comum even in Tacitus' day (as we learn from the Younger Pliny, *Epp.* 4.13). It seems likely that Ovid's father, who certainly sent his boys to Rome for the next stage of their education, in the so-called 'rhetorical schools' (a misleading title for modern ears), may well, like many other ambitious parents – such as Horace's – have also preferred a Roman *grammaticus* (*Tr.* 4.10.15–16 suggests this).

It is with his transfer to Rome that Ovid first came into direct contact with that influential soldier and statesman Marcus Valerius Messalla Corvinus (64 BC–AD 8), whose client he appears to have been (see below, p. 35). In addition to his public career, Messalla was an orator, a historian and a literary dilettante, the patron of a group of poets that included Tibullus, Sulpicia and – till the success of the *Monobiblos* led Maecenas to make overtures to him – Propertius. The patronage of Messalla, and the support he gave his young protégé's early poetical efforts – a welcome counterweight, no doubt, to the pragmatic disapproval expressed by the boy's father – formed a crucial factor in determining the course of Ovid's future career. Once he had joined Messalla's circle, realized the obsessional quality of his devotion to the poet's calling and sensed his potential creative powers, the final issue was never really in doubt.

From now on he spent more and more of his time in literary pursuits, to the horror of his father, who reminded him tartly that there was no money in poetry, that even Homer died a poor man (*Tr.* 4.10.21–2). The picture is a familiar one: it calls to mind (of all people) the rag-merchant Echion in Petronius' *Satiricon* (§46), discussing his own son's education: 'I've just bought the boy some law books, as I want him to pick up some legal training for home use. There's a living in that sort of thing. He's done enough dabbling in poetry and such like.' Ovid's sense of filial duty, which, as we shall see (below, p. 25), was stronger than many have supposed, made him do his best, very much against the grain, to replace poetry with prose, to train himself as a forceful speaker for the Forum and the law-courts. The frequent use in his work of legal imagery (see pp. 29 and 272) suggests that he may even have studied jurisprudence at home. In about 29 or 28 BC, at the age of fourteen or so, he entered upon the 'rhetorical' phase of his education, about which we have eyewitness evidence from the Elder Seneca (*Controv.* 2.2.1–12, esp. §§ 8ff.). Unlike his brother, who at once displayed a natural talent for oratory and legal debate, Ovid seems (as we might expect) to have exploited the rhetoricians – Arellius Fuscus, Porcius Latro, perhaps L. Junius Gallio, who became his personal friend – for anything that might improve his poetry, while impatiently discarding the rest.

As Higham well demonstrates ((1), pp. 41ff.), the rhetorical quality of Ovid's verse has been much exaggerated, and he seems to have given the rhetoricians at least as much as he got from them. Though Ovid had a habit (Sen. *Controv.* 2.2.8) of versifying Latro's aphoristic tags (cf. *Met.* 13.121–2, *Am.* 1.2.11–12), the process was a two-way one. Within a very few years it was Ovid the poet who had created a stock of erotic commonplaces (*sententiae*) on which would-be declaimers were encouraged to draw (Sen. *Controv.* 3.7.2, 10.4.25). There is no evidence to suggest that he pursued the art of *declamatio* once his education was over, and even during it the set debates (*controversiae*) clearly bored him (*Controv.* 2.2.12). *Even then*, Seneca believed, however pleasant and elegant

Ovid's talent may have been, his speeches were nothing but poetry masquerading as prose (cf. *Tr*. 4.10.26). The details of formal *argumentatio* he found tiresome; his mind worked in essentially poetic terms throughout.

Furthermore, he had already, to judge from our scanty evidence, begun his exploration of the ever-interesting topic – heterosexual passion – that was to engross his creative powers, more or less exclusively, till he was over forty. Seneca quotes at length (*Controv*. 2.2.9ff.) from one *controversia* that he did declaim, in which his main theme was that true love knows neither sense nor moderation, that to weigh one's words and actions, to calculate the odds, is a mark of elderly caution: *sic senes amant*, thus do old men love. Here is adolescent passion *in excelsis*. Because Ovid was no more than seventeen at the time, the significance of this declaration has been generally missed. Boissier, indeed, thought that the young poet thus revealed himself 'already at school . . . what he always was' – a most curious error, when we recall that the deathless passion here advocated is that *between husband and wife*, and set such innocent marital devotion – the world well lost for love – against that cynical exploitation of sex already apparent by the end of the *Amores*, and formalized as a literary seducer's manual in the *Art of Love*. How, and why, this advocate of passionate marriage transformed himself into Rome's self-styled *praeceptor amoris* – and cuckolds' scourge – is a problem that will bear closer examination than it has hitherto received.*

III

While Ovid and his brother were both still students in the rhetorical schools (*Tr*. 4.10.27–30) they assumed the *toga*

---

* At the same time it remains a nice irony that Ovid, the only Augustan poet to suffer official sanctions on moral grounds, was also the only one who ever married – let alone three times. Virgil seems to have been homosexual, Horace liked Greek flute-girls and mirror-lined bedrooms, Tibullus and Propertius suffered, with articulate masochism, under demanding or indifferent mistresses: Ovid may not have been the ideal husband, but at least he tried.

virilis, the garb of manhood, in their case with the broad purple stripe that marked them out as destined for a senatorial career. This step was normally taken, during the Augustan period, at about the age of sixteen, and heralded a privileged youth's entrance to public life, his apprenticeship in the *cursus honorum* of administrative and military service. In Ovid's case this formal recognition of maturity was also the occasion for the first of his three marriages. He was 'given' a bride, he tells us – i.e. his family arranged a match for him – while still 'a mere boy' (*paene puero*, *Tr*. 4.10.69–70). This suggests an early betrothal even by Roman standards. The average age of a girl at marriage seems to have varied between thirteen and sixteen, that of a boy between fifteen and eighteen – see, e.g., Balsdon (1), p. 121 – though the minimum legal age in each case was twelve and fourteen respectively. Ovid, then, will certainly not have been more than sixteen when he married his first wife, perhaps in 27 BC. The marriage, he says, was of short duration (though he does not tell us exactly how long it lasted); and he then goes on – almost forty years after the event – to dismiss his young wife, in one brief, bitter phrase, as 'neither worthy nor useful' (*nec digna nec utilis*).

Such a verdict, when we consider his subsequent reputation, is intriguing enough in itself; but it also needs to be related, chronologically, to the beginning of his literary career. Even before he assumed the *toga virilis* Ovid had been writing poetry (*Tr*. 4.10.19–30), and in this pursuit he was encouraged by his patron Messalla (*EP* 2.3.75–8, cf. 1.7.28–9), through whom he became acquainted with a wide circle of writers and *littérateurs*, including Propertius (see below, p. 32). Scarcely two years after his first marriage, at the age of eighteen or so ('when my beard had only been trimmed once or twice', *Tr*. 4.10.57–60), Ovid gave his first public readings. As he himself tells us (ibid.), the inspiration, and uniting theme, of the poems he then presented was provided by the mysterious girl – never yet convincingly identified, and often regarded as fictional – to whom he gave the pseudonym 'Corinna'. The poems, that is, were early drafts for the

Amores. Ex nihilo nihil fit; and when we have made all possible allowance for literary borrowings and inventive fantasy, it seems an almost irresistible conclusion that Corinna was based, at least in part, on Ovid's mysterious first wife.*

Various hints in the poems themselves tend to confirm such a supposition. It is striking how often Corinna seems to be more easily *available* to Ovid than would normally be the case with a mistress who was another man's wife or *maîtresse en titre*. At siesta-time she comes to his bedroom (1.5), while he is around in hers during the morning to watch her maid dress her hair (1.14.13–30), or, as dawn breaks, to enjoy post-coital slumber (1.13.5–8). He is behind the door, eavesdropping, while the old bawd instructs her on how to catch a wealthy lover (1.8.109ff.). The two of them visit the theatre (2.7.3) and the races (3.2) together. There is even a reference, when Corinna is planning a sea-voyage, to 'the household gods we shared, that familiar bed' (2.11.7–8). A surprising number of the poems acquire extra charm, irony and pathos if we consider their protagonists, not as common-or-garden lovers surmounting the usual social hazards, but as two married adolescents, exploring a booby-trapped world of adult passions and temptations, and playing private games, first with their society, then – *liaisons dangereuses* – with one another, and finally, in Ovid's case, with a literary audience. If we always sense the image, in the *Amores*, of Ovid the husband behind that of Ovid the lover, his marital portraits (e.g. the husband desperately anxious, against all the evidence, to believe his wife, 2.2.56ff.) take on a new dimension: in 3.4 he may even be talking to himself, and the nightmare of marital infidelity in 3.5 – generally regarded as a spurious addition to the canon – acquires a new argument in favour of authenticity. Similarly, if the two abortion poems (2.13,14) describe action by Ovid's wife, rather than

---

* I owe this suggestion to my student Mr Joseph A. Casazza, who has elaborated his *aperçu* – on the whole along rather different lines – in a University of Texas MA thesis, 'Corinna and the tradition of love elegy' (1979).

his mistress, then the narrator's doubts concerning his paternity (2.13.5-6) can be linked to the regular agonized complaints of infidelity in Bk 3, and the whole sequence be seen as arising from the break-up of a marriage rather than the end of an affair.*

If this theory has even an element of truth in it, it would go a long way towards explaining Ovid's psychological and literary metamorphosis during the years that followed. For whatever reason, he never wrote any poems like the *Amores* again: the vein – human or literary – was exhausted. The autobiographical *persona*, however much or little of a fictional construct it may have been, abruptly vanished, to be replaced in due course by that of the urbane and cynical *praeceptor amoris*, the seducers' friend. Only after his exile (see p. 48) did Ovid's special circumstances force him back into drawing on his own life and surroundings as material for his art. The romantic and naïve adolescent who had fallen passionately in love with his own wife (so unsmart: no wonder he kept Corinna's identity secret), and celebrated that relationship with a heartfelt student *controversia* on the irresistibility of marital passion, was soon to learn the agonies of loss and betrayal, the masks with which that hurt could be concealed – and transmuted into art. If 3.5 *is* genuine early work, it shows the mask, for once, slipping: the reduction of the *Amores* from five books to three for a second edition (see p. 267) must have given him the chance, *inter alia*, to excise over-explicit or otherwise tell-tale material. Yet numerous hints remain. Even as it stands, the *Amores* may begin in an unmistakable mood of happy innocence (like that first magical chapter of Hemingway's *A Moveable Feast*), but it ends with innocence lost. Behind the hard-shelled sophisticate of the *Art of Love* we occasionally glimpse the sensitive young lover of the *Amores*, compensating for the wound he had received as a husband by

---

* Casazza (Ch. iv, pp. 41-56) provides a useful survey of the main passages in the *Amores* where Ovid seems to be treating his relationship with Corinna in marital terms : e.g. 1.8.19, 1.14.39, 2.5 *passim*, 2.11.7-8.

a stylized assault on the whole marital condition, a Casanova-like commando raid against fidelity wherever it might be found.

IV

Ovid's first marriage, then, ended at about the same time as his training in the rhetorical schools – that is, when he had turned eighteen and was beginning to achieve public recognition as a poet. Soon afterwards he left Rome for nearly two years, travelling and sightseeing in Greece, Asia Minor and Sicily (*Tr.* 1.2.77–8, *EP* 2.10.21ff., *Fast.* 6.417–24). He makes no mention of this episode in his autobiographical elegy (*Tr.* 4.10). There was nothing unusual, however, about such a period abroad. Young men of good family, then as in the eighteenth century, very often rounded off their formal education by making the Grand Tour, visiting famous Greek sites, and studying for a while at Athens. After his divorce Ovid can hardly have found this change of scene anything but beneficial. We might have expected him and his brother to go abroad together, especially since he speaks (*Tr.* 4.10.31–2) of their closeness; but the brother died suddenly when only just twenty (ibid.), i.e. in the spring or summer of 24 BC, and it is a fair presumption that Ovid left Rome somewhat later.

It would be interesting to know more about Ovid's relationship with his father at this point. From his own account (*Tr.* 4.10.17ff.) it was his brother who satisfied the old man's family ambitions, Ovid who played the literary dilettante. When his brother died, however, Ovid became the sole heir, and was surely, as such, put under even stronger parental pressure to follow a public career. Perhaps he even persuaded his father to finance a Grand Tour by promising that he would, on his return, enter upon the official *cursus honorum*. No one has seriously examined the problem of Ovid's finances and familial obligations, yet they are crucial for an understanding of his life. He was, it is obvious, a *rentier*, living off the income from family capital. But who controlled it? Under Roman law at this period a son, *even after marriage*, remained wholly in his father's *potestas*, and could not hold property in his own right. He lived off an allowance, or sometimes a capital settlement (*peculium*), over which his father retained full jurisdiction. To free a son of this paternal control called for a complex legal device of double emancipation.* Though many fathers doubtless treated their sons' *peculium* 'as being in fact, what it was not in law, the son's absolute property', we have no reason to suppose that this was so in Ovid's case. What little we know of his father suggests a dominating provincial paterfamilias of the old school, tight not only with his own money (*Am.* 1.3.10), but also – to judge from the repeated complaints of poverty scattered through the *Amores* – with his son's allowance. When we consider Ovid's life-style, that is scarcely to be wondered at. As the old man survived to the age of ninety (*Tr.* 4.10.77–8), he must be reckoned a powerful, and enduring, influence in Ovid's life.

At this point, it is clear, he was still willing to risk a further substantial investment in his surviving heir's education, presumably with an eye to long-term political and financial recoupment from Ovid's future senatorial career. That Ovid had benefited financially from his marriage and divorce seems unlikely. At all events he now left Rome, in the company (and under the tutelage) of a poet named Macer, about whom, it is safe to say, we know a good deal less than might be assumed from the standard literary handbooks. Ovid lists him with other contemporary Roman poets (*EP* 4.16.6), and tags him 'Ilian' Macer: from other allusions (*Am.* 2.18.1–3, *EP* 2.10.13 –14) it appears that his *chef-d'œuvre* was a completion of the Trojan cycle dealing with events before and after the *Iliad*, and entitled *The War of Troy* (*Bellum Troianum*: Apul. *De Orthogr.* 18). He seems to have begun his literary career as a love-elegist, like Ovid or Tibullus (*Am.* 2.18.35–40, Tib.

---

* See Balsdon (1), pp. 117–18, with references, for an excellent brief account of this – in every sense – peculiar phenomenon.

2.6.1), only later transferring his attention to military epic. He was related to Ovid's third wife (*EP* 2.10.9–10), a long-term friend of Ovid himself (ibid.) and very probably a member of Messalla's literary circle. He is also supposed, with some plausibility, to have been the old acquaintance addressed in *Tr.* 1.8, on whom Ovid heaped reproaches for lack of sympathy and support at the time of his banishment.

That is all we can say about him with any confidence: it is impossible, on the evidence at our disposal, to identify him more closely. He was certainly *not* Aemilius Macer, the elderly didactic poet who read to Ovid his versified treatises on snakes and herbs (*Tr.* 4.10.44), since this gentleman died in 16 BC, and Ovid's travelling-companion was the addressee of a poem (*EP* 2.10) written in Tomis as late as AD 12–13. Most scholars since John Masson, in the early eighteenth century, have confidently identified him as M. Pompeius Macer, the naturalized Roman son of Pompey's Greek adviser Theophanes of Mytilene; but this ascription, sanctified though it has become by long tradition, and now endorsed by Syme, (2), p. 73, will not do either. Let us look at the evidence for it.

Pompeius Macer wrote a tragedy, *Medea* (Stob. *Flor.* 78.7), plus a handful of epigrams – all, as we might expect, in Greek. If he is the procurator of Asia mentioned by Strabo (13.2.3, C. 618) – and that is far from certain – he will have served there, as Augustus' appointee, from about 20 BC. He seems to have been a successful and ambitious politician, who later acted as Augustus' director of public libraries (Suet. *Div. Jul.* 56.7), and held high office under Tiberius, whose personal friendship he enjoyed (Tac. *Ann.* 1.72). It is improbable, to say the least, that the procurator of Asia – even if the dates squared, which they do not – would spend a year or more of his official time travelling around with Ovid, including a prolonged visit (*EP* 2.10.21–2, 29–30) to Sicily. It is inconceivable that Ovid could have written this man a flattering petition from exile (*EP* 2.10) which wholly ignored both his public career and his Greek literary work, treating him exclusively as an epic, and a Roman, poet –

characteristics nowhere else ascribed to him. The cognomen Macer is, unfortunately for us, an all too common one, and we shall, unless fresh evidence turns up, probably never be able to identify Ovid's friend with any certainty.

The tour seems to have been enjoyable for both of them. Elegiac and epic poet alike had opportunities to pick up local colour, at the site of Troy (*Fast.* 6.417–24), in Athens (*Tr.* 1.2.77), travelling from city to city down the Ionian coast (*Tr.* 1.2.78, *EP* 2.10.21) and, above all, in Sicily, where they spent the best part of a year (*EP* 2.10.29), and which is the only part of his trip that Ovid describes in any detail. The two of them apparently witnessed an eruption of Etna, which had been volcanically active for some years (Virg. *Georg.* 1.471, with Servius ad loc.; Appian *Bell. Civ.* 5.114,117; Dio Cass. 50.8.3). They visited Enna, and the shrine of the Palici near Leontini: both, interestingly, most famous for the slave-revolts that had been started there in the previous century (Diod. Sic. 34–5; 36.3.7, cf. 11.88,90). They travelled by boat and carriage, keeping up a non-stop discussion, as Ovid tells us (*EP* 2.10.33–8), of the most enjoyable sort, from dawn to dusk every long summer day. Years afterwards, from exile, his nostalgia could still evoke their journey in sharp and loving detail.

Ovid was back in Rome by the winter of 23/22 BC, and dutifully set about his planned career. As a prelude to his official duties, he must have studied public administration and law, as all young senatorial aspirants did at this stage, most often under an eminent jurisconsult (Cicero, earlier, had been a pupil of Scaevola): his legal training left its mark on his poetic vocabulary and imagery. This year or two of preparation was known as the *tirocinium fori*; it was normally followed by the *tirocinium militiae* (training for military service) after which the future senator would spend some time as a *tribunus militum*, or legionary staff officer, before resuming his more strictly political career. He would then hold one or more minor administrative offices until he reached the age of twenty-seven, when he became eligible to stand for the quaestorship. These four initial stages in the *cursus honorum*, beginning at the age of nineteen or twenty, thus generally lasted about two years each.

Now the interesting, and significant, point about Ovid's brief period of public life is that he avoided the *tirocinium militiae* altogether (*Am.* 1.15.1–4, *Tr.* 4.1.71). Though this omission may have been legitimate – Ovid hints that he was physically unfit for service (*Tr.* 4.10.37) – it brought him a good deal of adverse criticism, and goes far towards explaining his ambivalent, and somewhat self-conscious, attitude towards the soldier's life, his exaltation of the *militia amoris*. It also may well be the reason for his undertaking more than one vigintiviral office during the next few years. Such minor magistracies were almost certainly regarded as a bore, a mere tiresome stepping-stone to higher things. It is also true that disinclination to fulfil such political or military obligations had become fairly widespread during Augustus' reign. If there was a shortage of suitable candidates, Ovid may well have been glad to help out some more ambitious contemporary, who would doubtless be happier serving *his* apprenticeship as a military tribune on active service.

At all events, after completing his *tirocinium fori*, Ovid, as he tells us, duly held several different legal and administrative positions. He belonged to the three-man board of the *tresviri* (*Tr.* 4.10.34), though whether these were the *monetales* (who controlled the public mint) or the *capitales* (whose business, as Owen charmingly puts it, was 'to execute capital sentences, burn books, etc.') is not made clear; the general assumption that it was the latter may only reflect a Gilbertian instinct among scholars for heavy-handed prescient irony. He also belonged to the *decemviri stlitibus iudicandis* (*Fast.* 4.383–4), a board of ten which under Augustus had supervisory or presidential functions over the centumviral court, and in addition was himself a member of this court (*centumvir*: *Tr.* 2.93–6), which adjudicated in civil actions, mostly property or inheritance suits. Here, like Kipling in naval wardrooms, he picked up a good deal of technical jargon, which later resurfaced as more or less effective metaphor. Lastly, as an *eques* in good standing, Ovid was liable for duty as a *iudex privatus*, or private arbitrator, a responsible position which he prides himself (*Tr.* 2.95–6) on having discharged in an impeccable manner, and which, again, left its mark on his poetic vocabulary.

v

Till he was of age to hold the quaestorship – that is, in 16 BC – Ovid could postpone his final choice between public service and that leisured *vita umbratilis*, 'life in the shade', the poet's vocation (see pp. 37–8) to which he felt himself irresistibly drawn. Exactly how long he continued in the preliminary offices (or, indeed, how much of his time they took up) is uncertain. It seems likely, however, that his duties were not over-demanding, and left ample time for the literary life, since during this period (see p. 39) he composed enough poems to publish, *c.* 15 BC, as the first, five-book, edition of the *Amores*. He may also have preferred to postpone a final showdown with his father as long as possible. 16 BC, in fact, seems to have been a crucial date in his career. It formed a *terminus ante quem* for his decision whether or not to renounce the senator's broad purple stripe, and revert to equestrian status; it heralded his first formal publication as a poet; and, almost certainly, it marked the date of his second marriage. It is hard to believe that these events were not, in some way, causally linked, or that Ovid's father did not play a decisive part in them – perhaps insisting that if his son (spurred on no doubt by the phenomenal success of the *Amores*) insisted on retiring into private life, he should at least do his familial duty by taking another wife and getting an heir. As we have seen, any young man in Ovid's position would be financially (and doubtless emotionally) vulnerable to this kind of pressure.

As it happens, we can determine the date of Ovid's new marriage within fairly close limits. His one child, a daughter, was born to this second wife; she married young, at the earliest possible age (*prima iuventa*); and bore two children, by two successive husbands. At least before the second of these births, and perhaps before both of them, Ovid's father died, aged ninety (*Tr.* 4.10.75–8). Ovid was fifty at the time of his exile (AD 8); if his father had died in that same year, he would have been forty when Ovid was born. In fact, he must have died earlier, since his wife survived him, but both were deceased before the scandal of Ovid's exile broke (*Tr.* 4.10.80 –84). Though not impossible, it is unlikely that the father was much more than fifty when his younger son was born. We can, then, assume that he most probably died at some point between *c.* 5 BC and *c.* AD 5, with a median date of 1 BC or AD 1. If we further assume that Ovid's daughter bore her first child at about the same time, when not more than fourteen – fifteen at the outside – then her own birth will fall *c.* 14 BC on the median date, and in any case neither earlier than 19 nor later than 9. If Ovid was in fact pressured into his second marriage by his father after finally (and as late as possible) rejecting a public career, then the median dates of 16–14 BC for that marriage, and the subsequent birth of a child – which would have been its prime object – fit perfectly on all counts. Ovid's second marriage, like his first, was of short duration; but since he goes out of his way to acquit his second wife of wrongdoing (*Tr.* 4.10.71), it seems highly likely that the union was terminated by death (perhaps in childbirth) rather than by divorce.

It is also reasonable to assume that, on the occasion of his son's remarriage, Ovid's father made a more generous, and more permanent, financial settlement in his favour. Though the marriage itself cannot have brought him any great satisfaction (no male child, and, with the lady's early demise, no hope of one), the death of his elder son must have made it correspondingly easier for him to settle capital on Ovid. Further, the young poet could now demonstrate ten years' literary work in the newly published *Amores*, plus enthusiastic acclaim from an appreciative public. At this point, clearly, Ovid's father capitulated, since Ovid *did*, from now on, devote all his time and energies to the writing of poetry and the social pleasures of the metropolis. (Patronage may also have played its part. It is likely that Messalla contributed to preserving Ovid's financial independence and, hence, his equestrian status.) For about ten years he remained single (see below, p. 41), as he had done during the decade *c.* 25/4–16/15, thus leaving ample scope for any minor liaisons to match those described in the *Amores*, and boasted of at the beginning of the *Art of Love* (1.29–30). How far we can believe Ovid when he claims that no scandal touched his name (i.e. that he was never shown to have committed adultery with a respectable woman, or to have got even a lower-class wife pregnant, *Tr.* 2.349ff.) is a matter for speculation. Equally, how far the 'autobiographical' details he gives are fiction, how far fact, will never be known, though it seems safe enough to assume that they are a mixture of both.

Despite the undoubted social prejudice at Rome against writing – or indeed anything but business, farming, soldiering or law – as a professional career (cf. Fraenkel, pp. 9–10), Ovid had grown up in an age of intense, and often brilliant, literary creativity. When he first began to give public recitations (*c.* 25 BC), Virgil had already published his *Eclogues* (*c.* 37) and *Georgics* (30/29), Horace his *Epodes* and *Satires* (*c.* 30), Propertius the *Monobiblos* (28), and Tibullus Bk 1 of his elegies (*c.* 27). Of these poets Virgil he 'only saw' (*Tr.* 4.10.51); Horace he heard recite, but does not claim as an acquaintance; while his brief friendship with Tibullus was interrupted by one or other of them always being away from Rome, and cut short by Tibullus' premature death in 19 BC. Sextus Propertius, however (b. ? 50 BC, d. before 2 BC), was Ovid's close companion, bound to him by that untranslatable thing, *sodalicium* (Tr. 4.10.46), something both stronger and more formal than 'intimacy' or 'friendship'. Like Ovid, he was a provincial *eques*, a native of Assisi in Umbria; like Ovid again, he abandoned the advocate's profession for that of poet, the more easily in that his father had died during his childhood, and he therefore came into his inheritance – sadly diminished through requisitioning for the veterans of Antony

INTRODUCTION

and Octavian – on attaining his majority (Prop. 1.21, 22; 4.1.127–34). He now established himself in Rome, shortly before Ovid's arrival there as a schoolboy; fell, briefly, in love with a girl named Lycinna (Prop. 3.15.3–6); joined Messalla's literary circle; and, c. 30 BC, became totally infatuated with a woman whose real name, it seems, was Hostia (Apul. De Mag. 15), but to whom in his poems he gave the pseudonym of 'Cynthia', by which she remains better known to this day. She was probably an upper-class married lady (cf. Williams, pp. 529–35) rather than the freedwoman or courtesan of earlier scholarly tradition. The affair, and the poems it generated, must have been familiar to Ovid while he was still an impressionable adolescent. Propertius regularly read Ovid his work (Tr. 4.10.45–6), and Ovid, who had a retentive memory, repeatedly imitates, parodies, adapts or alludes to it in his own poems. This is not surprising. Propertius, too (Syme, (2), p. 188), 'speaks for the primacy of love and poetry'; reveals, indeed, a quietly subversive streak in his work, despite the fashionable imperial trappings he flaunts.

The other minor poets whom Ovid lists (Tr. 4.10.41ff., EP 4.16.5–38) suggest, with some force, the neoteric, post-Hellenistic tradition that preoccupied itself with mythology, didacticism and, above all, literary epic, the latter often a thinly disguised form of political flattery or propaganda. The tradition even developed a polite formula (recusatio) for refusing invitations to publicize and ennoble the exploits, generally military, of important men. The full achievement of Augustan poets such as Horace and Virgil can only be measured in terms of the agitprop pitfalls which they managed to transcend or avoid – as the Georgics and the Roman Odes bear ample witness. It is hard to believe, on the other hand, that Aemilius Macer (see above, p. 27) showed himself any more inspiring on the subject of snakes than did Nicander. Ponticus composed what was doubtless a very dull Thebaid, and Propertius dutifully compares him to Homer (Prop. 1.7.1 –4) 'if only the Fates are kind to his verse' – they weren't, alas; Bassus and his iambics failed even to rate a mention by

Quintilian. The group, like every literary circle the world over, clearly operated by mutual puffing, from which some members benefited more than others. There is something infinitely depressing about the roll-call of forgotten poetasters in Ovid's last published poem (*EP* 4.16; cf. Syme, (2), pp. 105–6): the rehashers of old mythological themes, the imitators of Callimachus, the nationalist drum-beaters and the scribblers of epic esoterica, sedulous pasticheurs, all, churning out that synthetic drivel which Persius and others were to castigate so fiercely half a century later.

VI

It is ironic when we reflect that the young Ovid regarded all these poets, without distinction, or at least said he did, as so many gods on earth (*Tr.* 4.10.41–2): that passage does not read as though written tongue in cheek. It is doubly ironic when we study the enormous social gap that existed between the literary world of Rome (not to mention Ovid's non-literary friends) and those powerful, well-connected, mostly aristocratic patrons on whom that world depended for its support and encouragement. Such support was not always, or indeed chiefly, financial in the strict sense, but rather a matter of social promotion, public relations, influence-peddling: the establishment of a salon, the authoritative endorsement of a reputation, the opening of the right doors. Few things are more striking in Ovid's work than the contrast between the literary-erotic exhibitionist of the *Amores*, the blasé *praeceptor amoris* of the *AA* and *RA*, the manipulator of gods and men in the *Metamorphoses* – a *persona* whose central element is brilliant self-assurance – and the humble petitioner who emerges in the poems of exile (see below, pp. 46ff.), revealing, with uncomfortable precision and clarity, just how socially precarious his position in Rome had always been (cf. now Syme, (2), p. 76). As Owen and others have pointed out, he uses a quite different tone when addressing his patrons from that which marks poems addressed to friends and associates. Significantly, the former are, for the most part, known and identifiable, while his closest intimates – Celsus, Brutus, Atticus, Carus – remain shadowy figures, social and historical ciphers only surviving from time's trash-heap because Ovid happened to mention them. He exalts *probitas* above pedigree (*EP* 1.9.39–40, *Met* 13.140–41), a sure mark of his own milieu.

Among his patrons the most influential was Messalla, who from the beginning encouraged his literary interests, and provided the salon in which Ovid, like Tibullus, could publicize his work to best advantage. M. Valerius Messalla Corvinus (64 BC – AD 8) served as *legatus* to Cassius at Philippi; he then switched his support to Antony, but abandoned him in disgust because of Antony's conduct in Egypt, and finally joined Octavian, holding a key command at Actium (31 BC). In 25, about the time of Ovid's emergence as a poet, he became Rome's first City Prefect, but, for what ever reason, resigned five days later,* devoting himself thereafter to a distinguished career at the bar. He died aged seventy-two, some months before Ovid's exile, and it is just possible that the loss of his powerful advocacy (he had been a close personal friend of Augustus) was what left the poet so fatally vulnerable to denunciation by enemies or rivals (see p. 43).

Messalla's patronage of Ovid was continued, though with differing degrees of enthusiasm, by his two sons, Messalinus and Cotta Maximus – both, we may note, strong supporters of Tiberius (see now Syme, (2), p. 117–34). In the case of Messalinus, a distinguished soldier but a political hack, this support came very close to fawning servility (Tac. *Ann.* 1.8.5, 3.18.3). Ovid did not know Messalinus well, and the poems he addresses to him (*EP* 1.7, 2.2) are couched in tones of the most abject and distant respect. With Cotta Maximus, however, who was about twenty years younger than he was,

---

* Jerome reports him as complaining that the power he exercised was *incivilis*, i.e. unjustifiably autocratic; Tacitus (*Ann.* 6.11.4) remarks, tartly, that he found he couldn't cope with the job. The two versions are not necessarily incompatible.

and whom he had known as a child, Ovid achieved something approaching genuine intimacy: perhaps the nearest he came to such a relationship with any of his patrons (but see below on Graecinus). Tacitus (*Ann.* 6.5,7; 4.20), Persius (*Sat.* 2.72 with schol.) and the Elder Pliny (*HN* 10.57) may dwell on Cotta's luxury, gourmandizing and spendthrift improvidence, but to Ovid he remained the spirit of loyalty and generosity (*EP* 2.3.29, 3.2.5, 103, 3.5.7). Other evidence confirms that this was not mere flattery on Ovid's part. It is interesting that Ovid was with Cotta on Elba in AD 8 (see p. 45) when news of the Emperor's displeasure reached him.

Another influential patron was the rich aristocratic dilettante Paullus Fabius Maximus (? 45 BC–AD 14), patron of literature (Juv. 7.95), the addressee of an ode by Horace (4.1), consul 11 BC, and a close intimate of Augustus: cf. Syme, (2), pp. 135ff. As his client, Ovid attended on him, was admitted to his dinner-table, read him new poems and even composed the epithalamium for his wedding (*EP* 1.2.129–35). Ovid's own third wife (see p. 41) had been a member of Fabius' household: probably a dependant or relative of his wife Marcia (ibid., 136–8), whose maternal aunt was the mother of Augustus. This connection probably also explains Ovid's acquaintance with the wealthy Sextus Pompeius (cos. AD 14), a collateral descendant of Pompey the Great, whose father had married Marcia's younger sister, thus ensuring himself at least a distaff relationship to the Imperial family. Though during Ovid's journey into exile Pompeius afforded him some protection, this does not in itself explain the tone of grovelling humility with which Ovid addresses the great man (see, e.g., *EP* 4.4 and 5, on Pompeius' consulship). The only other patrons whom Ovid mentions by name are two brothers, P. Pomponius Graecinus and L. Pomponius Flaccus, of whom he seems to have known the former somewhat better (cf. now Syme, (2), pp. 74–5, 83). Indeed, their acquaintance dated back to the period of the *Amores*, where (2.10.1–2) we find Graecinus arguing that to love two women at once is an impossibility; though in later years, to judge by the somewhat formal epistles that Ovid addressed to him from Tomis (*EP* 1.6, 2.6, 4.9), they had, perhaps inevitably, drifted apart. Graecinus and his brother (the latter another intimate of Tiberius) seem both (*EP* 1.10.37) to have done what they could to ease Ovid's lot in exile.*

With none of these persons, it is clear, was Ovid truly intimate. His real friends were drawn, as we might expect, from those who shared both his social status and his literary interests: Julius Hyginus, keeper of the Palatine Library (Suet. *De Gramm.* 20), fellow-poets such as Propertius and Macer, Ponticus and Bassus (above, pp. 27, 32–3), or the various scholars, soldiers and minor officials who crop up as recipients of many of the *Black Sea Letters*. Even those closest to him, as we have seen, remain mere names to us, a reminder of how ruthlessly time eliminates all but a fraction of the material essential to reconstruct any social group. All we know about Ovid's companions is what we can glean from his poems: that Celsus (who died during Ovid's exile) had dissuaded him from suicide, and even planned to visit him in Tomis (*EP* 1.9), that Atticus was his inseparable fellow-socialite and most valued critic (*EP* 2.4.13–20), that Brutus acted as his editor and publisher (*EP* 1.1, 3.9; cf. *Tr.* 1.7, 3.14, 5.1; Syme, (2), p. 80), that Carus wrote a poem on Hercules and was tutor to Germanicus' children (*EP* 4.13.11–12, 47–8; 4.16.7–8). Most of these figures moved on the fringes of Roman high society, and were dazzled by its exclusive glamour; none of them truly belonged to it. They were, in essence, middle-class intellectuals. Ovid and Propertius, old-fashioned *equites* from the provinces, probably enjoyed as much social prestige as any of them.

Such was the milieu in which, after renouncing his senatorial career, Ovid settled down to the leisured existence

---

* Ovid also sent hopeful missives (on approval, as it were, like Pindar's 'Phoenician goods') to Germanicus Caesar, Tiberius' nephew, the dedicatee (after Augustus' death) of the *Fasti* (*EP* 2.1), and to the Thracian Cotys, a barbarian prince with a taste for literature (*EP* 2.9); but these were not patrons, much less friends, merely great men to be courted for their potential favours.

of a poet with private means, a literary celebrity and man-about-town. To judge from his total output (see p. 39) he must have had ample time for the pleasures of the metropolis, the dinners and parties, the plays and ballets, days at the races and evenings over wine, of which we get so vivid and kaleidoscopic a picture in the amatory poems. It would be strange, too, if the self-portrait that emerges from the *Amores* and the *Art of Love*, of an urbane gallant with a perpetually roving eye, was an unadulterated fiction. Even if we credit him with unswerving marital fidelity during his brief second marriage, he was very soon fancy-free and on the town once more, sauntering through the shady colonnades, eyeing the flash of an ankle, the lift of a skirt, scanning the crowds in theatre audience or temple congregation for a promising pretty face.

Like many Romans, Ovid preferred to divide his time between town and country, using his house near the Capitol (*Tr.* 1.3.29–30) when socializing, but retreating to his country villa (*Tr.* 4.8.27–8) when he wanted to work in solitude. The latter was conveniently close, only three miles or so outside Rome, on a pine-clad hillside overlooking the junction of the Via Clodia and the Via Flaminia (*EP* 1.8.43–4); Ovid used to write out in his orchard (*Tr.*1.11.37), and much enjoyed gardening for relaxation (*EP* 1.8.45ff., cf. 2.7.69). Sometimes, too, he would make the ninety-mile journey to his father's estate at Sulmo (*Am.* 2.16). But the magic of the city always drew him back; even in exile, he confesses, it is not for the countryside that his heart yearns (*EP* 1.8.41). The nostalgic visions that haunt him are of temples and porticoes, public gardens, formal fountains; the only greensward he misses is that of the Campus Martius (ibid., 35–8). *Urbanitas* was his watchword.

VII

It is noteworthy that, for fifteen years or so, Ovid's rate of production, now he was at last enjoying the *vita umbratilis*, remained almost exactly what it had been during the decade (25–16) that he spent on the *Amores*, i.e. about 500 lines *per annum* of finished work, a figure not strikingly in excess of that achieved by Virgil, and some answer to those critics who accuse him of glib facility in composition. Original drafts certainly accounted for much more: as Ovid himself tells us (*Tr.* 4.10.61–2), he wrote a good deal, but burnt any material that failed to meet his own critical standards. During this period he published *Heroides* 1–15, his lost tragedy *Medea*, and all the material contained in the present volume: his revised three-book edition of the *Amores*, the *Art of Love*, the *Cures for Love* and the little didactic squib (of which only a fragment survives) *On Facial Treatment for Ladies*. But thereafter his production-rate, hitherto remarkably consistent, takes an enormous upward turn. The *Cures for Love* appeared in AD 1. Seven years later, at the time of his relegation to the Black Sea, he had written fifteen books of the *Metamorphoses*, totalling almost 12,000 lines, and six of the *Fasti*, which adds about 5,000 more. On the face of it this represents a jump from 500 to about 2,500 lines *per annum*; and however much we modify this figure – e.g. by treating the *Metamorphoses* as unrevised, and by assuming that work on both the *Metamorphoses* and the *Fasti* had begun long before AD 1 – there still remains a quite extraordinary burst of increased creativity to account for.*

What is more, the scope and subject-matter of his poetry were similarly transformed. There is a symbolic appropriateness, at every level, in his new architectonic, indeed epic, preoccupation with mythological metamorphosis, with 'young girls who watched' (in Caroline Preston's haunting phrase) 'strange feathers beginning to sprout from

---

* After his *relegatio* Ovid's production-rate drops back sharply again, as we might expect, though not to its original level. If to the 6,726 lines of the exilic poems we add the 644-line *Ibis*, we get a total of 7,370: spread over nine years this produces an 819-line average *per annum*. But there were few social distractions in Tomis. Ovid also tells us that he destroyed much of what he wrote in exile (*Tr.* 4.1.101ff., 5.12.61–2).

their delicate fingers'. His antiquarian investigations into the Roman calendar mark a striking change of mood, no less than topic, from that dedicated modernism he had shown in his work as *praeceptor amoris*, when he declared (*AA* 3.121–2): 'Let others worship the past; I much prefer the present, / Am delighted to be alive today', and went on to praise (127–8) modern 'Refinement and culture, which have banished the tasteless/ Crudities of our ancestors'. Above all, though Ovid retained all his old psychological acumen, he now, abruptly, abandoned that vein of fashionable eroticism which he had mined, with obsessional exclusiveness and great popular success, for over a quarter of a century. What lay behind so radical a change of direction, so remarkable an imaginative upsurge of new ideas?

It is, of course, possible that the vein was exhausted: after all, by AD I Ovid had reached his mid-forties, and could hardly go on writing exclusively about sex for the rest of his life. The age of Henry Miller still lay in the future. He may also have been scared off the subject. Augustus' draconian legislation against adulterers, beginning in 18 BC with the *Lex Iulia de adulteriis coercendis* (see pp. 71ff.), had forced him to modify, or at least to camouflage, the earlier elegiac convention of passionate devotion to, and pursuit of, someone else's wife. Hence his repeated, and wholly unconvincing, protestations that he was writing only for freedwomen and courtesans. Worse still, his *Art of Love* was published almost immediately after a scandalous *cause célèbre* involving Augustus' only daughter Julia, who in 2 BC found herself banished to a remote island, ostensibly (see p. 55) because of numerous and flagrant acts of adultery with an assortment of well-connected and politically embarrassing lovers (Vell. Pat. 1.100; Suet. *Div. Aug.* 19.64–5; Dio Cass. 55.10). But neither of these motives quite accounts for the sudden, and brilliant, change of poetic direction represented by the *Fasti* and the *Metamorphoses*. Can we, however tentatively, correlate this phenomenon with some significant change in Ovid's own personal circumstances?

His father's death and his third marriage both fall within the period under discussion. We have already seen (above, p. 31) that Ovid's father probably died *c.* 1 BC/AD 1: that is, about the same time as the publication of the *Art of Love*. When did Ovid remarry? We know that his third wife, by a previous husband, had a daughter who, at some point before AD 16 (Syme suggests AD 12), married P. Suillius Rufus. It is also virtually certain that this girl is the Perilla addressed by Ovid in *Tr.* 3.7, where he reminds her, wistfully, of how, before his exile, he guided her own youthful efforts at poetry.* Thus she must have been fourteen or fifteen, at the least, in AD 8, and born not later than 7 BC: it follows that Ovid is unlikely to have married her mother (unless he acquired her pregnant, as Augustus did Livia) before 6 or 5, and it could have been considerably later. At the time of Ovid's exile his wife must have been at least thirty: five years later we find him wondering (*EP* 1.4.47ff.) whether her hair, like his, has begun to turn grey, whether misfortune has aged her as it has him.

Just enough is known about her background to make us wish we knew more. She was related to Ovid's friend and travelling-companion, the poet Macer (above, p. 26). More important was her (not clearly defined) standing, intimate but dependent, in the household of Paullus Fabius Maximus, where Ovid, himself the great man's client (*EP* 1.2.129–35), probably met her. Through Fabius' wife Marcia she enjoyed at least a nodding acquaintance with the Empress Livia (*Tr.* 1.6.25, 4.10.73). Thus to Ovid she must have represented not only stability and maturity, but also a friend (in every sense)

---

* Perilla's identification as Ovid's stepdaughter was established, with cogent arguments, by Wheeler, 'Topics from the life of Ovid', AJPh 46 (1925) 26, and is now generally accepted. Other points may be noted. During the earlier years of his exile, Ovid carefully refrained, in the *Poems of Lamentation* (*Tristia*), from identifying the addressees of his verse-letters, in order not to expose them to possible reprisals as sympathizers with so notorious a political unperson. There are two exceptions only to this rule: Ovid's wife, and Perilla. The familial inference is clear. The epistle to Perilla also refers (*Tr.* 3.7.45) to Ovid's loss of 'country, home, *and you* [plural]', which clinches the matter: cf. *Tr.* 1.3.64.

at court. After her husband's banishment she remained in Rome to work for his recall; but it would be a mistake to treat their relationship as a mere *mariage de convenance*. Ovid vividly sketches the agony of their separation (*Tr.* 1.3.79ff.), and his letters to her from exile (*Tr.* 1.6, 3.3, 4.3, 5.2, 5.5, 5.11, 5.14; *EP* 1.4, 3.1) reveal a warmth, respect and intimate affection that contrast, often strikingly, with the underlying, or overt, attitude to women revealed in his earlier work. The largely narcissistic *Sturm und Drang* of the *Amores*, the chauvinistic Don Juanism of the *Art of Love*, the idea of love as pure sex, of sex as pursuit and capture – all this has vanished. For the first time ever, Ovid, or his poetic *persona*, is treating a woman as an equal, as an adult human being. The sad thing about this public correspondence – of which, of course, we have only one side – is the element of despair that finally permeates it: the exile's paranoia, the nagging anxiety that his wife, if not positively disloyal, could nevertheless, somehow, be doing more than she is to help him. The epistles, frequent at first, become more intermittent. After the long, half-irritable list of instructions and reminders (*EP* 3.1) dispatched late in AD 13, they cease altogether. But their cumulative impact makes it clear that not only was this marriage wholly different from Ovid's two previous ones; it marked a fundamental change in his concept of human relationships.

Thus it is very tempting to correlate his father's death, his third marriage and his new lease of poetic life into a causal nexus: to see his father's death as the psychological release that not only, at long last, gave him complete financial independence, untrammelled control of the family estates (see above, pp. 25–6), but also permitted – indeed perhaps encouraged – the new and more mature relationship into which he now entered; to see this intrapsychic metamorphosis as the trigger-release (also controlling flow and direction) of a creative surge that produced, within a remarkably short space of time, both the *Metamorphoses* and the *Fasti*. If this causal nexus is valid, we can then posit a probable chronological sequence: the death of Ovid's father, perhaps about 1 BC, when Ovid was still engaged on the *Art of Love*, followed by the poet's remarriage a year or two later, *c.* AD 2, and his new poetic efflorescence. At that point Ovid himself would have been forty-five, his new wife in her early twenties, and his stepdaughter about nine.* His own daughter by his second wife was already married, to one Cornelius Fidus, whose sole claim to fame (apart from this relationship) was that Domitius Corbulo referred to him, in the Senate, as 'that depilated ostrich', an insult which apparently (Sen. *De Const.* 17.1) reduced him to public tears.

Despite his new wife's highly placed connections, and the more officially acceptable turn his work was now taking – the *Fasti* in particular offered just that blend of traditionalism and *Romanitas* most calculated to please Augustus – Ovid's position in Rome was more vulnerable than he ever seems to have realized till it was too late. Like all fashionable, and successful, literary men, he made personal enemies, who would not be slow to denounce his activities or otherwise intrigue against him when the chance arose: the best-known of these was the anonymous figure whom he attacked under the pseudonym 'Ibis', in 644 lines of elegiac invective (c. AD 9), and to whom he refers elsewhere (*Tr.* 3.11, 4.9, 5.8). 'Ibis' – his identity remains quite uncertain: he may have been a professional informer, a *delator* – carefully drew Augustus' attention to Ovid's more *risqué* erotic verse (*Tr.* 2.77–80), slandered the poet behind his back (*Tr.* 3.11.20, *Ibis* 14), and did his level best to rob him of his property (*Tr.* 1.6.9–14) through sharp litigation. He seems to have been a man whom Ovid had once trusted (*Ibis* 19), thus confirming the naïvety of which the poet accused himself (e.g. *Tr.* 3.6.35, *EP* 1.6.20). Despite Thibault's reservations (pp. 16–17), it seems more than likely that 'Ibis', or someone like him, both

---

* I am only too well aware that this thesis depends on what French scholars so graphically term *une combinaison fragile*, and I advance it here with some diffidence on that account; but it does at least make sense of the scanty evidence at our disposal, and for that reason I feel inclined to let it stand.

denounced Ovid to Augustus and hoped, by inducing a charge of *lèse-majesté* (*laesa maiestas*), to get the informer's cut from his victim's property.

Ovid was clearly a tempting target for vultures of this sort. As he himself had been well aware since he first began to publish, literary fame could compete neither with true social exclusiveness nor with a cool million in the bank. His own range of patrons was respectable, but not overwhelmingly powerful, nor, indeed, always totally committed to his cause. Despite several appeals, it was not until AD 14 that Paullus Fabius Maximus agreed to petition Augustus on the poet's behalf – and then died before he got around to it. Though Ovid prided himself on staying out of politics, hostile critics could point to innumerable passages in his work that mocked just about every aspect of Augustus' regime, from its military imperialism (and recruiting problems) to its much-touted schemes of moral regeneration. Ovid had laughed, in his patronizing way, at the pomp of Roman triumphs, the stuffiness of Roman law, the *rusticitas* of Roman virtue; he had advocated the pleasures of *otium*, the notion of sexual as the moral equal of military conquest. Above all, he had published a pseudo-didactic handbook of seduction which not only (despite his literary disclaimers) presented adultery as a high-class social game, but had proved immensely, and lastingly, popular among the very people at whom Augustus' moral reforms were primarily directed. He had, in fact, built up against himself, all unknowingly, a quite remarkable reserve of official ill-will. When the time came, this ill-will was to be concentrated with some effectiveness, and the *Art of Love* offered it a handy excuse for action.

VIII

The facts of Ovid's banishment are well-known, its true reason mysterious. Ovid himself lists two causes for it (*Tr.* 2.207, 4.1.25–6): an immoral poem, the *Art of Love*; and a 'mistake' or 'indiscretion' (*error*), the nature of which he never fully reveals. This *error* was clearly the main precipitant of Augustus' anger, to which the poem, though a contributory offence, for the most part served as a cover (*EP* 2.9.75–6). Its secret remains one of the most tantalizing enigmas in history, and has evoked a corresponding variety of more or less specious explanations, now conveniently tabulated, analysed and (for the most part) exploded in Thibault's useful monograph, *The Mystery of Ovid's Exile* (1964), to which subsequent scholarship has added comparatively little. In default of new evidence the mystery may well (as Thibault thought) be insoluble: the best we can hope to do is narrow down the possibilities, laying out the essential evidence, such as it is, and eliminating all speculation that conflicts with it. The direct evidence all stems from Ovid himself: oddly, though the exile of so famous a poet must have been a *cause célèbre*, the first surviving source apart from Statius (*Silvae* 1.2.254ff.) to mention it is Jerome, in AD 381. We cannot prove that he is not lying, but he had good reason to tell the truth (if not the whole truth), and, like Thibault (p. 116), I start from the working hypothesis that his statements, consistent enough with one another, are self-serving but reasonably honest, that his worst fault is *suppressio veri*. Despite Augustus' stern veto on any publication of the facts, nevertheless, Ovid's obsession with posterity drove him, compulsively, to scatter hints, some of them highly suggestive.

In November AD 8, probably as a result of delation, information concerning some serious indiscretion (*error*) on Ovid's part came to the attention of Augustus, and to a restricted circle of other influential persons, including Ovid's patron and friend Cotta Maximus (*EP* 2.3.61ff.) At first Cotta was angry with Ovid; when he learnt the true facts of the case, however, anger turned to irritated sympathy ('they say you groaned over my mistakes', ibid., 66), and he quickly wrote Ovid a letter from Elba, where he was staying, saying he was sure Augustus could be placated. Before the Princeps took action Ovid travelled north to consult Cotta; yet even then, when Cotta asked him if the report was true, he still prevaricated, through a mixture of fear, shame and emotional distress (*EP* 2.3.85–90). It was now that the summons arrived ordering the poet back to Rome for a private hearing before Augustus. It appears that Ovid was subjected to a severe tongue-lashing (*Tr.* 2.133–4) by the outraged Emperor: there was, to ensure secrecy, no formal trial. Ovid was to be banished, in perpetuity, to the remote coastal settlement of Tomis, near the mouth of the Danube estuary, in the still unsettled province of Moesia. At least his life had been spared (*Tr.* 2.147, 4.4.45). The banishment was of the type known as *relegatio* (*Tr.* 2.135–8, cf. *Tr.* 4.4.46, 5.2.55–8, etc.), in which the victim retained his property and citizenship, but had his place of exile specified (others could, within limits, reside where they chose, provided it was a certain distance from Rome). In Ovid's case, his *Art of Love* was also banned – an unusual step – from Rome's three public libraries (*Tr.* 3.1.59–82, 3.14.5–18), and he was required to leave Rome by December (*Tr.* 1.3.5–6, 1.11.3), a stipulation which made his journey both unpleasant and dangerous (*Tr.* 1.4, 1.11.13ff.). This sentence was conveyed, both to Ovid and to the public at large, by an imperial edict (*Tr.* 2.135, 5.2.8). In the case of *relegatio* a pardon was always, in theory, possible, and the edict would become invalid, unless confirmed by his successor, on the death of the emperor who issued it (Owen (2), p. 46).

Whatever the specific reason for Ovid's banishment (see below pp. 49–59), it is impossible not to perceive a refinement of calculated cruelty behind the sentence chosen for him. Hope was not removed: there always remained a possible mitigation of sentence. Thus the poet who had so coolly mocked imperial aspirations would be reduced to a caricature of the toadying, grovelling courtier, addressing endless hyperbolic flatteries and pleas to those whose beliefs he had offended. He would, to borrow an expressive modern phrase, be left to dangle slowly in the wind (and a freezing wind at that), his pose of sophisticated superiority and indifference gone, forced into a humiliating public embracement of the

Augustan myth he had once found so risible, deification, triumphs and all (e.g. *EP* 3.4). No Communist show-trial ever staged so public, and prolonged, an exercise in recantation and self-abasement. While there was even the slimmest chance of recall, or even of being transferred to a less harsh environment, Ovid would continue to bombard the capital with fawning rhetoric, with gross endorsements of the regime he had hitherto treated, in his apolitical way, as a kind of bad joke. As a revenge for all the years of superior private sniping, the *de haut en bas* accusations of middle-class vulgarity and pompous propaganda, this particular punishment fitted the crime with quite horrific aptness.

To execute this social butterfly, who was, after all, the most famous living poet in Rome, would have been far too easy, and might well have provoked a serious outcry at a time when Augustus had other still more serious problems on his hands (see p. 55). *Relegatio* was a far better answer: it gave a spurious appearance of clemency and – the crucial point – let Augustus and his advisers dictate Ovid's place of residence. Tomis, from their viewpoint, was a psychological masterstroke. It robbed Ovid not only of Rome, but of that whole cultured milieu on which he depended for his inspiration. It showed him, the hard way, how the empire he so despised was run, exposing him daily not only to barbarian *mores* but also to the very real threat of enemy incursions. It struck at his instrument of expression, the Latin language, by marooning him in a linguistic wilderness of debased Greek, 'Sarmatian' and Getic: 'Composing a poem you can read to nobody', he complained bitterly (*EP* 4.2.33–4), 'is like dancing in the dark.' To the Getae, *he* was the barbarian (*Tr.* 5.10.37). Above all, it stripped him of his literary conceits, turned all his smart military and naval metaphors for the *vie amoureuse* into appalling fact. Now he sailed real stormy seas to reach his destination, suffered the cold of real winters, donned a real helmet to help fight off marauding tribesmen. By a supreme irony, the erstwhile *tenerorum lusor amorum* became totally indifferent to sex (*EP* 1.10.33–4). Life, as he himself recognized (*Tr.* 5.1.25–8), had indeed overtaken art in his creative world. Another exile, tougher and more self-reliant, might have transported his library to Tomis, completed the *Fasti*, made a final revision of the *Metamorphoses*, and divided the rest of his life between mythic fantasy, antiquarianism, and the exploration of the new and alien terrain in which he found himself. But Augustus knew his man. Ovid never really adapted his outlook to the bleak rigours of Tomis, and devoted almost all his energies to angling for an imperial pardon – thus denying himself the companionship of his loyal wife, who was left behind in Rome to work for his recall (*Tr.* 1.2.41, 1.3.81–8, etc.).

So, in the December of AD 8, after an agonized last night in Rome (*Tr.* 1.3), Ovid set out on his journey into exile. He was never to return. Sailing down the stormy Adriatic and through the Gulf of Corinth, he recalled making the same voyage, in happier days, as a student on his way to Athens (*Tr.* 1.2.77). From the Isthmus he took another ship to Samothrace, where he stopped for a while, clearly spinning out the trip as long as he could, and thence sailed for Tempyra in Thrace.* From here, in the spring of AD 9 (*Tr.* 1.10), he made his way to Tomis overland. He travelled slowly enough for news from Rome to catch up with him at various points (*Tr.* 1.6.15, 1.9.39–40). In addition to his abandonment by many of his friends, and the efforts of 'Ibis' to obtain his property at home (above, p. 43), he seems to have been robbed or otherwise swindled by the servants who accompanied him (*Tr.* 1.11.27ff., 4.10.101; *EP* 2.7.61–2). He reached Tomis by autumn, before the severe Black Sea winter set in. This outpost of empire was to be his home, though he did not then know it, for the rest of his natural life.

---

* His repeated claim (*EP* 3.4.59–60, 4.11.15–16) that an exchange of correspondence between Rome and Tomis could take up to a year is clearly based on his own leisurely progress, and calculated to emphasize the Black Sea's remoteness. Elsewhere, however (*EP* 4.5.5–8), he is considerably more realistic about the speed of the mail service.

IX

It is not only inevitable, but also reasonable, that the riddle of Ovid's *relegatio* should continue to attract such intense curiosity, and by no means only among scholars. By imperial fiat the greatest Roman poet of his day was plucked from the society which sustained his creative drive and subjected, over nearly a decade, to the kind of humiliating exile that might have been designed 'to arrest and freeze forever his generous stream of inspiration' (Owen (2), p. 36). At the very least we want to know *why*, since, *prima facie*, there is a disturbing irrationality about the whole proceedings. If the true cause of exile (as some still maintain) was the *Art of Love*, why did Augustus delay for so many years before taking action against its author? If the object of banishment was to stop Ovid's mouth, why was he allowed, indeed encouraged, to correspond freely with friends in Rome (*EP* 3.6.11–12)? If, as Ovid frequently asserted, he had committed no indictable crime (e.g. *EP* 2.9.71, cf. *Tr.* 3.1.51), why did Augustus remain so inflexible? Finally, in view of the punishment chosen, is there not a suspicion of calculated sadism and vindictive personal spite about the entire episode?

That the *Art of Love* was, in fact, one count of a double indictment (*Tr.* 4.1.25–6) Ovid assures us on innumerable occasions (Owen (2), pp. 10–11, Thibault, pp. 30–31). The main objection to the poem seems to have been its didactic quality, the notion of Ovid as a conscious propagandist for seduction reduced to a fine art, a teacher of adultery (*Tr.* 2.212, 348; *EP* 2.10.15–16, 3.3.47–8, 58). He makes it quite clear, however, that the second charge against him, referred to habitually as his 'mistake' or 'indiscretion' (*error*), was the more serious of the two (*EP* 3.3.71–6, also 2.9.72–6). While this does not justify our treating the *Art of Love* merely as a 'cover', designed to distract attention from the more sensitive area in which Ovid's *error* lay (*Tr.* 2.7–8, 345–6) – it is clear that Augustus found it a morally

subversive poem, as indeed by his (public) standards it was* –
it does focus our main attention on something that Ovid,
despite himself, was constrained (*Tr.* 2.207–12) to treat as a
top-level secret. Despite the efforts of countless investigators,
the enigma persists.

This official cloak of secrecy, referred to on various occa-
sions (*Tr.* 1.5.51–2, 3.6.32, 4.10.100, etc.) is one of the more
significant clues in our possession. Augustus' government, like
most modern ones, habitually, and effectively, suppressed the
general circulation of embarrassing or unpalatable facts (Dio
Cass. 53.19.3). In Ovid's case, however, 'everybody', i.e. the
usual inner circle of *cognoscenti*, knew very well what had
taken place (*Tr.* 1.1.23, 4.10.99, *EP* 1.7.39). This does not
imply (indeed, all our evidence suggests precisely the opposite)
any acquaintance with the true facts on the part of the general
public. Whatever Ovid's *error*, it could not have been con-
nected with a *well-known* public scandal – unless it somehow
involved additional sensitive evidence, which revealed that
scandal in a new light, and which Augustus was therefore de-
termined to suppress. Ovid at one point (*Tr.* 3.4.4) links his
downfall to ruinous connections in high places. The scandal
involved 'great names' (*magna nomina*), as indeed we might
have guessed from the strenuous campaign to suppress it. Had
it not been for this unfortunate intimacy, he adds (ibid., 13–
14), he might still be happily at large in Rome. It is just con-
ceivable, as Thibault argues (pp. 21–2), that the lost works of
Seneca, Aufidius Bassus, Cremutius Cordus or, above all,
Suetonius, contained the whole truth of the matter; but the
absolute silence of the next four centuries – and indeed of ex-
tant authors such as Tacitus – argues strongly against such *ex
post facto* knowledge. The balance of probability is that the
secret was indeed well kept, that few were privy to it, and that
for all practical purposes the truth died with Ovid, as he said it
should (*Tr.* 1.5.51).

---

* Ovid suggests at one point (*Tr.* 2.237–8) that Augustus has never read the
poem, only (like too many modern magistrates) heard carefully culled passages
read by ill-wishers (*Tr.* 2.77–80), a practice, as he rightly points out, liable to
inhibit fair judgement.

What other hints does Ovid give us? His *error* was unpremeditated (*Tr.* 4.4.43–4) and without any thought of personal gain (*Tr.* 3.6.33–4), yet the result of a complex chain of events (*Tr.* 4.4.37–8). It was not – a fact Ovid several times emphasizes, but which, as we shall see, conflicts with other aspects of his own testimony – a legally indictable crime (*Tr.* 1.2.97–8, 1.3.37–8, 3.1.51–2, 3.11.33–4, *EP* 1.6.25, 2.9.71, etc.). In particular, he had committed neither murder, poisoning nor forgery (*EP* 2.9.67–70), nor was he guilty of treasonable action (*Tr.* 1.5.41–2, 2.51–2, 3.5.45–6) or even treasonable talk (*Tr.* 2.446, 3.5.47–8) against Augustus. In fact, he had not *done* anything at all; rather he had *seen* a crime committed by others, which apparently, to begin with, he had not recognized for what it was (*Tr.* 2.103–4, 3.5.49–50), though he describes it (*Tr.* 3.6.28) as 'deadly' or 'fatal' (*funestum*), an ambiguous epithet (see below, p. 58). It was, he says, a 'more serious injury' (*gravior noxa*) than any legal crime (*EP* 2.9.71–2). Yet if he was a mere witness, wherein did his culpability lie? Clearly, in *not reporting* the incident: a word at the right moment could have saved him (*Tr.* 3.6.11–14, cf. *EP* 2.6.7–10). Why, then, did he keep silent? Again he gives us the answer: he was scared (*Tr.* 4.4.39, *EP* 2.2.17), and so did nothing, in the vain hope that the scandal would blow over.

From this it sounds as though Ovid's role in the affair was at best, peripheral: that of the smart but innocent man-about-town, the fashionable *praeceptor amoris* of the literary salons, taken up (rather like the late Stephen Ward) by Rome's promiscuous *beau monde*, who stumbled accidentally into a dangerous situation, and then panicked. He repeatedly castigates himself – just as we would expect in the circumstances – for having been naïve and gullible (*Tr.* 1.2.100, 1.5.42, 3.6.35; *EP* 1.6.20, 1.7.44, 2.2.17). Yet this mere error of judgement (*Tr.* 4.10.89–90, *EP* 1.7.39, 2.6.7, 3.3.73, etc.) was, nevertheless, an improper act (*Tr.* 5.2.60, 5.11.17; *EP* 1.1.66, 1.6.21, 2.2.105, 2.3.33, 2.6.5, etc.) of which he felt ashamed (*Tr.* 5.8.23–4). Worse, it caused deep personal pain to Augustus (*Tr.* 2.209–10, *EP* 2.2.57–8) and was, indeed, a direct offence against him (*Tr.* 1.10.42, 2.134, 3.8.39–40, 5.7.8,

5.10.52; *EP* 2.2.21) of the type (it has been suggested) known as *laesa maiestas* (*lèse-majesté*: *Tr.* 1.5.84, 2.123, 3.6.23, 4.10.98; *EP* 1.4.44). We should, however, note that though Ovid repeatedly describes the Princeps as *laesus*, the *maiestas* we have to infer for ourselves; and *maiestas*, however loosely defined, was without doubt a legal offence. Ovid may be splitting hairs for his own benefit, but whatever his actual *error*, it was indefensible (*Tr.* 1.2.95–6), and the Princeps could well have imposed the death penalty because of it (*Tr.* 1.1.20). Though the wave of public dislike for Ovid which his *relegatio* produced (*Tr.* 1.1.23–4, 2.87) can be explained by society's rejection of any official scapegoat, the immediate reaction even of Cotta Maximus (who not only learnt the facts but was Ovid's patron) seems to have been one of anger (*EP* 2.3.61ff.).

This fact gains in significance when we recall that Cotta Maximus and his brother Messalinus were both strong partisans of Tiberius (certainly from the time his accession was assured), since Tiberius and his mother Livia were, and remained, implacably hostile to Ovid. Ovid's own attitude to them, not surprisingly, is one of constrained, nervous and distant self-abasement (e.g. *Tr.* 2.161–6), in sharp contrast to the warm admiration (and hopes of favourable treatment) he displays during these last years when addressing or referring to Germanicus (*EP* 2.1, 2.5.41–6, 4.8.23–88), for whose succession he prays (*EP* 2.5.75) and to whom, after Augustus' death, he rededicated his *Fasti* (*Fast.* 1.3–6, cf. *Tr.* 2.551). Germanicus had the clemency and humanity (Suet. *Calig.* 3.3, Tac. *Ann.* 2.73) which Tiberius so conspicuously lacked; better still, he was not only Tiberius' natural nephew, but (on the insistence of Augustus) his adopted son (Dio Cass. 55.13), and thus in direct line for the purple. Had Ovid survived a year or two longer, his hopes would have been dashed yet again: in AD 19 Germanicus died, probably by poisoning (Tac. *Ann.* 2.69–73; Dio Cass. 57.18; Suet. *Calig.* 1–7), and Tiberius' position became virtually unassailable, since his other adopted son, Agrippa Postumus, the brother of Julia II, had been secretly executed (Tac. *Ann.* 1.6) immediately after Augustus' death.

Such is the evidence at our disposal, and as Thibault reminds us (pp. 115–16), we have to reject any explanation that shows inconsistency with any part of Ovid's own explicit testimony. It is more probable that he was hinting at the truth than lying; and if he *was* lying, the mystery, short of fresh evidence, becomes by definition insoluble. The most we can concede is that he was playing down his own culpability in order to win a reprieve. We are looking, to recapitulate, for an indiscretion that took place in high society, was unpremeditated but part of a complex situation, was not *per se* indictable(?), brought Ovid no profit, and in fact consisted of his having witnessed (perhaps without full understanding at the time) a crime committed by others. In particular he emphasizes that he had taken no treasonable action against Augustus, that he had committed neither murder nor forgery, poisoned no one. If he had reported the incident he might have remained a free man, but he was scared to do so. He was also, he says, both naïve and gullible. Further, his *error* caused Augustus deep personal pain, and could (Ovid's language suggests) be in some sense categorized as *lèse-majesté*. It *could* have brought Ovid the death penalty, and he was ashamed of it. It also caused especial resentment in Livia, Tiberius and their adherents. He was obliged to keep it secret, though a limited number of people in Rome seem to have known the truth.

Thibault has earned the gratitude of all subsequent investigators by the exemplary way in which he has analysed, and refuted, countless implausible theories as to the nature of Ovid's *error*. We no longer need to waste space wondering whether the *praeceptor amoris* saw Livia nude in her bath, or Augustus committing paederasty, or the younger Julia engaged in incest; whether he gate-crashed a neo-Pythagorean séance, or the rites of the Bona Dea. Till the nineteenth century the rule was *cherchez la femme*; then variations of political conspiracy became popular; latterly the *Zeitgeist* has had its turn, with Ovid's general attitude of smart atheistical urban hedonism provoking a violent reaction from the Augustan moral reformists. No specific theory advanced hitherto exactly fits the facts, and of the three main theories advanced, two can be dismissed out of hand. First, Ovid makes it clear that his *error* was a specific offence, so that though his social and religious attitudes may well have made him unpopular in official circles (cf. above, p. 44), they cannot have been the direct cause of his *relegatio*. Secondly, since he emphasizes that his *error* was to have kept quiet about something he had *seen*, we can rule out any personal involvement with a highly connected lady as being responsible for his downfall. Adultery, as Thibault reminds us (p. 54), is not an ocular offence.

Ovid's own statements, taken in conjunction with the pattern of historical events during the last decade or so of Augustus' reign, all point rather towards some sort of unwitting political *bêtise*, linked with the deadly factional struggle between Julians and Claudians for the succession, and carefully camouflaged by official public charges suggesting moral turpitude. This, as Syme has pointed out (*Tacitus*, Oxford, 1958, Vol. 1, pp. 403–4), was a useful device, particularly valuable in dealing with the two Julias, to conceal more serious, and politically sensitive, offences. Only in political and, probably, conspiratorial or otherwise treasonable circumstances does the lifelong *relegatio*, by private imperial edict, of a mere witness – let alone the danger of his execution over an arguably non-indictable offence – even begin to make any sense. As has long been recognized, such circumstances indeed existed in the years immediately prior to Ovid's exile.

In 2 BC a group of ambitious aristocrats had tried to establish themselves, through Augustus' daughter Julia, in a position where they could, after the death – whether natural or (Plin. *HN* 7.149) induced – of the Princeps, take over effective control of the empire (Syme, (2), pp. 193–8). The plot failed, and the scheme to murder Augustus, conceived by its more extreme proponents, surely in part dictated the Emperor's subsequent reluctant shift towards a 'Tiberian solution'. Significantly, it was Julia's sexual promiscuity that received most public attention when the scandal broke (see p. 40). The refusal of the 'Julian faction' to admit defeat, then or later, must surely be attributed to Augustus' own persisting ambivalence over the succession. By AD 4 two of his three grandsons were dead, in circumstances suspicious enough at least to start a rumour that Livia had somehow done away with them for her son's benefit (Tac. *Ann.* 1.3, Dio Cass. 55.10–11; cf. p. 345). Tiberius, whose earlier disgrace had encouraged the pro-Julian *coup*, had been adopted, *faute de mieux*, by the ageing Emperor; though at the same time, characteristically still hedging his bets, Augustus made the new heir apparent himself adopt, not only his nephew Germanicus, but also Augustus' last surviving grandson, Julia II's brother Agrippa Postumus. That the former, in due course, was poisoned, and the latter executed, need surprise no one. A little earlier, perhaps in response to the considerable public criticism which her banishment still provoked, Julia I had been transferred from the island of Pandateria to a less severe place of exile: Rhegium (Reggio) in southern Italy (Tac. *Ann.* 1.53.1, Suet. *Div. Aug.* 65.3, Dio Cass. 55.13.1: Augustus, for whatever reason, came to repent his earlier harshness, Sen. *De Benef.* 6.32.2).

The years that followed, particularly the period between AD 6 and 9, saw Augustus' regime pass through an acutely critical phase. There were wars and uprisings in Illyria and Pannonia (Dio Cass. 55.27), a serious recruiting problem, increased taxation of senators and *equites* (with the added risk of disaffection that this brought), famine in Italy, and growing rumours, sometimes confirmed, of rebellion and conspiracy. Such circumstances could not fail to provoke some sort of attempt by the 'Julian faction'. The natural figureheads for any 'succession plot' would be the two Julias and Agrippa Postumus; Tiberius and his supporters, recognizing this, devoted considerable time and ingenuity to neutralizing all three. The first victim of this process was Agrippa Postumus.

Despite his adoption, he did not, on his tardy assumption of the *toga virilis*, a year or so later, receive those honours which had marked his two brothers out for the succession (Dio Cass. 55.22.4). Busy rumours had been spread by the opposition about his intractable, brutish character (Vell. Pat. 2.112, Dio Cass. 55.32, Tac. *Ann.* 1.3). In AD 5 or 6 he was banished to Surrentum (Sorrento) (Suet. *Div. Aug.* 65.1, Vell. Pat., ibid.), and in late AD 7, by senatorial decree, his place of exile was changed to the remote island of Planasia (Pianosa) near Elba (Suet. *Div. Aug.* 65.4, Tac. *Ann.* 1.3.6, Dio Cass. 55.32). His banishment was made permanent, he was placed under military guard, and his property became forfeit to the state treasury. In normal circumstances only the gravest of crimes could have justified such harsh treatment. Tacitus claims that Agrippa had committed no offence; if this is true, it indicates the skill of his enemies' propaganda. On the other hand (a point to bear in mind when considering Ovid's identical disclaimer), political activists regularly assert their technical innocence of *crimes*. Even if we concede Agrippa's guilt, Augustus might well be anxious, in those troubled times, to suppress evidence of conspiracy in high places. From now on, indeed, the Princeps habitually referred to Agrippa Postumus and the two Julias as his 'three boils' (Suet. *Div. Aug.* 65.4), and was in the habit of quoting Homer (*Il.* 3.40) to the effect that he should never have married, and should have died without issue. When he said this it was, clearly, Scribonia and her offspring rather than Livia whom he had in mind. The anecdote offers a slight presumption of guilt on the trio's part, but *could* refer merely to their existential nuisance-value.

The following year (AD 8) saw the exile not only of Ovid (above, pp. 44ff.) but also of the younger Julia, to the island of Trimerus, off the Apulian coast, where, as an extra safeguard, she was made dependent for her subsistence on her grandmother Livia (Tac. *Ann.* 4.71). The ostensible reason for Julia's removal was, as in her mother's case, sexual promiscuity (Tac. *Ann.* 3.24, Suet. *Div. Aug.* 65.1.4), but the evidence is strikingly vague, and in all likelihood camouflaged a political offence or frame-up. Since Julia was convicted of *adultery* (Tac. *Ann.* 4.71) it follows, as Sir Ronald Syme reminds me, that her husband, L. Aemilius Paulus, was still living at the time. This is chronologically important, since Aemilius Paulus himself was said to have taken a leading part in a conspiracy against Augustus (Suet. *Div. Aug.* 19.1–2), in which Julia was clearly involved. The plot involved the release of both Agrippa Postumus and the elder Julia from their places of exile, and their subsequent presentation to the legions – in the hope, clearly, that Julia's popularity (Suet. *Div. Aug.* 65.3, Dio Cass. 55.13.1) would ensure her son's succession. The only possible date for this attempt (if it in fact took place) would thus be in 7/8 AD. At all events, Aemilius Paulus was executed (schol. Juv. 6.158) or banished (Syme, (2), pp. 210–11), and his wife exiled for life. On the other hand, her alleged lover, D. Junius Silanus (Tac. *Ann.* 3.24), was merely excluded from court circles, and in AD 20 returned to Rome with Tiberius' knowledge and consent. The contrast between his fate and that of the others is suggestive: more than ever it looks as though Julia's adultery was simply a cover for the charge (whether genuine or fabricated) of conspiracy and treason.

All this gives us some very clear pointers as to what Ovid's secret *error* may have been. His own apologia, and subsequent fate, tell us that he had incurred the implacable hostility of Livia and Tiberius; that if he looked anywhere for salvation after Augustus' death, it was to Germanicus. He had always been an ardent advocate, something striking in so apolitical a poet, of the Julian succession, writing fulsome tributes to Gaius Caesar, the grandson of the Princeps (*AA* 1.177ff., *RA* 155–6; even here he could not entirely restrain his *nequitia*, cf. p. 342). Later Christian tradition (Sidonius Apollinaris 23.157ff.) linked his name with that of the elder Julia. Though the notion that Julia was the model for Corinna sounds like mere clerical fantasizing, it is by no means implausible that the most fashionable elegiac poet in Rome should have moved on the fringes of Julia's circle. Her scandalous conduct – whether sexual, political, or both – caused her father Augustus deep personal pain (Suet. *Div. Aug.* 65.2–3), and a similar reaction could well be expected from him to any further conspiracy in which she was involved. Though Ovid goes out of his way to emphasize that *he* had done nothing treasonable, that he had not himself conspired against Augustus (e.g. *Tr.* 2.51–2, 3.5.45–6), such disclaimers strongly suggest the guilty witness (*Tr.* 2.103–4, 3.5.49–50 etc.) anxious to minimize his involvement as an accessory after the fact. In particular, it is curious that he should specifically deny having been guilty of murder, either by knife or poison, or of forgery (*EP* 2.9.67–70), since one of Aemilius Paulus' fellow-conspirators, Audasius, was charged – in what circumstances we do not know – with forgery, while an attempt on Augustus' life, just as in 2 BC, formed part of the plot (Suet. *Div. Aug.* 19).

If Ovid saw or overheard, however innocently, preparations for a *coup* of this sort, then the hints he gives us make complete and immediate sense. 'Great names' were indeed involved. The insistence on official secrecy is more than understandable. Ovid's unwillingness to go to the authorities sprang not only from fear, but also from a disinclination (which he could never afterwards acknowledge) to betray his Julian friends. The temptation to keep quiet and hope against hope for a successful outcome must have been immense. No thought of personal gain, indeed, but rather natural loyalty was involved: the situation governing the succession struggle was complex, and bred great evils (*Tr.* 4.4.38). What Ovid witnessed was indeed 'deadly' (*funestum*, *Tr.* 3.6.28): potentially to Augustus, in the event to Ovid himself. He had, very literally, been involved in a case of *lèse-majesté*; though he had taken no positive action ('Thou shalt not kill; yet need'st not strive, officiously, to keep alive'), his silence was in itself culpable, and could, just as he admits, have earned him the death penalty. The hostile reaction of highly placed individuals (especially supporters of Tiberius), the deadly and unforgiving enmity of Livia and Tiberius themselves – these now make complete sense. Though Ovid's constant snickering at the morals and dignity of the regime provided an extra incentive to those selecting his place of exile (above, p. 44), his prime function, ironically enough, was to provide convincing support for the cover-charges of sexual misconduct against the younger Julia – hence the public banning of the *Art of Love* a decade after its publication – and camouflage for the political realities that lay behind this salacious official version of events. The literary *praeceptor amoris* found himself, in the end, a political pawn.

X

Of all the many myths that have accumulated round Ovid, perhaps the most pernicious – and certainly the most persistent – is that of his straightforwardness, his lack of depth. He is, in fact, among the most complex, odd and elusive poets of antiquity. One of the most modern, too: Ovid's capacity to operate on multiple levels of awareness, his preoccupation with facets of identity and the divided self, both prefigure the emergence of a new psychological world. His seemingly simple verse draws us into a subtle labyrinth of ironic allusiveness; his mythical constructs reveal sociopolitical undertones; metamorphosis becomes a metaphor for the human condition, offering a bridge between the real world and that of the imagination. To what extent did Ovid's implied political attitudes penetrate his poetry? How far did his anti-Augustan temperament (cf. above, p. 47) colour those seemingly light-hearted pronouncements on love, war or the activities of prominent mythological figures, especially Jupiter? Above all, what is the relationship between the poet and his creative *persona*: between the historical Publius Ovidius Naso whose career we have just examined, and the witty, ironic womanizer, erotic *littérateur* and *praeceptor amoris* whom we meet in the *Amores* and the *Art of Love*? What congruity subsists between the thrice-married poet who rejected a senatorial career, and the literary hedonist, the heir to, and parodist of, an elegiac tradition going back to Callimachus?

The discussion of Ovid's *persona* has suffered badly from over-rigid schematization. The tradition which regarded Corinna as a 'real' character, and Ovid's erotic poetry as autobiographical in the fullest sense, provoked a critical reaction which held that Corinna was a fictitious creation, composed of the literary characteristics of mistresses in erotic poetry, set in traditional elegiac situations. According to this interpretation, not only Corinna but also the 'I' of the poems, the narrator, is a mask, a *persona*, sexual no less than political, which bears no necessary resemblance to Ovid the man. Ironically, proponents of this view support it with quotations from Ovid's own exilic apologia, composed to demonstrate, for the benefit of sceptical officialdom in Rome, his personal (as opposed to his literary) rectitude: 'My Muse is wanton, but my life is chaste' (*Tr.* 2.353–6). We are asked to choose between two convenient stereotypes: biographical character or fictional character, each in its tidy pigeon-hole. Both these attitudes strike me as misconceived; but due to an extremely influential antibiographical trend in modern literary criticism, which extends far beyond the field of classical studies, the question is too often treated as though it had been settled once and for all. This is very far from the case.

No one would, or should, deny that the *persona* as such exists, and plays a fundamental role in creative literature; but in recent years its critical exploitation has been something less than discriminate. We should bear in mind that neither a pure biographical portrait nor a pure fictional portrait ever in reality occurs. Just as the supposedly imaginary character will always betray elements of actual persons – *ex nihilo nihil fit* – so a conscious effort at portraiture will always end up creating something subtly different and *sui generis*. Self-portraiture in poetry is a uniquely complex problem; but it is worth bearing in mind that when we do have adequate evidence with which to check the *persona* against the biographical facts – Yeats,

Frost, Eliot, Pound, Sylvia Plath and Anne Sexton are instances that at once spring to mind – we find, despite the obvious and predictable differences, a far closer and more consistent nexus between the poet's life and the poetic *persona* than many modern critics care to assume. The same, arguably, will be true of Ovid. Person and *persona* are symbiotic: there can be no easy, schematic, rule-of-thumb distinction made between them.

Those who promote the '*persona* theory' tend to apply it, without over-nice discrimination of genre or occasion, to most categories of literature. Yet it makes an immense difference whether the author is writing declared fiction (e.g. drama, epic, a novel, an imaginary epistle) or a type of literature where the author speaks, or pretends to speak, in his own identifiable person, such as journals, diaries, autobiographies, memoirs, personal letters, personal lyric or elegiac poetry, and first-person satire. This distinction is not always drawn by critics, and is strikingly absent in Ovid's case. Arguments for an Ovidian *persona* have always concentrated, significantly, on the erotic poems, though these are by no means the only, or even the likeliest, poems by Ovid in which such a *persona* can be inferred. I have yet to hear any critic reassuring us that when Ovid describes Daphne turning into a tree, or Arethusa into a fountain (*Met.* 1.547–55, 5.632–6), he is not actually drawing on personal experience. Nor, for obvious reasons, has it ever been suggested that the letters in the *Heroides* are autobiographical: what we have here is a kind of fiction akin to that which Richardson practised in *Pamela*, developed within a familiar mythological framework. On the other hand, it would be hard to argue that the poems of exile are *not* substantially autobiographical. We can discount some of the horrors as propaganda designed for home consumption but here the fictive *alter ego* is reduced to a minimum, the voice we hear is Ovid's own. Life has overtaken the poet's mythologies; history and art intersect amid the snows of the Dobruja.

Thus to isolate the creative *persona* in Ovid's works we need to consider each group of poems separately, and on its own merits. The degree of autobiographical involvement, whether direct or oblique, is bound to vary a great deal. In some cases, e.g. the *Fasti*, it will be negligible. But the erotic poems are quite another matter. Here we have a substantial body of work which occupied Ovid's full time and energies from late adolescence until his early forties (see p. 40), the prime creative period of any poet's life. All of this poetry deals, in the most direct fashion, with sexual conquest, with erotic success or failure. It we discount the *Heroides* and the lost *Medea* (and even they offer thematic variations on the ever-interesting topic), Ovid's entire *œuvre* up to middle age embodies either what at least purports to be personal sexual experience, or advice based on such experience.

This leads to an interesting conclusion. Suppose we accept, for argument's sake, the proposition that the first-person lover or *praeceptor amoris* in these poems is a fictive projection quite distinct from Ovid himself. Suppose we further accept Ovid's own post-exilic assurance to Augustus (*Tr.* 2.349–58) that, while his verse may have been wanton (*iocosa*), his private life was irreproachable: then one inescapable inference presents itself. We have to do with an obsessional sexual fantasist, as resourceful (if not as vulgar) as Frank Harris, a creative writer whose entire erotic output depended on his imagination and what he had read in books. Even the argument (above, pp. 22ff.) that he drew much of his working material from his first marriage – thus, of course, vindicating his assertions of respectability in a hitherto unexpected way – runs directly counter to this concept of the erotic poems as a purely literary confection, a genre mish-mash combining Hellenistic motifs with imitation or parody of Ovid's predecessors (above all Propertius) in the Roman elegiac tradition.

Such a thesis is primarily sustained by lack of hard evidence. If we knew as much about Ovid's private life as we do, for instance, about Byron's, the odds are we would hear a good deal less about the 'Ovidian *persona*', and what we did hear would be better-balanced. Even on the literary side, the persistent belief in a subjective Hellenistic love-elegy, going back to Callimachus or Philetas, is mere wishful thinking on the part of scholars. No one would deny Ovid's bookishness. But is it inherently probable that he was the psychological forerunner of a writer such as Emily Brontë? His cheerfully pragmatic attitude to sex shows not a trace of that murky Gothic symbolism which always seems to hang about the parthenogenetic Heathcliffes of this world.

Put in such terms, the implausibility of Ovid's own protestations at once becomes apparent, and merely 'deepens when we recall how much of his early life, apart from two brief marriages, he spent as an unattached man-about-town (above, pp. 38ff.). Against this we have to balance all the familiar arguments advanced against any identification of poet with *persona*: Ovid's irony and frivolity, his addiction to parody and literary allusion, his exploitation of myth, his wholesale purloining of erotic and other commonplaces from his elegiac predecessors, above all the chameleon switches of mood and personality he displays, his concern, at every level, with metamorphosis. A writer who depends so much on books, the argument runs, is likely to have purloined his mistress from other men's poems. A poet who can describe himself, by turns, as a faithful lover, a promiscuous Casanova, the world's greatest stud and an impotent neurotic, is merely composing five-finger exercises on literary themes – however these characteristics might, or might not, later substantiate his *soi-disant* role as Rome's most articulate instructor in seduction.

Such arguments remain largely unconvincing. The human psyche, as Whitman well knew, is more paradoxical and varied than these tidily logical apriorisms would suggest. Artists and poets, fantasists almost by definition, often with a remarkable capacity for living exclusively in the present, tend to display an endemic weakness for what might be termed 'instant convictions', especially in the areas of sex and politics. A mood is true, perhaps overwhelmingly so, today; tomorrow may, with equal sincerity, reverse it. A poem will probably result from each stage in this process, and the poet's narcissism will ensure that both are preserved for posterity. Which, if either, is posterity to label 'insincere'? Posterity, alas, can be extraordinarily obtuse. In *Amores* 2.7 and 2.8 Ovid first indignantly denies Corinna's charge that he has been carrying on with her maid, then switches about and asks the maid herself who can have given their affair away. A likely enough situation (if Corinna was based on Ovid's first wife, positively Mozartian); and half the secret fun, for Ovid, must have lain in knowing both sides of the story, writing little poems about them separately, one for each protagonist, and then publishing them together later, when enough time had passed for the entire incident to be nothing but an enjoyable joke, recollected with pleasure if not in tranquillity.

But for the commentator, whose life has run in duller channels, such conduct defies belief. Easier (and less worrying) to write the whole baffling performance off as rhetorical variations on a *topos*, projected by some *persona* not identifiable with the author. The poems then at once become 'pure literature', i.e. can be as irrational as you please without anyone getting upset over them. *We do but jest, poison i' jest: no offence i' the world*. This arbitrary dichotomy between poet and *persona* has obscured the critical issue as nothing else could have done, since Ovid, more than most creative artists, revels in literary masks: his obsession with metamorphosis is fundamental to his poetic impulse. So long as the issue continues to be studied in simplistic terms, as a straight choice between 'autobiography' and 'fiction', it will remain insoluble – and no less unreal than the old battles between Unitarians and Separatists over the Homeric Question, which were similarly bedevilled by an artificial polarity of belief. In Ovid's case we cannot begin to understand the literary *persona* until we accept the fact that it constantly embodies and exploits material from the poet's life. If we discount his self-serving exilic propaganda from Tomis, explicitly designed to secure some mitigation of sentence (above, p. 47), it is a waste of time trying (for whatever motive) to present the *praeceptor amoris* as a respectable middle-class intellectual who, like Nabokov, just happened to have this purely literary obsession with the seamier side of sex.

Let us apply these findings to another pair of poems, which also, or so we are assured, cannot be reconciled with one another: *Amores* 1.3 and 2.4. In the first, Ovid swears eternal devotion to his girl of the moment (significantly unnamed): no sexual circus-rider he, he assures her. The second – largely ignored by Ovidians – offers about as categoric a profession of the Casanova creed as one could hope to find. The one proclaims fidelity, the other indefatigable concupiscence. *Ergo*, it is argued, either one or both must be a literary exercise. But why? The two moods frequently alternate (*experto credite*) in one person; and if that person happens to be a dedicated poet, why not exploit them both? Metamorphosis, in fact, is the name of the game, while Ovid's loving version of the Narcissus myth (*Met.* 3.341ff.) hints at the second dominant strain in his make-up. He could, by turns and without effort, assume the roles, or masks (*personae*), of devoted lover, social butterfly, avuncular rake, cynical Don Juan, literary gossip and *praeceptor* (as a change from *desultor*) *amoris*. But such switches of mood offer no evidence whatsoever that Ovid's erotic poems are purely literary fantasies. Equally invalid is the assumption that literary borrowings, if demonstrable, somehow *preclude* direct experience. Since Ovid's views in *Amores* 2.4 had been, to some extent, anticipated by Propertius (e.g. at 2.22.1–18 and 2.25.41–5), must we therefore conclude that Ovid is here merely writing variations on a *topos* – as though he had no mind of his own, and as though sexual emotions were not the most widely shared, and perennial, impulses to bedevil the human heart?

XI

The character, the *persona*-projected-from-the-person that emerges from an overall reading of Ovid's erotic poems, is consistent, credible, and increasingly camouflaged, as time goes on, behind a protective smokescreen of literary sophistication and cynical detachment. We have already seen (above, p. 24) some of the factors that may have contributed to this process. Indeed, Ovid charts his own development with what appears to be considerable candour. The appearance, of course, may be deceptive. To some extent he is almost certainly creating a kind of fictional poetic *Bildungsroman*: the question is, how far? The portrait projected is not only persuasive in itself but strikingly congruent, at every stage, with the known facts of his life. What we are shown, in essence, is the destruction of innocence, the forging of an Achilles' shield, bright and impenetrable, to protect over-sensitive emotions. Our first encounter with the poet of the *Amores* reveals an engaging enthusiast, in love with poetry, in love with love, dazzled by the senses, immensely creative and vulnerable. By the time we are through that carefully revised cycle, the narrator has plummeted to a nadir of despair and self-hatred: the world is not the glittering toy he thought it, human relations can hurt and perplex, disillusion has set in. It is at this point that Ovid creates his true *persona*, his protective carapace: the vulnerable lover's experiences become mere grist to the didactic mill of a new, untouchable protagonist, the *praeceptor amoris*, a brilliant, heartless, witty, articulate student of Roman manners and morals, the heterosexual Wilde or Coward of antiquity.

The mask, of course, is not quite consistent. In the *Art of Love*, flashes of kindness and human consideration from time to time break through that glittering façade. Yet from a very early point in his poetic career, Ovid's attitude to sex is presented as one of pure priapic functionalism (or, as in *Am.* 3.7, its antonym, impotence). Any feeling he may have retained for human relationships is carefully suppressed, and further distanced by a battery of recondite allusions. Here one suggestive modern parallel is Eliot's *Waste Land*, also the work of a bookish and allusive author, similarly given – perhaps, again, as a form of camouflage or self-protection – to literary quotation and parody. Could Ovid also claim 'These fragments have I shored against my ruins'? The release of new material since

Eliot's death has shown that *The Waste Land* is deeply rooted in unhappy personal experience, an all-too-accurate reflection of the poet's psychological and sexual problems at the time when it was written. The *persona*, in both cases, is there, but symbiotic with the living face behind it. Cynicism and irony, too, can be defensive masks, as we see from the poems and stories of Dorothy Parker, who transmuted the raw material of a sensuous, desperately neurotic life into brittle and witty works of art.

The chief reason why Ovid *qua* eroticist can only be tolerated by so many people as a literary *farceur* is, I suspect, because he almost wholly lacked – or perhaps very early suppressed – the romantic instinct, as his elegiac predecessors most certainly did not. Catullus and Propertius both had incendiary affairs with that highly modern figure, the *femme fatale*, whom they celebrated in burning verses; they understood, all too well, what Mario Praz has labelled the Romantic Agony, and counted all well lost for love. But in Ovid's mind the Romantic Agony was to be neutralized by irreverent laughter. Originally, we may surmise, for self-protective reasons, he seems to have treated all grand passions, political no less than erotic, as lacking in *urbanitas* if not positively vulgar. It did not take long for the pose to become habitual, to engender a coolly assured attitude to life. The ironic parodist in him turned Rome's governmental and marital clichés inside-out; the two interpenetrated to form a scathing in-depth appraisal of Augustan society (see above, p. 44). *Militat omnis amans*: the lover, in Ovid's scale of values, has no less tough a time, and deserves no less well of society, than the soldier or the statesman. Ovid is as indifferent to Roman middle-class values, seemingly, as to the glories of empire (it took exile to make him tone down both attitudes, and even then with a specific end in view); Augustus and his friends must have found such a poet, *ab initio*, not only frivolous but also subversive.

Today, of course, things have changed. Few critics now take exception to Ovid's alleged political attitudes, much less attribute them to a *persona*: not surprisingly, since they might have been custom-made to suit modern Western liberals. The notion of an authoritarian regime, sniped at by literary intellectuals who wrap up their message in myth and symbol, has a contemporary, and all too familiar, quality about it. Looked at in this way, Ovid at once becomes an acceptable figure in the anti-totalitarian resistance movement – a movement of which the later Roman heroes, and casualties, included Lucan, Seneca, Petronius and Juvenal. His withdrawal from a senatorial career in favour of poetry and sex (two notoriously private, if not anti-social, activities) can be construed as a deliberate rejection of Augustus' civic, moral and political ideals.

Yet though Ovid's politics may have become respectable nowadays, his public attitude to sex (whatever its more sensitive antecedents may have been) remains a perennial embarrassment: hence one strong motive (cf. above, pp. 59ff.) for assuming a distinct *persona* in the erotic poems. Above all in the *Art of Love*, but already to some extent in the *Amores*, we see a man to whom women are, fundamentally, *sexual objects*. This is not a universal Roman attitude: Propertius and Tibullus, to look no further, tell a very different story. It is significant how often, particularly in the *Art of Love*, Ovid refers to the object of his desire in the neuter: *quod ames*, he says, '*something* for you to love' (see, e.g., *AA* 1.91–2, 175, 263; other instances abound). Even the word 'love', with its romantic connotations for modern ears, is subtly misleading. What Ovid has in mind throughout is not love (in the sense that Meredith or Erich Segal would understand it) but straightforward sexual seduction. The man's sole concern is to get the woman into bed, while the woman holds out for as many fringe benefits as she can collect before surrendering her one trump card: her elusiveness. *Do ut des*. Take away the high poetic finish, the sophisticated wit, the brilliant instinct for parody, and what remains, far less coarsely expressed, is, in essence, the attitude of Henry Miller as formulated in his *Tropic* novels or *The Rosy Crucifixion*: women as objects of pursuit, reduced to their ultimate vaginal function – or as mere grit in the poetic oyster, a stimulus to elicit immortal verse and, more important, immortal fame.

To borrow Ovid's own favourite image, what he offers, particularly in the *Art of Love*, is a guide to sexual siege-warfare and night-exercises (*Am.* 1.9, *AA* 2.233ff.). Pursuit, moreover (cf. p. 134), forms the essence and major attraction of the game. For Ovid a woman, to be attractive, must be hard to get: easy marks leave him cold. He spends nearly three books of the *Art of Love* telling men and women how to manoeuvre during the chase, and no more than a few perfunctory lines (*AA* 3.769–808) instructing them how to act when their quarry is safely bedded. Everyone, he assures us in a casual aside (*Am.* 1.5.25), knows about *that*. Like 'Walter', the author of that pathological casebook *My Secret Life* (which spells out, embarrassingly, just what the *Art of Love* would mean in practice), Ovid seems to have been obsessed by the idea and practice of seduction as an end in itself: we may speculate as to his original motives (above, p. 24), but the fact remains. His wiry physique, his natural abstemiousness, are only mentioned to demonstrate that he kept himself fit for the job.

How far, despite his much-vaunted psychological prowess, did he ever understand, or even really like, women as such? More, perhaps, than we might guess from the didactic poems alone, where his formulas for dealing with them almost all derive from popular, and perennial, masculine fantasies – on occasion, indeed, bearing an unfortunate resemblance to the kind of advice handed out in the editorial columns of *Playboy*. Even Bk 3 of the *Art of Love*, on the face of it designed to accommodate women, ends up by advising them to behave in ways that will please and flatter men. Yet against this one has to set the adolescent who declaimed in favour of passionate marital love (above, p. 21), the poet whose uxoriousness was in such striking contrast to the irregular bachelor lives of his literary contemporaries, who reveals so genuine a relationship with his third wife in his epistles from exile. The mask, as I have suggested, may well have been protective camouflage for a too-vulnerable sensitivity, hurt at an impressionable age and determined never to be hurt again: the modern example of Somerset Maugham offers some suggestive parallels. This does not require us to believe Ovid *au pied de la lettre* when he asserts, in his apologia to Augustus from Tomis (*Tr.* 2.339–58), that his erotic poems are to be construed as mere fiction. Why should we trust such self-exculpation more than his equally firm assertion, written in happier days (*AA* 1.28–9), that 'This work is based / On experience: what I write, believe me, I have practised'?

As should by now be clear, almost everything that Ovid wrote in exile was self-serving propaganda of a peculiarly desperate sort, its prime object being to pave the way for his reprieve (or at least some amelioration of his punishment) by refurbishing his tarnished moral credentials. In particular he was determined to separate himself, *qua* man and citizen, from that unfortunate *carmen* with which everyone identified his image. Hence his emphatic assertion (*AA* 1.31–4, 2.599–600, 3.483–4; cf. *EP* 3.3.51–2) that the women for whom he wrote the *Art of Love* were not freeborn married ladies but *demi-mondaines* and therefore fair game, an argument which I find, in all senses of the word, meretricious (cf. p. 73). Gordon Williams has argued, with some cogency (pp. 538–52), that not only Catullus, but also Tibullus and Propertius, cultivated mistresses who, far from being courtesans, or even freedwomen, were married Roman ladies of superior rank. This, he argues, was the elegiac convention that Ovid inherited, one not unlike that of the Provençal troubadours, with a lover undertaking to serve his married, and therefore enticingly unavailable, mistress.*

---

* If Ovid derived a good deal of his early erotic material from his first wife (see p. 23), this would not only provide an excellent motive for keeping the identity of 'Corinna' a secret (since tradition demanded an elusive mistress rather than a legally available wife: imagine the literary snickers if the truth got out!), but would, for this period at least, also give an unexpected and ironic truth to his claim, from exile, that his Muse may have been wanton, but his life was chaste. Equally ironic, of course, was the poet who, in such circumstances, wrote poems about the adultery game, only to have his wife take off to practise what he preached.

If this is true, and I think it is, then the *paraclausithyron* (see p. 274) and the whole concept of 'enslavement to passion' (*servitium amoris*) at once make excellent sense, which was not the case when scholars applied them to call-girls, since the latter are not paid (except in special pathological cases) to shut their clients out or otherwise treat them like dirt, and would hardly make a living if they did. But an upper-class married lady indulging herself in a little discreet adultery on the side is a quite different proposition, which at once eliminates all those puzzling social paradoxes in which Ovid's erotic poems *prima facie* abound. Why should any Roman gentleman need a manual of *social* seduction techniques to crack the defences of women who, supposedly, (a) did not belong to his own class, and (b) were in any case virtually defined by their availability? Why all the elaborate but, on the face of it, quite irrelevant stage-props: presents and lady's-maids, go-betweens and confidantes, hall-porters, secret messages and carefully planned assignations? When Ovid claims *not* to be writing for respectable (or not-so-respectable) married women, his protestations sound as conventional, and as hollow, as the novelist's guarantee that his characters are wholly imaginary and not based upon any living persons. With his motives for such a caveat we are brought back, sharply, to the political and social realities of Augustan Rome.

XII

Probably in 18 BC, Augustus passed the first stage of his legislation for social and moral reform, including the *Lex Iulia de maritandis ordinibus* and the *Lex Iulia de adulteriis coercendis*. The first aimed at encouraging larger families and discouraging obdurate bachelors, *inter alia* by restricting their right to accept legacies. It had proved unpopular with the landowning gentry, and Augustus had been compelled to accept substantial revisions to the original draft (Suet. *Div. Aug.* 34.1). Later, such resentment did it arouse, in particular among the equestrian order (Dio Cass. 56.10), that we find it jettisoned altogether (AD 9), and replaced by the far milder consular *Lex Papia Poppaea*. But it is the second – equally unpopular – law which most concerns us here. Its object was to stamp out adultery, in particular at senatorial or equestrian level, and to this end it embodied a series of positively draconian penalties for the guilty. Both parties were relegated to different islands for life, the paramour losing half his property, and the woman a third, as well as half her dowry. Such legislation, as Tacitus remarked (*Ann.* 3.24.2), was an affront to Roman tradition. It also divided free women into two categories, *matrones honestae*, with whom any sexual liaison was illegal, and those *in quas stuprum non committitur*, who were beyond contamination, i.e. prostitutes.

No ruler, let alone so canny a politician as Augustus, would impose these stringent punishments unless adultery had long since become the upper class's most popular diversion – which is exactly what we might guess from a first perusal of the Roman elegiac tradition. Further, since Ovid's *Art of Love* (which formalized several generations of classy fun-and-games into an erotic quadrille with its own sophisticated rules) had come out, to immense publicity, almost two decades after the *Lex Iulia de adulteriis coercendis* was first promulgated, it seems a fair assumption that this ordinance had been honoured, so to speak, more in the breach than the observance. Yet a general flouting of the law (as with comparable modern regulations concerning, say, homosexuality or marijuana) offered no protection against its enforcement. Once it was on the statute-book, however rarely it might be invoked, the whole existing convention of erotic elegy, with its married mistresses and titillating *servitium amoris*, became overnight an explosively dangerous commodity. Julia I's disgrace, politically motivated though that may have been, provided an all-too-graphic demonstration of what was at stake. Was it due to bravado, *naïveté*, pro-Julian sentiment or pure accident that Ovid brought out his *Art of Love* right in the wake of that resounding scandal?

He had begun writing the *Amores* about 25 BC, in a

freer atmosphere: attempts at moral legislation some three years earlier seem to have come to nothing, and the conventions developed by poets from Gallus to Propertius could still be exploited. Yet by the time the original five-book edition of the *Amores* appeared, probably in 16 or 15 BC (see p. 30), the *Lex Iulia de adulteriis coercendis* hung like a Sword of Damocles over the private lives and literary fashions of upper-class Rome. Ovid therefore camouflaged his views, but in an arrogantly perfunctory way; he certainly did not change them. Numerous poems in the *Amores* – even as revised – still present what are obviously married ladies of breeding engaged in adulterous pursuits (e.g. 1.4, 1.10, 2.2, 2.4, 2.7, 2.12, 3.2, 3.4, 3.14). The fiction of their status as freedwomen or courtesans is meant to impress no one except the authorities, like Ovid's claims (above, p. 70) about the audience for whom he allegedly composed the *Art of Love*. Like a child, he was playing with fire: life, and love, were a game of words to him; it is unlikely that he ever understood, till the blow fell, just how vulnerable a stance he had taken up. His pretences are perfunctory. Occasionally, too, the mask slipped. 'It's so provincial/To object to adulterous wives' he observes at one point (*Am.* 3.4.37–8). Don't stand on your marital rights, he adjures the husband: your wife's affairs will bring you presents and influential friends.

The long passage in the *Black Sea Letters* (*EP* 3.3.49–64) where Ovid yet again swears that he has steered clear of married women, and only written about, or for, freedwomen and *meretrices*, quite openly alludes to Augustus' 'stern law' on adultery and the hopelessness of his exile ever being rescinded if he is believed to have written a textbook for upper-class adulterers – '*vetiti si lege severa/credor adulterii composuisse notas*'. It was the *belief* that had to be dissipated: the truth was another matter. The eleventh commandment in such circles, Augustan or Edwardian, has always run: 'Thou shalt not be found out' – an attitude which Ovid hints at strongly elsewhere (*Tr.* 2.418), when he complains to the Princeps about writers who are free and successful despite having published erotic literature, and *not having kept quiet* about their sexual affairs, *concubitus non tacuere suos*. The operative word is *tacuere*. If we assume, as I think we must, that Ovid's main preoccupation, when protesting his personal innocence in the pre-exilic poems, was to insure himself against the more unpleasant consequences of the Augustan adultery laws, then much that would otherwise remain contradictory at once falls into place. The mask, to this extent, was no literary device, but – in a highly personal sense – self-protection. As we approach 1984, we should be able to recognize, and appreciate, his dilemma.

XIII

It is not possible, within the scope of this already over-extended introduction, to give an adequate analysis of the many literary problems which Ovid's erotic poems present. That would require a separate monograph, which I hope in due course to write, and for which the problems already discussed, here and in the body of the notes, provide some sort of starting-point. The establishment of a firm biographical and literary chronology, the precise relationship of the poet himself, at each successive stage, to his creative *persona* – these form essential prolegomena to any useful evaluation of the poems. Many further topics then call for discussion: some are lightly touched on in the present work, others not treated at all (which should not be taken as evidence that I do not have them very much in mind). They include the evolution of Ovid's creative method between the *Amores* and the *Art of Love* (and, *a fortiori*, between the *Art of Love* and the *Metamorphoses*); the precise significance of those lengthy illustrative digressions (e.g. the story of Daedalus and Icarus, *AA* 2.21–96) with which the poet breaks up and enlivens his didactic precepts; his use of imitation and parody to exploit – and criticize – the elegiac tradition that he inherited; his oddly limited and repetitive imagery, mostly drawn from farming, sailing or the racecourse; his mythic parallels; his calculated ambiguities, often for the purpose of double entendre; his attitude to magic as, at its highest level, poetic metaphor (a recurrent preoccupation which goes back at least as far as Gorgias and Plato); his cool attitude to religion and philosophy, in particular the Epicureanism of Lucretius; above all, his complex structural patterns and thematic orchestration.

Structuralism, indeed, has become a kind of academic growth industry in Ovidian studies, with both good and bad results. It is by now a truism that both the Augustan elegists and the Hellenistic poets whose general literary tradition they inherited employed (as we might expect) various principles of formal book-arrangement when putting their collections together for publication, as well as similar internal principles for the articulation of longer works. The most common devices were (i) the use of *variatio*, i.e. the separation of poems with similar topics, addressees or (where appropriate) metres, (ii) the positioning of key poems at points of emphasis, in particular the beginning, middle or end of a book, with the central poem often acting as a pivot balancing the first and second half, and (iii) the deployment of poems in pairs or cycles.

Various scholars have applied these principles, with greater or lesser success, to Theocritus, Callimachus, Catullus, Virgil, Horace and, above all, to Tibullus, Propertius and Ovid. Their application offers a salutary reminder that pattern-spotting and pattern-making, as processes, too often lack any clear distinction from one another in the mind of the critic, with the result that, as Dryden said of translation, 'many a fair precept . . . is, like a seeming demonstration in the mathematics, very specious in the diagram, but failing in the mechanic operation.'

Since the setting up of structural models is an activity dangerously deficient (at least as far as literature is concerned) in external scientific controls, it is not to be wondered at that the theorists, like Gibbon's Byzantine heretics, contradict one another at every turn. The situation has been further complicated, in particular as regards the *Amores*, by a self-defeating tendency to look for numerical correspondences, either in line-groupings or individual poems. When such correspondences proved elusive, the temptation to juggle the three books into shape, by uniting or dividing poems, and thus producing a neat 15 + 20 + 15 pattern, was irresistible, but a shaky basis on which to construct further hypotheses. My own feeling is that while Ovid clearly planned the overall structure of the *Amores* in a general sense, attempts to pin him down to an over-rigid schematization are doomed *ab initio*.

The *Amores* as we have them (see p. 267) constitute a second, much-reduced edition of an original five-book publication. Ignoring the vexed question of how much, if anything, *Amores*[2] added to the canon, we can say with confidence that a great deal was jettisoned: the equivalent of two whole books. The criteria for the exclusion of these juvenilia need not have been exclusively literary. If my biographical reconstruction is valid, and the development of Ovid's literary *persona* was dictated at least in part by a need for emotional self-protection (above, pp. 22ff); if, in particular, Am. 3.5 can be taken as a youthful exercise surviving accidentally from *Amores*[1] rather than as non-Ovidian pastiche – then, it seems safe to assume, much that was excised from *Amores*[2] went out not only because it was prentice work in the literary sense, but because of its embarrassing candour. As the collection stands, Ovid moves in three books through the entire paradigm of direct sexual experience, from fancy-free *nequitia* to disillusionment and rejection, all counterpointed against a literary exploration of the elegiac mode, with Elegy herself personified (e.g. in 3.1) as an erotic tease. In each book key poems, literary or thematic, top and tail the collection, though central 'pivots' are harder to prove.* It may be significant that Bk 1 shows most evidence of structural planning, and has, as a result, elicited a greater than usual degree of consensus among

---

* 'Frame' poems include 1.1, 1.15, 2.1, 2.18 (? to be placed after 2.19), 3.1 and 3.15, all on the pursuit of elegy; the only indisputable 'pivot' poem is 1.8, the bawd's sermon on the advantages of gold-digging.

structural critics. The inference could be that, because of its relatively upbeat mood, it suffered least from revision and suppression: that what Ovid was most concerned to excise were over-candid poems, in the Propertian manner, of *marital* heart-break and betrayal. *Am.* 3.5, the 'dream poem', would fit precisely into this category.

The *Art of Love* is an altogether different proposition, consisting of three (four including the *Cures*) long related poems on a common theme, which presumes a more tightly knit and consciously organized structure. I have made a detailed analysis of this structure, which I hope to publish elsewhere. A brief general survey must suffice here, for two reasons. First, full-scale structural investigations have no place in a book of this sort, though their findings may be of interest; and second, because of that lack of external control from which such analyses suffer, I do not flatter myself that the patterns I have extrapolated – against my own expectations and instincts – are necessarily any more cogent than their predecessors.

What I isolated was a series of thematic groupings, each internally subdivided, with no discernible numerical pattern, but relying heavily on balanced correspondences involving ring-composition and hysteron-proteron devices, and signposted by strategically placed metaphors and images, mythic *exempla* or personal statements. Thus (to begin at the beginning) Bk 1 for me consists of five major divisions: (A) Proem and Partitio (1–40): (B) Part One: Hunting Grounds for Women (41–252): (C) a central linking passage, with the coda to Part One (253–62) leading into the introduction to Part Two (263–8); (D) Part Two: Hunting Techniques (269–754): (E) Coda and Envoi (755–72). It should at once be clear that just as (A) and (E) balance one another, so do (B) and (D), while (C) functions as a double central pivot.

Within these major groupings I have detected others, internal to each individual section, but at the same time setting up counterpointed correspondences throughout the book as a whole. To take a particularly striking example, the first section of the proem (1–22), the introductory sections of (B) and

(D) 41–66, 269–350), and the coda and envoi (755–72) are all organized in a hysteron-proteron pattern. Where P = personal statement, M = metaphorical illustration, and E = *exemplum* (mythic or otherwise), the following respective sequences occur: PMEPEMP; PMEMP; ME (M + E) EM; MEMEM. Similarly with the other books, where the main units of division (apart from proem and coda) are individual 'lessons', articulated with pivot and link sequences, I found the same internal thematic symmetries, the same external counterpointing between sections. Though I have not attempted a full analysis here, the reader will find some discreet typographical signposting in the section-divisions of my translation of the *Art of Love*, which on occasion diverge from those commonly accepted by editors. Research in this area has a long way to go still; no conclusions – my own least of all – can be described as anything more than tentative.

XIV

Ovid has suffered, more than most Roman poets, from overclose association with the eighteenth century – an association which automatically guaranteed his depreciation during the Romantic revival, and from which he is only slowly recovering today. This relationship was given formal expression by the habit of translating his work into stopped rhyming couplets – a practice which obstinately survived even such hazards as the Ovidian habit of joking about Elegy's 'one lame foot' when referring to the pentameter. 'Let my verse rise with six stresses,' Ovid says, 'drop to five on the downbeat' (*Am.* 1.1.27): the traditional translator, presumably unable to count, with cheerful impartiality gives him five on both. Even in the *Metamorphoses* the use of rhymed couplets to express hexameters sets up associations wholly alien to the original movement of the verse; yet just such a version, that by A. E. Watts, came out as recently as 1954, to be reinforced by L. P. Wilkinson's illustrative extracts in *Ovid Recalled* a year later. It took the pioneering efforts of Guy Lee, whose version of the *Amores*

(1968) remains a landmark in Ovidian studies, to break the tyranny of this singularly inappropriate medium; and even Lee did not face the simple fact that, however one sets about translating a Latin elegiac couplet, the first line, to achieve any sort of structural correspondence, has to be longer than the second.

The problem of the hexameter had already been tackled, with some success, by Day Lewis and Richmond Lattimore, who saw that the trouble with an English stress-equivalent to strict classical metre was that it lacked all counterpoint and tension: having neither fixed vowel-quantities nor (except in the most rudimentary sense) inflections, English could match neither the plangent and mosaic sonorities of Latin nor the flexible springiness of Greek on their own terms. On the other hand, there had to be some attempt to produce the *effect* of the original, since otherwise we would still be stuck with the tradition of 'local equivalence': blank verse, rhyming quatrains or other even less apposite English growths (for a full discussion of this problem see my *Essays in Antiquity*, London 1960, pp. 185ff.). Day Lewis and Lattimore went for the beat, the ictus, and let the metre take care of itself. They worked out a loose six-beat (occasionally five-beat) line, generally, though not always, with a feminine ending, that at least caught the precipitate striding movement of the hexameter, while preserving its fundamental structure. It was the late Gilbert Highet – an excellent occasional verse-translator in addition to his other multiple talents – who first extended these ideas to the elegiac couplet in the extracts he used to illustrate *Poets in a Landscape* (1957), representing the pentameter by a variable short-stopped line with anything from five to two main stresses.

This, in essence, is the principle I have adopted for the present version of Ovid. It gives ample scope for rhythmic variety, something fundamental to all poetry based on stress, a compensation for the absence of those contrapuntal resonances only achievable in a language with the full resources of fixed-quantity metre at its disposal. While at least suggesting the

highly formal (yet never boring) elegiac pattern that Ovid used
to such subtle effect, it also gives great scope for changes of
pace and emphasis, often through a casual enjambment that
works more easily in English than it might in Latin. It is not
the perfect solution – no translation can offer that – but at
least (I flatter myself) it achieves some sort of workable com-
promise between the false associations of home-grown form
and the impossible demands of alien metrics. The greatest pit-
fall, to be avoided at all costs, is the self-indulgent contempo-
rary pastiche, dated almost before it is written. When I feel
tempted, as I have at times done, to satisfy a weakness for
loose historical parallels by translating Ovid's exilic poems in
the manner of *Rock Drill* or the *Pisan Cantos*, I need only pick
up Pound's own execrable version of Sophocles' *Women of
Trachis*, and sanity rapidly returns. *Homage to Sextus Prop-
ertius* is another matter altogether, yet equally inapplicable:
what we have here is not a translation, not even a
'metaphrase', but a poem in its own right.

It is now over forty years since I first read Ovid in Latin,
and twenty since I first published a critical evaluation of him
(see *Essays in Antiquity*, pp. 109–35). The present study has
occupied my not over-generous leisure moments for more than a
decade, and has steadily deepened my appreciation of Ovid's at
times almost Empsonian complexities, the richness and variety
of his poetic vision, his wit, his irony, his bubbling sense of fun,
his elusive and delicate sensibilities, his changing moods and
masks, his life-long love affair with the infinite subtleties of the
Latin language. Much of what I wrote about him in 1960 I
would still maintain: the supremacy of his early love-poetry and
the exilic elegies, his ability to transcend the carapace of wit and
fashion with which he protected himself, his failure fully to
control an extended *magnum opus* (apparent even in the *Cures
for Love*, let alone in the *Metamorphoses*). On the other hand I
have, I hope, come to a better appreciation of the deep prob-
lems inherent in his creative *persona*, and the relationship of
that *persona* to his public and private life. I have lived with him
now for many years: admiration has deepened into affection,

and as I write these words I feel I am offering a tribute to some old and dear personal friend. If I can, in my translation, convey even a fraction of the continuing pleasure and enlightenment Ovid has brought into my life, then all my labours will have been well worth while.

Athens – Methymna – Los Angeles – Austin
1969 – 81

THE POEMS

THE AMORES

Epigram by the Poet

We are our author's book. Before, we comprised five sections,
    Now we're cut down to three. The decision was his.
You still may derive no pleasure from reading us – but
    remember,
    With two of us gone, your labour is that much less.

BOOK I

I

Arms, warfare, violence – I was winding up to produce a
  Regular epic, with verse-form to match –
Hexameters, naturally. But Cupid (they say) with a snicker
  Lopped off one foot from each alternate line.
'Nasty young brat,' I told him, 'who made *you* Inspector of
5   Metres?
  We poets come under the Muses, we're not in your mob.
What if Venus took over the weapons of blonde Minerva,
  While blonde Minerva began fanning passion's flame?
Who'd stand for Our Lady of Wheatfields looking after rides
  and forests?
10 Who'd trust the Virgin Huntress to safeguard crops?
Imagine long-haired Apollo on parade with a pikestaff
  While the War-God fumbled tunes from Apollo's lyre!
Look, boy, you've got your own empire, and a sight too much
  influence
  As it is. Don't get ambitious, quit playing for more.
15 Or is your fief universal? Is Helicon yours? Can't even
  Apollo call his lyre his own these days?
I'd got off to a flying start, clean paper, one magnificent
  Opening line. Number two brought me down
With a bump. I haven't the theme to suit your frivolous metre:
20 No boyfriend, no girl with a mane of coiffured hair –'
When I'd got so far, presto, he opened his quiver, selected
  An arrow to lay me low,
Then bent the springy bow in a crescent against his knee, and
  Let fly. 'Hey, poet!' he called, 'you want a theme? Take *that*!'
25 His shafts – worse luck for me – never miss their target:
  I'm on fire now, Love owns the freehold of my heart.
So let my verse rise with six stresses, drop to five on the
  downbeat –
  Goodbye to martial epic, and epic metre too!

86

Come on then, my Muse, bind your blonde hair with
    a wreath of
Sea-myrtle, and lead me off in the six-five groove!   30

2   Love hurts

What's wrong with me nowadays, how explain why my mattress
    Feels so hard, and the bedclothes will *never* stay in place?
Why am I kept awake all night by insomnia, thrashing around
    till   can't sleep
    Every weary bone in my body aches?
If Love were my assailant, surely I'd know it – unless he's   5
    Craftily gone under cover, slipped past my guard?
Yes, that must be it: heart skewered / by shafts of desire,
    the raging
Beast, passion, out at prowl in my breast.
Shall I give in? To resist might just bank up the furnace –
    All right, I give in. A well-squared load lies light.   10
Flourish a torch, it burns fiercer. I know, I've seen it. Stop the
    Motion, and pouf! it's out.
Yoke-shy rebellious oxen collect more blows and curses
    Than a team that's inured to the plough.
Your restive horse earns a wolf-curb, his mouth's all bruises;   15
    A harness-broken nag scarcely feels the reins.
It's the same with Love. Play stubborn, you get a far more
    thorough
    Going-over than those who admit they're hooked.
So I'm coming clean, Cupid: here I am, your latest victim,
    Hands raised in surrender. Do what you like with me.   20
No need for military action. I want terms, an armistice –
    You wouldn't look good defeating an unarmed foe.
Put on a wreath of myrtle, yoke up your mother's pigeons –
    Your stepfather himself will lend you a fine
Chariot: mount it, drive in triumph through the cheering   25
    Rabble, skilfully whipping your birds ahead,
With your train of prisoners behind you, besotted youths and
    maidens,

Such pomp, such magnificence, your very own
Triumph: and I'll be there too, fresh-wounded, your latest
30   Prisoner – displaying my captive mind –
With Conscience, hands bound behind her, and Modesty, and
    all Love's
    Other enemies, whipped into line.
You'll have them all scared cold, while the populace goes crazy,
    Waves to its conquering hero, splits its lungs.
35 And what an escort – the Blandishment Corps, the Illusion
    And Passion Brigade, your regular bodyguard:
These are the troops you employ to conquer men and
      immortals –
    Without them, why, you're nothing, a snail unshelled.
How proudly your mother will applaud your triumphal progress
40   From high Olympus, shower roses on your head;
Wings bright-bejewelled, jewels starring your hair, you'll
    Ride in a car of gold, all gold yourself.
What's more, if I know you, even on this occasion
    You'll burn the crowd up, break hearts galore all round:
With the best will in the world, dear, you can't keep your
45   arrows idle –
    They're so hot, they scorch the crowd as you go by.
Your procession will match that of Bacchus, after he'd won
      the Ganges
    Basin (though *he* was drawn by tigers, not birds).
So then, since I am doomed to be part of your – *sacré* triumph,
50   Why waste victorious troops on me now?
Take a hint from the campaign record of your cousin, Augustus
    Caesar – *his* conquests became protectorates.

3

Fair's fair now, Venus. This girl's got me hooked. All I'm
    asking from her
Is love – or at least some future hope for my own
Eternal devotion. No, even that's too much – hell, just let me
    love her!

(*Listen*, Venus: I've asked you so often now.)
Say yes, pet/I'd be your slave for years, for a lifetime.   5
  Say yes – unswerving fidelity's my strong suit/
I may not have top-drawer connections, I can't produce
  blue-blooded
  Ancestors to impress you, my father's plain middle-class,
And there aren't any squads of ploughmen to deal with *my*
  broad acres –
  My parents are both pretty thrifty, and need to be.   10
What *have* I got on my side, then? Poetic genius, sweetheart,
  Divine inspiration. And love. I'm yours to command –
Unswerving faithfulness, morals above suspicion,
  Naked simplicity, a born-to-the-purple blush.
I don't chase thousands of girls, I'm no sexual circus-rider;   15
  Honestly, all I want is to look after you
Till death do us part, have the two of us living together
  All my time, and know you'll cry for me when I'm gone.
Besides, when you give me yourself, what you'll be providing
  Is creative material. My art will rise to the theme   20
And immortalize *you*. Look, why do you think we remember
  The swan-upping of Leda, or Io's life as a cow,
Or poor virgin Europa whisked off overseas, clutching
  That so-called bull by the – horn? Through poems, of course.
So you and I, love, will enjoy the same world-wide publicity,   25
  And our names will be linked, for ever, with the gods.

4

'So your man's going to be present at this dinner-party?
  I hope he drops down dead before the dessert!
Does this mean no hands, just eyes (any chance guest's
  privilege) –
Just to *look* at my darling, while *he*
Lies there with you beside him, in licensed embracement   5
  And paws your bosom or neck as he feels inclined?
I'm no longer surprised at those Centaurs for horsing around
  over

Some cute little filly when they were full of wine –
I may not live in the forest, or be semi-equipped as a stallion,
10   But still *I* can hardly keep my hands to myself
When you're around. Now listen, I've got some instructions
      for you,
      And don't let the first breeze blow them out of your head!
Arrive before your escort. I don't see what can be managed
      If you do – but anyway, get there first.
When he pats the couch, put on your Respectable Wife
15   expression,
      And take your place beside him – but nudge my foot
As you're passing by. Watch out for my nods and eye-talk,
      Pick up my stealthy messages, send replies.
I shall speak whole silent volumes with one raised eyebrow,
20   Words will spring from my fingers, words traced in wine.
When you're thinking about the last time we made love
      together,
      Touch your rosy cheek with one elegant thumb.
If you're cross with me, and can't say so, then pinch the bottom
      Of your earlobe. But when I do or say
25 Something that gives you especial pleasure, my darling,
      Keep turning the ring on your finger to and fro.
When you yearn for your man to suffer some well-merited
      misfortune
      Place your hands on the table as though in prayer.
If he mixes wine specially for you, watch out, make him
      drink it
30   Himself. Ask the waiter for what *you* want
As you hand back the goblet. I'll be the first to seize it
      And drink from the place your lips have touched.
If *he* offers you tit-bits out of some dish he's tasted,
      Refuse what's been near his mouth.
Don't let him put his arms round your neck, and oh, don't
35   lay that
      Darling head of yours on *his* coarse breast.
Don't let his fingers roam down your dress to touch up
      Those responsive nipples. Above all, don't you dare

Kiss him, not once. If you do, I'll proclaim myself your lover,
    Lay hand upon you, claim those kisses as mine.   40
So much for what I can see. But there's plenty goes on under
    A long evening wrap. The mere thought worries me stiff.
Don't start rubbing your thigh against his, don't go playing
    Footsy under the table, keep smooth from rough.'
(I'm scared all right, and no wonder – I've been too successful   45
    An operator myself, it's my own
Example I find so unnerving. I've often petted to climax
    With my darling at a party, hand hidden under her cloak –)
'– Well, *you* won't do *that*. But still, to avoid the least
    suspicion,
    Remove such natural protection when you sit down.   50
Keep pressing fresh drinks – but no kisses – on your husband,
    Slip neat wine in his glass if you get the chance.
If he passes out comfortably, drowned in sleep and liquor,
    We must improvise as occasion dictates.
When we all (you too) get up and leave, remember   55
    To stick in the middle of the crowd –
That's where you'll find me, or I you: whenever
    There's a chance to touch me, please do!'
(Yet the most I can win myself is a few hours' respite:
    At nightfall my mistress and I must part.)   60
'At nightfall he'll lock you inside, and I'll be left weeping
    On that cold front doorstep – the nearest I can come
To your longed-for embraces, while *he's* enjoying, under
    licence,
    The kisses, and more, that you give me on the sly.
What you *can* do is show unwilling, behave as though you're
    frigid,   65
    Begrudge him endearments, make sex a dead loss.'
(Grant my prayer, Venus. Don't let either of them get
    pleasure
    Out of the act – *and certainly not her!*)
'But whatever the outcome tonight, when you see me
    tomorrow
    Just swear, through thick and thin, that you told him No.'   70

5

A hot afternoon: siesta-time. Exhausted,
   I lay sprawled across my bed.
One window-shutter was closed, the other stood half-open,
   And the light came sifting through
5 As it does in a wood. It recalled that crepuscular glow at sunset
   Or the trembling moment between darkness and dawn,
Just right for a modest girl whose delicate bashfulness
   Needs some camouflage. And then –
In stole Corinna, long hair tumbled about her
10   Soft white throat, a rustle of summer skirts,
Like some fabulous Eastern queen *en route* to her
      bridal-chamber –
Or a top-line city call-girl, out on the job.
I tore the dress off her – not that it really hid much,
   But all the same she struggled to keep it on:
15 Yet her efforts were unconvincing, she seemed half-hearted –
   Inner self-betrayal made her give up.
When at last she stood naked before me, not a stitch of clothing,
   I couldn't fault her body at any point.
Smooth shoulders, delectable arms (I saw, I touched them),
20   Nipples inviting caresses, the flat
Belly outlined beneath that flawless bosom,
   Exquisite curve of a hip, firm youthful thighs.
But why catalogue details? Nothing came short of perfection,
   And I clasped her naked body close to mine.
25 Fill in the rest for yourselves! Tired at last, we lay sleeping.
   May my siestas often turn out that way!

6

It's a dog's life for you, porter, chained to the wall. You're
     entitled
   To something better. Come on now, let's hear that door
Creak open, sweet music of rusty hinges. I'm not demanding
   Any outsize favour. Just give me a wide enough crack

To squeeze through sideways. Love's melted off my poundage, 5
    I'm a shadow, a skeleton. One inch – or two – is enough.
Love will teach you to creep undetected past watchful sentries,
    He'll never let you put a foot wrong.
I used to be scared of the dark and its empty phantoms,
    Was amazed by anyone who went out at night. 10
Then came a snicker of laughter – quite audible – from Cupid
    And his sexy mother. 'You too can be brave,' they said,
And presto! I was in love. Nowadays neither flitting ghosts nor
    Murderous footpads cause me the slightest qualms.
It's just *you* I fear. You're stubborn. You alone need my
      flattery; 15
    You hold the bolt that could finish me off.
Just look at this doorpost, all wet with my tears. (If you want a
    Really good view of it, why not undo the bars?)
When you were stripped for that flogging, and all ashiver,
    Didn't I get your mistress to let you off? 20
Have you the gall to suggest that the favour I once showed you
    Can be paid with any lesser service in return?
One good turn merits another. Here's your chance to get what
    you're after –
The night is passing: slide that doorbolt free!
Just slide it – I tell you, you'll win reprieve from your long
      bondage, 25
    Goodbye to the endless bread and water of servitude! –
No good. You're a hard case, porter. All my entreaties
    Fall on deaf ears. The door stays barred. Such tough
Oak-battened defences are fine when a city lies under
    Siege – but where's the invader now, 30
In peacetime? Shut out a lover, what's left for your enemies?
    The night is passing: slide that doorbolt free.
No army marches behind me, I'm innocent of weapons –
    If it weren't for that incubus Love
I'd be on my own. But *he* can never be got rid of: 35
    Simpler, for me, to tear body and soul apart.
One poet, then, mildly fuddled, with Love as escort
    And a cock-eyed wreath set askew

On his sticky-damp hair. Who'd shrink from such an attacker?
40   *The night is passing: slide that doorbolt free.*
Still obstinate? Or asleep? God damn you, have my entreaties
      Been wasted on empty air?
Yet, as I recall, when first I tried to slip past you,
      You stayed awake till all hours
45 Watching the stars wheel round. Got a girl in your cubbyhole?
      If so, you're one up on me.
Only give me the same chance – I'd take on your shackles.
      The night is passing: slide that doorbolt free.
Listen – didn't I catch the creak of hinges, the labouring
50   Scritch of an opened door? –
No such luck. Just a random gust, rattling the woodwork,
      Blowing my hopes sky-high.
Boreas, flame of a north wind, remember your air-raped
      Bride, come thunder these deaf posts down for me!
55 Silence throughout the city: damp with bright dewfall.
      The night is passing: slide that doorbolt free.
I've a sword and a torch, I'm ready to storm this standoffish
      Mansion by frontal assault –
Darkness, desire and drink don't make for moderation,
60   Night removes self-restraint; the others, fear.
I've exhausted my repertoire. Neither threats nor entreaties
      Can shift you. You're tougher than the door itself.
Guarding pretty girls isn't your forte. Man, you'd do better
      As a warder in some top-security gaol.
65 [Already the morning star's at its frosty zenith, and cockcrow
      Shatters poor workers' dreams.]
I'm not exactly happy. Well, I'll take off this garland
      And leave it lying right on the front step.
Come morning, my mistress will find it there, mute witness
70   To this wasted vigil of mine.
I'd better be off now. You stuck to it. Duty is duty,
      No Lovers Admitted. So, goodbye,
You and your door, slaves both. For unfeeling toughness
      You're just about evenly matched.

7

Any friend of mine here? Then tie up my hands (proper
   shackles
  Are what they deserve) until
This frenzy has blown itself out. I went mad, I assaulted
  My mistress. The poor girl's hurt, and in tears.
My rage was such, though, I could have beat up my own
   parents,   5
  Horsewhipped the blessed gods.
Well, there *are* precedents – like sevenfold-shielded Ajax
  When he ran amok through the meadows, slaughtering
   sheep,
Or Orestes the mother-killer, sick instrument of paternal
  Vengeance, all ready to knock off   10
His pursuing Furies. What I did (no excuses!) was mess up
  Her new coiffure. Like that, in disarray,
It looked splendidly windswept. Oh, her beauty – like
   Atalanta's
  (I suppose) while hunting game on the Arcadian hills,
Or Ariadne's, all tears as the cruel sirocco lifted   15
  Theseus, ship and promises, out of her life; –
And what price Cassandra, about to be raped, in chaste
   Athena's
  Shrine, on her knees? But she was a priestess, so
Wore her hair in a snood. Unanimous verdict: I'd been a
   brute, a
  Madman. Only she said nothing. She was too scared.   20
Yet her silent, frozen expression still condemned me, her
   speechless
  Tears proclaimed my guilt.
I'd sooner have had my arms fall from their sockets – easier
  To forego a part of myself. I found
A madman's strength – but it turned to my disadvantage,   25
  My toughness did me no good.
Hands, agents of crime and violence, I disown you!
  Clap on the gyves. The charge is sacrilege.

issue of domestic violence

earnest or parody

If I beat up Rome's lowest bum, *and he was a citizen*,
30 I'd be for it. Have I any more right to hit my girl?
Well, Diomede started it. He set me a bad example –
First man to strike a goddess. I came next.
Yet Diomede proved less culpable. *His* fury was expended
On an enemy. *I* hurt the girl I said I loved.
35 Come on now, conquering hero, enjoy your magnificent
Triumph, wear laurel, give thanks to the gods –
And hark to the crowd, as it surges behind your chariot, calling
'Up the brave boyo who defeated – a girl!'
She'll walk ahead, poor sweet, hair all dishevelled, dead-white
40 Except for the scratches on her cheeks –
My one and only captive. Bruised lips, bites around neck and
shoulders
Would have made more appropriate scars.
Last point: if I *had* to boil over like some furious torrent,
Transported with sheer rage,
45 Couldn't I just have scared her by shouting, bawled her
Out in fine style, made threats – but have known
When to stop? I could have ripped down her dress from neck
to waistline –
The belt would have stopped me there.
Instead, I grabbed the hair off her forehead, tore at those
ladylike
50 Cheeks with my nails. I admit it. I was a brute.
She stood there, bewildered. Her face had gone pale and
bloodless
As new-sawn marble, I watched
The numbness grip her, a shudder run through her body
Like a breeze in the poplar-leaves,
55 Or rippling across a reedbed, or ruffling catspaws
Sketched on the skin of the sea.
Tears brimmed in her eyes, spilled over at last, descended
Like drops from melting snow.
It was then that I first began to feel the enormity
60 Of what I had done. Those tears she shed were my blood.
Three times I tried to kneel before her in supplication

96

And clasp her feet. Three times
She thrust off those nightmare hands. Don't hesitate, darling,
    Scratch my face back. Revenge
Will lessen the agony. Eyes, hair, have your will of them: 65
    Anger lends strength to a weak hand.
Or else at least remove the signs of my misdemeanour –
    Just rearrange your hair as it was before!

8

There's a certain – well: any reader in need of a procuress?
    Listen,
Try Dipsas. A certain bitch, snake, hag.
Dipsas, dipso, well-named. If *she* ever saw pink horses
    At sunrise, they weren't the Dawn's.
She's a witch, mutters magical cantrips, can make rivers   5
    Run uphill, knows the best aphrodisiacs –
When to use herbal brews, or the whirring bullroarer,
    How to extract that stuff from a mare in heat.
She can control the weather, make a day overcast with
    Cloud at will, or brilliant and clear;   10
I've known times (believe it or not) when the moon turned
    bloody,
    And blood dripped from the stars.
It wouldn't surprise me if the old bitch grew feathers at
    nightfall
    And went flapping round like an owl –
I've heard rumours, it's possible. What's more, she's got double   15
    Pupils, a twin light glinting from each eye.
She conjures up long-dead souls from their crumbling
    sepulchres
    And has incantations to split the solid earth.
Well: this old hag undertook to suborn *our* relationship,
    And a glibly poisonous tongue she had for the job.   20
By pure chance I overheard her. The big double doors stood
    open.
    Here, then, is what she said: 'You know,

Dearie, you made a great hit with that rich young gentleman
    Yesterday. He'd got eyes for nobody else –
And why should he have? There's no girl more beautiful.
25   Such a pity
    Your turn-out doesn't match your face.
I'd like to see you become as wealthy as you're good-looking –
    Once get you in the money, I shan't ever starve.
The stars were against you, dearie, Mars stood in opposition,
30   But now Mars has wheeled off, and today
Venus is in the ascendant. Look how her rising favours
    Your lot: a rich suitor, and anxious to oblige!
Dead handsome, too, just about as pretty as you are – if he
    wasn't
    Bidding himself, why, people would bid for *him*.
Ah, that got a blush! Pale faces need colour, but Nature's
35   method
    Is so unpredictable. Safer to stick to Art.
Keep your eyes on your lap. Look demure, scale your responses
    To the size of each lover's gifts.
In the old days it was different. Those Sabine women stuck to
40   One husband apiece. But then *they* didn't wash.
Today Mars is so taken up with foreign campaigning
    That Venus has made a clean sweep of Rome,
Her own Aeneas' city. Pretty girls have a ball. No virgins
    Except the unasked – and a smart kid asks for herself.
45 Prissy-faced women are worth close scrutiny: you'll discover
    A frown can hide a multitude of sins.
Bending that bow made trial of Penelope's young wooers,
    A good stiff horn proved too much for them.
Volatile time slips past us without our knowledge
50   Like a swift-gliding river. Brass shines
With constant usage, a beautiful dress needs wearing,
    Leave a house empty, it rots.
Lack of exercise withers your beauty, you need to take lovers –
    And the treatment calls for more than one or two.
55 Run a string, take your pick. It's safer, less troublesome:
    Wolves that raid flocks eat best.

That poet of yours, now, what does he give you, except his
    latest
  Verses? Find the right lover, you'd scoop the pool.
Why isn't he richer? The patron god of poets
  Wears gold, plays a gilded lyre.   60
Look, dear, stop worshipping genius, try generosity
  Just for a change. To give is a fine art.
And don't you look down your nose at some slave who's
    purchased
  His freedom. Chalked feet are no crime.
Don't let yourself be fooled by ancestral portraits. Your
    lover's   65
  Broke? Then give him the boot, and his pedigree too.
When he asks for a night on the house because he's so
    handsome
  Tell him No. His boyfriend can foot the bill.
While you're spreading your net, go easy. Don't show too
    rapacious
  Or your bird may fly off. Once you've caught him, anything
    goes.   70
Some show of love does no harm: let him fancy himself your
    darling,
  But take good care you collect a *quid pro quo*.
Don't say Yes every night. Pretend that you have a headache,
  Or make Isis your excuse, then you can plead
Religious abstention. Enough's enough, though – he may get
    accustomed   75
  To going without, over-frequent rebuffs may cool
His passion off. Take gifts, but be deaf to entreaties –
  Let the lucky man hear his rival cursing outside.
You've hurt him? *He* started it. Throw a quick tantrum.
    This kind of
  Counter-attack will very soon choke him off.   80
But never stay angry too long. A festering quarrel
  Can make permanent enemies.
Another trick you must learn is control of the tear-ducts,
  How to weep buckets at will –

99

And when you're deceiving someone, don't let perjury scare
85   you:
    Venus ensures that her fellow-gods
Turn a deaf ear to such gambits. You must get yourself a
    houseboy
    And a well-trained maid, who can hint
What gifts will be welcome. Don't let them demand exorbitant
90   Tips for themselves. Little presents soon add up.
Your sister and mother, your nurse, these can all help fleece a
    lover –
    Many hands make quick loot.
When you've run through all other excuses for getting presents
    Say it's your birthday, show him the cake.
95 Don't let him get cocksure, without any rivals:
    Love minus competition never wears well.
Leave the bed suspiciously rumpled, make sure he sees it,
    Flaunt a few sexy bruises on your neck –
Above all, show him his rival's presents (if none are
    forthcoming
100   Order some yourself, from a good shop).
When you've dug enough gold, then protest he's being far too
    generous
    And ask him for a *loan* – which you'll never repay.
Beguile with sweet words, and blandish while you despoil him:
    A taste of honey will mask the nastiest dose.
105 These tactics are guaranteed by a lifetime's experience,
    So don't ignore them. Follow my advice.
And you'll never regret it. Ah, many's the time you'll bless me
    While I'm alive, and pray that my old bones
Lie easy after I'm gone –'
                    At this point my shadow
110   Betrayed me. I was dying to get my hands
On those sparse white locks, to tear at the old hag's raddled
    Cheeks and drink-bleary eyes.
May the gods strip the roof from her head, end her days in
    poverty,
    Send her horrible winters and an eternal thirst!

*love
and war*

● 9

Every lover's on active service, my friend, active service,
    believe me,
    And Cupid has his headquarters in the field.
Fighting and love-making belong to the same age-group –
    In bed as in war, old men are out of place.
A commander looks to his troops for gallant conduct,   5
    A mistress expects no less.
Soldier and lover both keep night-long vigil,
    Lying rough outside their captain's (or lady's) door.
The military life brings long route-marches – but just let his
    mistress
    Be somewhere ahead, and the lover too   10
Will trudge on for ever, scale mountains, ford swollen rivers,
    Thrust his way through deep snow.
Come embarkation-time *he* won't talk of 'strong north-easters',
    Or say it's 'too late in the season' to put to sea.
Who but a soldier or lover would put up with freezing   15
    Nights – rain, snow, sleet? The first
Goes out on patrol to observe the enemy's movements,
    The other watches his rival, an equal foe.
A soldier lays siege to cities, a lover to girls' houses,
    The one assaults city gates, the other front doors.   20
Night attacks are a great thing. Catch your opponents sleeping
    And unarmed. Just slaughter them where they lie.
That's how the Greeks dealt with Rhesus and his wild
    Thracians
    While rustling those famous mares.
Lovers, too, will take advantage of slumber (her husband's),   25
    Strike home while the enemy sleeps: getting past
Night patrols and eluding sentries are games both soldiers
    And lovers need to learn.
Love, like war, is a toss-up. The defeated can recover,
    While some you might think invincible collapse;   30
So if you've got love written off as an easy option
    You'd better think twice. Love calls

*explore metaphor
of lover as soldier*

For guts and initiative. Great Achilles sulks for Briseis –
    Quick, Trojans, smash through the Argive wall!
35 Hector went into battle from Andromache's embraces
    Helmeted by his wife.
Agamemnon himself, the Supremo, was struck into raptures
    At the sight of Cassandra's tumbled hair;
Even Mars was caught on the job, felt the blacksmith's meshes –
40 Heaven's best scandal in years. Then take
My own case. I was idle, born to leisure *en déshabillé*,
    Mind softened by lazy scribbling in the shade.
But love for a pretty girl soon drove the sluggard
    To action, made him join up.
And just look at me now – fighting fit, dead keen on night
45   exercises:
  If you want a cure for slackness, fall in love!

10

I had all the parallels for you. You were my Helen, Troy-bound
    From Sparta, the cause of war
Between first and second husbands. You were Leda, conned
      and swanned by
    That adulterous god on the make
5 In his birdsuit of white plumage. You were Amymone
    Plodding through dusty fields
With a waterpot on her head. I got nervous at bulls and eagles,
    Trying to figure what shape Zeus might take for sex
When it could be *your* turn next. But now I don't care any
    longer,
10 I've come to my senses, your profile leaves me cold.
Why am I different? you ask. I'll tell you. *Because you keep*
    nagging
    For presents. That's what turns me off.
At first you were guileless. Then I loved you, soul and body –
    But now this inner flaw's eclipsed your looks.
15 Love is a child, and naked. Childhood spells innocence;
    Nakedness, open ways. Why invite

This son of Venus to sell himself? He's got no pocket
  In which he can stash away his gains.
Neither mother nor son are military experts – soldiers'
  Pay, my dear, is not for unwarlike gods.   20
Even the prostitute, screwing a wretched livelihood out of
  Her body, game for any man with the cash,
Still curses her grasping bully. She's *forced* to hustle –
  You have a free choice.
Consider the beasts of the field. Too bad if unreasoning   25
  Brutes turn out kinder than you!
Do mares demand gifts from their stallions? Do cows solicit
  Their bulls? Must a ram
Court ewes with offerings? Only a woman glories
  In fleecing her males. She alone   30
Rents out her nights, is up for bids, plays the seller's market,
  Lets her pleasure adjust the price.
When sex gives equal enjoyment to both partners
  Why should *she* sell it, *he* pay?
If a man and a woman perform the same act together, is it   35
  Fair for you to profit by it, while I lose?
It's disgraceful for witnesses to sell false testimony,
  Disgraceful for jurymen to pocket bribes;
When defending counsel is bought, that's a crying scandal,
  Like a corruptly wealthy Bench.   40
It's scandalous to cash in on the proceeds of fornication
  Or prostitute your looks for gain.
Such services, freely given, deserve our thanks, but
    whenever
  You put out for cash, we're quits –
One payment finally discharges all obligations,   45
  The debts of common kindness are written off.
You beauties should think twice before putting a price-tag
  On bedroom amusements. Highly unpleasant results
Can ensue from such sordid traffic. The Vestal Tarpeia
  Bargained for Sabine armlets, but was crushed   50
Under Sabine arms. Eriphyle betrayed her husband
  For a necklace – and got

Her son's sword straight through her vitals. Still, there's no
    objection
  To dunning the rich for gifts –
They can afford such demands. Pick your grapes from the
55   most prolific
  Vineyard, and if it's apples you want, then try
Alcinous' orchard. Let courtesy, trust, devotion
  Be the poor man's tribute. From each
Lover his all – but according to his resources. *My* gift
60   Is poetry, the praise
Of beautiful girls. I can make them immortal. Fine dresses,
  Jewellery, gold, all perish. But the fame
Bestowed by my verse is perennial. I'm not ungenerous,
  it's being
  Asked I detest. Quit wanting, and I'll give.

II

Let me tell you about Napë. Though she's expert at setting
  Unruly hair, she's no common lady's-maid.
She fixes our private assignations, arranges meetings,
  Is the perfect go-between.
5 She's often fast-talked a too-hesitant Corinna
  Into coming over. She's never let me down.
Hey, Napë! Here's a note I've written your mistress –
  Please deliver it *now*, without delay.
You're not iron-hearted. There's no flinty streak in your nature,
10   And you're nobody's fool. You must
Have taken a hit or two yourself in the wars of passion?
  Then help me – we're fighting on the same side.
If she asks how I am, say I live in longing. My letter
  Provides all the details. Quick,
15 Don't let's waste time talking. Catch her at a free moment,
  Give her the note – and make sure
She reads it at once. Watch her face and eyes as she does so,
  Expressions can be revealing of things to come.
And take care she replies on the spot, with a good long letter –

Half-blank tablets drive me mad, 20
So get her to crowd up her lines, and fill the margins
    From side to side. But wait –
Why should she weary her fingers with all that scribbling?
    One single word is good enough: '*Come.*'
Then I'd wreathe my victorious writing-tablet with laurel 25
    And hang it in Venus' shrine
With this inscription: '*To Venus, from Ovid, for services rendered,*
    One cheap wooden writing-tablet – now beyond price.'

12

I need sympathy. I'm downhearted. That wretched
        writing-tablet
    Is back, with a dismal *No, can't make it today.*
There's something in omens. Just as she was departing
    Napë stubbed her toe on the doorsill, and stopped.
Next time you're sent out, girl, remember to be more careful 5
    While negotiating the threshold. Pick up your feet,
Keep off the bottle.
                    To hell with that damned obstructive
    Tablet, its coffinwood frame
And *no*-saying wax (which I bet was extracted from hemlock
    Honey, as specially gathered by Corsican bees), 10
That off-red surface, dyed – I'd supposed – with a tincture
    Of cinnabar. Not true. It had tasted blood.
Cheap useless object – I'll dump you at some crossing
    For a laden wagon to splinter with its wheels!
The craftsman who fashioned you from untrimmed timber – 15
    I'll swear he had guilty hands. The tree itself
Must have been used as a gibbet, then turned into crosses
    For some executioner. In its nasty shade
Hoarse nightjars lurked, a mass of vultures and screech-owls
    Infested its branches, hatching eggs. 20
Was *this* the stuff to which I entrusted such loving
    Messages for my mistress? I must have been mad.
Such a tablet would better suit the most prolix of legal

Documents, stuff to be droned out
By some gravel-voiced lawyer. It should lie with accounts and
25   ledgers
Recording the bad debts of a glum tycoon.
You in every way two-faced tablet! *Two* – that number
Was unlucky from the start. How vent
My fury? Curse you, may dry rot riddle your crumbling
30   Frame, and filthy white mildew blanch your wax!

13

She's on her way over the sea from her doddering husband,
    The blonde day-bringer, wheels all aglint with frost –
What's the hurry, Aurora? Take it easy, let Memnon's spirit
    Enjoy the yearly sacrifice by his birds!
5 Now, if ever, I love to lie in my mistress's tender
    Embrace, feel her close by my side,
At this cool hour of deep sleep, with liquid bird-song
    Tremulous in the air.
What's the hurry? All lovers, men and girls, resent your coming:
10   Exert those rosy fingers, rein in awhile!
Seamen out in deep water, eyes fixed on the constellations,
    Steer closer before your rising, don't yaw off course.
Even the weariest traveller's out to greet you,
    Every soldier's armed and ready by the time you arrive.
You're always up first. You challenge the weary peasant,
15   trudging
    Along with his mattock. You call
The ploughman to yoke up his weary oxen. You rob young
    Children of sleep, drive them out to school
And the cruel cane. You send cultured guarantors crowding
20   Down to the courts, where a one-
Word pledge may lose them a fortune. Pleaders and advocates
    Resent your summons, forcing them to resume
The daily legal grind. When a woman might still be resting
    You jerk her back to dull domestic chores.
25 I could put up with everything else – but only a crusty

Misogynist, surely, would stand
For girls getting up at dawn? The times I've prayed that
   darkness
   Might stand fast against you, and the stars
Not vanish before your countenance, that a hurricane
   Would crack your axle, or your horses fall   30
Headlong through blinding cloud! Why hurry, spoilsport?
   Are you black-hearted because your son was black?
[*Could it be that she never burned up for that Ethiopian?*
   Or does she suppose her naughtiness unknown . . .?]
How I wish Tithonus could spill the truth about you – no
   distaff   35
   Reputation in heaven would drop so low.
You hurry away from him because he's so much older,
   To mount the chariot he weakly hates –
But if it was your love, your Cephalus, you were embracing,
   You'd cry: 'Run slowly, horses of the night!'   40
Why should I suffer in love just because your husband's senile?
   Did you marry the old buffer on my advice?
Just think how long a sleep the Moon allowed her beloved
   Endymion – and she's as beautiful as you!
The Father of Gods himself was so averse to seeing you,   45
   Once, that he ran two nights of love into one.
Ah: that last crack must have gone home – I saw her blushing.
   But the sun still (as usual) rose on time.

14

I *told* you to stop using rinses – and now just look at you!
   No hair worth mentioning left to dye.
Why couldn't you let well alone? It grew so luxuriantly,
   Right down to below your hips,
And fine – so fine you were scared to set it, like silken   5
   Threads in a vivid Chinese screen,
Or the filament spun by a spider, the subtle creation
   That she hangs beneath some deserted beam.
It was neither dark nor blonde, but a brindled auburn,

10   A mixture of both, like some tall cedar when
        The outer bark's stripped off, in a dew-wet precipitous
            Valley of Ida. Not to mention the fact
        That it was so tractable, could be dressed in a hundred styles,
            and
        Never made you get cross. With no pins
15 Or curlers to make it go brittle, no bristling side-combs,
        Your maid could relax. I've been there
    Often enough while she fixed it, but never once saw you
        Pick up a hairpin and stick it in her arm.
    If it was early morning, you'd be propped up among lilac
20   Pillows and coverlets, your hair
    Not yet combed out. Yet even in tangled disorder
        It still became you. You looked like a wild
    Exhausted Maenad, *al fresco*.
                                        Poor down-fine tresses,
        What torture they had to endure!
25 You decided on corkscrew ringlets. The irons were heated,
        Your poor hair crimped and racked
    Into spiralling curls. 'It's a crime,' I told you, 'a downright
        Crime to singe it like that. Why on earth
    Can't you leave well alone? You'll *wreck* it, you obstinate
        creature,
30   It's *not for burning*. Why, in its natural state
    It'd make the best perm look silly –' No good. Her crowning
        Glory, that any mod god might well
    Have envied, sleek tresses like those that sea-wet naked
        Dione holds up in the picture – gone, all gone.
35 Why complain of the loss? You silly girl, you detested
        That waist-length tangle, so stop
    Making sad *moues* in your mirror. You must get accustomed
        To your own New Look, and forget
    Yourself if you aim to attract. No rival's incantations
40   Or tisanes have harmed you, no witch
    Has hexed your rinse, you haven't – touch wood – had an
        illness;
            If your hair's fallen out, it's not

Any envious tongue that's to blame. You applied that
    concoction
  Yourself. It was you that did it. *All your fault.*
Still, after our German conquests a wig is easily come by –   45
  A captive Mädchen's tresses will see you through.
You'll blush, it's true, when your borrowed plumage elicits
  Admiration galore. You'll feel that the praise (like the hair)
Has been bought. Once you really deserved it. Now each
    compliment
  Belongs to some Rhine maiden, not to you.   50
Poor sweet – she's shielding her face to hide those ladylike
  Blushes, and making a brave effort not to cry
As she stares at the ruined hair in her lap, a keepsake
  Unhappily out of place. Don't worry, love,
Just put on your make-up. This loss is by no means
    irreparable –   55
  Give it time, and your hair will grow back as good as new.

15

Why, gnawing Envy, impute an idler's existence to me?
  Why dismiss the poet as a drone?
What's your complaint? That I've failed (though young and
    healthy) to follow
  Tradition, or chase the dusty rewards
Of a soldier's career? That I haven't mugged up dull lawsuits,   5
  Or sold my eloquence like a whore
In the courts and Forum? Such labours are soon forgotten.
  What *I* seek is perennial fame,
Undying world-wide remembrance. While Ida and Tenedos
  Still stand, while Simois still runs swift to the sea,   10
Old Homer will live. While clustering grapes still ripen
  And wheat still falls to the scythe
Hesiod's works will be studied. The verse of Callimachus –
  Weak in imagination, strong on technique –
Has a worldwide readership. Sophoclean tragedy   15
  Is safe from Time's ravages. While sun and moon

Survive, so will Aratus. While the world holds one devious
    servant,
  Stern father, blandishing whore, or ponce on the make
Menander's immortal. Rough Ennius, spirited Accius
20   Have names time will never destroy. What age
  Will not cherish great Varro's epic of Argo's voyage,
    Jason's quest for the Golden Fleece?
The work of sublime Lucretius will prove immortal
    While the world itself endures;
25 And so long as Rome's empire holds sway over the nations,
    Virgil's country poems, his *Aeneid*, will be read.
While Cupid's armoury still consists of torch and arrows
    Tibullus' elegant verse
Will always be quoted. From lands / of sunset to sunrise,
    Gallus,
30   Gallus and his Lycoris, will be renowned.
Though Time, in time, can consume the enduring ploughshare,
    Though flint itself will perish, poetry lives –
Deathless, unfading, triumphant over kings and their triumphs,
    Richer than Spanish river-gold. Let the crowd
35 Gape after baubles. To me may golden Apollo proffer
    A cup, brimming over, from the Castalian spring
And a wreath of sun-loving myrtle. May my audience always
    Consist of star-crossed lovers. Never forget
It's the living that Envy feeds on. After death the pressure
40   Is taken off. All men get their due in the end.
So when the final flames have devoured my body, I shall
    Survive, and my better part live on.

BOOK 2

I

A second batch of verses by that naughty provincial poet,
  Naso, the chronicler of his own
Wanton frivolities; another of Love's commissions (warning
  To puritans: *This volume is not for you*).
I want my works to be read by the far-from-frigid virgin   5
  On fire for her sweetheart, by the boy
In love for the very first time. May some fellow-sufferer,
  Perusing my anatomy of desire,
See his own passion reflected there, cry in amazement:
  'Who told this scribbler about my private affairs?'   10
One time, I recall, I got started on an inflated epic
  About War in Heaven, with all
Those hundred-handed monsters, and Earth's fell vengeance,
      and towering
  Ossa piled on Olympus (plus Pelion too).
But while I was setting up Jove – stormclouds and
      thunderbolts gathered   15
  Ready to hand, a superb defensive barrage –
My mistress staged a lock-out. I dropped Jupiter and his
      lightnings
  That instant, didn't give him another thought.
Forgive me, good Lord, if I found your armoury useless –
  Her shut door ran to larger bolts   20
Than any *you* wielded. I went back to verses and compliments,
  My natural weapons. Soft words
Remove harsh door-chains. There's magic in poetry, its power
  Can pull down the bloody moon,
Turn back the sun, make serpents burst asunder   25
  Or rivers flow upstream.
Doors are no match for such spellbinding, the toughest
  Locks can be open-sesamed by its charms.
But epic's a dead loss for me. I'll get nowhere with swift-footed

30 Achilles, or with either of Atreus' sons.
   Old what's-his-name wasting twenty years on war and travel,
     Poor Hector dragged in the dust –
   No good. But lavish fine words on some young girl's profile
     And sooner or later she'll tender herself as the fee,
35 An ample reward for your labours. So farewell, heroic
     Figures of legend – the *quid*
   Pro quo you offer won't tempt me. A bevy of beauties
     All swooning over my love-songs – that's what *I* want.

2

One moment, Bagoas. Since you're your mistress's protector,
  A word, pray, with you – brief, but to the point.
Yesterday afternoon, while strolling down that cloister
  Where all the Danaid statues are on display
I saw her. Love at first sight. I dashed off a note – with
5   suggestions –
  And got the nervous answer: *It's not allowed.*
Why not? I wrote back. It turned out that *you* were the trouble,
  An over-strict guardian. Look,
If your head's screwed on, watchdog, you'll quit making
     enemies –
10 Get feared, men soon wish you dead.
Her husband's a fool, too. Why spend all that effort guarding
  What loses nothing when ignored?
Still, if he wants, let him cherish his love-struck illusions
  And believe that his toast of the town
15 Is a model of chastity! Just allow your mistress her freedom –
  On the quiet – and she'll repay you in kind.
Make a deal, you'll find the lady in thrall to the servant;
  ** Make a deal. If you're windy, turn a blind eye.
She's reading a note on the quiet – it's from her mother.
20 A stranger appears – in two shakes he's an old friend.
When she wants to visit some girlfriend she claims is unwell,
     don't
  Argue – accept the illness as a fact.

[If she's late coming back, don't wait up, that's too exhausting.
    Get your head down, take forty winks.]
Don't ask what games can be played in the precinct of linen-   25
    Draped Isis; don't let the packed
Theatre disturb you. Accomplices get their rake-off **
    And silence costs little effort. Such an aide
Enjoys high favour. Indiscipline brings no beatings
    To *him*, he's top dog, the rest trash.   30
To hoodwink the lady's husband, ingenious cover-stories
    Must be concocted: a tale that satisfies *her*
Will be swallowed by *him*. He may frown, or pull damnable
    faces,
    But it's what Baby Doll says that goes.
Now and then, of course, she must stage a noisy altercation   35
    With you too – call you a monster, pretend to cry,
While you bring some charge against her she can prove
    ill-founded –
    One false accusation, and who'll credit the truth?
Thus your position – and savings – will grow more substantial
    Daily. Take my advice, and you'll soon be free.   40
It's informers (as doubtless you've noticed) who get iron collars
    Around their necks. Break faith, and a dank
Prison awaits you. Loose talk left Tantalus thirsty for ever
    Though up to his neck in water, clutching at fruit
Always just out of reach. Io's too-conscientious protector   45
    Died young – she was deified. I've seen
A man's legs rotting in shackles because he compelled some
    Reluctant husband to admit himself *cocu*.
He deserved far worse. Such a ploy was doubly malicious –
    Killed X's self-respect, *and* his wife's good name.   50
Charges of this sort, believe me, are anathema to a husband;
    Even when he listens, they're no help.
If he's cool, your officious tattling will be met with indifference;
    If in love, he'll be badly upset. What's more,
Most adultery (flagrant or not) remains non-proven –   55
    A husband's judgement always favours his wife.
Though he be an eyewitness, he'll still believe her denials,

Discredit his own eyes, deceive himself.
If he sees her tears, he'll start crying too, and threaten
60   The slanderer with a writ. Why bother to fight
When the odds are so stacked against you? You're sure to be
    beaten
(Note pun) with the lady perched on her judge's lap.
We're not hatching some crime, we don't come together for
    the decoction
Of poisonous doses. No dagger glints in *my* hand.
65 All we need is your consent to some quiet love-making –
It's hard to imagine a more harmless request.

3

Bad luck that your mistress should have a keeper who's
    neither
Male nor female, who can't enjoy true sex!
The man who was first to sever boys' genital members
Should have been castrated himself.
5 If you'd ever fallen in love, your attitude would be different:
More obliging, complaisant with my demands.
But you weren't born to ride a warhorse, or handle weapons –
A spear in your hand would look out of place.
Leave such things to real men, abjure male aspirations,
10   Be content to soldier under your lady's flag.
Give her devoted service, and she'll reward you; without her
What use would you have? She's the right
Age for all sportive pleasures. She's attractive. A thousand
    pities
To waste that figure out of sheer neglect!
And despite your strict reputation, she *could* have got round
15   you –
A really determined couple is hard to resist.
Still, it seemed more appropriate to try persuasion first, and
Give you one last chance to cash in on the deal.

4

I wouldn't attempt to defend my spotty morals, or whitewash
  My flaws with aggressive lies.
If it's any help, I confess. Admission of guilt. Then why not
  Go the whole hog, indict
My faults myself? I hate what I am, yet (try as I may) can't   5
  Not be the thing that revolts me. It's hell
Being stuck with what you can't kick. I lack all firmness
  And strength to control my moods, get whirled away
Like a skiff in a current. There's no one type of beauty
  That arouses my longing: if I'm always in love   10
Blame my wide-ranging interests. Shyness and modesty
    spark me
  Off every time – a demurely lowered face
And I'm hooked. But it's just the same if she's pertly forward:
  Sophistication promises well in bed.
A primly old-fashioned appearance, then? I always suspect
    that's   15
  Mere camouflage for unacknowledged desire.
A bluestocking turns me on with her intellectual powers,
  A featherbrain ditto just by being naïve.
Then there's the girl who tells me Callimachus is a bungler
  Compared to me – I always go for my fans –   20
Or the critical termagant who slates both poems and author:
  How I long to be laid by her as well!
One's got a slinky walk: *that* gets me. Another's uptight –
  She can be softened out with a little sex.
A fine operatic voice, for me, is a standing temptation   25
  To smother the singer with kisses in mid-song.
Guitar-lessons help. Watch those fingers – the chords, the
    glissandos!
  How fail to fall in love with such clever hands?
Then think of the floor-show dancer, arms weaving in rhythm,
  Doing undulant bumps and grinds: 30

Never mind about me (I'm just omnisusceptible), make pure
    Hippolytus watch her act
And even *he'd* go priapic.
                  You're tall, like the heroines of
    legend,
    Lie the full length of a bed;
35 But petite girls, too, are attractive. I'm sold on *both* sizes –
    Long and short alike are equally to my taste.
The fashionable I enjoy at their face-value, the unsmart
    For all that they *could* be, *à la mode*.
I'm crazy for girls who are fair-haired and pale-complexioned –
40   But brunettes make marvellous lovers too:
The sight of dark tresses against a snow-white neck reminds me
    That Leda was famed for her black curls,
While a flaxen poll calls up thoughts of blonde Aurora –
    My sex-life runs the entire
45 Mythological gamut. My tastes are equally all-embracing:
    Young girls have the looks – but when it comes to technique
Give me an older woman. In short, there's a vast cross-section
    Of desirable beauties in Rome – *and I want them all!*

5

'Time and again all I've wanted was to die, and end it.
    (Get behind me, Cupid!) No love
Is worth *that* much. You've been hell for me since the
    beginning,
    I feel like death whenever I recall
5 The way you deceived me. It wasn't a half-erased letter-tablet
    That laid bare your activities. No secret gifts
Pointed the finger. I wish – *how* I wish! – that my case was
    hopeless:
    Why does it have to be so damnably good?
Lucky the man who dares go bail for his lady-love's
10   Reputation, who knows she can say
"I didn't do it." Iron-hearted, not to mention masochistic,
    Is the prosecutor who aims

To draw blood, to get his conviction. No, I was an eyewitness
  Of your crime: not (as you thought) asleep
From the drinking after dinner, but sober, and well aware of   15
  Those eyebrow-signals, those eloquent nods,
Œillades and smiles, little messages traced on the table
  By your finger, in wine; the remarks
Loaded with hidden meaning, the code-words given
  A private significance. When   20
Most of the guests were gone, and the table had emptied
    (except for
  One or two of the boys, out cold),
I saw you exchanging the most outrageous kisses, acquaintance
  Of tongues well under way: by no means the style
In which a nice girl would peck at her prissy brother,   25
  But intimate, passionate, a lovers' embrace.
I can't imagine Diana bestowing such torrid kisses
  On Phoebus: Venus and Mars
Was more like it. "What are you doing?" I cried. "This is
    alienation
  Of lovers' rights – mine. I claim   30
An exclusive monopoly. What's yours and mine is private –
  No third party is going to share my goods."'
Thus I raged on at her, half angry, half miserable,
  While a blush of guilt rose to her cheeks –
Like the dawn sky tinged faint red by the bride of Tithonus   35
  Or a girl when she sees her betrothed,
Or roses bright among lilies, or the enchanted
  Face of a harvest moon,
Or the stain that some Lydian woman can put upon ivory
  To stop it turning yellow with the years: 40
Such, or something much like it, was her complexion – she'd
    never
  Looked prettier, though the effect
Was quite accidental. A downcast gaze became her, nothing
  Brought out her beauty like remorse.
I felt like tearing her hair out, new set and all, I wanted   45
  To rake my nails across her delicate cheeks –

But one glimpse of that sweet face and my violence evaporated:
  My girl's best defence, as always, was herself.
I abandoned the strong-arm act, turned suppliant, begged her
50   For some equally juicy kisses. She laughed,
And complied with enthusiasm – the kind of sizzling
      performance
  Guaranteed to stave off even the triple bolt
Of Jupiter in his fury. Yet one fear still torments me:
  Did *he* get the same? I could wish
55 That those kisses had been less torrid, not *so* much better
    Than the ones I taught her. She'd learnt
Something new, it would seem. There's pleasure too keen for
      comfort –
  Why did our tongues ever meet?
That's not all I'm alarmed by, either. If this connection
60   Makes an intimacy of tongues
What else might not be conjoined? Such kisses could only
  Be learnt in bed. Some *maestro* has been well paid.

6

Parrot, that feathered mimic from India's dawnlands,
  Is dead. Come flocking, birds,
To his funeral: come, all you godfearing airborne
  Creatures, beat breasts with wings,
5 Mourn, claw your polls, tear out soft feathers (your hair), and
    Pipe high your sad lament.
Philomela, nightingale, the ancient crime of Tereus
  Which you lament is long past –
Divert your grief to the obsequies of a rare and modern
10   Bird: poor Itylus' case was tragic, but antique.
All wing-borne voyagers through the clear empyrean
  Lament now, and above all
His friend the turtle-dove. They lived in complete agreement,
  Their bond of faith held firm to the end.
15 What Pylades was to Orestes of Argos, that, Parrot,
  Turtle-dove was to you – while Fate allowed.

loves the parrot more than the poet

Yet of no avail your devotion, your rare and beautiful plumage,
  Your adaptable mimic's voice;
Not even the care that my darling lavished on you –
  Poor Polly, paragon of birdhood, is dead.   20
So green his feathers, they dimmed the cut emerald; scarlet
  His beak, with saffron spots.
No bird on earth could copy a voice more closely
  Or sound so articulate.
Fate, jealous, removed him – that unaggressive creature,   25
  That talkative devotee of peace,
With his tiny appetite, whose love of conversation   29
  Left him little leisure for food,   30
Who lived on a diet of nuts, used poppy-seed to encourage   31
  Sound sleep: kept his thirst at bay   32
With nothing but water. Quails spend their whole life fighting – 27
  Maybe that's how they reach a ripe old age.   28
Carnivorous vultures, kites gyring high in the heavens,
  Weather-wise jackdaws, prophets of rain to come,
All are long-lived – while Minerva's *bête noire*, the raven,   35
  Can outlast nine generations. Yet Parrot is dead,
That loquacious parody of human utterance, that bonanza
  From the eastern edge of the world.
Greedy death almost always picks off the best ones early –
  It's the third-raters who reach a ripe old age.   40
Thersites attended the funeral of Protesilaus; Hector
  Was ashes while his brothers still lived.
What point in recalling the desperate prayers my sweetheart
    uttered?
  Some stormy sirocco blew them out to sea.
Six days he survived, and then, at dawn on the seventh,   45
  His thread of destiny ran out.
Yet somehow, though dying, he could still find utterance,
  And the last words he ever spoke were: 'Corinna, farewell!'
Beneath a hill in Elysium, where dark ilex clusters
  And the moist earth is for ever green,   50
There exists – or so I have heard – the pious fowls' heaven
  (All ill-omened predators barred).

Parrot is a parody of the poet.

Harmless swans roam after food there, there dwells the
    phoenix,
    That long-lived, ever-solitary bird;
55 There Juno's peacock spreads out his splendid fantail
    Amid the billing and cooing of amorous doves;
And there, in this woodland haven, the feathered faithful
    Welcome Parrot, flock round to hear him talk.
His bones lie buried under a parrot-sized tumulus
60   With a tiny headstone bearing these words:
R.I.P. Polly: this tribute from his loving mistress:
    'Articulate beyond a common bird'.

7

Am I always to be on trial against new accusations?
    Pleading my case so often, win or lose, is a bore.
Suppose we're at the theatre: one backward glance, and your
    jealous
    Eye will deduce a mistress up in the gods.
5 Any good-looking woman need only quiz me – at once you're
    Convinced it's a put-up job.
If I say a girl's nice, you try to tear my hair out;
    If I damn her, you think I'm covering up.
If my complexion is healthy, that means I've gone off you;
10   If pale, then I'm dying of love for someone else.
How I wish I'd some genuine infidelity on my conscience –
    The guilty find punishment easier to take.
But by such wild accusations and false assumptions
    You devalue your rage. Don't forget
15 How the wretched long-eared ass, when too heavily beaten,
    Gets stubborn, goes slow.
And now this fresh 'crime' – I've been having an affair with
    Cypassis, your lady's-maid!
If I really wanted some fun on the side, I ask you, would I
20   Pick a lower-class drudge? God forbid –
What gentleman would fancy making love to a servant,
    Embracing that lash-scarred back?
Besides, she's an expert coiffeuse, her skilful styling

Has made her your favourite. What?
Proposition a maid so devoted to her mistress?   25
   Not likely. She'd turn me down – and blab.
By Venus and the bow of her winged offspring,
   I protest my innocence!

8

O expert in creating a thousand hairstyles, worthy
   To have none but goddesses form your clientele,
Cypassis! – and (as I know from our stolen pleasures)
   No country beginner: just right
For your mistress, but righter for me – what malicious gossip   5
   Put the finger on us? How did Corinna know
About our sleeping together? I didn't blush, did I,
   Or blurt out some telltale phrase?
I'm sorry I told her no man in his proper senses
   Could go overboard for a maid –   10
Achilles fell madly in love with *his* maid, Briseis,
   Agamemnon was besotted by the slave-
Priestess Cassandra. I can't pretend to be socially up on
   Those two – then why should I despise
What's endorsed by royalty? Anyway, when Corinna   15
   Shot *you* a dirty look, you blushed right up.
It was *my* presence of mind, if you remember, that saved us,
   When I swore that convincing oath –
(Venus, goddess, *please* make the warm siroccos
   Blow my innocent perjury out to sea!)   20
I did you a good turn. Now it's time for repayment.
   Dusky Cypassis, I want to sleep with you. Today.
Don't shake your head and play scared, you ungrateful
     creature,
   You're under a condominium of two
And only one's satisfied. If you're silly enough to refuse, I'll 25
   Reveal all we've done in the past, betray my own
Betrayal. I'll tell your mistress just where we met, and how
     often,
   And how many times we did it, *and* in what ways!

9

No terms could be strong enough, Cupid, to express my
    resentment
  At the treacherous way you've settled yourself in my heart.
What's your grudge against me? Have I ever once deserted
  Your standards? Then why should I
Be the one who gets shot from behind? How come your torch
5   and arrows
  Are turned against friends? Small renown
From a military walkover. Remember how Achilles, after
  Spearing Telephus, rendered him first-aid?
For the hunter, pursuit is all. Once caught, his quarry
10   Is forgotten, while he harks off on a new trail.
Against stubborn opposition you're slow in coming forward:
  It's we, your faithful supporters, who suffer worst.
Passion has worn me down to a living skeleton: why blunt
  Barbed arrows on skin and bone?
15 There are so many loveless people, both men and women –
  If you want a popular triumph, try *them*.
Had Rome not advanced her power the wide world over
  She'd still be a straggle of thatched huts.
The worn-out soldier retires on his State allotment, an ageing
20   Racehorse gets put out to grass,
Warships are dry-docked, the discharged gladiator
  Hangs up his wooden sword.
Well, I'm a veteran too – see my sexual campaign-ribbons –
  And it's high time I quit the field.

9B

[25] If I heard a voice from heaven say 'Live without loving,'
  I'd beg off. Girls are such exquisite hell.
When desire's slaked, when I'm sick of the whole business,
  Some kink in my wretched nature drives me back.
It's like riding a hard-mouthed horse, that bolts headlong,
5   foam flying

122

From his bit, and won't answer the rein –   [30]
Or being aboard a ship, on the point of docking, in harbour,
   When a sudden squall blows you back out to sea:
That's how the veering winds of desire so often catch me –
   Hot Love up to his lethal tricks again.   10
All right, boy, skewer me. I've dropped my defences,   [35]
   I'm an easy victim. Why, by now
Your arrows practically know their own way to the target
   And feel less at home in their quiver than in me.
I'm sorry for any fool who rates sleep a prime blessing   15
   And enjoys it from dusk to dawn   [40]
Night in, night out. What's sleep but cold death's reflection?
   Plenty of time for rest when you're in the grave.
My mistress deceives me – so what? I'd rather be lied to   20
   Than ignored. I can live on hope. Today
She'll be all endearments, tomorrow throw screaming
    tantrums,   [45]
   Envelop me one night, lock me out the next.
War, like love, is a toss-up. If Mars is inconstant, he gets that
   From you, his stepson. You're quite
Unpredictable, Cupid, with your lucky-dip favours,   25
   And more volatile than your own wings.   [50]
Maybe you'll hear my appeal, though – your delectable mother
   Might help there – and settle in as king of my heart?
Then admit the flighty sex *en masse* to your dominions
   And you'd have guaranteed popularity all round.   30

10

It was *you*, no doubt about it, Graecinus: I clearly remember
   How you said no man could possibly fall in love
With two girls at once. I believed you. I dropped my defences.
   Result – double love-life. Embarrassing. All your fault.
There's nothing to choose between them for looks. They both
    dress smartly,   5
   On performance they're just about neck and neck –
I can't make up my mind which I find more attractive,

But fancy first A, then B,
Swung to and fro like a yacht in a choppy crosswind,
10 My erotic psyche torn
Between rival claimants. Didn't one girl produce sufficient
    Anxiety for me, Venus? Why double my load?
If it comes to that, why put extra stars in heaven,
    Top up the sea with water, releaf the trees?
Still, things could be worse. At least I'm not starved of
15   affection.
    A celibate life is something I'd only wish
On my very worst enemies. Just imagine sleeping
    Plumb in the middle of a double bed!
Give me some wild love-making to disrupt dull slumber,
20   With congenial company between the sheets,
And no holds barred. If one girl can drain my powers
    Fair enough – but if she can't, I'll take two.
I can stand the strain. My limbs may be thin, but they're
        wiry;
    Though I'm a lightweight, I'm hard –
25 And virility feeds on sex, is boosted by practice;
    No girl's ever complained about *my* technique.
Often enough I've spent the whole night in pleasure,
        yet still been
    Fit as a fighting cock next day.
What bliss to expire in Love's duel – that, God willing,
30   Is the way *I'd* choose to die!
Let the soldier stick out his chest as a target for hostile
    Arrows, purchase eternal renown with blood;
Let the cash-hungry merchant make one voyage too many
    And wash the lies down his throat
With the brine of the trade-routes. But I'd like to reach
35   dissolution
    In mid-act, die on the job.
Easy enough to guess what some mourner will say at my
        funeral:
    'His death was all of a piece with his life.'

11

The trouble began when they felled those pines on Pelion
    And the barren sea-lanes beheld
Argo, amazing Argo, on her reckless quest for the Golden
    Fleece, threading the Clashing Rocks.
Why didn't she spring a fatal leak? If only no man   5
    Had ever bothered the wide
Seas with an oar! Corinna has plans for a voyage, leaving
    The household gods we shared, that familiar bed.
Sweetheart, why make your poor poet freeze in conventional
    Panic at all those high rhetorical winds?   10
Besides, the sea's *so* unattractive – no cities or woodlands,
    Just an endless blue expanse;
And don't think those delicate shells, those variegated pebbles
    That you find at the water's edge
Exist in mid-ocean. Paddle barefoot along the foreshore,   15
    It's safe for girls there. Don't plunge in
Or you'll find yourself out of your depth. Why not learn about
    maelstroms,
    Sea-monsters and tempests, from other travellers' tales?
Let *them* evoke rock-fanged and towering coastlines, or African
    Quicksands. Take every word on trust –   20
Credulity costs nothing, suffers no shipwreck,
    Is immune to the fiercest storm.
Too late to gaze back at dry land when you've cast off hawsers
    And your vessel is driving out to sea.
While the anxious lookout blenches at violent crosswinds,   25
    Sees death in the crowding waves.
And suppose some power whips those waves to a fury, just
    watch
    The colour drain from your face,
Just hear you invoking the patron gods of sailors,
    Envying anyone ashore on dry land!   30
Safer to stay in bed, read books, and practise
    Fingerwork on your lute –

But if your mind's made up, if I'm wasting exhortations
    On the wind, then may all marine
Deities grant you smooth sailing – I'll hold the whole lot of
35   them
    Responsible if you drown.
Remember me while you're away, and may a stronger following
    Wind fill your sails on the homeward run! .
May storm blasts and tidal waves (with divine direction)
40   Get the sea running this way – one word
From you, and a westerly breeze will swell your canvas
    (You can haul on the sheets yourself).
I'll keep watch from the shore, I'll sight your familiar vessel
    Before anyone else. 'My goddess is aboard,'
45   I'll tell the crowd. I'll bring you ashore on my shoulders,
    Cover you with kisses, offer up
The victim I promised for your safe return. We'll have a picnic,
    Use some dune as a table, heap sand
For our couch, and over the wine you'll tell me endless stories
50   Of how your ship nearly went down
In a raging storm – but of course *you* weren't scared by sudden
    Typhoons, or dark nights, you were on your way back
To me. I'll believe all you say, I don't care if it's fiction –
    Why shouldn't I indulge my own desires?
55   May bright-dazzling Lucifer whip up his celestial
    Horses, and bring me that moment – soon!

12

A wreath for my brows, a wreath of triumphal laurel!
    Victory – Corinna is here, in my arms,
Despite the united efforts of husband, door, and porter
    (That unholy trinity) to keep her secure
5   From all lovers, however artful. This bloodless conquest
    Demands a super-triumph. Look at the spoils.
What did my generalship win? Some town with crumbling
    defences
    And a shallow moat? Oh no, *I* captured a *girl*!

When Troy fell at last, after that ten-year struggle,
  How much of the credit went to the High Command,   10
And how much to the troops? There's no army to share *my*
    glory,
  The credit is mine alone, I'm a one-man band,
Commander, cavalry, infantry, standard-bearer, announcing
  With one voice: *Objective achieved.*
What's more, mere luck played no part at all in *my* triumph: 15
  Unswerving perseverance did the trick.
No novelty, either, about the cause of warfare. Europe
  And Asia would never have been
Embroiled without Helen's abduction. It was a woman
  Brought Centaurs and Lapiths to blows   20
Over the wine at that wedding. A woman, Lavinia, got the
  Trojans fighting again, for the second time,
When they set foot on Latin soil. While our City was still
    new-founded
  Those Sabine girls screaming rape
Provoked most bloody reprisals. I've seen two bulls battling   25
  Over a snow-white heifer – she egged them on.
You could say I'm Cupid's conscript, called up, like so many
    others,
  For front-line service – but no shedding of blood.

13

Corinna got pregnant – and rashly tried an abortion.
  Now she's lying in danger of her life.
She said not a word. That risk, and she never told me!
  I ought to be furious, but I'm only scared.
It was me by whom she conceived – or at least, I assume so: 5
  I often jump to conclusions. Ilithyia, Queen
Of the Afric shore, whose presence broods over alluvial
  Canopus, Memphis, palmy Pharos and that
Broad delta where swift Nile discharges seaward
  In seven meandering streams: 10
By your sistrum I beg you, by the holy head of Anubis

127

(So may Osiris evermore love your rites,
The slow snake writhe through your sanctuary, the horned bull
    Apis grace your processions!), ah look down
15 In mercy, Goddess: through one spare both of us; in your
    Hands her life lies – and mine in hers.
She has kept your holy days, a regular worshipper,
    Asperged by the eunuch priests
With dripping laurel-switches – and your compassion
20   For girls in labour is well-known.
Ilithyia, Goddess of Childbirth, hear my entreaties, save her –
    She's worth it, truly. Just say the word,
And I'll robe myself in white, burn incense on your smoking
    Altar, lay at your feet the gifts I vowed,
With a label reading 'From Ovid, in grateful thanks for
25   Corinna's
Recovery' – ah, please make it all come true!
Look, sweetheart, I know how you're feeling, I know it's no
    time for
Recriminations – but *never* try that again!

14

What's the point of a girl being exempt from active service –
    No shield-drill, no column-of-route
Marching away to the wars – if she uses weapons against her
    Self, suffers hurt from her own hand?
5 The woman who first ripped foetus from placenta should have
    Died by such butchery herself.
Would you *really* chance your arm in that bloody arena
    Just to keep your belly unwrinkled? Suppose
Mothers in olden times had caught on to such practices,
10   Mankind would be quite extinct,
And we'd need a new-style stone-throwing demiurge
    To repeople our empty world.
Who would have cracked Priam's might if the sea-goddess
        Thetis
    Had refused to carry her load?

Had Ilia ripped those twins from her swollen belly   15
  Our City's Founder would have been lost.
Had Venus aborted the unborn Aeneas, no Caesars today would
  Exist in the world. You too
Would have perished, your beauty still embryonic, had your
  Mother attempted the same game   20
Take my own case – I'd rather die from a surfeit of loving
  Than find myself mother-scuppered before birth.
Why cheat the laden vine when grapes are ripening
  Or strip an apple-tree while the fruit's still green?
Let all things mature in season, come forth, develop –   25
  Have patience. Life is a prize
Well worth the waiting. Why probe your entrails with lethal
  Instruments? Why poison what's still unborn?
Child-blood on Medea's hands excites our horror, dismembered
  Itys brings tears to the eye: 30
Parental savagery rampant. Yet both these women had bitter
  Cause to destroy their own dear flesh –
Revenge on a husband. But *you* – what Tereus or Jason
  Drives *you* to commit this deadly self-abuse?
No Armenian tigress would foul her den with such actions: 35
  No lioness would destroy her own cubs.
Yet tender young girls do this – though not with impunity:
    often
  The uterine murderess dies herself,
Dies, and is carried out for cremation, hair all dishevelled,
  To cries of 'Serve her right!' from the passers-by.   40
May these utterances of mine be scattered down the wind, and
  No weight attach to such ill-omened words!
Be merciful, Gods. Let her first offence go unpunished,
  That's all I ask. If she errs again – then strike!

15

Ring of mine, made to encircle my pretty mistress's finger,
  Valuable only in terms of the giver's love,
Go, and good welcome! May she receive you with pleasure,

Slip you over her knuckle there and then.
5 May you fit her as well as she fits me, rub snugly
    Around her finger, precisely the right size!
Lucky ring to be handled by my mistress! I'm developing
    A miserable jealousy of my own gift.
But suppose I could *be* the ring, transformed in an instant
10 By some famous magician's art –
Then, when I felt like running my hand down Corinna's
    Dress, and exploring her breasts, I'd work
Myself off her finger (tight squeeze or not) and by crafty
    Cunning drop into her cleavage. Let's say
15 She was writing a private letter – *I'd* have to seal it,
    And a dry stone sticks on wax:
She'd moisten me with her tongue. Pure bliss – provided
    I didn't have to endorse any hostile remarks
Against myself. If she wanted to put me away in her jewel-
20 Box, I'd cling tighter, refuse to budge.
(Don't worry, my sweet, I'd never cause you discomfort,
    or burden
    Your slender finger with an unwelcome weight.)
Wear me whenever you take a hot shower, don't worry
    If water runs under your gem –
Though I fancy the sight of you naked would rouse my
25 passions, leave me
    A ring of visibly virile parts . . .
Pure wishful thinking! On your way, then, little present,
    And show her you come with all my love.

16

I am here in Sulmona, my own Pelignian riding,
    A small place, but lush with streams:
Though the ground parch and crack under a blazing summer
    Sun, though the Dog Star glares
Like brass, clear rills still wander through these fertile
5 meadows,
    The grass remains fresh and green.

Wheat yields well in this soil, the vine still better; in places
   You can glimpse an olive grove,
And along the slow river-bank, by knee-deep pastures,
   The turf grows rank and moist.   10
But my flame isn't here – or rather, to change the image,
   Though my heart's on fire, the kindling spark is away.
Offered a place in the sky between Castor and Pollux,
      I'd still say
   No. What's heaven worth minus you?
May those who have scored the world with endless highways   15
   Lie uneasy in dank clay graves!
If they *had* to cut trunk-roads, they should have made it a rule
   that
   Girls were obliged to travel with their beaux.
Suppose I was crossing the Alps in a blizzard, all goose-pimples –
   With my girl along I'd take the trip in my stride.   20
With her, I'd cheerfully sail through sand-shoals, or put to sea
   when
   A gale was blowing full blast;
I'd baulk at nothing – the monsters yelping from Scylla's
   Virgin groin, the reefs of Cape Malea,
Those maelstrom waters that wreck-glutted Charybdis   25
   Spews up and sucks down by turns –
Even suppose a typhoon took charge of us, and towering
   Waves washed our guardian gods away,
You could wind your white arms about my shoulders – so lissom
   A weight would be easy borne: 30
Think of the times young Leander swam over to Hero, till that
   Last night when the lamp blew out
And he was lost. But without you, my sweet, even this, my
   favourite
   Landscape – these water-meadows, the rows
Of teeming vines, a cool breeze stirring the treetops, some
   peasant   35
   Singing away as he waters his patch of land –
Looks barren and strange, un-Pelignian, somewhere else,
   quite different

From the farm on which I was born:
More like Scythia, or the bloody rock of Prometheus,
40   With such neighbours as Britons in woad
Or wild Cilician pirates. Elm loves vine, vine sticks with elm –
      then
Why must my mistress and I
Be parted so often? You swore you'd stay with me always,
      On my life you swore it, by
45 Your eyes, those stars of my heart; but a girl's oath is lighter
      Than leaves in autumn, whirled
Away by wind or wave. Yet if you've a glimmer of feeling
      Left for me, then make your promises deeds,
Get out the trap, harness your quick-stepping ponies,
50   Shake up the reins, and away,
Wild manes flying! May all winding roads and valleys
      Be straight where you pass, and the high hills lie down for
         you!

17

Anyone who considers enslavement to girls disgraceful
   Will undoubtedly write me off as a disgrace.
It's not losing my name I mind – I just wish the goddess
   Of Paphos and sea-girt Cythera would cool it off
5 In her dealings with me; and if I *had* to fall for a beauty
   Why couldn't she have been kind?
But a profile breeds pride, and Corinna's loveliness makes her
   Treat me like dirt. She knows herself too well,
Gets her haughty ways (I suspect) from her mirror-image –
      and never
10   Looks at it till she's made up.
You're a spoilt beauty, darling, your face is too seductive
   (One look at it and I'm hooked) –
But you *still* have no call to despise me, when lesser
   Breeds can aspire to greatness. We know
15 How the nymph Calypso lost her heart to a mortal
   And held him against his will;

132

A sea-nymph (the story goes) bedded down with Peleus, Egeria
   Made it with Numa the Just,
And Vulcan has rights over Venus, despite his smithy
   And that shameful twisted limp.   20
Well, look at the metre I'm using – *that* limps. But together
   Long and short lines combine
In a heroic couplet. So take me, darling,
   On your own terms (to lay
Down the law in bed would become you). I shan't be an
     accusation   25
   You're glad to get rid of; our love
Won't ever require disowning. I have capital assets,
   Good poems – and many women aspire to fame
Through my art. I know one who goes round saying she's
     Corinna:
   What wouldn't the poor thing give for her dream   30
To be true? But poplar-fringed Po and icy Eurotas flow ever
   Apart: none but you shall be sung
In my verses, you and you only shall give my creative
   Impulse its shape and theme.

18

While you are taking your poem up to the wrath of Achilles
   And arming your oath-bound heroes for the fray,
Love-in-idleness, Macer, and the shades of dalliance
   Preoccupy *me*. That tender erotic urge
Shatters my high-flown intentions. The times I've ejected   5
   My mistress, only to have her nestle back
In my lap. I'm ashamed, I told her. Weeping, she whispered:
   'Ashamed of loving poor me?' and wound her arms
Tight round my neck, sabotaged me with unending
   Kisses. So, I'm surrendering, have recalled   10
My imagination from military active service, to cope with
   A sex-war on the domestic front.
Still, I *did* assume the sceptre, began writing a tragic opus –
   Tragedy suited my style, I was going well,

But Love guffawed at my costume: that cloak, those crimson
15   buskins,
    The sceptre I'd grabbed in my plebeian paw.
Once again the will of my obstinate mistress checked me,
    And passion has triumphed over the tragic bard.
Now I stick to my proper last – verse-lectures on seduction
20   (I tend to be wrong-footed by my own advice!),
Or love-lorn heroines' letters – Penelope to Ulysses,
    Phyllis' tearful complaint on being ditched;
Appeals to Paris, Macareus, ungrateful Jason; something
    Calculated to stir Hippolytus *and*
25 His father; or the Final Message Department – Dido clutching
    A naked sword, and Sappho her Lesbian lyre.
My friend Sabinus has played international postman
    With uncommon speed – replies
From all over the world are now in: Penelope remembers
30   Ulysses' hand, Phaedra has read the note
Hippolytus penned; Aeneas (turned pious) has answered
    Poor Dido's appeal; there's even a *billet-doux*
For Phyllis, if she's alive still; for Hypsipyle an unpleasant
    Comeback from Jason; Sappho, whose love is returned,
35 Gives the lyre she vowed to Apollo. Even you, friend Macer,
    – Insofar as it's safe for a martial poet – lace
Your warfare with 'Love the Golden': Paris, adulterous Helen
    (Noble but Naughty), Laodameia (True
Unto Death). If I know you, you'll get more pleasure from
        that lot
40   Than from warfare – so why not give up and join *my* camp?

19

You may not feel any need (and more fool you) to guard that
    Girl of yours – but it sharpens *my* desire,
So would you oblige? What's allowed is a bore, it's what isn't
    That turns me on. What cold clod
Could woo with his rival's approval? We lovers need hope and
5   despair in

Alternate doses. An intermittent rebuff
Makes us promise the earth. Who wants a beautiful woman
  When she never deceives him? I can't
Love a girl who's not intermittently bitchy. Corinna spotted
  My weakness (full marks!) and saw how   10
To use it against me. The times she invented a headache,
  And when I still hung around, just threw me out,
Or pretended she'd had an affair, looking horribly guilty
  When in fact she'd done nothing at all –
And having thus quickly rekindled my cooling ardour   15
  Would suddenly switch her mood
To the ultra-compliant. Her compliments, her sweet nothings,
  Her kisses – oh God, her kisses! So you too,
My latest eye-ravisher, must ensnare me at times by pretending
  To be frightened: must – on occasion – say No,   20
And leave me there, prostrate on your doorstep, to suffer
  Long hours of frosty cold, the whole night through.
Act thus, and my love will endure, grow stronger with each
    passing
  Year – that's the way I like it, that feeds the flame,
Love too indulged, too compliant, will turn your stomach   25
  Like a surfeit of sweet rich food.
Had Danaë never been locked in that brazen turret, would
    Jupiter
  Ever have got her with child?
When Juno transmogrified Io into a horned heifer
  She increased the girl's sex-appeal.   30
If you're after what's lawful and easy, then why not gather
  Leaves from the trees, or drink
Water out of the Tiber? To prolong your dominion over
  Your lover calls for deception. (I hope I won't
Have cause to regret that statement.) Yet come what may,
    indulgence   35
  Irks me. I flee the eager, pursue the coy.
And as for *you*, man, so careless of your good lady,
  Why not start locking up at night?
Why not ask who it is comes tapping, ever so softly,

40   On your front door – or why it is the dogs
Start barking at midnight? What about all those to-and-fro
    missives
    The maid delivers? How come your wife now sleeps
Alone so often? Why can't you get really worried just
Once in a while, allow me to display
45   My skill at deception? To covet the wife of a dummy
    Is like stealing sand off the beach.
I'm warning you: put your foot down, play the heavy husband,
    Or I'll start going cold on your wife!
I've stood it quite long enough, always hoping you'd lock her
50   Away out of sight, so that I
Could outwit you. But no. You clod, you put up with things
    no husband
    Should stand for a moment. Let me have the girl
And there's an end to my passion. Won't you *ever* deny me
    Entry, won't you beat me up one night?
55   Can't I ever feel scared? have insomnia? sigh in frustration?
    Won't you give me some good excuse
To wish you dead? I've no time for complaisant, pimping
    husbands –
    Their kinkiness spoils my fun.
Find someone else, who *likes* your easy-going habits, or if you
60   Must have me as a rival, then *get tough*!

BOOK 3

I

There's this ancient wood – no axe has thinned it for ages,
    It might well be some spirit's home.
At its centre, a sacred spring, an arched limestone grotto,
    And sweet birdsong all around.
While I was strolling here, through an overwoven   5
    Dapple of shade, and wondering just what task
My Muse should embark on next, there appeared before me
    Elegy, perfumed hair caught up in a knot,
And short – I think – in one foot: good figure, nice dress,
    a loving
Expression. Even her lameness looked chic.   10
Behind her stalked barnstorming Tragedy, fraught brow
    hidden
By flowing hair, mantle atrail in the dust,
Left hand waving a royal sceptre, high Lydian
    Boots encasing her calves.
'Won't you *ever*', she asked me, 'have done with love as a
    subject?   15
Why get stuck in the same old poetic rut?
Your efforts to shock make gossip for drunken parties,
    a buzz at
Every street-corner. As you walk by
Fingers point, people whisper: 'Look, there goes that poet
    With the ultra-combustible heart.'   20
All this shameless parade of your sexual activities makes you
    The talk of the whole town – and what do *you* care?
It's high time your inspiration chose a loftier model:
    You've idled enough. Start on some major work.
Your present theme cramps your style. Try the deeds of
    heroes –   25
    A subject (you'll find) more worthy of your art.
You've been playing at poetry – ballads for girl-adolescents,

Juvenile stuff, the eternal *enfant terrible*.
Now why not turn *my* way, make Roman tragedy famous,
30   Give me the inspiration that I need?'
With that she nodded three or four times, her scarlet buskins
      Holding her upright against the weight of her hair.
At this point, or so I recall, a mischievous expression
      Crept over Elegy's face. (Had she got
35   A myrtle-wand in her hand? I think so.) 'You posturing
      Windbag,' she cried, 'do you *have* to be such a bore?
Can't you *ever* stop your pomposity? At least you condescended
      To attack me in elegiacs, you turned my own
Metre against me – not that I'd ever dream of comparing
40   Your high palatial vein with my own
Minuscule talent. Besides, I'm frivolous, like my subject,
      And equally unheroic. All the same,
Without me Our Lady of Passion would be plain vulgar –
      She needs my help as adviser and go-between.
45   The door your tough buskin can't break down flies open
      At one flattering word of mine;
Corinna took lessons from me, how to hoodwink porters
      Or spring the most foolproof lock,
How to slip out of bed in her nightdress and move with
            unerring
50   Feet, like a cat, through the night.
Yet I've earned my advantage. I've beaten you by submitting
      To indignities which your pride
Would recoil from in horror. The times I've been nailed to
            indifferent
      Front doors, for any passer-by to read!
55   Why, I even remember lying snug in a maid's bosom
      Till some crusty chaperone took off –
Not to mention the time I was sent as a birthday present
      To that frightful girl who just tore me into shreds
And flushed me away. It was I who awakened your dormant
60   Poetic genius. If *she's* after you now
It's me you should thank for it.' 'Ladies, please listen,'
      I told them
Nervously, 'don't take offence –

One of you honours me with sceptre and buskins: high-flown
   Utterance springs to my lips at her touch.
But the other offers my passions undying glory: come then,   65
   Short foot and limping metre, it's you I choose!
I'm sorry, Tragedy. Just be patient awhile. Your service
   Demands a lifetime. *Her* needs are quickly met.'
The goddess forgave me. I'd better get on with this little
   volume
   While I may – my subconscious is hatching a masterpiece.   70

2

I don't come here to watch horses, I'm no bloodstock-fancier –
   Though of course I hope your favourite wins.
To sit at your side and talk with you is what *I'm* after –
   I want you
   To know the havoc you've wrought in my heart.
You watch the chariots, I you – that way we'll both see   5
   Just what we want, a feast
For your eyes and mine alike. How lucky that charioteer is
   Who enjoys your support! How I wish
I could be in *his* shoes - away at a flying gallop
   From the start of the race, flat out,   10
Now a touch of the whip, now give them their head
   and shave the
   Post at the turn with my nearside wheel!
But if I saw *you* in mid-gallop I'd falter, the reins would drop
   from
   My hands – like that time when a spear
Nearly killed Pelops at Pisa, while he was gazing, besotted,   15
   In Hippodameia's eyes, though of course
As her chosen favourite he won, just as I hope your driver
   And I both manage to do.
It's no use your edging away. The seating regulations
   Of the Circus have one advantage – they pack us close.   20
Hey, you on the right there, whoever you are, please remove
   your elbow
   From this lady's ribs, and you

In the row behind, would you mind *not* sticking your bony
    Knees in her back? Sit up, sir! My sweet,
25 Your dress is brushing the ground, you really should gather
    It up – no, let me. There you are. Oh dear,
What a mean old dress to keep such beautiful legs hidden!
    M'm. The more one looks – what a mean old dress!
Just the sort of legs that belonged to Atalanta, that Milanion,
30   Hot on her heels, was mad to touch,
Or that painters bestow on Diana the huntress, running
    With tucked-up skirts, and wilder than the wild
Beasts she pursues. But *yours* – I was hot enough when I hadn't
    Seen them, and now–! It's like adding flame
35 To a bonfire, or wet to the sea. And what other treasures
    May not be hidden under that summer dress?
Feeling hot? Would a cooling breeze be welcome? There,
    let me
    Fan you a little. Or is the heat all in my own
Too-fevered head? Is it just my romantic imagination
40   That's burned up by your girlish charms?
Oh dear – while I was talking a little dust just settled
    On your white dress. Shoo, dirty dust, from so
Spotless a body! Oh look, here comes the procession! Quiet,
    And give them a hand. The golden procession's here,
45 Victory in the lead, with wings outspread – O Goddess,
    Hear me, and grant that my love prevail!
Next comes Neptune. Sailors, a round of applause there!
    Me, I'm a landsman. The sea's no concern of mine.
Ah, here's Mars – clap him, soldiers! Myself, I can't *stand*
    fighting,
50   Peace is my thing. You know: make love not war.
Here's Apollo for soothsayers, Artemis for hunters,
    And Minerva for craftsmen. Now,
You countryfolk, up on your feet, give a cheer for gay
    Bacchus
    And Ceres! All boxers and jockeys, defer
55 To Castor and Pollux. But *our* applause goes to amorous
    Venus, and her child with the deadly bow.

(Help this new venture, Venus: soften up my prospective
    mistress
    Till she loves me – or anyway till she lets *me* love *her*.)
I'm in luck – she nodded. I won't demand more of you,
    sweetheart,
    Than the goddess has promised already. You'll be   60
(Forgive me, Venus!) a greater divinity. By these spectators,
    By the gods in procession, I swear it, I want you as mine
For ever and ever – Oh my, your feet are dangling, why not
    Try propping them on the rail in front? They've cleared
The track for the star event. Look, four-horse chariots!   65
    There goes the praetor's signal. They're away –
And, yes, I can see your favourite! Anyone that you back is
    Just bound to win. Even the horses seem
To know what you want. Oh God, he's taking that corner
    Far too wide – the next man's edging him out.   70
What are you playing at, fool? You'll disappoint the lady!
    Hard on your left rein! I fear we've backed
A loser. Come on, then, everyone, wave your togas, make the
    Stewards order a restart! Hold it – yes,
They're calling them back. Mercy, don't let all those flapping   75
    Garments disturb your coiffure! Just lean
Close to me, I'll protect you. Look, up go the starting-gates
    Again, and they're off, all in a close-packed bunch
Of different colours. Go *on*, get through that opening,
    Don't disappoint me and my girl this time!   80
Bravo, he's done it, he's won! Well, love, *you're* not
    disappointed –
    But what about *me*? *My* prize is still to win.
She smiled, eyes bright, inviting – That'll do, now.
    Keep the rest for – another place.

3

Gods exist? Don't tell me. She went back on her sworn word –
    yet
    Her face looks no whit less pretty than before

That act of gross perfidy, her long hair has got no shorter
  Since she spat in divinity's eye. Her fair
Peaches-and-cream complexion is just as it was, the same
5   delicate
  Flush warms her ivory cheek.
Those sweet little feet of hers are as tiny as ever; graceful
  And tall she was – graceful and tall she remains.
Bright eyes she had – they still shine like stars. Yet how many
10   Times did the treacherous creature invoke
Them falsely to my deceit? Oh, I know the gods in heaven
  Forgive a girl's lies; true beauty enjoys divine
Status as such. Why, she swore an oath only the other
  Day, by the eyes of us both – but mine
Were the ones that suffered. Come clean, Gods – if she
15   bamboozled
  You with impunity, why should *I* have to pay
For another's offences? [Isn't it bad enough that you ordered
  Andromeda to be sacrificed for her mama's
Crime of excessive beauty?] Worse still, that I find you puffball
20   Witnesses, so that she fools
Us both with a laugh, unpunished. To redeem her perjury
  Must *I* pay the price, be stuck with a double con?
Either God is a word without substance, an empty bogey
  To play on the dumb credulity of the mob,
25 Or if he exists he's besotted by girls, allows them
  Exclusive rights, carte blanche.
We men aren't so lucky. Mars girds on his deadly broadsword
  Against us, Pallas Athene wields her spear
In unconquered might. Against us the bow of Apollo
30   Is bent, and Jupiter poises his bolt,
Arm upflung – yet these same gods are scared of chastizing
  A pretty blasphemer, they fear
Those who don't fear *them*. Then why bother to burn incense
  On their altars? We men should display
More courage. Jupiter's bolts blast his own high places and
35   sacred
  Groves – but he's careful never to hit

142

A perjured lady. So many deserved it, yet only wretched
    Semele died, burnt up by her own zeal.
What, pray, would have happened if she'd resisted her lover's
    Advances? No motherly stint for divine Papa   40
Delivering Bacchus. Oh, what's the point of bombarding
    The sky with complaints? Gods have eyes, have hearts –
If *I* was divine, I'd legitimize ladies' barefaced
    Whoppers, let them take my godhead in vain.
Why, I'd even swear it was truth the little darlings were telling – 45
    I wouldn't be one of those mean old gods.
Still, darling, I'd be glad if you strained their forbearance
    A little less often – or left my eyes out of it.

4

Being tough's no good, man. Guarding your girl won't help
    you.
    Try exploiting her feminine instincts. Remove
All restraints. If she's *still* chaste, that's genuine chastity. If she
    Only holds back from compulsion, then the first
Chance that she gets, she'll do it. With body mewed up,
    her urges   5
    Are whorish as ever. No watchdog can stopper desire –
Or even sequester the person. Bolt each door, bar every lover.
    Adultery still will lurk within.
But give her free scope, she'll get bored – with full endorsement
    The itch for illicit affairs   10
Very quickly subsides. Believe me, your prohibitions
    Exacerbate vice. Why not try a permissive regime?
It's far more effective. Just lately I saw a tight-reined stallion
    Get the bit in his teeth and bolt
Like lightning – yet the minute he felt the reins slacken,   15
    Drop loose on his flying mane,
He stopped dead. We eternally chafe at restrictions, covet
    Whatever's forbidden. (Look how a sick man who's told
No immersion hangs round the bath-house.) Though Argus
    had hundreds

20   Of eyes – in the back of his head, too! – yet Love
    Still got past his guard single-handed. Poor Danaë was a virgin
      When she entered her iron-barred turret, and then
    Gave birth. Penelope had no guard, yet remained unmolested
      Among all those young bucks. Desire
25 Mounts for what's kept out of reach. A thief's attracted
      By burglar-proof premises. How often will love
    Thrive on a rival's approval? It's not your wife's beauty,
        but your own
      Passion for her that gets us – she must
    Have *something*, just to have hooked you. A girl locked up
      by her
30 Husband's not chaste but pursued, her fear's
    A bigger draw than her figure. Illicit passion – like it
    Or not – is sweeter. It only turns me on
    When the girl says 'I'm frightened.' Not but what it's illegal
      To imprison a freeborn girl. Keep tricks like that
35 As a sanction for aliens. Besides, do you want her warder
      To go around saying 'I did it'? Why keep
    Her chaste if a slave gets the credit? And it's so provincial
      To object to adulterous wives – a deplorable lack
    Of that *ton* for which Rome is famous. The City's founders –
40 Romulus, Remus: Ilia's Martian twins –
    Were bastards. If all you wanted was virtue, why pick a beauty?
      The two things just *never* coincide.
    If you're wise, you'll play up to her. Stop pulling damnable
      faces,
      Don't stand on your marital rights.
    She'll bring you scads of good friends: take care to cultivate
45   them –
      A minimal effort, a substantial return:
    Freedom for you to drink with the boys, while endless
      Presents – from others – greet your eye at home.

5

'Darkness, sleep drowning my weary eyes – and then a
  nightmare

That scared me silly. This was the way of it:
Picture a sunlit hillside, with thick-clustering ilex
   On its lower slopes, and birds
Everywhere in the treetops, a grassy meadow beyond, and   5
   One lush green overgrown spot
With a *drip-drip-drip* of water. It was hot. I sought shelter
   under
   Those leafy branches – yet even there the heat
Oppressed me still. Then, suddenly, a white heifer
   Came into sight, cropping the flowery grass,   10
Whiter than fresh-fallen snowdrifts, before they've melted
   To wet slush, whiter than sheep's
Milk as it hisses and froths in the bucket at milking-time
   Straight from the udder. A bull,
Her privileged mate, was with her, and settled down on   15
   The meadow-grass by her side:
Lay there, ruminant, slowly chewing the grassy
   Cud as it rose in his throat, till I saw
Him begin to nod, and sleepily lower that great horned
   Head to the ground.   20
Then a carrion-crow swooped down on widespread pinions
   And sat cawing there in the grass:
Three times, with mischievous beak, it pecked at the heifer's
   Breast, and tore out a snow-
White tuft. The heifer at last abandoned bull and meadow,   25
   A livid bruise on her throat,
And seeing other bulls at pasture in the distance,
   Bulls in the distance, and fine
Pasturage to be had, moved over and joined them,
   In quest of more fertile fields,   30
A richer diet. So tell me, my unseen expounder
   Of dreams (if such dreams do have significance), what
Does mine portend?'
                The interpreter pondered on all
   I'd told him,
    Then answered: 'That heat you tried
To escape from by sheltering under the breeze-stirred
   branches,   35

Yet in vain, was the heat of desire.
The heifer stood for your girl – white, a most appropriate
    colour –
The bull, her companion, was you.
The sharp-beaked crow that pecked at her breast was some
    elderly
40   Bawd fast-talking her into another affair.
Just as the heifer, at last, after long hesitation,
    Left her bull, so you too will be left
Alone in your own cold bed. The bruise on her breast bears
    witness
To the stain of adultery.'
                    There
His interpretation ended. At those words the blood ran
45   freezing
    From my face, and the world went black before my eyes.

6

Reed-choked and muddy river, would you please mind
    stopping
    Your flow for a moment? I'm late
For a date with my girl. There's no bridge, no cable-ferry
    To get me across without oars.
5   I remember you as a shallow stream, easily fordable, only
    Just deep enough to wet
My ankles – but look at you now, all swollen with melted
    Mountain snow, turbid, whirling down in spate!
What was the point of my hurrying? Why did I ever bother
10   To go without sleep, to travel on night and day
If I've still got to waste time here, if I can't think up any
    Ingenious method of reaching the far bank?
If only I had winged sandals, like Danaë's heroic
    Son Perseus, when he cut off Medusa's head
15   With its crawling coiffure of snakes, or that airborne chariot
    From which the first seed-corn fell
On earth's virgin soil! (All lies, old poetic nonsense

That never really happened – and never will.)
Look, river, your banks are capacious enough – why don't you
   Stay within them? (So may you flow   20
For ever!) Believe me, if it gets known that you held up
   Me, a poet in love, then your name
Will stink to high heaven. Why, rivers should help young
   lovers –
   Rivers know all about love themselves.
Inachus pined, we're told, for Melia the Bithynian –   25
   At her touch, his icy shallows thawed.
While Troy still stood her siege, Xanthus was dazzled
   By Neaera's beauty. And wasn't it true love
For Arcadian Arethusa that drove Alpheus underseas to
   Syracuse? Think of Creüsa, betrothed   30
To another, but ravished away and hidden in Phthiotis
   By Peneus – or so they say. Why should I tell
The tale of how Mars' daughter Thebe caught Asopus'
   Fancy – and bore him five girls in a row?
Where are your horns, Acheloüs? Broken off in a fury   35
   By Heracles' strong right arm:
Not for all Calydon, all Aetolia would he have done it,
   But Deianeira – alone – was worth the lot.
Rich Nile, who hides so well the region of his rising,
   Whose waters flow seaward through   40
Those seven wide mouths, is said to have nursed for Evanthe,
   Asopus' daughter, a flame his own mighty flood
Could never extinguish. Enipeus, red-hot to embrace Salmonis
   Without getting her wet, said *Back*!
To his waters – and back they went. Then there's Anio,
   tumbling   45
   Down through rocks amid Tibur's orchards – he
Lost his heart to Ilia, didn't mind her unkempt appearance,
   The grief-stricken way she tore at her cheeks
And hair as she wandered barefoot through the wilderness,
   mourning
   Mars' lust, and her uncle's crime.   50
At the sight of her swift-flowing Anio's head surged upward

From his loud midwaters, and thus
He spoke: 'Oh why do you pace my bank so forlornly, Ilia,
    Daughter of Ilium's royal line?
55 Why must you wander alone, your finery discarded,
    Hair falling down your back, no white
Ribbon to bind it? Why are you crying, why in such frenzy
    Beating your naked breast?
The man who could look on your tears and feel no pity must
    have a
60   Heart compounded of iron and flint.
Ilia, don't be afraid. My palace is ready for you, my waters
    Will do you honour. Ilia, don't be afraid.
A hundred nymphs and more you shall have to attend you –
    a hundred
    And more my streams contain.
65 Don't reject me, not that, I beseech you, dear Trojan lady –
    Say "Yes" and you'll reap a still richer reward
Than all I have promised.'
                  She kept her eyes modestly
    lowered,
    Warm tears soaking her bosom. Three times she tried
To escape from those mighty waters, but found herself
    powerless,
70   Frozen with fear. Then, at last,
Hands clutching her hair, voice tremulous, she somehow
    Broke into bitter words: 'O that my bones
Had been gathered and laid to rest in the tomb of my
    ancestors
    While I was a virgin still! Ah why
This offer of marriage? My vows, I broke my vows as a
75   Vestal –
    Whorish, unclean. No right to the sacred fire.
Why linger, a butt for cheap pointing fingers? The brand of
    Shame is on my face: so, wipe it out!'
With that she raised up her robe before her swollen
80   Eyes, and hurled herself into the swift
Flood, but the lubricous River, it's said, swam his hands up

Under her breasts, and bedded her as his Queen.
Has some girl warmed *you* up, too? I suppose it's just credible –
  This woodland greenery would make a fine
Camouflage for such crimes.
                     Your stream (I declare)
  has widened   85
  While I've been talking! Those banks
Aren't deep enough to contain it. What's your grudge against
  me, though?
  Why interrupt my journey, postpone the joys
Of a lovers' meeting? If only you were a proper river,
  Well-known internationally, on the map,   90
And not this anonymous product of *ad hoc* drainage,
  With no settled source or route,
Dependent instead upon flash floods and melting snows, the
  Largesse that dull winter bestows!
If it's winter you're muddy-turbulent; then, come summer,   95
  A desert of stones and dust.
What traveller ever slaked thirst in *your* waters, or wished you
  Long life, a perennial flow?
In spate you're a menace to fields and cattle – though that's a
  problem
  For others, not me; I'm more concerned with my own   100
Troubles. I must have been crazy, telling you tales of rivers
  That fell in love, dropping the names
Of Inachus, Acheloüs, Nile and the rest of them
  To a no-name dribble like you!
May you get what you deserve, you fouled-up torrent –   105
  Heatwave all summer, and in winter, drought!

7

I can't fault the girl on looks, or style, or sophistication –
  And I'd tried for her often enough. *But*
There we lay, in bed, embracing, and all to no purpose:
  I was limp, disgusting, dead.
Heaven knows I wanted it badly, and so did my partner;   5

But still I failed to measure up.
She tried every trick – wound her arms (whiter than snow or
    Ivory) around me, pressed
Her thighs up snug under mine, plied me with sexy kisses,
10   Tongue exploring like mad,
Whispered endearments, called me her master, tried me
    With nice four-letter words – they often help.
No good. My member hung slack, as though frozen by hemlock,
    A dead loss for the sort of game I'd planned.
15 There I lay, a sham, a deadweight, a trunk of inert matter,
    Not even sure if I was alive, or a ghost.
What sort of old age shall I have (if I ever reach it)
    When I can't make out as a youth?
I'm ashamed, at my age. Little good in being young and virile
20   If as far as *she* could tell
I was neither. She left my bed with sisterly decorum,
    Pure as a Vestal off to tend
The sacred flame. But it's not all that long since I made it
    Twice with that smart Greek blonde, three times
25 With a couple of other beauties – and as for Corinna,
    In one short night, I remember, she made me perform
Nine times, no less. Perhaps some Thessalian hell-brew
    has ruined
    My physical urges, maybe I'm a victim of spells
And herbal concoctions. Perhaps some witch is busy transfixing
30   My image, and name, in red wax,
Sticking pins through my liver. Magic spells can transform
    wheatfields
    Into barren tares, can dry up springs at source,
Charm acorns off oaks, grapes from vines, strip orchards
    bare of
    Their fruit without human aid – so what's to stop
35 Some magician giving my member a local anaesthetic?
    Maybe *that* was the trouble, made worse
By embarrassment when I couldn't, the final humiliating
    Blow to my masculine pride.
Such a marvellous girl – her own dress couldn't cling closer

Than I did to her: I eyed her, touched her, but that   40
Was as far as it went. Put Nestor in my position,
   Tithonus even, and despite their decrepitude
They'd rise to the test like boys. I'd the chance to possess her,
   But she got no deal. What can I pray for now?
I'm sure the gods must regret the gift with which they
    endowed me –   45
   Just look at the way I've messed it up! I got
Everything that I hoped for, an enthusiastic welcome,
   Kisses, the girl on her own: yet where
Did all my good fortune take me? What's ownership minus
   Possession? To leave such wealth intact   50
Was a trick fit for misers. I lay there like Tantalus, parching
   Because of his indiscretion, eyes on the fruit
That always hung just out of reach. I mean, one just *doesn't*
   Get up simon-pure after a night with a girl –
And it's not that she wasn't seductive, just think of those
    marvellous   55
   Kisses she wasted on me, the tricks she tried!
She could have shifted an oak-tree, broken hard adamant,
   Worked up unfeeling stones:
A living, virile partner, for her, was a pushover – but just then
   I lacked both virility and life.   60
What joy can a blind man get from a painted picture?
   What's the use of a singer performing for the deaf?
I imagined every variety of erotic pleasure, invented
   No end of positions – in my head –
But still my member lay there, an embarrassing case of   65
   Premature death, and limper than yesterday's rose.
Yet *now* – what perverse timing! – just look at it, stiff and
    urgent,
   Eager to go campaigning, get on the job.
(Oh why can't you lie down? I'm ashamed of you, you bastard –
   I've been caught by your promises before.   70
You let me down, it was *your* fault I landed weaponless
   In this embarrassing and expensive fix.)
My girl tried everything, even some gentle massage

Of the offending part –
75 Yet *still* it wouldn't come up. All her varied resources
   (She saw) left it quite unmoved.
Then she really got mad. 'You're sick,' she told me. 'Stop
      wasting
   My time. Who sent you along
To gatecrash my bed? Look, either some witch has hexed you
80 Or you've just been making love with another girl.'
That did it. She jumped out of bed, her nightdress flying,
   with a
   Delectable flash of bare feet,
And to stop her maids from guessing nothing had happened
   Splashed around with some water – as though it had.

8

Does anyone nowadays look up with admiration
   At the liberal arts, or believe
Love-elegies rate a dowry? Time was when poetic talent
   Came dearer than gold, but today
To lack cash is plain vulgar. When my poems please my
5   mistress
   They can go in where *I* can't.
A few pretty compliments, and the front door slams behind me –
   Me, genius, out in the cold,
Traipsing round like a fool, replaced by some new-rich soldier,
10 A bloody oaf who slashed his way to the cash
And a knighthood. Darling, how could you *bear* to embrace
      him
   With those exquisite arms – much less let *him* hug *you*?
That headpiece (let me remind you) once wore a helmet,
      those loins
   That serve you were strapped with a sword,
15 On the left hand a knight's gold ring, new, inappropriate,
   Replaces a shield. The right –
Yes, touch it – has shed men's blood. Can you hold hands
   with a killer?

Whatever became of your tender heart?
Just look at his scars, mementoes of old battles –
  That body earned him all he's got.   20
Maybe he'll even tell you how many human carcases
  He's butchered. Such give-away hands
Surely choke your gold-digging instincts? Yet I, pure priest
  of the Muses
  And Apollo, declaim in vain to a locked door.
If you want to be with it, don't learn what we layabouts know,
  but   25
  Train as a front-line soldier, rough it in camp:
Make centurion, don't make good verses. A spot of active
  service
  And Homer would qualify for a classy lay.
When Jupiter realized gold's sovereign potency, presto,
  He coined himself to raise   30
The price of a quick seduction. Without the profit motive
  Father was adamant, the girl a prude,
Her tower of iron brass-bolted. But when this smart seducer
  Cashed down on her, crying 'Give!'
She gave with a will. When old Saturn ruled in heaven   35
  Earth's wealth lay deep underground
Where he'd stored it away – bronze, silver, gold, and the
  ponderous
  Weight of cold iron. Ingots were still unknown.
Yet Earth had better to offer – crops without husbandry,
  Fruit there for the picking, honey in hollow oaks;   40
No ploughshares to break up the landscape, no surveyors
  Pegging out the boundaries of estates,
No oars to churn up the seaways – men travelled no further
  Than the shoreline in those days.
Ingenious human nature, scintillatingly self-destructive,   45
  So clever you cut yourself – what
Use is it ringing your cities with turreted fortifications?
  Why stir up enemies to fight?
Was the sea your domain? Best have stuck to terra firma:
  Why not stake out a third realm, in the sky?   50

(Though as far as you can you *do* reach heavenwards:
        Bacchus,
    Hercules, Romulus, and now Caesar too
All have their temples.) Today we dig the earth, not for
        produce
    But for solid gold. Soldiers get wealth through blood,
55 And not their own, either. The Senate's barred to a pauper,
    Income grades honours. Thus, the grave judge;
Thus, the stern knight. Let them own the lot, Campus and
        Forum
    At their command, theirs to decide
For peace or brute war – so long as they don't bid up the
        prices
60   On our lovers, so long as they leave
The poor man his bone, it's enough. As things are, were my
        girl as prudish-
    Chaste as a Sabine, Sugar-Daddy still calls the shots.
So the porter won't let me in, and she's scared (she says) of
        her husband
    When I'm around. But if I could *pay* those two
They'd leave us the house to ourselves. Why can't neglected
        lovers
65   Have their own god, who'd turn ill-gotten gains to dust?

9

If Memnon's mother, if the mother of great Achilles
    Lamented their sons, if grievous death
Can touch high goddesses, then, O Elegy – all too truly
    Now named for sorrow – unbind your hair
And weep tears of loss. Tibullus, your pride, your laureate
5   poet
    Lies on the high pyre, a husk
Winnowed by flame. Cupid's there, quiver reversed,
        bow broken,
    Holding a burnt-out torch.
See how sadly he walks, poor child, wings drooping,
10   How he beats at his bared breast,

How the tears rain down on his hair, now lying all tangled
    About his throat, and his mouth's a loud O of grief.
Thus he looked, they say, long ago, when he saw his brother
    Aeneas to the grave
From Iulus' palace. Venus is mourning too, the death of   15
    Tibullus has hit her as hard .
As the boar-tush that gashed the groin of young Adonis.
    We poets
    Are called sacred, beloved of the gods – by some
Even divinely inspired. But importunate Death profanes
    all that's
    Sacred, lays obscure hands   20
On each mortal alike. What good were divine parents to
    Orpheus?
    Could the songs that spellbound beasts
Save even him? His father Apollo sang 'Woe for Linos!'
    (They say) in the wild woods
To a reluctant lyre. Great Homer, perennial well-spring   25
    Of inspiration for poets, one day sank
Under hell's black waters, drowned in eternity. Only
    Songs, spells, escape the greedy flame,
Only the poet's work endures, the tale of that Trojan
    High endeavour, the nightly guile   30
That unwove an immortal web. Thus Delia, thus Nemesis,
    Old love and new, are assured of lasting fame.
Did religion give them as much? What use, now, those
    Egyptian
    Rattles, those nights of chaste solitude? When
Good men die untimely I'm tempted – forgive my bluntness –   35
    To deny that the gods exist. A holy life
Is still closed by death. The most pious of worshippers
    Will yet be dragged from his temple to the grave.
Is creative magic your touchstone? Look, there lies Tibullus,
    Great talent rendered down   40
To an urnful of ashes. Did flames devour *your* body, poet,
    Make bold to feed on *your* heart?
Such blasphemous fire would scarcely have baulked at
    burning

The gilded temples of the gods.
45 Venus, Queen of high Eryx, averted her countenance, shed sad
    Tears, it is said, despite herself.
    Still, better this way. Suppose you had died, still unknown,
        of that illness
    Long ago on Corfu, had mouldered in some cheap grave?
    Here, your swimming eyes were closed, as the spirit fled them,
50 By a mother's hand. She paid
    Your ashes the final rites, with your sister as fellow-mourner
    Tearing unkempt hair. Next-of-kin
    Kisses mingled with those of Nemesis and your previous
    Mistress – you weren't left to burn away alone.
55 Stepping down from the pyre, 'I was lucky in love,' said Delia,
    'The spark I kindled in you
    Spelt life.' 'No, the loss is mine,' cried Nemesis. 'Why should
        you feel
    Sorrow? It was me he clung to as he died.'
    Yet if human survival means more than a ghostly reputation,
60 Tibullus must surely dwell in Elysium,
    Welcomed by young Catullus, ivy-garlanded, poet and scholar,
    With his Calvus, and perhaps (should that charge
    Of friendship dishonoured prove false) you too, Gallus,
        over-lavish
    Of your own blood, your dear life.
    With these, if some ghostly substance survive the body,
65   your ghost will
    Be numbered, an elegant newcomer to the ranks
    Of the blessed dead. May your bones rest undisturbed in their
        guardian
    Urn, I pray, and on your ashes the earth lie light.

 10

High summer has brought round Ceres' yearly festival
    And my darling lies alone in her empty bed.
Flaxen Ceres, your fine hair wreathed with wheat-ears,
    why must

Your rites inhibit our fun?
People the wide world over extol your munificence, Lady: 5
    No other goddess lavishes more on mankind.
In earlier times a hirsute and ignorant peasantry never
    Parched corn, hadn't heard
About threshing-floors. Oak-trees, those primitive oracles,
    yielded
    Them acorns: acorns and herbs   10
Made up their diet. Ceres first taught the seed to ripen
    In the furrow, first scythed
The golden cornstalks, broke ox to yoke, drove ploughshare
    Through virgin soil. Can *this*
Be a goddess who battens on lovers' sorrows, finds proper
    worship   15
    In the torment of sexless nights?
Yet though fertile fields are her special delight, she's no simple
    Rustic herself – nor is her heart untouched
By love, as the Cretans will tell you – and not *everything* Cretans
    Say is a lie. Why, Crete once stood proud nurse   20
To Jove himself: there he, who sways the starry vault of
    Heaven, sucked milk
As a newborn babe. Unimpeachable evidence, evidence
    backed by
    Crete's foster-son: Ceres should plead
Guilty. The facts are well-known. Out on the slopes of Ida   25
    She met with that keen
Marksman Iasius hunting. Fire coursed through her marrow,
    Passion and shame at odds. But shame
Lost out to passion. Oh, then you could see the furrows
    Turn barren-dry, then seed   30
Yielded a meagre harvest. Though labourers had sweated
    With mattocks and crooked share
To crack those recalcitrant clods, though the seed was
    broadcast
    Field-wide and even, their hopes
Went all for nothing. Thicket-deep the goddess of increase   35
    In dalliance lay, the wheatspike wreath

Tumbled from her long tresses. Only Crete enjoyed fruitfulness
    That year. Wherever she came was harvest-home –
Crops rioted amid the very forests of Ida, wild boar
40   Trampled spelt in the woods.
Minos the law-giver prayed for more such seasons: better
    He had prayed for Ceres' love to last.
Just because lonely nights were hell for you, dear golden
    Goddess, why put *me* through the same
Torture during your festival? Why should I be sad? Your
45   daughter's
Found again, and now queens it over a realm
Second only to Juno's. This festive day calls for wine, for
    love-making
And song – what fitter tribute to all-powerful gods?

11A

I've stood enough, for too long. Heart and patience are both
    exhausted
    By this fickle obsession. So – *out*!
That's right, I've slipped the chain, achieved emancipation,
    Can blush – now – for what I once
5   Bore so unblushingly. Triumph: passion spurned and trodden
    Under my feet. A tardy access of horn-
Stiff will. Keep it up, stand firm. Such suffering's bound to
    Pay off in the end. Nasty medicine does you good.
How *could* I have swallowed such insults? The times I was
    driven
10   Away from your door, to grovel on the bare
Pavement – *me*, a gentleman! The times I stood guard,
    slave-like,
    Outside your shuttered house (while you
Made love to God knows who) and was forced to watch your
    lover
    Lurch home exhausted, done in!
15   Yet even this hurt less than *him* seeing *me* – I could wish my
    Bitterest enemy no worse a fate.

Was there ever a day when I failed to act as your personal
    Watchdog, companion, shadow, lover, friend?
And wasn't it our relationship made you a public sweetheart,
    One love-affair generating so many more?   20
Why remind you of all your sordid lies, those broken
    Promises, worthless oaths
You swore to my undoing, the young men who gave you
    private
    Signals at parties, coded exchanges? 'She's sick,'
They told me: at once I hurried back like a madman, found
    you   25
    The picture of health – and in my rival's arms.
Such incidents (there were others I'd sooner omit) have
    hardened
    My heart at long last. So go find
Some other more willing victim. My vessel lies safe in harbour,
    Garlanded, indifferent to the swelling storm outside.   30
Leave off your blandishments. The old line's lost its magic
    Hold on my senses. I'm not the fool I was.

IIB

My capricious heart's a cockpit for conflicting emotions,
    Love versus hate – but love, I think, will win.
I'll hate if I can. If not, I'll play the reluctant lover:
    No ox loves the yoke – he's just stuck with what he hates.
A fugitive from your vices, I'm lured back by your beauty: 5
    Your morals turn me off, your body on.
So I can live neither with nor without you, I don't seem
    To know my own mind. I wish you were
Either less beautiful or more faithful: such a good figure
    Doesn't go with your bad ways.   10
The facts demand censure, the face begs for love – and gets it,
    Eclipsing (to my cost) its owner's crimes.
By the bed we shared, by all those gods who so often
    Let you take their names in vain,
By your face, that image for me of high divinity,   15

By those eyes which captivated mine,
Spare me! And mine you'll always remain, whatever your
    nature;
Just choose – would you rather I loved
Freely or by constraint? Let me spread sail, cruise with a
    following
20   Breeze – make me want what I can't resist!

12

What day was it, birds of ill omen, that you croaked your
    portents
Above this eternally love-struck head of mine?
What unlucky star has crossed me, what gods are planning
My downfall? That girl whom the town
5 Spoke of – till lately – as *mine*, my solitary obsession,
    I fear I must now share
With all comers. Could my poems have made her a public
    figure?
That's it: *she* was prostituted by *my* art,
And serve me right for trumpeting her beauty abroad! If my
    darling's
10   On the market, it's all my fault –
I've pimped her charms, I've marked up the route for lovers,
    It was I who let them in at her front door.
What good have my poems done me? They've brought
    nothing but trouble,
    Made men envy my success.
Thebes could have been my theme, or Troy, or Caesar's
15   exploits,
    But only Corinna sparked me off.
Why couldn't the Muse, and Apollo, have withheld their
    inspiration
    When I first turned my hand to verse?
Yet poets' statements aren't normally taken as gospel – I never
20   Meant such light stuff to carry weight.
Myth's more our field. We created Scylla, who raped her
    father's

Lock, and keeps packs of mad
Dogs in her groin and womb. We snaked up Medusa's
    hairstyle,
    Winged Hermes' heels, gave Perseus his flying horse,
Stretched Tityos the giant till he covered nine acres,
    found three   25
    Heads for dragon-tailed Cerberus, made
Enceladus, windmilling spears with his thousand arms;
    drew heroes
    Ravished by Siren voices, shut the winds
Of Aeolus in a wineskin for Odysseus, worked the
    water-torture
    On treacherous Tantalus – a thirst   30
For ever unsatisfied – turned Niobe to flint, made Callisto a
    she-bear,
    Philomela a nightingale,
Let Jupiter masquerade in feathers or showers of gold, or
    Swim off as an ocean bull
With some hapless virgin up. Then there's Proteus, and the
    Theban   35
    Sown teeth of the dragon, those oxen snorting fire,
Phaëthon's sisters weeping amber tears, sea-goddesses
    Conjured from ships, the sun
Wheeling back in the heavens at sight of Thyestes' ghastly
    Cannibal feast, rocks bouncing along in the wake   40
Of strumming Amphion – oh, creative poetic licence
    Is boundless, and unconstrained
By historical fact. You ought / to have taken my praise of
    Corinna
    As fiction. Now *your* credulity's done *me* harm!

13

We had come to Falerii – good orchard land: once captured by
    Camillus:
    And (the why of our visit) my wife's home-town.
Priestesses were busy with Juno's chaste festival – sacrifice
    Of a local heifer: crowded games.

5 Despite an exhausting journey over mountain roads, to witness
       This ritual more than made up for the delay.
   There stood the goddess's grove, dark-shadowed, immemorial –
       One step inside, and you know
   That some spirit haunts the place. There's a rough old altar
10   Where worshippers burn incense, mutter a prayer.
   Hither, through garlanded streets, with solemn chanting
       To the skirl of flutes, and cheers
   From the bystanders, comes a once-yearly procession, leading
           snow-white
       Heifers, sleek on Falerian pasture, young
   Calves with no lowering menace – as yet – abud in their
15   foreheads,
       Humble pigs from the sty (placate
   God at cut rates) and old / bell-wethers with backward-curving
       Horns on their bony skulls. Only the goat
   Is banned, as Juno's *bête noire*. When she fled Jove, and
           sought shelter
20   Deep in the forest, a goat's bleat gave her away.
   So to this day little children still throw spears at the tattler,
       And whoever scores first wins
   A nannygoat prize. Ahead of the goddess walk youths and shy
           maidens,
       Skirts sweeping the broad street,
25 The girls' hair all entwined with gold and jewels, gilded
       Shoes peeping out from beneath
   Ceremonial mantles. Veiled, white-robed in the ancestral
       Greek fashion, they bear on their heads
   The sacred vessels. Then the crowd hushes in reverence
30   As Juno herself goes past on a gilded float
   Drawn by her priestesses. The ritual came from Argos:
       On Agamemnon's murder Halaesus fled
   The scene of the crime, fled his heritage: after long wanderings
       By land and sea, he founded these city-walls
35 And taught his prosperous burghers the worship of Juno.
       Lady, look kindly always on me, on them.

14

I don't ask that you should be faithful, you're far too attractive:
    I'd just prefer *not* to know about your affairs –
So depressing. My principles aren't based on exclusive
        possession,
    But they *do* require some attempt
To cover one's tracks. Any girl who can swear she didn't,   5
    Didn't. Only admission ruins her name.
What lunacy to expose nocturnal business in daylight
    And broadcast one's private acts! Even a tart
About to perform with some nameless gentleman keeps the
        public
    Outside by bolting her door   10
Before they begin – whereas *you* feed gossip succulent titbits
    Of scandal, turn informer on your own misdeeds.
Show a little more decency (or at least pretend to): then I
    Can think you faithful even when you're not.
Keep on with your present life, *just don't admit it.* A modest   15.
    Persona, in public, shouldn't prove too bad
An embarrassment. Impropriety has its special off-limits
    Enclave, where every kind of fun is the rule
And restraints are unheard-of. But the moment you walk out,
        drop all
    Wanton behaviour. Keep your misconduct for bed,   20
Where stripping off need occasion no embarrassment, nor the
    Twining of thigh over thigh:
The proving-ground for countless varieties of passion,
    Tongue thrust between cherry-ripe lips,
Non-stop whispered endearments, ecstatic moans, the bedstead 25
    Shaking away like mad:
But reassume, with your clothes, a highly respectable
        expression.
    A virtuous air which abjures the very thought
Of illicit sex. Lay them all, but allay my suspicions, leave me
    In ignorance, let me cling   30

163

To my foolish illusions. All those to-and-fro notes – need I see
    them?
    Couldn't you even smooth out the bed
Or tidy your hair? (That degree of dishevelment takes more
    Than sleeping alone.) *Must* you flaunt the bites
On your neck? All you draw the line at is doing it in my
35   presence –
    If you don't care for your good name, please think of me!
Each time you confess a liaison it kills me by inches, my reason
    Blanks out, I'm covered in a cold sweat.
Then love's overlaid by vain hatred for what I can't help
    loving,
40   Then I wish I were dead – with you.
I'll make no inquiries, won't probe into your secrets:
    Self-deception will be my official line.
But if ever you're caught in the act, if I actually witness
    Your shameful conduct with my own eyes,
45 Make sure you contradict the evidence of my senses,
    And then I'll accept your word
Against what I saw. No trouble in defeating a would-be loser –
    Just let your tongue
Remember that phrase 'Not guilty'. Two words will free you.
    Your case may
50   Be weak – but then so is your judge!

15

Mother of tender loves, you must find another poet:
    My elegies are homing on their final lap.
Postscript concerning the author: of Paelignian extraction,
    A man whose delights have never let him down,
5 Heir – for what that's worth – to an ancient family,
    No brand-new knight jumped up
Through the maelstrom fortunes of war. Mantua boasts her
    Virgil,
    The Veronese their Catullus. *I* shall become the pride
Of my fellow-Paelignians – a race who fought for freedom,

Freedom with honour, in the Italian wars   10
That scared Rome witless. I can see some visitor to Sulmona
  Taking in its tiny scale, the streams and walls,
And saying: 'Any township, however small, that could breed so
  Splendid a poet, I call great.' Boy-god,
And you, Cyprian goddess, his mother, remove your golden   15
  Standards from my terrain –
Horned Bacchus is goading me on to weightier efforts, bigger
  Horses, a really ambitious trip.
So farewell, congenial Muse, unheroic elegiacs –
  Work born to live on when its maker's dead!

THE ART OF LOVE

BOOK I

Should anyone here in Rome lack finesse at love-making,
    let him
  Try me – read my book, and results are guaranteed!
Technique is the secret. Charioteer, sailor, oarsman,
    All need it. Technique can control
5 Love himself. As Automedon was charioteer to Achilles,
    And Tiphys Jason's steersman, so I,
By Venus' appointment, am made Love's artificer, shall be
    known as
  The Tiphys, the very Automedon of Love.
He's a wild handful, will often rebel against me,
10   But still just a child –
Malleable, easily disciplined. Chiron made young Achilles
    A fine musician, hammered that fierce heart
On the anvil of peaceful artistry. So this future terror
    To friend and foe alike went in awe, it's said,
15 Of his elderly teacher, at whose bidding the hand that in after-
    Time bore down Hector was held out for the tawse.
As Chiron taught Achilles, so I am Love's preceptor:
    Wild boys both, both goddess-born – and yet
Even bulls can be broken to plough, or spirited horses
20   Subdued with bridle and bit.
So Love shall likewise own my mastery, though his bowshots
    Skewer my breast, though his torch
Flicker and sear me. The worse the wounds, the deeper the
    branding,
    That much keener I to avenge
25 Such outrage. Nor shall I falsely ascribe my arts to Apollo:
    No airy bird comes twittering advice
Into *my* ear, *I* never had a vision of the Muses

Herding sheep in Ascra's valleys. This work is based
On experience: what I write, believe me, I have practised.
   My poem will deal in truth.   30

Aid my enterprise, Venus! Respectable ladies, the kind who
   Wear hairbands and ankle-length skirts,
Are hereby warned off. Safe love, legitimate liaisons
   Will be my theme. This poem breaks no taboos.
First, then, you fledgling troopers in passion's service,   35
   Comes the task of finding an object for your love.
Next, you must labour to woo and win your lady;
   Thirdly, ensure that the affair will last.
Such are my limitations, such the ground I will cover,
   The race I propose to run.   40

While you are fancy-free still, and can drive at leisure,
   Pick a girl, tell her, 'You're the one I love.
And only you.' But this search means using your eyes: a
     mistress
   Won't drop out of the sky at your feet.
A hunter's skilled where to spread his nets for the stag, senses   45
   In which glen the wild boar lurks.
A fowler's familiar with copses, an expert angler
   Knows the richest shoaling-grounds for fish.
You too, so keen to establish some long-term relationship,
   Must learn, first, where girl is to be found.   50
Your search need not take you – believe me – on an overseas
     voyage:
   A short enough trek will bring you to your goal.
True, Perseus fetched home Andromeda from the coloured
     Indies,
   While Phrygian Paris abducted Helen in Greece,
But Rome can boast of so many and such dazzling beauties   55
   You'd swear the whole world's talent was gathered here.
The girls of your city outnumber Gargara's wheatsheaves,
   Methymna's grape-clusters, all
Birds on the bough, stars in the sky, fish in the ocean:

60 Venus indeed still haunts
    Her son Aeneas' foundation. If you like budding adolescents
        Any number of (guaranteed) maidens are here to delight
    Your roving eye. You prefer young women? They'll charm you
        By the thousand, you won't know which to choose.
65 And if you happen to fancy a more mature, experienced
        Age-group, believe me, *they* show up in droves.

    Here's what to do. When the sun's on the back of Hercules'
        Lion, stroll down some shady colonnade,
    Pompey's, say, or Octavia's (for her dead son Marcellus:
70   Extravagant marble facings, R.I.P.),
    Or Livia's, with its gallery of genuine Old Masters,
        Or the Danaids' Portico (note
    The artwork: Danaus' daughters plotting mischief for
            their cousins,
        Father attitudinizing with drawn sword).
75 Don't miss the shrine of Adonis, mourned by Venus,
        Or the synagogue – Syrian Jews
    Worship there each Sabbath – or the linen-clad heifer-goddess's
        Memphian temple: Io makes many a maid what *she*
    Was to Jove. The very courts are hunting-grounds for passion;
80   Amid lawyers' rebuttals love will often be found.
    Here, where under Venus' marble temple the Appian
        Fountain pulses its jets high in the air,
    Your jurisconsult's entrapped by Love's beguilements –
        Counsel to others, he cannot advise himself.
85 Here, all too often, words fail the most eloquent pleader,
        And a new sort of case comes on – his own. He must
    Defend *himself* for a change, while Venus in her nearby
        Temple snickers at this reversal of roles.

    But the theatre's curving tiers should form your favourite
90   Hunting-ground: here you are sure to find
    The richest returns, be your wish for lover or playmate,
        A one-night stand or a permanent affair.
    As ants hurry to and fro in column, mandibles

Clutching grains of wheat
(Their regular diet), as bees haunt fragrant pastures   95
  And meadows, hovering over the thyme,
Flitting from flower to flower, so our fashionable ladies
  Swarm to the games in such crowds, I often can't
Decide which I like. As spectators they come, come to be
    inspected:
  Chaste modesty doesn't stand a chance.   100
Such incidents at the games go back to Romulus –
  Men without women, Sabine rape.
No marble theatre then, no awnings, no perfumed saffron
  To spray the stage red:
The Palatine woods supplied a leafy backdrop (nature's   105
  Scenery, untouched by art),
While the tiers of seats were plain turf, and spectators shaded
  Their shaggy heads with leaves.
Urgently brooding in silence, the men kept glancing
  About them, each marking his choice   110
Among the girls. To the skirl of Etruscan flutes' rough triple
  Rhythm, the dancers stamped
And turned. Amid cheers (applause then lacked discrimination)
  The king gave the sign for which
They'd so eagerly watched. Project Rape was on. Up they
    sprang then   115
  With a lusty roar, laid hot hands on the girls.
As timorous doves flee eagles, as a lambkin
  Runs when it sees the hated wolf,
So this wild charge of men left the girls all panic-stricken,
  Not one had the same colour in her cheeks as before –   120
The same nightmare for all, though terror's features varied:
  Some tore their hair, some just froze
Where they sat; some, dismayed, kept silence, others vainly
  Yelled for Mamma; some wailed; some gaped;
Some fled, some just stood there. So they were carried off as   125
  Marriage-bed plunder; even so, many contrived
To make panic look fetching. Any girl who resisted her pursuer
  Too vigorously would find herself picked up

And borne off regardless. 'Why spoil those pretty eyes with
    weeping?'
130   She'd hear, 'I'll be all to you
That your Dad ever was to your Mum.' (You alone found
    the proper
    Bounty for soldiers, Romulus: give me that,
And I'll join up myself!) Ever since that day, by hallowed
    custom,
    Our theatres have always held dangers for pretty girls.

135   Don't forget the races, either: the spacious Circus offers
    Chances galore. No need,
Here, of private finger-talk, or secret signals,
    Nods conveying messages: you'll sit
Right beside your mistress, without let or hindrance,
140   So be sure to press against her wherever you can –
An easy task: the seating-divisions restrict her,
    Regulations facilitate contact. Now find
Some excuse to engage in friendly conversation,
    Casual small-talk at first –
145   Ask, with a show of interest, whose are those horses
    Just coming past: find out
Her favourite, back it yourself. When the long procession
    of ivory
    Deities approaches, be sure you give
A big hand to Lady Venus. If some dust should settle
150   In your girl's lap, flick it away
With your fingers; and if there's no dust, still flick away –
    nothing:
    Let any excuse serve to prove your zeal.
If her cloak's trailing, gather it up, make a great business
    Of rescuing it from the dirt –
155   Instant reward for your gallantry, a licensed peep at
    Delectable ankles, and more.
Keep an eye on whoever may be sitting behind you,
    Don't let him rub his knee
Against her smooth back. Light minds are captivated by trifles:

Plumping out a cushion can often help,   160
Or fanning the lady, or slipping a little footstool
    Under her dainty feet.

Such approaches will the Circus afford to a new courtship,
    Such, too, the crowded forum with its grim
Sanded arena, where Cupid's a regular contestant,   165
    Where the blood-and-guts fancier gets bloodied himself:
While he's chatting, and touching her hand, and checking the
        programme,
    And anxious (once he's placed his bet) to know
Which contestant will win, the winged steel has transfixed him,
    He groans at the wound, becomes part   170
Of the show he was watching. When Caesar lately staged that
    Naval mock-battle between Persians and Greeks,
Young men and girls converged from east coast and west,
        the whole wide
    World was packed into Rome –
With such a throng, who could fail to find what caught his
        fancy?   175
    Many a man was singed by some foreign flame!

Now Caesar is planning to fill in the final gaps of
    Empire: now the furthest East will be ours,
Revenge fall on Parthia, joy lighten the grave of Crassus,
    Redeem the standards profaned   180
By barbarian hands! The avenger's prepared, proclaims his
    Captaincy, though of green years: embraces a war
No boy – no other boy – could direct. Why cravenly reckon
    The age of a god? These Caesars come to courage young,
The surge of heavenly spirit outstrips mere calendars,   185
    Takes mean delays ill. A mere babe
Was Hercules when he strangled those two serpents: even
    In the cradle he proved worthy of Jove.
And you, Bacchus, still a youth, what age were *you* when
        conquered
    India bowed before your rod?   190

171

With the years – and luck – of your father, boy, you'll fight this
    Campaign: with his years – and luck – you'll win.
Such a debut befits so great a name: today prince of
    The youths, tomorrow of their seniors! Since
195 You have brothers, avenge these brothers' insults; since a
    Father is yours, uphold a father's rights.
Your father, your country's father, has armed you for battle;
    Your enemy has wrested *his* kingdom from
A reluctant sire. Your righteous javelins shall match his
200 Treacherous arrows. Justice and right shall march
Before your banners. May these lost-cause Parthians likewise
    Lose every fight, may my prince bring the wealth of the East
Back home! Mars and Caesar – one god, one god-to-be –
    endow him
    With your paternal powers as he sets forth!
205 I prophesy victory for you, vow a song in your honour,
    Will extol you with loud praise:
You'll stand and exhort your troops in words I have written –
    May my words, I pray, not fall short
Of your valour! I'll speak of Parthian backs, of Roman courage,
210 Of the shafts discharged by the foe
As he retreats on horseback. If a Parthian flees to conquer
    What's left him for defeat? That's a bad
Omen for warfare already. The day will come, most splendid
    Of beings, when you'll ride in gold behind
215 Four snow-white steeds, preceded by captive chieftains, fetters
    About their necks to prevent the flight that brought
Them safety before. Cheering youths will look on, and girls
    beside them,
    A day to make every heart run wild for joy;
And when some girl inquires the names of the monarchs,
220 Or the towns, rivers, hills portrayed
On the floats, answer all her questions (and don't draw the
    line at
    Questions only): pretend
You know even when you don't. *Here comes Euphrates*, tell
    her,

With reed-fringed brow; those dark
Blue tresses belong to Tigris, I fancy; there go Armenians,   225
   That's Persia, and that, h'r'm, is some
Upland Achaemenid city. Both those men there are generals –
   Give the names if you know them; if not, invent.

Banquets, too, give you an *entrée*, offer
   More to the palate than wine: 230
There flushed Love has often clasped the horns of reclining
   Bacchus in a seductive embrace,
And when wine has sodden Cupid's bibulous pinions
   He's grounded, too sluggish for the sport he's begun.
Still, it takes *him* no time to shake out his damp plumage –   235
   But if Love merely brushes the breast
You're wounded, it hurts. Wine rouses the heart, inclines to
     passion:
   Heavy drinking dilutes and banishes care
In a sea of laughter, gives the poor man self-confidence,
   Smooths out wrinkles, puts paid   240
To pain and sorrow. Then our age's rarest endowment,
   Simplicity, opens all hearts, as the god
Dissipates guile. Men's minds have often been enchanted
   By girls at such times: ah, Venus in the wine
Is fire within fire! Night and drink can impair your eye for
     beauty: 245
   Don't trust the lamplight too much,
It's deceptive. When Paris examined those goddesses, when
     he said, 'You
   Beat them both, Venus,' he did it in broad
Daylight. But darkness hides faults, each blemish is forgiven:
   Any woman you name will pass   250
As a beauty at night. Judge jewels or fine fabrics,
   A face or a figure, *by day.*

How list every female resort with prospects for the hunter?
   Sand-grains are fewer. Why tell of Baiae with
Its yacht-fringed beaches and hot sulphurous thermal   255

Baths? I met one tourist who came back
Home from there with a nasty hole in his heart, said the waters
    Weren't half as healthy as report made out.
Then there's Diana's woodland shrine, not far from the city,
260   With its murderous slave-priest –
Diana's a virgin, detests the shafts of Cupid: that's why
    People who go in the woods
Always get hurt, always will.
                              So far my elegiacs
    Have taught you which coverts to draw, where to spread
265 Your erotic nets. What follows is more subtly artistic –
    How to snare the girl of your choice.
All you gallants, mark and attend now; and you, the common
    People, encourage my task with a thumbs-up!

The first thing to get in your head is that every single
270   Girl can be caught – and that you'll catch her if
You set your toils right. Birds will sooner fall dumb in
        springtime,
    Cicadas in summer, or a hunting-dog
Turn his back on a hare, than a lover's bland inducements
    Can fail with a woman. Even one you suppose
275 Reluctant will want it. Like men, girls love stolen passion,
    But are better at camouflaging their desires:
If masculine custom precluded courtship of women
    You'd find each besotted girl
Taking the lead herself. A heifer amid lush pastures
280   Lows to the bull, a mare
Whinnies at stallions; but our male libido's milder,
    Less rabid: man's sex has bounds
Imposed by convention. Incest is out. Think of wretched
        Byblis –
    Burned up by her brother, expiating her crime
285 With a suicide's noose. Myrrha loved her father (but hardly
    As a daughter should), and now she's straitjacketed
Behind tree-bark, oozing those fragrant tears we use for
    Perfume, named after her: myrrh.

174

Once in the shady valleys of woodland Ida
    There roamed a milk-white bull,   290
Pride of the herd, spotless save for one single
    Black mark between his horns:
The heifers of Crete all yearned to sustain that burden
    On their backs; but Pasiphaë
Proudly rejoiced in her role as bull's mistress, eyed his   295
    Cows with envious hate.
What I say is well-known: not even Crete of the hundred
    Cities, for all her mendacious ways,
Can deny it. With unpractised hands – they say – the lady
    Plucked leaves and lush grass   300
For this bull, went off with the herds, unrestrained by
    concern for
Her husband. A bull won out
Over Minos himself. Why dress richly, Pasiphaë?
    Your lover's blind to your wealth.
Why bother with mirrors when the company you're seeking   305
    Is upland cattle? Why keep fixing your hair,
You silly girl? You're no heifer (on *that* you can trust your
    mirror) –
But oh, how you wish you could sprout horns!
If you love Minos, steer clear of *all* adulterers; if you
    Choose to cuckold your man, then at least   310
Cuckold him with a man!
                 See the queen desert her bower
    For woods and glens, like some god –
Frenzied maenad: ah, the times she eyed a cow in fury,
    Crying, 'What can my lord ever see
In *that*? Just watch the silly creature frisking before him   315
    Down there at pasture – I suppose *she* thinks
She's a raving beauty.' With that, she would have the wretched
    Cow dragged from the herd to be yoked to the plough
Or poleaxed at the altar in a bogus sacrifice, just to
    Let her – a rare pleasure – get her hands   320
On her rival's entrails. The times she slaughtered such heifers
    To appease the gods, and cried, as she held out

Their guts, 'Go see how he likes you *now!*' Now she craves to
    be Io,
    Now Europa: bovine, or bull-borne.
325 Yet the herd-leader, taken in by a wooden cow, contrived to
    Fill her: their offspring betrayed
    Its paternity. Had Aerope restrained her love for Thyestes
    (And to forego even one man
    Is a serious matter), Phoebus would never have turned
    backwards
330   In mid-flight, have driven his steeds
    And chariot Dawnwards. From Nisus his daughter stole that
    purple
    Lock – and now fights down
    The mad dogs that swarm from her groin. Agamemnon lived
    through battles
    On land, and great storms by sea,
335 To become his wife's victim. Who's not wept for flame-racked
    Creüsa, for the children whose bloody death
    Stained Medea's hands? Amyntor's son Phoenix wept tears
    From sightless orbs; fright-maddened horses tore
    Hippolytus limb from limb. Ah Phineus, why blind your
340   Innocent sons? On your own head the same
    Horror will fall. Each one of these crimes was prompted
    By woman's lust – lust that far
    Outstrips ours in keenness and frenzy. Why doubt that you
    can conquer
    Any girl in sight? Few indeed
345 Will turn you down – and (willing or not) a male proposition
    Is something they all enjoy. Draw a blank,
    Rejection brings no danger. But why should you be rejected
    When new thrills delight, when what's not ours
    Has more allure than what is? The harvest's always richer
350   In another man's fields, the herd
    Of our neighbour has fuller udders.

                        But first you must
    get acquainted
    With your quarry's maid – she can help

In the early stages. Make sure she enjoys the full confidence
  Of her mistress: make sure you can trust
Her with your secret liaison. Corrupt her with promises, 355
  Corrupt her with prayers. If
She's willing, you'll get what you want. She'll await the
    propitious
  Time (like a doctor) when her mistress is in
A receptive, seducible mood, when she's bursting out all
    over
  With cheerfulness, like a wheat-crop in rich soil. 360
When hearts are rejoicing, and have no sorrow to constrict
    them,
  They're wide open, Venus can steal
In by persuasive guile. Grim Troy long faced her besiegers,
  But a light-hearted change of mood
Fell for that troop-gravid horse.
                           Another time to try her 365
  Is when she's been miffed by a rival. Make it your job
To ensure she gets her revenge. Prime her maid to egg her on
    while
  Combing her hair each morning, put an oar in
To boost Ma'am's plain sailing, sigh to herself, and murmur:
  'What a pity it is you can't just pay him out 370
With a tit-for-tat,' then talk about *you* in persuasive
  Language, swear you're dying of mad
Passion. But lose no time, don't let the wind subside or
  The sails drop slack. Fury, like brittle ice,
Melts with delay. You may ask, does it pay to seduce the 375
  Maid herself? Such a gambit involves great risk.
Bed makes one girl jealous, takes the edge off another:
    will she
  Want you for her mistress – or for *her*?
It can go either way. Though the situation calls for
  Bold risks, my advice is, *Don't*. I'm not the sort 380
To climb precipitous paths, sharp peaks. With me for leader
  No young man will be caught. But if,
While she carries your letters back and forth, it's not just
  Her zeal but her figure that tickles your fancy, then make

385 Mistress first, maid second. Never *begin* your wooing
     With the lady's companion. And here's one piece of advice
(If you trust in my skill at all, if the greedy winds don't
     Blow my words out to sea):
Lay off – *or make sure of her.* Once she's involved, and guilty,
390   There's no longer any fear
That she'll turn informer against you. What's the use of liming
     A bird's wings if it escapes? A loose-netted boar
That breaks free is no good. Play your fish on the hook she's
     taken,
     Press home your assault, don't give up till victory's won.*
397 But keep such relationships secret: with a secret informer
     You'll always know every move your mistress makes.

It's wrong to suppose that only shipmen and toiling farmers
400   Must observe due season. Grain
Cannot always be trusted to the treacherous furrow, nor
     curving
     Hulls to the green deep; likewise
It's not always safe to pursue young girls: the occasion
     Will often condition success. Thus, avoid
405 Her birthday; and April the First (the feast of Venus
     In conjunction with Mars); and when
The Circus is decorated, not, as before, with gew-gaws
     But with the wealth of kings: never make
Your attempt at such times – then storms are roughest, the
     Pleiads
410   Sinking horizonwards, or the Kid washed down
Under the waves. Best to sit tight: those who venture
     On the high seas now, limp home
With a dismembered vessel. Begin on a day of mourning:

---

* Lines 395–6 do not appear in two of the better MSS, and are omitted as
spurious by some editors. I am in two minds about this verdict, so translate
them here:

Then guilty complicity will keep her from betraying you,
     And you will learn of all your mistress says or does.

The anniversary of Rome's bloody defeat
At the Allia – or perhaps on the Jewish sabbath: many   415
   Shops will be shut then. Regard
Your mistress's birthday with superstitious horror,
   Set a black mark against
Any day when you have to buy presents. Yet avoid it as you
     may, she'll
   Collect all the same. Every woman knows just how   420
To fleece her panting lover. When she's got a spending mood
     on,
   Some loose-garbed pedlar will come and spread out his
     wares
With you sitting by. She'll ask you to look at the stuff, show
     off your
   Expert knowledge. Kisses will follow. Then
She'll insist that you buy it, swear it'll satisfy her   425
   For years, say she needs it now, now's a good
Time to buy it. Tell her you haven't the cash in the house,
     she'll
   Ask for a note-of-hand – just to make
You sorry you learnt how to write. There's the birthday-cake
     gambit,
   A broad hint for presents: she's born x times a year   430
As the occasion demands. Or she'll come up weeping,
     pretend she's
   Lost one of her ear-bobs. Such girls
Are always borrowing things that, once they've had loaned
     them,
   They never return. Your loss in this sort of case
Isn't even offset by gratitude. To list the tricks such
     gold-digging
   Tarts employ, I'd require ten mouths, ten tongues.   435

Let wax pave the way for you, spread out on smooth tablets,
   Let wax go before as witness to your mind –
Bring her your flattering words, words that ape the lover:
   And remember, whoever you are, to throw in some good   440

Entreaties. Entreaties are what made Achilles give back
    Hector's
    Body to Priam; even an angry god
Is moved by the voice of prayer. Make promises, what's the
    harm in
    Promising? Here's where anyone can play rich.
445 Hope, once entertained, is enduring: a deceptive
    Goddess – but useful. Your gift
Once made, you can be abandoned, and with good reason:
    She'll have fleeced you, past tense, at no
Loss to herself. But a present withheld breeds expectations:
450   That's how farmers, so often, are fooled by a barren field,
That's why the inveterate gambler doubles his losses
    To stave off loss, why the dice-box beckons his hand
Back again and again. *This the task, this the labour*, to win her
    Gift-free: she'll continue to give
455 Lest she lose what she's given already. A persuasive letter's
    The thing to lead off with, explore her mind,
Reconnoitre the landscape. A message scratched on an apple
    Betrayed Cydippe: she was snared by her own words.
My advice, then, young men of Rome, is to learn the noble
460   Advocate's arts – not only to let you defend
Some trembling client: a woman, no less than the populace,
    Elite senator, or grave judge,
Will surrender to eloquence. Nevertheless, dissemble
    Your powers, avoid long words,
465 Don't look too highbrow. Who but a mindless ninny
    Declaims to his mistress? An over-lettered style
Repels girls as often as not. Use ordinary language,
    Familiar yet coaxing words – as though
You were there, in her presence. If she refuses your letter,
470   Sends it back unread, persist:
Say you hope she'll read it later. Time breaks stubborn oxen
    To the plough, time teaches a horse
To accept the bridle. An iron ring's worn by constant
    Friction, the furrowed soil
475 Rubs away the curved ploughshare. What is softer than water,

What harder than stone? Yet the soft
Water-drip hollows hard rock. In time, with persistence,
   You'll conquer Penelope. Troy fell late,
But fall it did. Suppose she reads your notes, but won't answer?
   Don't press her, just keep up   480
Your flattering *billets-doux*. The girl who reads letters
   Will reply to them in the end: affairs like these
Go by degrees and stages. First you may get an angry
   Note saying 'Don't pester me, please.'
She's really afraid you'll stop: what she wants (but says she
     doesn't)   485
   Is for you to go on. Press hard, you'll win through in the end.

What else? If she's out, reclining in her litter,
   Make your approach discreet,
And – just to fox the sharp ears of those around you –
   Cleverly riddle each phrase   490
With ambiguous subtleties. If she's taking a leisurely
   Stroll down the colonnade, then you stroll there too –
Vary your pace to hers, march ahead, drop behind her,
   Dawdling and brisk by turns. Be bold,
Dodge in round the columns between you, brush your person 495
   Lingeringly past hers. You must never fail
To attend the theatre when she does, gaze at her beauty –
   From the shoulders up she's time
Most delectably spent, a feast for adoring glances,
   For the eloquence of eyebrows, the speaking sign.   500
Applaud when some male dancer struts on as the heroine,
   Cheer for each lover's role.
When she leaves, leave too – but sit there as long as she does:
   Waste time at your mistress's whim.

Don't torture your hair, though, with curling-irons: don't
     pumice   505
   Your legs into smoothness. Leave *that*
To Mother Cybele's votaries, ululating in chorus
   With their Phrygian modes. Real men

Shouldn't primp their good looks. When Theseus abducted
    Ariadne
510   No pins held up *his* locks;
Hippolytus was no dandy, yet Phaedra loved him; Adonis,
    That creature of woodland, allured
A goddess. Keep pleasantly clean, take exercise, work up an
    outdoor
    Tan; make quite sure that your toga fits
515 And doesn't show spots; don't lace your shoes too tightly
    Or ignore any rusty buckles, or slop
Around in too large a fitting. Don't let some incompetent
    barber
    Ruin your looks: both hair and beard demand
Expert attention. Keep your nails pared, and dirt-free;
520   Don't let those long hairs sprout
In your nostrils, make sure your breath is never offensive,
    Avoid the rank male stench
That wrinkles noses. Beyond this is for wanton women –
    Or any half-man who wants to attract men.

525 Lo! Bacchus calls to his poet: Bacchus too helps lovers,
    Fosters that flame with which he burns himself –
As Ariadne discovered, ranging the unfamiliar
    Sea-strand of Naxos, crazed
Out of her mind, fresh-roused from sleep, in an ungirt
530   Robe, blonde hair streaming loose, barefoot,
Calling 'Ah cruel Theseus!' to the deaf waves, tears coursing
    Down her innocent-tender cheeks.
She wept, she besought, yet contrived to remain appealing
    Despite all: not even those tears
535 Could imperil such beauty. Hands beating her soft bosom,
    'He's gone,' she cried, 'he's betrayed me: what, ah what
Will become of me now?' Then, presto, the whole shore echoed
    With frenzied drumming, the clash
Of cymbals. She broke off, speechless, fainted
540   In terror, the blood fled
From her pale inert limbs, as wild-tressed Bacchanals, wanton

Satyrs, the god's forerunners, appeared,
With drunken old Silenus, scarce fit to ride his swaybacked
   Ass, hands clutching its mane
As he chased the Maenads – the Maenads would flee and rally – 545
   A dizzy rider, whipping his steed ahead
Till he pitched off the long-eared ass on his head, and the
     satyrs
   All shouted: 'Up with you, Dad!
Come on up there!' And then came the god, his chariot
     grape-clustered,
   Paired tigers padding on as he shook 550
The golden reins. Poor girl: lost voice, lost colour – lost
     Theseus.
   Thrice she tried to run, thrice stood frozen with fear,
Shivering, like the thin breeze-rustled cornstalk,
   Or osiers in a marsh. 'I am here
For you,' the god told her. '*My* love will prove more faithful. 555
   No need for fear. You shall be
Wife to Bacchus, take the sky as your dowry, be seen there
   As a star, the Cretan Crown, a familiar guide
To wandering vessels.' Down he sprang from his chariot,
     lest the
   Girl take fright at the tigers; set his foot 560
On the shore, then gathered her up in his arms – no
     resistance –
   And bore her away. No trouble for gods to do
Whatever they please. Loud cheers, a riotous wedding:
     Bacchus
   And his bride were soon bedded down.
So when the blessings of Bacchus are set out before you 565
   At dinner, with a lady to share your couch,
Then pray the Lord of Darkness and Nocturnal Orgies
   To stop the wine going to your head!
Here double-talk is the vogue: lace your conversation
   With ambiguous phrases designed to make the girl 570
Feel they're specially meant for her. Write flatteries on the
     table

In wine, let her read herself your heart's
   Mistress: gaze deep in her eyes with open passion –
   One silent glance can speak
575 Whole volumes. Make sure you're the first to snatch the cup that
   Her lips have touched: drink from where she has drunk;
And if there's some piece of food she's fingered, take it,
   Brushing her hand as you reach out.
Let it be your concern, too, to please your lady's escort –
580 He'll be more use to you as a friend.
When you're dicing to settle the drinking-order, let him take
    your
   Place, give him the garland off your head,
Never mind if he's placed below you or with you, still let him
   Be served first every time, defer to his words.*
I'll give you specific advice, now, on just what limits
590 You should set to your drinking. Keep mind and feet
Steady. Above all, avoid drunken quarrels, don't get
   Into a fight too fast.
His stupid swilling killed off Eurytion the Centaur;
   Wine over dinner was rather meant to promote
Fun and games. So if you've a voice, then sing; or if your
595   movements
   Are graceful, dance. Please with whatever gifts
You possess to give pleasure. And though real drunkenness
    can harm you,
   To feign it may prove useful. Let your devious tongue
Stutter and slur: then, however licentious your words or
600 Actions, they'll be blamed on the wine. 'A health
To the lady,' you'll cry, 'a health to the man she sleeps with!'
   – While silently wishing her present partner in hell.
But when the tables are cleared, and the guests departing,

---

* Lines 585–8 are a spurious (and moralizing) insertion by some post-Ovidian hand:

   It's a safe, well-trodden path to deceive in friendship's name: safe
   And well-trodden perhaps, but still
The path of guilt. That way a collector collects more
   Than is due him, looks to care for more than his charge.

And in the confusion you perceive your chance
To make contact, then join the crowd, discreetly approach her   605
   On the way out, let your fingers brush against
Her side, touch her foot with yours. Now's the time for
      chatting
   Her up, no clodhopping bashfulness – the bold
Are favoured by Chance and Venus. Don't think that your
      eloquence
   Must conform to poetic canons. Just pitch in   610
And you'll find yourself fluent enough. You must play the
      lover,
   Ape heartache with words, use every subtle device
To compel her belief. It's not hard – what woman doesn't
      believe she's
   A natural object for love, or, however plain,
Isn't thrilled by her own appearance? Besides, very often   615
   That passion a gallant feigns in his opening round
Will become the real thing. (So, girls, show more kindness to
      pretenders:
   True love may spring tomorrow from today's
False declaration.) Press on, undermine them with devious
   Flatteries: so a stream will eat away   620
Its overhanging bank. Never weary of praising
   Her face, her hair, her slim fingers, her tiny feet.
Even the chaste like having their good looks published,
   Even virgins are taken up with their own
Cute figures. Why does it still bother Juno and Pallas   625
   That they didn't win first prize in the Phrygian woods?
When it's praised, then Juno's peacock displays its plumage;
   If you stare without comment – no show.
Even racehorses, back in the paddock, respond with pleasure
   To a combed mane, a pat on the neck.   630

Don't be shy about promising: it's promises girls are undone
      by;
   Invoke any gods you please
To endorse your performance. Jupiter smiles from heaven

On foresworn lovers, lets all their perjuries blow
Away unrequited. (*He* used to swear falsely, by Styx, to
635   Juno –
So looks now with favour on others who do the same.)
The existence of gods is expedient: let us therefore assume it,
    With gifts of incense and wine on their antique hearths –
No carefree repose, like a drowsy siesta, keeps them
640   Remote after all. So, lead an innocent life:
Divinity's nigh. Honour bonds, don't embezzle deposits,
    Avoid murder and fraud. If you're wise
Gull only girls, they're no danger. In this one deception
    It's good faith that ought to make you blush.
They're cheats, so cheat *them*: most are dumb and
645   unscrupulous: let them
Fall into the traps they've set themselves.
Egypt had drought for nine years once, no rain to quicken
    Her harvest-fields. Then Thrasius the sage
Told King Busiris the gods could be propitiated
650   With a stranger's spilt blood.
Busiris replied: '*You* shall be the gods' first victim, you the
    Stranger who brings water to Egypt's soil.'
So Perillus, the inventor of Phalaris' brazen bull, was
    The first, unlucky man, to roast in his own
665   Cruel contrivance. Both kings did right. No fairer statute
    Than that which condemns the artificer of death
To perish by his art. So let perjuries gull the perjured,
    Let Woman smart from the wounds she first dealt out!

Tears, too, will help: with tears you'll shift adamant.
    Flaunt wet
660   Cheeks – if you can – for *her* to see:
But if tears won't come (and they sometimes fail in a crisis)
    Just wipe a moist hand across your eyes!
What sensible man will not intersperse his coaxing
    With kisses? Even if she doesn't kiss back,
665   Still force on regardless! She may struggle, cry 'Naughty!',

Yet she wants to be overcome. Just take care
Not to bruise her tender lips with such hard-snatched kisses,
    Don't give her a chance to protest
You're too rough. Those who grab their kisses, but not what
    follows,
    Deserve to lose all they've gained. How short were you   670
Of the ultimate goal after all your kissing? That was
    Gaucheness, not modesty, I'm afraid . . .

It's all right to use force – force of *that* sort goes down well
    with
    The girls: what in fact they love to yield
They'd often rather have stolen. Rough seduction   675
    Delights them, the audacity of near-rape
Is a compliment – so the girl who *could* have been forced, yet
    somehow
    Got away unscathed, may feign delight, but in fact
Feels sadly let down. Hilaira and Phoebe, both ravished,
    Both fell for their ravishers. Then there's another tale,   680
Well-known, but well worth retelling, which recounts how
    Achilles
    Made a girl on Scyros his:
It was after the goddess had won that beauty-competition
    Against her peers on Ida, and had given her own
Reward to Paris; after Priam had welcomed his foreign   685
    Daughter-in-law, and a Greek wife came to dwell
Within Troy's walls. All swore allegiance to the injured
    Husband. So one man's hurt became
A national cause. But Achilles – to his shame, were the act not
    prompted
    By a mother's prayers – concealed his manhood beneath   690
A girl's long robe. What's this? Wool-spinning's not your
    business,
    Achilles: it's quite another of Pallas' arts
Through which you'll find fame. What have you to do with
    baskets?

Your arm should support a shield. Why does the hand
That will one day slay Hector carry a skein? Cast aside your
695   spindle
With its laborious threading: the Pelian spear
Is what *you* should wield.
                       The king's daughter, Deidamia,
Who shared his room soon proved
That manhood through rape. Her seduction must have been
     forceful,
700   But to *be* forced was what she desired.
'Don't go,' she cried, when Achilles was hastening from her,
Distaff forgotten, a warrior under arms.
Where's that violence now? Why coax the perpetrator
Of your rape to remain, Deidamia? If you take
The initiative, it's true, you may feel some embarrassment:
705   better
To let *him* – and more fun when you submit.
Any lover who waits for his girl to make the running
Has too much faith in his own
Irresistible charms. The first approaches, the pleading,
710   Are the man's concern: *her* place
Is to hear his smooth line with kindness. To win her, ask her:
She's dying to be asked. Just provide a good excuse
For her to fulfil your wishes. Jupiter wooed those antique
Heroines as a suppliant. No girl seduced
715 The Almighty. But if you find that your pleading induces
Puffed-up disdain, then ease off,
Take a step back. Many women adore the elusive,
Hate over-eagerness. So, play hard to get,
Stop boredom developing. And don't let your entreaties
720   Sound too confident of possession. Insinuate sex
Camouflaged as friendship. I've seen ultra-stubborn creatures
Fooled by this gambit, the switch from companion to stud.

For sailors a pale complexion is inappropriate,
They should be tanned and dark,
725 Fetchingly weatherbeaten; so should husbandmen

Who spend their time out of doors
With plough and harrow; so should the champion athlete —
    If *they're* white, it looks all wrong.
But let every lover be pale: here's the proper complexion
    For lovers; this gambit, please note,   730
Has worked on every occasion. Pale was Orion, roaming
    The woodlands, pining for Side; pale
Daphnis (ah, unkind Naiad!). Look lean and haggard
    As proof of your passion, don't baulk
At hooding your lustrous curls. Sleepless nights, the pangs
        and worry   735
    Of consuming love — these will reduce young men
To a thin nothing. If you mean to achieve your purpose
    Be an object of pity, so that the passers-by
Will say at once, 'He's in love'.

                            Now should I complain,
        or warn you,
    That no one now distinguishes right from wrong?   740
Friendship and honour are empty words, it's not safe to praise
        your
    Girl to a friend — if he believes what you say
He'll be in there himself. You may ask, 'Did Patroclus
        cuckold
    Achilles? Wasn't Phaedra perfectly chaste
With Pirithoüs? Didn't Pylades love Hermione as Apollo   745
    Loved Pallas, or Castor his twin?'
If anyone nurses *that* hope, he'll believe that apples grow on
    Tamarisks, that honey's to be found in midstream.
The base alone gives pleasure; men seek only their own
        enjoyment,
    And find that sweet when it springs from another's pain.   750
How outrageous, when it's not their enemies that lovers
    Most need to fear! Nowadays you'll be safe enough
If you shun those you trust. Cousins, brothers, loyal
        comrades —
    Here's where your real trouble lies.

755 One word more before I stop. The characters of women
    All differ. To capture a thousand hearts demands
A thousand devices. Some soils are better for olives,
    Some for vines, or for wheat: you can't
Raise them all in one field. Hearts have as many changing
760   Moods as the face has expressions. A wise man
Will adapt to countless fashions, will resolve himself,
      like Proteus,
    Into water, now lion, now tree,
Now bristling boar. Some fish are trawled, some netted,
    Some caught with line and hook:
765 And don't try the same technique on every age-group,
    An old doe will spot the trap
From much further off. If a simpleton finds you too highbrow
    Or a prude over-coarse, they'll feel
Self-distrust and dismay. That's how the girl who shies off
    decent
770 Lovers will cheapen herself by giving in
To some low cad.
               This concludes the first part of my venture –
Now throw out the anchor, let my craft ride secure!

BOOK 2

Cry hurrah, and hurrah again, for a splendid triumph –
   The quarry I sought has fallen into my toils.
Each happy lover now rates my verses higher
   Than Homer's or Hesiod's, awards them the palm
Of victory. He's as cheerful as Paris was, sailing away from   5
   Warlike Sparta, the guest who stole a bride,
Or Pelops, the stranger, the winner of Hippodameia
   After that chariot-race.
Why hurry, young man? Your ship's still in mid-passage,
   And the harbour I seek is far away.   10
Through my verses, it's true, you may have *acquired* a
     mistress,
   But that's not enough. If my art
Caught her, my art must keep her. To guard a conquest's
   As tricky as making it. There was luck in the chase,
But *this* task will call for skill. If ever I needed support from   15
   Venus and Son, and Erato – the Muse
Erotic by name – it's now, for my too-ambitious project
   To relate some techniques that might restrain
That fickle young globetrotter, Love. He's winged and flighty,
   Hard to pin down. Just so   20
Minos might block every line of escape, yet his guest still
     found a
   Daring way out – by air.
When Daedalus had built his labyrinth to imprison
   The bull-man, man-bull, conceived through a queen's guilt,
He said: 'Most just Minos, put a term, now, to my exile,   25
   Let my native soil receive
My ashes. Since unkind fate would not let me live there,
   Grant me at least to die
In my own country. Release / the boy, if you hold his father's
   Services cheap; spare me if you will not spare   30
My son.' So much he said – but might have gone on pleading
   For ever in vain: the king

Would not grant his request. When Daedalus perceived this,
   Now, now is the time, he told himself, *to deploy*
35 *All your skill and craft. Minos rules earth, rules ocean:*
   No escape by sea or land. All that remains
   Is the sky. So, through the sky we'll seek our passage –
   God in high heaven, forgive
   Such a project! I do not aspire to touch your starry dwellings:
40   *This is the only way I have to escape*
   My master. Were there a way by Styx, through Stygian waters
   We'd swim to freedom. I must devise new laws
   For human nature. Necessity often mothers invention.
   Who would have believed man could ever fly?
45 But Daedalus fashioned birds' oarage, trimmed it with
     feathers
   Bonded the flimsy fabric with linen thread,
   Melted wax to glue wings in place. Very soon his novel
   Craftsman's task was achieved:
50 Excitedly the boy studied wings and wax, not guessing
   The gear had been made for his own
   Shoulders and arms, till his father said: 'These are the craft
     which
   Must bear us home, with their aid
   We must escape from Minos. Though he's blocked all other
55   Routes to us, he cannot master the air – as you
   Can do, through my device. But take care, don't go stargazing
   At belted Orion or the Bear:
   Take these pinions, fly behind me: I'll go ahead, you
   Follow my lead. That way
   You'll be safe. If we fly too close to the sun, through the
60   upper
   Air, then the wax will be softened by the heat;
   If we stoop too low seaward, then our thrashing pinions
   Will grow waterlogged from the spray.
   So, my son, set a middle course – and watch out for turbulent
   Air-currents: spread your wings
65 To the steady breeze, go with it.' While he talked, he was
     fitting
   The boy's gear, showing him how to move

Like a mother bird with her fledglings. Then he fixed his own
    harness
To his shoulders, nervously poised himself for this strange
New journey; paused on the brink of take-off, embraced his
    Son, couldn't fight back his tears.   70
They'd found a hilltop – above the plain, but no mountain –
    And from this they took off
On their hapless flight. Daedalus flexed his wings, glanced
    back at
His son's, held a steady course. The new
Element bred delight. Fear forgotten, Icarus flew more   75
    Boldly, with daring skill. The pair
Were glimpsed by an angler, line bobbing, who at the sight of
    them
Dropped his rod in surprise. They left
Naxos and Paros behind them, skirted Delos, beloved of
    Apollo, flew on east: to the north   80
Lay Samos, southward Lebynthos, Calýmne with its shady
    Forests, and Astypálaea, set amid fish-rich shoals.
Then the boy, made over-reckless by youthful daring,
    abandoned
His father, soared aloft
Too close to the sun: the wax melted, the ligatures   85
    Flew apart, his flailing arms had no hold
On the thin air. From dizzy heaven he gazed down seaward
    In terror. Fright made the scene go black
Before his eyes. No wax, wings gone, a thrash of naked
    Arms, a shuddering plunge   90
Down through the void, a scream – 'Father, father, I'm
    falling –'
Cut off as he hit the waves.
His unhappy father, a father no longer, cried: 'Icarus!
    Icarus, where are you? In what part of the sky
Do you fly now?' – then saw wings littering the water.   95
    Earth holds his bones; the Icarian Sea, his name.
So Minos failed to clip the wings of a mortal – yet here am
    I now, planning to pin down the winged god.

*

Delusions abound. Don't mess with Thessalian witchcraft –
100   That love-charm torn from the brow
Of a foal is no good. Not all Medea's herbs, not every
     Spell and magical cantrip will suffice
To keep love alive – else Circe had held Ulysses,
     And Medea her Jason, by their arts alone.
Giving girls aphrodisiac drugs, too, is useless – and
105   dangerous:
     Drugs can affect the brain, induce madness. Avoid
All such nasty tricks. To be loved you must show yourself
     lovable –
     Something good looks alone
Can never achieve. You may/be handsome as Homer's Nireus,
110   Or young Hylas, snatched by those bad
Naiads; but all the same, to avoid a surprise desertion
     And keep your girl, it's best you have gifts of mind
In addition to physical charms. Beauty's fragile, the passing
     Years diminish its substance, eat it away.
115 Violets and bell-mouthed lilies do not bloom for ever,
     Hard thorns are all that's left of the blown rose.
So with you, my handsome youth: soon wrinkles will furrow
     Your body; soon, too soon, your hair turn grey.
Then build an enduring mind, add that to your beauty:
120   It alone will last till the flames
Consume you. Keep your wits sharp, explore the liberal
     Arts, win a mastery over Greek
As well as Latin. Ulysses was eloquent, not handsome –
     Yet he filled sea-goddesses' hearts
125 With aching passion. How often Calypso lamented
     His haste to be off, swore the sea
Was too rough for rowing! Again and again she'd beg him
     To recount Troy's fate, made him find fresh words
For the same old tale. They'd pace the shore; pretty Calypso
130   Would say: 'Now tell me how King Rhesus met
His bloody end.' Then Ulysses would take the stick he was
     holding
     And sketch in the wet sand whatever scene

She'd demanded. 'Here's Troy,' he'd say, making walls of
  shingle,
  'And here's the river. Let's call this bit my camp.
This was the plain –' he levelled it – 'where we butchered
  Dolon,   135
  The spy-by-night, as he dreamed
Of Achilles' horses. There stood the tents of Rhesus;
  I rode back home that night
On the King's captured steeds –' As he spoke, a sudden
  breaker
  Washed away Rhesus, his camp, and Troy itself.   140
Then the goddess exclaimed: 'You'd trust *these* waves for your
  voyage?
  Look at the great names they've destroyed!'
So don't rely too much on looks, they can prove deceptive
  Whoever you are: have something more than physique!

Nothing works on a mood like tactful tolerance: harshness   145
  Provokes hatred, makes nasty rows.
We detest the hawk and the wolf, those natural hunters,
  Always preying on timid flocks;
But the gentle swallow goes safe from man's snares,
  we fashion
  Little turreted houses for doves.   150
Keep clear of all quarrels, sharp-tongued recriminations –
  Love's sensitive, needs to be fed
With gentle words. Leave nagging to wives and husbands,
  Let *them*, if they want, think it a natural law,
A permanent state of feud. Wives thrive on wrangling,   155
  That's their dowry. A mistress should always hear
What she wants to be told. You don't share one bed by legal
  Fiat, with you love substitutes for law.
Use tender blandishments, language that caresses
  The ear, make her glad you came.   160
I'm not here as preceptor of loving to the wealthy; a suitor
  With gifts doesn't need my skills –
Anyone attractive who says 'Here's something for you,'

Has genius of his own. To such a one
165 I give place: he's got my tricks beat. I'm the poor man's poet,
     Was poor myself as a lover, couldn't afford
Gifts, so spun words. Poor suitors must woo with caution,
     Watch their tongues, bear much that the rich
Would never put up with. I recall how once in anger
170   I pulled my girl's hair. The days I lost through that
Little outburst! I don't think I tore her dress, I wasn't
     conscious
     Of doing so – but *she* said I did, and the bill
Was paid for at my expense. Avoid (if you're wise) your
     teacher's
     Errors, shun what may cost you dear.
175 Fight Parthians, but keep peace with a civilized mistress,
     Have fun together, do all that induces love.

If the girl's curt and unreceptive to your wooing,
     Persist, be obdurate: the time will come
When she's more welcoming. Go with the bough, you'll
     bend it;
180   Use brute force, it'll snap.
Go with the current: that's how to swim across rivers –
     Fighting upstream's no good.
Go easy with lions or tigers if you aim to tame them;
     The bull gets inured to the plough by slow degrees.
185 Was there ever a girl more prickly than Atalanta?
     Yet tough as she was, she went down
Before a man's prowess. Milanion, roaming the forest,
     Kept bewailing his lot, and the girl's
Unkindness. She made him hump hunting-nets on his back,
     he
190   Was for ever spearing wild boars;
His wounded flesh learnt the strength of Hylaeus the
     Centaur's
     Taut bow – yet his keener pangs
Came from another bow, Cupid's. I'm not suggesting

You have to go lugging nets up mountain glens
Or play the hunter, or bare your breast to flying arrows –   195
  A cautious lover will find the rules of my art
Undemanding enough. So, yield if she shows resistance:
  That way you'll win in the end. Just be sure to play
The part she allots you. Censure the things she censures,
  Endorse her endorsements, echo her every word,   200
Pro or con, and laugh whenever she laughs; remember,
  If she weeps, to weep too: take your cue
From her every expression. Suppose she's playing a
    board-game,
  Then throw the dice carelessly, move
Your pieces all wrong. At knucklebones, when you beat her,   205
  Exact no forfeit, roll low throws yourself
As often as you can manage. If you're playing halma,
    permit her
  Glass piece to take yours. Open up
Her parasol, hold it over her when she's out walking,
  Clear her a path through the crowd.   210
When she's on her chaise-longue, make haste to find a
    footstool
  For those dainty feet of hers, help her on and off
With her slippers. At times she'll feel cold: then (though
    you're shivering
  Yourself) warm her tiny hand
In your bosom. Don't jib at a slavish task like holding   215
  Her mirror: slavish or not, such attentions please.
When his stepmother Hera tired of sending him monsters
  To vanquish, then the hero who won a place
In the sky he'd formerly shouldered took to the distaff
  And basket, spun wool among Ionian girls.   220
If Hercules, then, obeyed *his* mistress's orders, will you
  Flinch from enduring what he endured?
She says you've a date in town? Be sure you always get there
  Ahead of time; don't give her up
Till it's *really* late. If she asks you to meet her somewhere,   225

197

Put everything off, elbow your way through the crowd
At the double. When she comes home, late at night, from a
    party,
    You still must attend, like her slave,
If she summons you. It's the same when she's in the country:
230   Love detests laggards. You've no transport? Walk.
Don't be put off by bad weather, or a heatwave,
    Or snowdrifts blocking your road.

Love is a species of warfare. Slack troopers, go elsewhere!
    It takes more than cowards to guard
These standards. Night-duty in winter, long route-marches,
235   every
    Hardship, all forms of suffering: these await
The recruit who expects a soft option. You'll often be out in
    Cloudbursts, and bivouack on the bare
Ground. We know how Apollo pastured Admetus' cattle,
240   Dossed down in a herdsman's hut. What mere
Mortal's too good for conditions a god accepted? Is lasting
    Love your ambition? Then put away all pride.
The simple, straightforward way in may be denied you,
    Doors bolted, shut in your face –
245 So be ready to slip down from the roof through a lightwell,
    Or sneak in by an upper-floor window. She'll be glad
To know you're risking your neck, and for her sake: that will
    offer
    Any mistress sure proof of your love.
Leander might, often enough, have endured Hero's absence –
250   But swam over to show her how he felt.
Don't think it beneath you to cultivate madam's houseboys
    And her more important maids:
Greet each one by name (the gesture costs you nothing),
    Clasp their coarse hands in yours – all part of the game.

255 On Good Luck Day, if you're asked for a present, even
    By a slave, then give: the expense
Will be minimal. See that the maids, too, get a handout
    On *their* day (the day those Gauls

Were figged by some dressed-up slaveys). It pays, believe me,
   To keep in with the servants – especially those who watch   260
Her front-door or bedroom entrance.
                                  Don't give your mistress
   costly
Presents: let them be small, but chosen with skill
And discretion. At harvest-time, when fields are full, boughs
   heavy,
   Send round a basket of fruit –
Say it came from your country estate (though you really
   bought it   265
   At some smart city shop). Give her grapes,
Or the chestnuts to which Amaryllis was so devoted –
   No, not chestnuts, she's off them these days:
Much too cheap. Why not try a poulterer's hoop of thrushes
   By way of remembrance? (It's shameful to use such gifts   270
In the hope of a death, to bribe the elderly or barren:
   I've no time for those who give presents a bad name.)
Would you be well advised to send her love-poems?
   Poetry, I fear, is held in small esteem.
Girls praise a poem, but go for expensive presents: 275
   Any illiterate oaf can catch their eye
Provided he's rich. Today is truly the Golden
   Age: gold buys honours, gold
Procures love. If Homer dropped by – with all the Muses,
   But empty-handed – he'd be shown the door.   280
There *are* a few cultured girls (not many, it's true), and
   others
   Who'd like to be cultured, but aren't;
Flatter any of these with poems: a bravura declamation
   Even of trash – this will suffice to win
Their approval. Clever or stupid, they'll take a poem
   fashioned   285
   In the small hours, for *them*, as a cute little gift.

Make your mistress ask as a favour for what you intended,
   All along, to do yourself
In the way of self-interest. You've promised manumission

290   To one slave? See that he begs it, first, from her.
     You plan to spare another his flogging, or the chain-gang?
       Then put her in your debt for a 'change of heart'
     That never existed. The benefit's yours, give her the credit,
       Waste not want not, while she
     Plays the Lady Bountiful. You're anxious to keep your
295   mistress?
       Convince her she's knocked you all of a heap
     With her stunning looks. If it's purple she's wearing, praise
       purple;
       When she's in a silk dress, say silk
     Suits her best of all; if her mantle's gold-embroidered
300   Say she's dearer than gold to you; if tweeds
     Take her fancy, back tweeds. She's in her slip? She inflames
       you
       (Tell her) with passion – but ask, at the same time,
     Very shyly, 'Aren't you cold?' Compliment the way she's
       parted
       Or curled her hair. Admire
305 Her singing voice, her gestures as she dances,
       Cry 'Encore!' when she stops. You can even praise
     Her performance in bed, her talent for love-making –
       Spell out what turned you on.
     Though she may show fiercer in action than any Medusa,
310   Her lover will always describe her as kind
     And gentle. But take care not to give yourself away while
       Making such tongue-in-cheek compliments, don't allow
     Your expression to ruin the message. Art's most effective
       When concealed. Detection discredits you for good.

315 Often in early autumn, when the year's at its sweetest,
       When grapes glow purple and full,
     One day we'll be chilled to the bone, the next get
       heat-exhaustion,
       Our bodies made listless by the changing air.
     Let's hope your girl keeps well – but if this unhealthy
320   Season turns her sickly, sends her to bed,

Then let her see, beyond doubt, how she's loved and
    cherished,
    Then sow your seed: you'll reap a bumper crop
When the time is ripe. Bear with her fretful sickness,
    Attend in person to all she'll let you do;
Let her see you weeping, comfort her with kisses   325
    Day in, day out; let her parched
Lips drink your tears. Invent cheerful dreams to tell her,
    Make vows galore – and all of them aloud.
Bring round some old crone to purify bed and bedroom,
    Eggs and sulphur clutched in her tremulous hands.   330
All this will be proof of your willing care: such tactics
    Have often led to a legacy. But don't
Let your services risk incurring the invalid's displeasure –
    Sedulous zeal should know its proper bounds.
Never restrict her diet, never make her drink unpleasant   335
    Medicines: leave your rival to deal with such things.

Remember, the wind you spread your sails to when leaving
    Harbour should not be used out on the high
Seas: let your young love, fancy free, gather strength through
    Experience. Nourish it well, in time   340
It will grow steadfast. The bull you now fear began as
    The calf you stroked; the tree
Beneath which you recline was once a sapling. A river's
    Small beginnings swell with progression, embrace
Many confluent waters. Get her accustomed to you: 345
    Habit's the key, spare no pains till that's achieved.
Let her always see you around, always hear you talking,
    Show her your face night and day.
When you're confident you'll be missed, when your absence
    Seems sure to cause her regret,   350
Then give her some respite: a field improves when fallow,
    Parched soil soaks up the rain.
Demophoön's presence gave Phyllis no more than mild
    excitement;
    It was his sailing caused arson in her heart.

355 Penelope was racked by crafty Ulysses' absence,
    Protesilaus, abroad, made Laodameia burn.
Short partings do best, though: time wears out affections,
    The absent love fades, a new one takes its place.
With Menelaus away, Helen's disinclination for sleeping
360   Alone led her into her guest's
Warm bed at night. Were you crazy, Menelaus?
    Why go off leaving your wife
With a stranger in the house? Do you trust doves to falcons,
    Full sheepfolds to mountain wolves?
365 Here Helen's not at fault, the adulterer's blameless –
    He did no more than you, or any man else,
Would do yourself. By providing place and occasion
    You precipitated the act. What else did she do
But act on your clear advice? Husband gone; this stylish
      stranger
370   Here on the spot; too scared to sleep alone –
Oh, Helen wins my acquittal, the blame's her husband's:
    All *she* did was take advantage of a man's
Human complaisance. And yet, more savage than the tawny
    Boar in his rage, as he tosses the maddened dogs
375 On lightning tusks, or a lioness suckling her unweaned
    Cubs, or the tiny adder crushed
By some careless foot, is a woman's wrath, when some rival
    Is caught in the bed *she* shares. Her feelings show
On her face. Decorum's flung to the wind, a maenadic
380   Frenzy grips her, she rushes headlong off
After fire and steel. Deserted, barbarian Medea
    Avenged her marital wrongs
On Jason by killing their children – like Procne the swallow,
    Another ruthless mother, breast stained red
385 With blood. Such acts destroy the most strongly bonded
    Passions: all prudent men should avoid
Set-tos of this sort. Such a ruling, though, won't condemn you
    (God forbid!) to one girl alone. No bride can expect
That degree of devotion. Have fun, but play it discreetly –
390   Don't broadcast your intrigues
As a boost for your ego. Don't make regular assignations,

Don't give X presents that Y might recognize.
Don't always meet in the same place: the lady may catch you
    If you haunt the milieux that she knows –
And whenever you write, make sure all previous letters   395
    Have been erased from your tablets: many girls read
More than was ever sent them. Venus, when affronted,
    Hits back, inflicts on you
All that she suffered. So long as Agamemnon was faithful,
    Clytemnestra stayed chaste. It was her husband's crimes   400
Turned her to the bad. She'd heard how Chryses, sacerdotal
    Fillet on head and laurel in hand, had failed
To win back his daughter. She'd heard the sad tale of abducted
    Briseis, knew how shameful delay
Had prolonged the war. Yet all this was mere hearsay: Priam's daughter   405
    Cassandra she'd *seen*, the conqueror shamefully caught
By his own captive. It was then she welcomed Thyestes' son to
    Her heart and bed, avenged her husband's ill deed.

Should your carefully camouflaged actions be brought not notwithstanding
    To light, then deny them still, through thick and thin;   410
Don't be over-subservient, don't flatter her more than usual –
    Such traits are clear proof of guilt.
Go to it in bed: that's the one way you'll get round her,
    With cocksmanship so fine it *has* to disprove
Any earlier peccadillo. Some advise taking aphrodisiac   415
    Herbal concoctions – they're poison, believe you me.
Some crush up pepper with nettleseed, an urticant mixture,
    Or blend yellow camomile in vintage wine;
But the goddess worshipped high on Eryx's leafy mountain
    Won't let her joys be forced this way –   420
Try white Megarian onions, and salacious colewort
    Picked from your kitchen-garden; eat eggs;
Enrich your diet with Hymettus honey, with the needled
    Pine-tree's delectable nuts.

*

Why digress on such hocus-pocus, Muse? I must guide my
425   chariot
      Straight down the innermost lane,
Grazing the rail. Just now, at my urging, you were ready
      To keep your affairs a secret. Now change tack
– At my urging – and publish them. Don't chide me for fickle
430   Impulses: no ship is always blown
By the same prevailing wind. We veer to every quarter
      As the breeze fills our sails. Watch how
A charioteer will handle his horses, first letting them gallop,
      Then skilfully reining them in.
435 Some women just don't react well to timid complaisance:
      If there's no competition in sight
Their love wanes. Success will often breed presumption,
      It's hard to keep your head
Through a run of good luck. You've seen the fire that
      smoulders
440   Down to nothing, grows a crown of pale ash
Over its hidden embers (yet a sprinkling of sulphur
      Will suffice to rekindle the flame)?
So with the heart. It grows torpid from lack of worry,
      Needs a sharp stimulus to elicit love.
445 Get her anxious about you, reheat her tepid passions,
      Tell her your guilty secrets, watch her blanch.
Thrice fortunate that man, lucky past calculation,
      Who can make some poor injured girl
Torture herself over him, lose voice, go pale, pass out when
450   The unwelcome news reaches her. Ah, may I
Be the one whose hair she tears out in her fury, the one whose
      Soft cheeks she rips with her nails,
Whom she sees, eyes glaring, through a rain of tears; without
      whom,
      Try as she will, she cannot live!
How long (you may ask) should you leave her lamenting her
455   wrong? A little
      While only, lest rage gather strength
Through procrastination. By then you should have her sobbing

All over your chest, your arms tight round her neck.
You want peace? Give her kisses, make love to the girl while
    she's crying –
That's the only way to melt her angry mood.   460

When she's been raging at you, when she seems utterly hostile,
    Then is the time to try
An alliance in bed. She'll come through. Bed's where
    harmony dwells when
The fighting's done: that's the place
Where loving-kindness was born. The doves that lately fought
    now   465
    Call softly, bill and coo.
The world at first was mere mass, confused and patternless,
    one great
    Mingled vista: stars, earth, sea. But soon
Heaven was set above earth, land ringed with water,
    And the void withdrew to its own place.   470
Birds made their home in the air, beasts in the forest:
    Deep underwater, fish lurked.
Mankind was nomadic then, went wandering through an
    empty
    Landscape, mere muscular brutes
Whose home was the woodland, who ate / gràss, used leaves
    for bedding,   475
    Went solitary, long avoided their own kind.
What softened those fierce hearts? Voluptuous pleasure
    When a man and a woman stopped
In the same place. They found what to do by themselves. No
    teacher
    Was needed. Venus saw the sweet game through   480
Without subtle trimmings. The bird has his mate, the fish will
    Find a partner out in the deep,
Hind follows stag, serpent tangles with serpent,
    Dog mounts random dog, the ewe
Thrills to be covered, bulls rouse their heifers, the snub-nosed   485
    She-goat's back sustains

Her rank male partner. Mares are driven to frenzy,
    Cross rivers in hot pursuit
Of their stallions. So get moving with this potent medicine
490   When your lady's angry: nothing else will relieve
Her fierce distress, this dose surpasses even Machaon's
    Drugs: if you've been unfaithful, this will make your peace.

As I was reciting these lines, Apollo abruptly
    Materialized beside me, thrumming a chord
495 On his gilded lyre, bay in hand, bay wreathed about his sacred
    Hair (to poets he will sometimes appear
In visible form). 'Preceptor,' he told me, 'of wanton
    Love, come, lead your disciples to my shrine,
Show them the world-famous sign, that brief commandment:
500   *Know yourself*. Only with true
Self-knowledge will a man love wisely, pursue the matter
    By exploiting the gifts he's got.
If nature's made him handsome, let him flash his best profile;
    If smooth-skinned, he should recline
505 Bare-shouldered. The brilliant talker can fill in those awkward
    Silences; the good singer should sing,
The good drinker – drink. But brilliant declamations
    And highflown poetic recitals are out of place
In common-or-garden discourse.' Such was Apollo's counsel,
510   Counsel to be obeyed: this god speaks truth.
Back to my theme, then. Any intelligent lover
    Will win in the end: my techniques
Are sure to bring him fulfilment. Not every sown furrow
    Repays its investment with interest, not every wind
515 Blows your wandering ship on course. Lovers get less pleasure
    Than pain: let them steel their hearts
To endless hardship. As thick as Sicily's swarming
    Bees, or hares on Athos, or the grey
Olive-tree's clustering yield, or shells on the shore, so many
520   Are the pains of love: there's gall for us in those pricks.

She's out, they'll announce, although you well may glimpse her

Somewhere inside. So, she's out,
You were seeing visions. Suppose she locks the door against
    you
    Come the promised night? Then doss down
On the bare ground. It's dirty? Too bad. Even when some lying 525
    And snotty maid asks, 'What's this
Fellow hanging around for?' still coax door and cruel mistress,
    Take off your wreath of roses, hang it up
On the knocker. When she's willing, move in; when she
    avoids you,
    Take yourself off: no gentleman should become 530
An importunate bore. Why force your mistress to say, 'You
    Just can't get rid of old so-and-so'? She won't
Always be set against you. And don't think it demeaning
    To endure a girl's blows or curses, to kiss her feet.

Why waste time over trifles? My mind's on greater matters, 535
    Great themes will I tackle – your full
Attention, please, reader! The task will be arduous – but no
    credit
    Otherwise: hard and exacting the toil
My art demands. Bear patiently with a rival, and victory
    Will be yours, you'll triumph in the end. 540
Take this not as mere human opinion, believe it rather
    Prophetic utterance: nothing in my art
Is of greater importance. Put up with her flirtations,
    Leave her billets-doux alone, let her come or go
As she pleases. Husbands allow this latitude to lawful 545
    Wives – they nod off, let sleep assist the fun.
At this game, I must confess, I fall short of perfection,
    But what to do? I just can't follow my own
Instructions. What, sit by while someone's making passes
    At my girl? Let that go, not blow my top? 550
Her own incumbent, as I remember, had kissed her: I resented
    The kisses: my love abounds with wild
Uncivilized instincts (a fault that has caused me trouble
    On more than one occasion). Wiser the man

555 Who oils doors for his rivals. But it's best to know nothing,
     Let guilty secrets be hidden; don't make her confess,
     Spare her blushes. Observe, you young blades, don't catch out
          your girls: no,
     Let them cheat you – and while they're cheating, believe
     They've eluded discovery. Passion's fanned by detection,
560   A guilty pair revealed will always persist
     In the love that undid them. Take one famous example –
          Vulcan's crafty snaring of Mars
     And Venus. Driven wild by a frantic passion
          For the goddess, Mars was transformed
565 From grim captain to lover. Nor did Venus play the rustic
          And hold out against his entreaties: there's no
     Goddess more willing. Ah, the times she mocked her
          husband's
     Limp, the wanton, or his hands, made hard
     By toil at the forge and bellows! To ape him in Mars' presence
570   Lent her chic, gave added charm
     To her beauty. At first they concealed their adulterous
     Meetings: guilt blushed, shame kept
     The affair quite dark. But who could deceive the Sun? He
     Saw all – and told Vulcan what acts
575 His wife was performing. Sun, that's a bad example
          You set there. Just ask, she'll oblige
     You too in return for your silence. So Vulcan set hidden
          Snares round and over the bed (no eye
     Could detect them), then put about he was off to Lemnos.
          The lovers
580 Met as arranged, were trapped
     In the toils, lay naked: tableau. Then Vulcan invited
          All the gods round. Venus came close to tears –
     She and Mars couldn't cover their faces, couldn't even
          Move a hand to their private parts.
585 Someone laughed and said: 'If you find your chains a burden,
          Brave Mars, transfer them to me!'
     At Neptune's urging, reluctantly, Vulcan released them:
          Venus ran off to Paphos, Mars to Thrace.

So much for Vulcan's plotting: once their shameful
   Secret was out, the lovers did as they pleased   590
Without thought for concealment. Later Vulcan admitted
   His folly, they say, and would curse the fatal skill
He'd deployed to catch them. So, be warned by the fate of
     Venus,
   Don't set up the kind of snare
She had to endure. Don't organize traps for your rivals,   595
   Don't intercept secret letters – that's a job
More proper to husbands (if they reckon such correspondence
   Worth interception). Once more, let me repeat,
There's no sport here that isn't legitimate, no long-skirted
   Respectable ladies figure in *my* fun.   600

Who'd dare to profane the rites of Ceres, who would publish
   The high mysteries held on Samothrace? To keep
Silence is no great virtue, but blurting out religious
   Secrets – that's a most heinous crime.
Garrulous Tantalus, vainly reaching up for apples,   605
   In water, yet parched with thirst,
Deserved his fate: Venus expressly commands that her holy
   Rites be kept private. I'm warning you, let no
Kiss-and-tell gossip come near them. These mysteries may not
   Lurk in a box, may not echo to the wild   610
Clash of bronze cymbals; yet, though so popular among us,
   Among us they still insist
On concealment. Venus herself, when she poses naked,
   Bends down, places one hand
Over her mons. Brute beasts may couple in public,   615
   Promiscuously, a sight to make girls blush
And avert their eyes; but our more furtive passions call for
   Locked doors and bedrooms, we hide
Our private parts under the bedclothes, and prefer, if not
     darkness,
   At least something less than bright   620
Noonday, a touch of shadow. In the old days, when sun and
     weather

Weren't yet kept off by roof-tiles, when oaks
Provided both food and shelter, love-making was restricted
    To caves or woods. Even these simple folk
Would have blushed to be seen in the act. But now we flaunt
625   our prowess
    At such nocturnal pursuits, pay a high price
Just for the kick of bragging. Will you give every girl
    in town the
Treatment, just to be able to tell your friends
'I had her, too'? Will you find some circumstantial scandal
630   To repeat about each as she's mentioned, never lack
For a victim to point at? That's mild, though: some fabricate
    stories
    They'd deny if true, claim there's no
Woman they haven't slept with. If they cannot touch girls'
    Bodies, they'll smear their names: though the flesh escape
635   Defilement, repute is tarnished. So, bar the lady's chamber,
    You crabby old doorkeeper, fix on a hundred bolts –
What's left secure when her name's fair game for 'adulterers'
    Who work to convince the world of what never took place?
Myself, I remain discreet about my erotic encounters
640   Even when they're true: keep such secrets under seal.

Take care not to criticize girls for their shortcomings: many
    Have found it advantageous to pretend
Such things didn't exist. Andromeda's dusky complexion
    Left wing-footed Perseus silent. Although
645   Everyone else thought Andromache too large a woman,
    To Hector alone she looked
Just the right size. Habit breeds tolerance: a long-established
    Love will condone much, whereas
At first it's all-sensitive. While a new graft's growing
650   In the green cortex, a light
Breeze can detach it; but soon, time-strengthened, the tree will
    Outface all winds, hold firm,
Bear adopted fruit. Time heals each physical blemish,
    The erstwhile flaw will fade:

Young nostrils cannot abide the stink of tanning leather,   655
    But age inures them to it, after a while
They don't even notice the smell. Labels minimize feelings –
    She's blacker than pitch? Try 'brunette'.
If she squints, compare her to Venus. She croaks? She's
    Minerva!
    A living skeleton? 'Svelte' is the word. Call her 'trim'   660
When she's minuscule, or 'plumpish' when she's a Fat Lady –
    Use proximate virtues to camouflage each fault.

Don't ask her age, don't inquire under just which consul
    She was born – leave that kind of chore
To the Censor's office, especially if she's past her girlish   665
    Prime, and already plucking those first
White hairs. Such ladies, in this (or even a higher) age-group
    Are good value, a field worth sowing, ready to bear.*
Besides, they possess a wider range of knowledge   675
    And experience, the sole source
Of true skill: they make up for their years with sophistication,
    Camouflaging their age through art; they know
A thousand postures – name yours – for making love in,
    More ways than any pillow-book could reveal.   680
They need no stimuli to warm up their passions –
    Men and women should share the same
Pleasures. I hate it unless both lovers reach a climax:
    That's why I don't much go for boys.
I can't stand a woman who puts out because she has to,   685
    Who lies there dry as a bone
With her mind on her knitting. Pleasure by way of duty
    Holds no charms for me, I don't want
Any dutiful martyrs. I love the sighs that betray their rapture,
    That beg me to go slow, to keep it up   690

---

* Editors have often remarked that lines 669–74 are out of place here, but no
truly satisfactory place was found for them until it was shown that they properly
belong at the *end* of Book 2, between lines 732 and 733. I have therefore trans-
posed them in the present version.

Just a little longer. It's great when my mistress comes, eyes
    swooning,
  Then collapses, can't take any more
For a long while. Such joys attend you in your thirties:
  Nature does not bestow them on green youth.
695 For the hasty, new-bottled wine; for me, a vintage
  Laid down long years before.
Only an ageing plane-tree can block the sunlight,
  Bare feet are crippled by a new-grown field.
Would you rate Helen's daughter Hermione over Helen?
  Was Medusa
700 An improvement on *her* mother? Any man
Willing to get involved with mature passions,
  And to stay the course, will win a worthwhile prize.

So the bed, as though consciously, has received its two lovers.
  And the door is shut. Muse, you must wait outside:
They don't need you, now, to prompt their whispered
705   endearments,
  Their hands won't be idle, fingers will learn
What to do in those hidden parts where Love's unnoticed
  Darts transfix the flesh.
Andromache got this treatment from most valiant Hector –
710   His talents extended beyond war:
Captive Briseis was handled thus by the great Achilles,
  Who came, battle-weary, to her soft bed.
Those hands, Briseis, you let those bloody hands caress you
  Though daily they claimed their stint
Of Phrygian dead. Or was that just what you found so
715   exciting –
  The hands of a conqueror on your limbs?
Believe me, love's acme of pleasure must not be hurried,
  But drawn insensibly on – and when you've found
Those places a woman adores to have touched up, don't let any
720   Feeling of shame prevent you, go right in.
You'll see that tremulous glint in her eyes, like the dazzle
  Of sunlight on a lake;

She'll moan and gasp, murmur words of sweet endearment
    Well matched to the sport you're playing, heave soft sighs.
But take care not to cram on sail and outrace your mistress,   725
    Or let *her* overtake *you*; both should pass
The winning-post neck and neck – that's the height of pleasure,
    When man and woman lie knocked out at once.
This is the pace you should keep when time's no object,
    And your stolen pleasures take no prick from fear;   730
When delay isn't safe, though, it helps to press on regardless,
    Step up the strike-rate, spur that galloping horse.
While strength and age permit it, keep at such labours: 669
    Bent age will come soon enough   670
On stealthy feet. Cleave the sea with oars, the soil with a
    ploughshare,   671
    Turn your fierce hands to war –   672
Or expend your strength and toil and vigour on women: 673
    This too is military service, this too needs sweat.   674

My task is ended: give me the palm, you grateful   733
    Young lovers, wreathe myrtle in my scented hair!
As great as Podalirius was among the Achaeans   735
    For his healing arts, or Achilles for his strength,
Or Nestor in counsel, or Calchas as prophet, or Ajax
    In arms, or Automedon as charioteer,
So great am I at the love-game. Sing my praises, declare me
    Your prophet and poet, young men: let my name   740
Be broadcast world-wide. As Vulcan made arms for Achilles,
    So have I done for you: then use
My gift, as he did, to conquer! And when you've brought
    down your
    Amazon, write on the trophy *Ovid was my guide*.

Now the girls (hullo there!) are begging me for lessons: 745
    The next part of this poem will be yours.

BOOK 3

I've armed Greeks against Amazons: now I must fashion
    weapons
  For Penthesilea and her girls.
A well matched fight is best, with victory granted
  Through the favour of kind
5 Venus, and Venus' earth-girdling son. Unfair for naked
  Ladies to meet armed troops: a victory gained that way
Would disgrace our gallants. 'But why lend venom to serpents?'
  I hear you ask, 'why betray a fold of sheep
To the ravening she-wolf?' Don't pin the evil reputation
10 Of one or two on them all, judge each girl by
Her own proper merits. It's true that Helen and Clytemnestra
  Must face sisterly charges from both
The sons of Atreus; it's true that what Eriphyle plotted
  Sent Amphiaraus and his horses down,
15 Still living, to Styx; yet Penelope stayed constant
  For ten years, while her husband was at the wars,
And ten more of his wanderings. Look at Protesilaus
  And Laodameia – who cut short her span on earth
To follow the man she loved. Alcestis redeemed Admetus'
20 Life by pledging her own, was borne to the grave
In his stead. Evadne cried, 'Ah take me, Capaneus!
  We'll mingle our ashes,' and sprang
On to the pyre. Virtue herself, by name and fashion,
  Is a lady: naturally she has her own
25 Followers to please, though my art doesn't call for such strict
  Principles – my little craft
Can manage with smaller sails. Only wanton passions
  Are learnt through me, I'll teach
How a woman should be courted. You seldom see the ladies
30 Using bows and flaming arrows on their men --
Men are often deceivers, girls hardly ever: inquiries
  Will prove the feminine cheat

A rare bird indeed. Medea, already a mother, was dumped by
  Perfidious Jason for another bride,
And as far as Theseus knew, deserted Ariadne   35
  Had long been food for gulls
On that lonely beach. How did Nine Ways get its title?
  How did the very woods come to shed their leaves
And weep for Phyllis? Remember that guest with the reputation
  For *piety*? *He* left poor Dido a sword –   40
And a motive for suicide. What ruined all these ladies?
  Erotic ineptitude, lack of technique. It takes
Technique to make love last – and they'd *still* be inept,
    had Venus
  Not appeared to me in a vision, made it clear
That my job was to teach them. 'Poor girls,' she said, 'what
    have *they* done,   45
  Weak defenceless lot, to be thrown
To the armed male wolves? Two books you've written
    instructing
  Men in the game: high time the opposite sex
Got benefit from your counsels. Stesichorus cursed Helen
  To begin with, but ended – better luck for him –   50
Singing her praises. If I know you, you'll be seeking their
    favour
  Till the day you die – so don't go mean on them now.'
With that she gave me a leaf from the garland of myrtle
  Binding her hair, and a few
Of the berries. Taking them, I sensed her numinous   55
  Power: air shone more brightly, my heart
Rose buoyant and carefree. While my inspiration lasts, then,
  Take lessons from me, girls (those of you whom the law,
And modesty, and your code, will permit): be mindful of
    creeping
  Old age, don't waste precious time –   60
Have fun while you can, in your salad days; the years glide
  Past like a moving stream,
And the water that's gone can never be recovered,
  The lost hour never returns.

65 Use your youth to the full: youth vanishes too swiftly,
   And what follows can never match
That first freshness. The beds of violets I remember
   Are withered weeds now; these thorns
Once shaped some charming garland. There'll come a time
      when
70   You who today lock out your lovers will lie
Old and cold and alone in bed, your door never broken
   Open at brawling midnight, never at dawn
Scattered roses bright on your threshold! Too soon – ah horror! –
   Flesh goes slack and wrinkled, the clear
75 Complexion is lost, those white streaks you swear date back to
   Your schooldays suddenly spread,
You're grey-haired. A snake husks off old age with its fragile
   Discarded skin; cast horns
Leave the stag in its prime. Unaided, a woman's charms will
80   Vanish away. Pluck the flower; left unplucked
It will wither and fall. Youth's span is shortened yet further
   By childbirth: overcropping ages a field.
Endymion on Latmos brought no blush to the Moon, nor was
      Cephalus
   A prize for which Aurora, the roseate Dawn,
85 Felt any shame. Though mourning Venus be granted
   Her Adonis, who was it sired
Harmonia and Aeneas? So, mortal women, follow
   The goddesses' example, don't deny
Such pleasures to eager lovers. They'll deceive you?
      Why worry?
90   Life holds firm. Let them come to the well
A thousand times, nothing's lost. Iron and flint are
      diminished,
   Worn down by use, but *that part*
Endures without fear of loss. Who'd forbid us to kindle
   Our lamp from a proffered flame, who'd hoard
95 The boundless deep at sea? So why should any woman
   Say 'No'? Tell me why – all you waste
Is douche-water. I'm not encouraging promiscuous conduct,
   Just warning you not be scared

216

Of shadows. Your favours forfeit you nothing. We're still in
    harbour –
Let me catch the light breeze, leave strong winds for outside. 100

I begin with self-cultivation: you get the best vintage
    From well-cared-for grapes, the wheat
Grows tallest in well-dug fields. True beauty's a gift of
    The gods, few can boast they possess it – and most
Of you, my dears, don't. Hard work will improve the picture: 105
    Neglect your looks, and they'll go to pot, even though
You're a second Venus. Young girls didn't cultivate their
    persons
    In the old days, true; but they didn't have cultured men
To live up to. Andromache wore a simple smock of sacking, 110
    And why not? She was the wife
Of a rough soldier. If you'd been married to Ajax, would you
    Dress up for a man who went around behind
Seven layers of oxhide? Crude simplicity's old-fashioned,
    Rome's all gold now, possesses the vast wealth
Of the conquered world. Consider the Capitol, past and
    present – 115
    You'd think today's version belonged
To a different god. Our Senate (august assembly!) now boasts
    A worthy chamber – first built, in Tatius' reign,
Of wattle and daub. The Palatine, where Apollo and our
    princes
    Now lord it, once pastured oxen for the plough. 120
Let others worship the past; I much prefer the present,
    Am delighted to be alive today – not for
The stubborn gold we mine, or the rare shells gathered
    For our delight from foreign shores,
Not for the marble quarried from crumbling mountains,
    the palaces 125
    Pier-built over the bay, but for
Refinement and culture, which have banished the tasteless
    Crudities of our ancestors. So, don't burden your ears
With precious pearls, once dived for by dusky natives
    In green tropic seas; don't come out 130

Wearing dresses that sag with the weight of the gold sewn on
    them:
  Wealth displayed to allure us may often repel.

What attracts us is elegance – so don't neglect your hairstyle;
  Looks can be made or marred by a skilful touch.
135 Nor will one style suit all: there are innumerable fashions,
  And each girl should look in her glass
Before choosing what suits her reflection. Long features go
    best with
  A plain central parting: that's how
Laodamia's hair was arranged. A round-faced lady
140   Should pile all her hair on top,
Leaving the ears exposed. One girl should wear it down on
  Her shoulders, like Apollo about to play
The lyre; another should braid it in the style of the huntress
  Diana, when she's after some frightened beast,
145 Skirt hitched up. Some need to keep it loose and windswept,
  Others to pin it back;
Some like tortoiseshell combs, some prefer to brush it
  Out in soft flowing waves –
But you can't count all the acorns on an oak's branches,
150   Or Hybla's bees, or wild beasts in the Alps,
And *I* can't be comprehensive about hair-fashions
  When every day brings out a chic new style.
Besides, the Neglected Look suits many girls: quite often
  You'd think it untouched since yesterday, though in fact
It's fresh-combed. Art simulates chance. When Heracles
155   entered that fallen
  City, and caught one glimpse of Iole's wild curls,
'That's the girl for me,' he exclaimed. So wind-blown Ariadne
  Was whirled off by Bacchus, to loud cheers
From his satyrs. Nature's too kind to feminine beauty,
160   Women have so many ways to offset defects!
We men are stripped bare, relentlessly; just as a north wind
  Brings down the leaves, so our hair
Falls out with age. But a woman can use imported rinses

To touch up those white streaks, produce
A better-than-natural tint; a woman goes out in a built-up   165
   Purchased postiche, replaces her own hair
With a wig, cash down – and unblushingly: boutiques display them
   Under Hercules' nose, right beside the Muses' shrine.

A word, I suppose, about dress. I have no time for flounces,
   Or purple-dyed woollen fabrics: when you've the choice   170
Of so many cheaper colours, it's just plain madness
   To carry such an investment on your back.
There's pale sky-blue, like the cloudless vault of heaven
   On a warm spring day, with no
Western breeze blowing up rain; or light gold, like the rescuer 175
   Of Phrixus and Helle from Ino's deep-sea wiles,
Or the colour that's like a wave, sea-green, named after
   The deep itself – fit garb
For the Nymphs. There's saffron: the dewy dawn-goddess is veiled in
   A saffron robe as she drives up her light-   180
Bringing horses; there's myrtle-leaf, there's amethyst-purple,
   Rose-white, the grey of a Thracian crane,
Chestnut (your turn, Amaryllis), almond-blossom, the beeswax
   Brown of a fleece – as many as or more
Than the flowers that blossom in springtime, when warm weather   185
   Puts buds on the vines, when barren winter's fled,
Are the dyes that wool will imbibe. So pick the right ones:
   Not all of them go well on every girl.
Dark grey suits pale complexions: grey suited Briseïs –
   She even wore grey into captivity.   190
A swarthy skin does better in white: Andromeda's white-clad
   Beauty drove jealous gods to punish her island home.

I was about to warn you against rank goatish armpits
   And bristling hair on your legs,
But I'm not instructing hillbilly girls from the Caucasus,   195

Or Mysian river-hoydens – so what need
To remind *you* not to let your teeth get all discoloured
   Through neglect, or forget to wash
Your hands every morning? You know how to brighten your
   complexion
200   With powder, add rouge to a bloodless face,
Skilfully block in the crude outline of an eyebrow,
   Stick a patch on one flawless cheek.
You don't shrink from lining your eyes with dark mascara
   Or a touch of Cilician saffron. My little tract
205 *On Facial Treatment* lists the most effective preparations –
   It may be short, but no end
Of hard work went into it, it's full of tips for restoring
   Faded beauty: my art is active on your behalf.
But don't let your lover find all those jars and bottles
210   On your dressing-table: the best
Make-up remains unobtrusive. A face so thickly plastered
   With pancake it runs down your sweaty neck
Is bound to create repulsion. And that goo from unwashed
   fleeces –
   Athenian maybe, but my dear, the *smell*! –
215 That's used for face-cream: avoid it. When you have company
   Don't dab stuff on your pimples, don't start cleaning your
   teeth:
The result may be attractive, but the *process* is sickening –
   Much that is vile in the doing gives pleasure when done.
A statue – signed, let's say, by that industrious sculptor
220   Myron – began as a mere lump
Of deadweight marble; the gold for your ring must first be
   Worked and shaped, your woollen dress was made
From greasy yarn; that splendid representation of Venus
   Posed naked, wringing out her seawet hair,
225 Was a rough and uncut stone once. So leave us to imagine
   You're asleep while you're at your toilet: only emerge
When the public picture's complete. I don't want to know how
   That complexion's built up. Shut your door,
Don't reveal the half-finished process. Most of your actions

Would offend if you didn't conceal them: there's a lot   230
Men are better not knowing. Look closely at those splendid
  Gold statues adorning the theatre – thin gilded foil
On a wooden frame! That's why the public can't come near
    them
  Till they're finished – and that's why you
Should keep men out while you're making up. Still, I don't
    forbid you   235
  To let them watch you comb your rippling hair
Out down your back – but mind you don't lose your temper
  As you tear at those tangled knots!
Don't vent your spleen on your lady's-maid: I detest a girl who
  Claws the poor creature's face, or stabs   240
Her arm with a needle. The victim will curse her mistress'
    head while
  She dresses it, and, while she bleeds, drop tears
Over the hated tresses. If you've difficult hair, keep a guard on
  Your boudoir door – or have your styling done
In a ladies-only temple! I once called on some woman who
    wasn't   245
  Expecting me. In her flurry she fixed her wig
On back to front. May such cause for embarrassment undo
    only
  My enemies! May this disgrace afflict none but wild
Parthian girls! There's nothing so ugly as hornless cattle,
  Bald fields, bare bushes – or a head sans hair.   250

Who are my clients? Not Semele, not Leda, not Phoenician
  Europa, cruising off on that pseudo-bull's
Broad back, or Helen (understandably, Menelaus
  Wanted her back; understandably, Paris kept
His prize for himself). It's the ordinary run of women,   255
  Pretty or plain, who consult me (the plain
Always outnumber the pretty). What help or instruction
  Do beauties require from art? They have their own
Potent dowry – natural good looks. When it's calm, the captain
  Relaxes; but in a storm all hands are piped.   260

A flawless face is a rarity: mask each blemish,
  Hide your physical faults – as far as you can.
Sit, if you're short, lest standing you seem to be sitting;
  Stretch out that pint-sized form,
Recline on a couch (but discourage rude measurement by
265   spreading
  A wrap or blanket across your legs).
The over-lean girl should wear more amply textured
  Dresses, a robe that's draped
Loose from her shoulders. Puce stripes offset a pallid
270 Complexion, while Nilotic linen transforms
The swarthy. Got ugly feet? Just keep them hidden
  In smart white bootees. Scrawny calves? Don't raise
Your skirt above the ankle. Protruding collar-bones? Mask them
  With pads. Is your trouble a flat bust?
275 Wear a good bra. If you have rough nails, coarse fingers,
  Don't gesture too much while you talk.
Bad breath? You should never converse on an empty stomach
  And keep your mouth well back from your lover's face!
If your teeth are decayed, or horsy, or protruding,
280 A guffaw can cost you dear. Believe it or not,
Girls even learn how to laugh: in their quest for decorum
  This is one more skill they must acquire.
Don't open the mouth too wide, control those dimples,
    keep your
  Teeth concealed behind your lips.
285 Don't split your sides with endless hilarity, but rather
  Laugh in a restrained, a ladylike way –
Some women distort their features with lop-sided guffaws, some
  Get so cross-eyed with mirth
You'd swear they were weeping. Others utter a harsh unlovely
290 Braying noise, like a she-ass hitched to the mill.
Where does art not enter? Girls learn / to make even tears
    attractive,
  To cry when and how they please.
Indeed, some mispronounce words with deliberate affectation,
  Bring them lispingly off the tongue:

222

Charm lurks in such errors of consciously faulty diction –   295
    What grace of speech they had they soon unlearn.
These hints are useful, so pay them proper attention –
    And mind you learn to walk in a feminine way!
No mean part of elegance derives from gait and carriage:
    These can attract or repel   300
Admiring strangers. One girl sways her hips artfully, catches
    The breeze with her flowing mantle, points her feet
In short dainty steps; another – like some red-cheeked peasant
      housewife –
    Clumps and waddles along, with hearty strides.
Moderation's best, as so often: don't play the country
      bumpkin,   305
    But equally, don't lay your affectations on
Too thick. No harm, though, in baring your left-hand shoulder
    And upper arm: for those
With a milk-white skin this works wonders – just let me see it,
    And I'm mad to press kisses on the naked flesh!   310

The Sirens, those sea-monsters, with their delectable voices
    Would draw in the swiftest ships:
At the sound of them Ulysses almost struggled loose from
    The ropes that tied him (his comrades' ears were stopped
With wax). Oh, music's seductive: girls should take
      singing-lessons –   315
    For many, it's the voice, and not the face,
That plays bawd. You should know the latest vaudeville
      numbers,
    The slinkiest hits from the Nile:
Any girl I'd call accomplished must know how to play a
    Stringed instrument, handle a quill.   320
Orpheus moved rocks and beasts with his lyre, held Tartarus
      spellbound,
    Tamed hell's three-headed dog;
When Amphion played (he who so nobly avenged his mother)
    The stones of Thebes moved with a will,
Sprang into walls. A dolphin, though dumb, responded   325

To human music – or so the famous tale
Of Arion alleges. Learn to play the two-handed Phoenician
    Harp as well, for a party it's ideal.
Have a smattering of the poets – Callimachus, Coan
330   Philetas, wine-flown Anacreon: don't forget
Sappho (what, I ask you, could be more wanton?),
    Or Menander's sugar-daddies, always gulled
By some tricksy slave. Be able to quote Propertius,
    Tibullus, or Gallus, in sentimental mood;
335 Learn passages from epic: the high-flown *Golden*
    Fleece by Varro (poor Helle!), or – what else? –
Virgil's *Aeneid* (those wanderings, great Rome's origins,
    The most publicized Latin poem of all time . . .).
Perhaps, too, my own name will be included
340   Among theirs, and my works escape
Oblivion: maybe some pundit will say: 'Here, read our
    Maestro's
    Polished advice on love (for both sexes), or choose
Some pieces from the three books of his *Amores*
    To declaim in a soft, enchanting voice,
345 Or, for dramatic recitation, one of the *Heroines'*
    Letters – an art-form he invented himself.'
So grant it, Apollo! You spirits of bygone poets,
    O Bacchus, O Muses, *make it all come true!*

Of course, I also insist that a girl should be a dancer,
350   Trained to shimmy delectably while the wine
Goes round after dinner. Lead actresses, ballerinas,
    These are idolized for their sinuous charms.
Some minor points I'm almost ashamed to mention: let her
    Know how to play board-games, to roll the bones –
355 And skilfully, planning her throws in advance, deciding
    At which point to hazard a piece, just when to huff.
The contest of halma should find her cunning rather
    than reckless
    When her pieces are taken by a two-pronged attack,
When her fighting men are exposed and struggling, in isolation,

Against a foe who comes back, and back again,   360
At her weakest point. She should have a sure hand for
    jackstraws –
Lift endless spillikins, never disturb the pile.
Then there's that other piece-game, the kind of backgammon
    Played on a twelve-point board (twelve points,
Twelve months in the year), or merels – like noughts and
    crosses   365
    With marbles – three in a row to win.
Countless pastimes await you – too bad if a girl doesn't
    Know how to play: games often provide a quick
Lead-in to love. But using your throws to the best advantage
    Is of minor importance: what matters is self-control.   370
This is when we lack caution, when our very zest betrays us,
    And our true self shows naked – all for a game!
Ugly anger creeps up on us, lust for a cash killing,
    Quarrels and brawls, anxiety, despair;
Accusations fly to and fro, the air's a clamour, angry   375
    Gods are invoked all round; but there's no
Trusting those tables. The things / that players will pray for!
    They'll even
    Quite often (I've seen them) dissolve in tears.
If you want men to find you attractive, may the gods in heaven
    Keep you well clear of all such disgusting tricks!   380

These, then, are the sports that indolent nature has given
    To women. Men have a richer choice:
They can play fast handball, throw the javelin or discus,
    Fence in armour, show-jump a horse. But you
Ladies aren't seen in the Field of Mars, you don't use the
    athletes'   385
    Cold baths, you don't swim in the Tiber. Where
You can stroll to your profit, of a scorching August noonday,
    Is under those shady arches down Pompey's colonnade;
Visit the Palatine, sacred to belaurelled Apollo
    (Whose power sank Cleopatra's fleet);   390
See the monuments raised by our Leader's wife and sister,

See his son-in-law, head wreathed with naval renown!
Genuflect at the incense-wreathed altars of the Memphian
   Cow, visit all three theatres (get front-row seats);
395 Patronize the Circus, see hot blood splash the arena,
   Watch a close-run chariot-race.
Out of sight's out of mind; what you don't know you can't
   covet –
   Fruitless, the pretty face that goes alone.
Though you can out-sing every legendary prima donna,
400   Music unheard gives little joy.
If Apelles of Cos had never contrived that pose for Venus
   She'd still be hidden deep
Under the ocean. What else do our dedicated poets
   Pursue but fame? This is the goal of all
405 Our labours. Poets were once the chosen of gods and monarchs:
   In olden times their choirs
Won great rewards; high honour, a venerable title,
   These a bard had – plus large
And regular cash donations. Take Ennius: born a Calabrian
410   Peasant, yet interred in the Scipio family vault
Because of his art. Today, though, the ivy lies unhonoured,
   And a life of poetic toil
Gets you labelled a drone. Still, to slave for recognition
   Does help. If the *Iliad*, that immortal work,
415 Had never been published, who'd have heard of Homer –
   Or of Danaë, if she'd reached old age still shut
Away in her tower? You pretty girls need your public,
   So mind you parade round the town
As often as you can make it. The wolf, to seize one sheep, will
420   Pursue the whole flock; an eagle plummets down
Into a flight of birds. So, the beauty must court her public –
   Perhaps, among so many, she'll find one man
Worth attracting. To get run after means full time on the party
   Circuit, means concentrating her whole
425 Mind on projecting that glamour. Besides, luck's a constant
   Factor, so keep your hook dangling: you'll take a fish

From the stream you'd least expect. Often hounds will range
    the mountain
    Thickets in vain, – and then a stag will plunge
Into the toils undriven. Could shackled Andromeda ever
    Have dreamt her tears would attract a lover? But then   430
Loose hair and abandoned weeping are sexy: her husband's
    funeral
    Is often where your widow looks out for the next man.

But keep clear of smart young beaux who make elegance a
    profession,
    Flaunt handsome profiles, are always fixing their hair:
The tale they tell you they've told to a thousand girls already,   435
    They're fancy-free, never stick to a constant love.
What's a woman to do when her lover's smoother than she is,
    And probably has more men on the side as well?
It's hard to believe, but true, that Troy would still be standing
    If the Trojans had followed poor Cassandra's advice.   440
Some make their assault behind a false mask of passion,
    use such
    Approaches to snatch – at shameful gain:
Don't be deceived by their hair, all sleek and perfumed,
    Their tight-laced shoe-tongues, the stuff
Of their togas, so finely textured, the rings that glitter –   445
    One, two, or more – on their fingers. The most
Elegant dandy among them may well be a sneak-thief
    Consumed with love for your dress,
Not your person. 'That's mine, give it back!' the victims
    clamour,
    'Give it back!', while the public square   450
Re-echoes their complaints, while Venus from her gilded
    Temple, and from their fountain the Appian nymphs
Look on unmoved. Some men have notorious reputations,
    Many have ditched a mistress. Learn in time
From some other girl's cries of distress to beware the prospect   455
    Of getting distressed yourself. Don't open that door

To some treacherous male. Don't believe the perjured oaths of
    Theseus,
    Athenian maids: those deities he invokes
He long since forswore. And his son Demophoön, heir to
460   Bad blood and broken faith – what girl would trust *him*
After he'd left poor Phyllis? Match promise with promise;
    If they keep their word, then you
Can come through too. That girl could snuff the undying Vestal
    Fire, loot Isis' temple of its sacred gear,
465 Or slip her lover a mixture of aconite and hemlock –
    Who denies her favours *after* taking gifts!

I must concentrate my theme more. Muse, rein in there,
    Quit your headlong gallop down the course!

A lover should pave the way with letters: make sure you detail
470   A trustworthy maid to act as your go-between.
Examine each message, deduce from his own expressions
    Whether it's faked, or written with genuine
Heartfelt distress. Wait a little before you reply: a lover's
    Honed up by delay – provided it's not too long.
475 Don't yield too easily to a lover's entreaties,
    But, equally, don't overdo
Those stubborn refusals. Scare him, yet leave him hopeful;
    Let each letter reduce his fear, increase his hopes.
A girl should write elegantly, but in everyday language –
480   Familiar phrases have their own appeal.
How often a hesitant lover takes fire from letters –
    And how often a barbarous style
Will undo the prettiest writer! Even though you're not married
    You're anxious to fool your men,
485 So have slave-boy or handmaid write your letters for you,
    Don't compromise yourself with each new beau;
489 Only a cad, it's true, would hang on to such proofs of passion –
490   But as evidence they pack a thunderbolt punch.
487 I've seen girls, pale with terror, submitting, wretched creatures,
488   To blackmail for life, all because of a letter. In my view

To counter fraud by fraud is permitted – the law will sanction
  Arms for self-defence against an armed attack.
So practise writing in a number of different
  Hands (bad cess to those who make such advice
Essential!), and take care, always, to erase the wax completely   495
  Before you use it: avoid any legible trace
Of a previous message. Transmute the sex of your lover
  Whenever you mention him: write 'her' instead.

Now, if I may, I'll turn from such lesser matters
  To more serious themes, spread full my swelling sails.   500
A pretty face should control mad fits of temper: radiant
  Peace is for men, raw fury marks the beast.
Anger swells up your countenance: veins throb and darken
  With pulsing blood, an ultra-Gorgonish fire
Darts from your eyes. When Pallas looked into the river,   505
  And saw her puckered expression, 'Away with you, flute!'
She cried, 'You're not worth it!' Take a glass to your tantrums,
  And which of you would recognize your own
Familiar features? It does just as much harm to look haughty –
  A gentle expression will best   510
Encourage love. I detest – and believe me, I know it – the over-
  Disdainful air: too often a silent face
Holds the seeds of hatred. Return his smiles and glances;
  If he beckons, acknowledge the gesture with a nod.
After such foreplay Cupid, the foils abandoned, empties   515
  His quiver of its keen darts.
What else? Glum girls are a bore. Leave Ajax to love
    Tecmessa:
  We men are a cheerful breed, it's bright
Girls who best charm us – if I were choosing a mistress
  Andromache or Tecmessa would never be *my* choice;   520
I find it hard to believe they ever slept with their masters
  (Though their parturitions inform me I must be wrong).
Could that dreary woman, I ask you, have ever called Ajax
  'My darling', or warmed his heart with lovers' words?

*

229

525 Who'll veto my trick of using great matters as examples
　　To illustrate small? Why shun the Leader's name?
　　Just as our good Leader makes X a squadron-commander,
　　　Y a centurion, entrusts the colours to Z,
　　So do you, too, consider how we can serve your advantage,
530　　Then place each one of us in his proper slot!
　　Let the rich man give you presents, the professional lawyer
　　　Be on call to defend you in court with skill
　　And eloquence: we, the poets, should stick to sending you
　　　poems –
　　　As a group, we're pre-eminent at dealing with love.
535 Far and wide we can broadcast the loved one's beauty: think of
　　　Nemesis, Cynthia – both household names!
　　Lands in the East and West all know of Lycoris; countless
　　　People keep asking me who my Corinna is.
　　What's more, there's no place in a poet for stratagems and
　　　deceptions:
540　　Vocation and art combine to fashion forth
　　His essential nature. We stay untouched by ambition or love
　　　of profit,
　　　Despise the forum, prefer a couch in the shade.
　　But we're easily hooked, we burn with vehement passions,
　　　And know – too well – how to give
545 Unswerving love. Our natures are made more pliant
　　　By our gentle art: an attitude to life
　　Grows from our studies. So, girls, be generous with poets:
　　　They're the Muses' darlings, contain
　　A divine spark. God is in us, we have dealings with heaven:
550　　Our inspiration descends
　　.From celestial realms. It's a crime to look for presents
　　　To such skilled bards – but a crime (I very much fear)
　　Which no girl shuns. But don't look openly rapacious,
　　　Dissemble a little: if he glimpses the net
　　A raw lover will baulk. No horseman would use the same
555　　　bridle
　　　On a fresh-broken colt and a well-
　　Trained hack; nor should you follow the same methods

To capture stable maturity and green youth.
This raw recruit, a novice in Love's campaigns, who's made it –
    Your latest victim – through the bedroom door,   560
Make sure he knows you alone, cleaves to none other:
    Plant high hedges all around
So tender a crop. Shun rivals: just keep him to yourself and
    You'll win the day. Love, like a king's throne,
Cannot share its rights. Your old soldier will come to loving   565
    Cautiously, by degrees, will put up with much
No recruit would endure; will not break down doors, or burn
    them;
    Will not go for a mistress's soft
Cheeks with his nails, will not rip up her (or his) clothing,
    Will not make her weep by tearing out her hair.   570
Such things may be expected from young blades hot in passion;
    But a veteran will bear the worst of wounds
With steadfast heart, will burn with slow-smouldering heat,
    like
    Damp hay, or green timber freshly cut
On the mountain slopes. His love is more sure; the other
    richer,   575
    But brief – pluck such transient fruit before it's gone!

We've unbolted the gates to the foe: let's make a general
    Surrender, in faithless betrayal keep our faith.
What's easily given ill nourishes any long-term passion –
    You should mix in the odd rebuff   580
With your cheerful fun. Shut him out of the house, let him
    wait there
    Cursing that locked front door, let him plead
And threaten all he's a mind to. Sweetness cloys the palate,
    Bitter juice is a freshener. Often a small skiff
Is sunk by favouring winds: it's their husbands' access to
    them,   585
    At will, that deprives so many wives of love.
Let her put in a door, with a hard-faced porter to tell him
    'Keep out', and he'll soon be touched with desire

Through frustration. Put down your blunt foils, fight with
    sharpened weapons
590   (I don't doubt that my own shafts
Will be turned against me). When a new-captured lover
    Is stumbling into the toils, then let him believe
He alone has rights to your bed – but later, make him conscious
    Of rivals, of shared delights. Neglect
These devices – his ardour will wane. A racehorse runs most
595   strongly
    When the field's ahead, to be paced
And passed. So the dying embers of passion can be fanned to
    Fresh flame by some outrage – I can only love,
Myself, I confess it, when wronged. But don't let the cause of
600   Pain be too obvious: let a lover suspect
More than he knows. Invent a slave who watches your every
    Movement, make clear what a jealous martinet
That man of yours is – such things will excite him. Pleasure
    Too safely enjoyed lacks zest. You want to be free
As Thaïs? Act scared. Though the door's quite safe, let him
605   in by
    The window. Look nervous. Have a smart
Maid rush in, scream 'We're caught!', while you bundle the
    quaking
    Youth out of sight. But be sure
To offset his fright with some moments of carefree pleasure –
610   Or he'll think a night with you isn't worth the risk.

I was going to omit the ways of eluding a crafty husband
    Or vigilant guard – let the bride
Respect her husband, let brides be guarded securely: that's
    proper:
    Modesty, law, and our Leader so prescribe.
615   But watch *you*? A woman still scarcely used to her freedom?
    Intolerable! Let me instruct you in all
The ways of deceit, and then (if you're properly determined)
    With as many watchers around you as Argus had eyes
You'll outsmart them all. Can a guard stop you writing letters

When you're shut in the bathroom? Will he find   620
All the places where your girl-accomplice can hide them –
    tablets
  Snugly tucked in her bra,
A package of papers strapped to one calf, a seductive message
  Slipped between sandal and foot?
If such tricks become known to the guardian, use your
    confidante's   625
  Body for paper, scribble a note on her back.
Then there's invisible writing, in milk: when you want to
    read it
  Just spread powdered carbon over the wax –
A reliable deception. Or write in moist oil of linseed:
  The seemingly blank tablet will preserve   630
Your hidden words. Think of Danaë's father, and all the
    trouble
  He took to protect his daughter – yet she contrived
To make him a grandfather. The city's full of theatres,
  Girls love the races – what
Can a guardian do? Say she worships Egyptian Isis,   635
  And goes where no watchful male
May follow, clashing her sistrum? What about the Good
    Goddess,
  Banning men from her temple (except her own
Chosen adherents)? The public baths provide plenty of private
  Fun for girls – while their guardians sit outside   640
In charge of their clothes. How cope with the sharp girlfriend
  Who's 'ill' on demand (but never too ill to vacate
Her bed for the length of a visit)? How counter those
    duplicate
  And duplicitous passkeys? How block the door – and all
Those other ways in? A guardian's wits can be fuddled   645
  With plenty of wine – cheap stuff,
Any Spanish rotgut, will do. There are knockout potions,
  Drugs to induce deep sleep,
Or your confidante can seduce the hateful creature,
  Keep him occupied, spin out time.   650

But what's the point of such unimportant digressions, when
    any
  Guard can be bought with a trifling bribe?
Bribes – believe me – will purchase gods no less than mortals:
  Even Jupiter can be placated by gifts.
655 What's the wise man to do? When fools enjoy such presents
  Why not accept the offering, hold your tongue?
But you'll need to purchase your guardian on a long-term basis:
  The favours he bestows he'll repeat *ad lib*.

I remember once complaining that you had to watch out for
660   Your friends: it's not men alone
To whom this applies. If you show yourself over-trustful,
  Other women will reap your pleasures: the hare
You started, they'll hunt. Watch that girl with the spare
    bedroom
  Who's so eager to help you – believe me, I've
Been in there more than once. And don't have a maid who's
665   too pretty –
  She's often usurped her mistress's role with me –
I must be crazy going on like this. Why charge bare-breasted
  Against the foe? Why testify to my own
Betrayal? Game birds don't notify the fowler
670   Where he can take them; no hind sets a savage pack
On her own trail –
            Damn advantage! I'll stick to my purpose,
  Arm the girls with Lemnian swords, expose my heart
To their thrusts. Just make us believe we're loved – a simple
  Assignment: desire is quick to kindle faith
675 In what it seeks. Let a woman glance sweetly at her lover,
  Sigh deeply, ask him why he's so late,
Then start crying, pretend to be cross about some rival,
  Claw his face with her nails –
That'll convince him in no time, he'll soon start feeling
680   Sorry for her, say 'Why, the poor little thing,
She's just crazy about me!' And if he's smart, if his mirror
  Flatters his profile, then (he thinks) goddesses too

Will compete for his favours. But however badly he wrongs
   you,
  Don't look put out. When there's talk of some other girl,
Keep calm, don't jump to conclusions: just how dangerous
   snap judgements   685
Can be, the story of Procris should demonstrate.

High under flowery Hymettus' violet hillside
  Flows a sacred spring: soft earth,
Lush turf, a little spinney of trailing arbutus,
  Dark myrtle, rosemary, scented bay,   690
Thick-burgeoning boxwood, the brittle tamarisk, slender
  Lucerne, domestic pines, a gentle stir
And rustle of warm spring breezes through that variegated
  Leafage, an airy caress blown over the grass.
Here Cephalus came to enjoy his siesta, hounds and huntsmen 695
  Abandoned, here he'd stretch out
When weary. 'Come hither,' he'd cry, 'come, changeable Aura,
  Come to my bosom, relieve my sultry heat!'
Some stupid tattling busybody remembered this utterance,
  Told it to Cephalus' wife.   700
Poor Procris thought 'Aura' was the name of a rival –
  She fainted, struck dumb with sudden grief,
Turned pale as late vine-leaves, caught by winter's onset
  When the clustering grapes have been picked,
Or ripe quinces, bending the bough they hang from, or cornel- 705
  Berries while they're still unfit to eat.
When she came round, she rent her flimsy garments,
  Raked nails down her innocent cheeks,
And at once rushed out down the street, hair all dishevelled,
  Like a thyrsus-crazed Maenad. When   710
She got near the spot, she left her companions in the valley
  And tiptoed bravely into the wood, alone.
What went on in your mind as you lurked there, jealous-crazy,
  Procris? What fire consumed your frantic heart?
Any moment she'd come now, this Aura, you thought, whoever 715
  She might be, and you'd see their shame

With your own eyes. Now you regretted coming (you never
  Wanted to catch him at it), now you were glad,
As love spun you every which way. Name, place, informer,
720 *All urged belief; and always, what the mind*
Fears may be true it thinks is true.

                                    When she saw the flattened
  Grass where a body had lain, her heart beat fast
In her trembling bosom. By now it was noon, the shadows
    shrunken
  At the midpoint between dawn and dusk,
And – look! – mercurial Cephalus came back through the
725   woodlands,
  Rinsed his hot face at the spring, while Procris lay
Hidden, taut, anxious. He settled down in his usual
  Grassbed. 'Soft Zephyrs, gentle Aura, blow
On me!' he called. Poor girl, when she grasped her
    more-than-welcome
730 Misunderstanding, the colour flowed back to her face
And the sense to her brain: up she sprang, thrashed through
    the foliage,
  A wife making a beeline for her beloved's arms.
He – thinking the movement a beast's – with youthful
    swiftness
  Jack-knifed to his feet, spear poised. *You fool,*
735 *What are you at? That's no beast, hold back your weapon! –*
Too late, ah God, you've hit her, the shaft's
Through your girl!
                    'My love'; she whispered, 'you've pierced
    this loving
  Heart of mine yet again, the last
Of so many wounds from Cephalus! Though I pass untimely,
740 No rival's displaced me: *that* will make the earth
Lie light on my bones. Now the breeze that I mistrusted
  Gathers my yielding spirit: I faint, I'm gone –
Close my eyes with your dear hand –'
                                    He clasped her dying
  Body to his, rained tears on the cruel wound,
745 And as the last breath ebbed from her (poor rash lady!)

The lips of her sad lover gathered it in.

Enough of digressions! If I'm to steer my weary vessel
    Safe into harbour, I needs must tackle the bare
Facts of the case. You're anxiously expecting me to escort you
    To parties: here too you solicit my advice.   750
Arrive late, when the lamps are lit; make a graceful entrance –
    Delay enhances charm, delay's a great bawd.
Plain you may be, but at night you'll look fine to the tipsy:
    Soft lights and shadows will mask your faults.
Take your food with dainty fingers: good table-manners
    matter: 755
    Don't besmear your whole face with a greasy paw.
Don't eat first at home, and nibble – but equally, don't
    indulge your
    Appetite to the full, leave something in hand.
If Paris saw Helen stuffing herself to the eyeballs
    He'd detest her, he'd feel her abduction had been   760
A stupid mistake. But drinking, for girls, is another matter –
    It suits them: desire and wine go well
In tandem. Note, too, that a strong head makes for steady
    Feet and a clear mind, no seeing double. The girl
Who's passed out drunk is the most disgusting object,   765
    Deserves to be laid by anyone in sight;
And falling asleep when the table's cleared is just as
    Risky: pudendal things befall a snoozing girl.

What's left I blush to tell you; but kindly Venus
    Claims as uniquely hers   770
All that raises a blush. Each woman should know herself,
    pick methods
    To suit her body: one fashion won't do for all.
Let the girl with a pretty face lie supine, let the lady
    Who boasts a good back be viewed
From behind. Milanion bore Atalanta's legs on   775
    His shoulders: nice legs should always be used this way.
The petite should ride horse (Andromache, Hector's Theban
    Bride, was too tall for these games: no jockey she);

If you're built like a fashion model, with willowy figure,
780　　Then kneel on the bed, your neck
A little arched; the girl who has perfect legs and bosom
　　Should lie sideways on, and make her lover stand.
Don't blush to unbind your hair like some ecstatic maenad
　　And tumble long tresses about
785　Your upcurved throat. If childbirth's seamed your belly
　　With wrinkles, then offer a rear
Engagement, Parthian style. Sex has countless positions –
　　An easy and undemanding one is to lie
On your right side, half-reclining. Neither Delphi nor Ammon
790　　Will tell you more truth than my Muse:
Long experience, if anything, should establish credit: trust my
　　Art, and let these verses speak for themselves!
A woman should melt with passion to her very marrow,
　　The act should give equal pleasure to them both:
795　Keep up a flow of seductive whispered endearments,
　　Use sexy taboo words while you're making love,
And if nature's denied you the gift of achieving a climax,
　　Moan as though you were coming, put on an act!
(The girl who can't feel down there is really unlucky,
800　　Missing out on what both sexes should enjoy.)
Only take care that you make your performance convincing,
　　Thrash about in a frenzy, roll your eyes,
Let your cries and gasping breath suggest what pleasure
　　You're getting (that part has its own private signs).
805　After the pleasures of sex, though, *don't* try to dun your lover
　　For a present: such habits defeat
Their own ends. And don't open all the bedroom windows:
　　Much of your body is better left unseen.

Our sport is ended: high time to quit this creative venture,
810　　Turn loose the swans that drew my poet's car.
As once the young men, so now let my girl-disciples
　　Inscribe their trophies: *Ovid was my guide.*

CURES FOR LOVE

'Wars,' said Love, after reading this booklet's name and title,
   'I see wars are being planned against me.' 'Please don't charge
Your favourite poet with such a crime, Cupid,' I answered,
   'Think of the times I've borne, under your command,
The colours you gave me! No Diomede I, to wound your   5
   Mother, so that she fled to the rarified heights
Of heaven in Mars's chariot: some young men may grow tepid,
   But I've always been a lover, and if you should ask
What I'm up to now – I'm in love. Besides, I've published a
     system
   For winning you over: what was pure instinct once   10
Is now done by rule. Dear boy, I'm betraying neither
   You nor my art; this new Muse will not reweave
Or unravel past work. Good luck to the happy lover, let him
   Rejoice in his passion, sail on with a following wind –
But for those who suffer the whims of an unworthy mistress   15
   Help is at hand: learn the comfort which my art
Has to bestow! Why does one poor lover fasten
   A noose round his neck, and swing – depressing load –
From the roofbeam, or another run a sword through his
     gizzard?
   You, Love, you peace-lover, *you* get blamed   20
For their slaughter. Let the man who'll die (unless he lays off)
   Of helpless passion, lay off – then you'll have no deaths
On your conscience. Besides, you're a child, should play
     games only:
   So, play: a mild regime goes well with your years.
You might have employed the naked arrows of warfare,   25
   But *your* shafts are untainted by deadman's blood.
Let your stepfather wield the sword and sharp spear, striding

Victorious through the carnage, red with gore:
Stick to your mother's arts, for them we practise safely –
30   No mother's bereavement is ever their fault;
Cause doors to be battered down by midnight brawlers,
    And many a garland to be hung
On their lintels; bring young men and shy girls together,
    Teach them the tricks to outwit
35 Suspicious husbands; show a shut-out swain on the doorstep
    How to curse and flatter by turns,
How to sing doleful ditties – such tears should well content
        you,
    Why risk the reproach of death? Yours isn't the torch
To light hungry funeral pyres.' Then Love, all golden, moving
40   His jewelled wings, said: 'Finish your purposed task.'

Attend to my precepts, then, you disappointed gallants,
    All those whom their loves have utterly betrayed.
Let him who taught you to love now teach you love's cure –
    Take succour from the hand that struck the wound!
45 Herbs healing and noxious grow in the same hedgerow,
    And often the rose will bloom
Close by the nettle; Achilles' spear, that wounded
    Telephus, also healed the wound it made.
(Whatever I tell the men, please believe me, ladies, is meant
        for
50   You too: I'm giving arms to both sides,
And even though some point may not directly concern you,
    Yet much can be learnt by example.) To quench
The fierce flames of desire is a profitable objective –
    Don't let your heart be enslaved
55 To its particular vice. Had Phyllis obeyed my precepts,
    She'd have lived to retread the path she took
That ninth and fatal time; had poor doomed Dido, never
    Would she have stood on that high tower and watched
The Trojan fleet spread sail; had Medea, jealous outrage
60   Would have drawn the line at killing her sons to spite
Their father Jason. Had Tereus, so besotted with Philomela,

Used my techniques, *he* could have avoided rape –
And life as a hoopoe. Give me Pasiphaë, she'll abandon
Her taurine fixation; give me Phaedra, her taboo
Desires will evaporate. Entrust Paris to me, and Helen's   65
Safe with her husband, the Greeks will never bring
Troy's citadel down. Had Scylla perused my pamphlets, Nisus
Wouldn't have lost that purple lock.
With me for leader, men, control your ruinous urges;
With me for leader, let ship and crew run straight!   70
When you were learning the love-game, you had to study Ovid:
You still need to read him now.
I am your public deliverer, will lighten hearts hard mastered
By passion: so welcome, each one of you, the rod
That proclaims your freedom! My opening prayer, Apollo,   75
Inventor of music and all healing arts,
Is to you: may your laurel protect me, help poet and healer
Alike, since the labours of both are your concern.

If you change your mind, then stop at the very first threshold
While you still may, while the impulse stirring your heart   80
Is moderate still. Crush out the bad seed of this sudden
Disease before it can grow, let your horse hold back
At the outset. Waiting breeds strength, time ripens tender
Grapes, turns the green herbage of bristling corn.
The tree that now spreads its welcome shade for travellers   85
Began life planted as a fragile slip
In the topsoil: one hand would have been enough to uproot it –
Now it towers immense, made great by its own strength.
With sharp and circumspect mind search out the nature
Of that which you love: if the yoke   90
Might one day gall, throw it off! Resist at the beginning:
When the disease has fed fat on long delay
Medicine comes too late. So make haste, don't wait for
tomorrow –
If you're unready today, by then you'll be
Even less prepared. Love's a con, feeds on delaying tactics: 95
Tomorrow is always the best day

For making your break to freedom. Few rivers start from
    mighty
  Sources, most broaden as they flow, fed full
By tributary streams. Had Myrrha realized sooner
100   How heinous the crime she was planning, she'd not be
A myrrh-tree today, bark hiding her blushes. I've seen a
    wound that
  Could have been healed on the spot, but went bad
When neglected too long. Yet because we love to reap the
    harvest
  Of Venus, we always say: 'Tomorrow will do
105 Just as well' – and meanwhile the silent flames are creeping
  Into our guts, while the evil tree's roots thrust
Down deeper still. Thus if the first-aid season's
  Been missed, if love's set firm in a captive heart,
A tougher problem remains. But because I'm summoned
110   Late to the patient's bedside, that doesn't mean
I must abandon the case. Philoctetes should have severed,
  With a firm hand, the gangrene from his flesh –
And yet, the tale goes, he was healed years later, living
  To strike the final blow that brought Troy down.
115 There: a moment ago I was hastening to expel your
  Ills at first blush, but now the help I bring
Comes late in the day. When you're trying to extinguish
  A fire, either catch it quick or let it burn out.
While its fury's on course, then cede to that coursing fury:
120   All such impetuous power is hard to face.
Any swimmer's a fool who thrashes against the current
  When he could have gone slantwise, downstream.
The impatient and still intractable temper rejects my
  Art with contempt, abominates every word
125 A counsellor gives. Best wait till the victim will let me examine
  His wounds, till he's ready to hear the truth.
Who but a fool would try to stop a mother weeping
  At her son's graveside? That's no place for advice.
When her tears are all shed, when her heartache's had
    appeasement,

Then use your words to ease the knot of pain.   130
Good timing's an art, a medicine almost: wine given
    At the right time's a boon, at the wrong
Can do positive harm. If you pick an unsuitable moment
    Your veto will irritate, inflame the disease.

So the moment you feel yourself treatable by my system,   135
    Act as I tell you. *No leisure* – that's rule
Number one. Leisure stimulates love, leisure watches the
    lovelorn,
    Leisure's the cause and sustenance of this sweet
Evil. Eliminate leisure, and Cupid's bow is broken,
    His torches lie lightless, scorned.   140
As a plane-tree rejoices in wine, as a poplar in water,
    As a marsh-reed in swampy ground, so Venus loves
Leisure: if you want an end to your loving, keep busy –
    Love gives way to business – and you'll be safe.
Listlessness, too much sleep (no morning appointments),
    nights at   145
    The gambling-tables, or on the bottle – these
Inflict no wounds, yet ruin your moral fibre, open
    A way for insidious Love to breach your hearts.
Cupid homes in on sloth, detests the active – so give that
    Bored mind of yours some really absorbing work: 150
Public business, the law-courts, a friend in need of Counsel –
    Join the smart urban-legal civilian set!
Or else be a soldier (the young man's proper profession),
    And watch your erotic frolics quit the field!
The fugitive Parthian, fresh cause of glorious triumph,   155
    Sees Caesar's troops come crunching across his steppes;
So conquer Love's *and* the Parthians' arrows together,
    Score a double, bring home to your country's gods
Not one but two trophies. When pricked by Diomedes' weapon
    Venus quit fighting, left her lover Mars   160
To bear the brunt of the battle. Why do you think Aegisthus
    Became an adulterer? Easy: he was idle – and bored.
Everyone else was away at Troy on a lengthy

Campaign: all Greece had shipped
165 Its contingents across. Suppose he hankered for warfare? Argos
    Had no wars to offer. Suppose he fancied the courts?
Argos lacked litigation. Love was better than doing nothing.
    That's how Cupid slips in; that's how he stays.

What else diverts the mind? Country matters, good farming –
170 These can oust all other concerns.
Tame and yoke oxen, set them to ploughing, make them
    Force the share through your hard soil;
Bury your seed-corn in the upturned furrow, coax your
    Land into yielding a bumper crop.
175 Look, there are branches so heavy with clustering apples
    The tree can scarcely support the weight of its own
Fruit; look beyond, at the chuckling water-channels,
    At the sheep as they crop lush grass;
There go the goats up the fells and rocky outcrops,
180 Soon they'll be back with full
Udders to suckle their kids. The shepherd plays his
    pan-pipes,
    Well-trained dogs at heel. From the depths
Of a nearby wood there comes the sound of anxious lowing
    As a cow calls her missing calf.
185 Don't forget the business of smoking out your bees and
    Raiding their hives for the combs –
Autumn brings fruit, while summer's rich with harvests
    And spring offers flowers; a fire
Takes the edge off winter. Your countryman picks the ripened
190 Grapes in due season, has a time to tread
The vintage, a time for reaping and binding, a time to
    Harrow the stubbled soil. You yourself
Can plant out shoots in your well-irrigated garden,
    You yourself can channel the water's flow.
195 In the grafting season make one branch cleave to another,
    Let the tree stand covered with foliage not its own.
When once the mind begins to delight in such pleasures
    Love's done for, flutters away

On enfeebled wings. What else? You could take up hunting:
  Venus
Has often been shamefully forced to quit the field   200
By Diana. Now set your beagles to chase the streaking
  Jack-hare, now spread your nets
On high leafy cols; scare the shy deer from its covert,
  Meet the boar's charge, bring it down
With a shrewd spear-thrust. You'll go to bed exhausted,   205
  Enjoy sound sleep, no girl
To keep you awake. Less taxing, but still a proper occupation
  Is catching small birds with net and snare,
Or camouflaging a fish-hook under exiguous
  Bait for some greedy fish to devour.   210
With these or other devices, till you unlearn your passion,
  You must con yourself on the sly.
Though the chains that hold you are strong, you just need to
      make a lengthy
  Journey, go far away: you'll weep, your mind
Will dwell on the name of your deserted mistress,   215
  Your foot often hesitate midway
Through your travels. The less you're anxious to go,
      the more you
  Should make sure of going, persist,
Force yourself to hurry regardless. Don't pray for rain,
      don't let those
  Foreign sabbaths delay you, or days   220
Of ill-omen. Don't ask how many miles you've covered,
  Or how many still remain; don't fake delays
To keep you around; don't count time, don't keep looking over
  Your shoulder to Rome. Get out, take Parthian flight –
That's worked so far. Some may call my precepts cruel: cruel 225
  I confess they are; yet to recover health
Demands much suffering. When sick, I often swallowed
  Bitter medicines (with an effort), denied myself food.
To cure the body you'll put up with cauterization, suffer
  The knife, let no water pass your parching lips.   230
What won't you do, then, to keep a well-balanced psyche

(Though this part of you costs more
Than the body)? Still, my technique is toughest at the outset –
    Your only task: to survive those first few days.
235 Have you seen how their first yoke galls fresh-broken oxen,
    And the racehorse is chafed by a new girth?
Going abroad is a step you may well find irksome,
    But go you will – and then you'll long to return,
Drawn not by home and country, but by love for your mistress,
240   And camouflaging your weakness with fine words.
Still, once you've set forth, there'll be innumerable distractions:
    The countryside, travelling-companions, that long, long road.
Just a short trip, you reckon? *No good.* Prolong your exile
    Till flame fades to embers, embers to dead ash.
245 If you hasten home without the proper resolution
    Love will renew the battle, war hard
Against you. Despite your absence you'll come back thirsty,
      greedy,
    Your whole venture abroad a dead loss.

If anyone fancies that Thessaly's noxious herbals
250   Or magic arts can help him, that's his affair.
Witchcraft's ways are outdated: Apollo, my patron, offers
    Innocuous aid through the spell
Of holy song. Under my guidance no spirits will be summoned
    Up from their graves, no crone will split the earth
Asunder with horrid cantrips, ripe crops won't jump the
255   hedges
    Into some neighbour's field, the sun's bright orb
Won't fade without warning. All will be just as usual –
    The Tiber flowing seaward, the moon aloft
Bright-riding in heaven. No heart will exorcise its passion
260   By incantations, it takes more than sulphur to drive
Love out. What use were the herbs of Colchis to Medea
    When she wanted to remain in her native home?
Of what avail to Circe her mother's enchantments
    When a favouring wind bore Ulysses' ships away?
265 She tried every trick to stop her crafty guest from leaving –

Yet he hoisted sail and took off. She tried
Every trick to avoid being inflamed by savage passion,
    But Love long dwelt in her unwilling breast.
She could subject men to a thousand metamorphoses:
    The laws of her own heart she could never change.   270
When Ulysses stood, impatient, on the brink of departure
    She still attempted (it's said) to hold him back
With these words: 'I'm not begging you, now, to be my
        husband –
    Though this, I recall, was at first
My fondest hope; though I would have made you a worthy
        consort,   275
    Being a goddess, child of the mighty Sun.
All I want is more time: please, don't be over-hasty –
    What less could I ask of you?
You can see how rough the sea is, you ought to fear it:
    Later the wind will sit better for your sails.   280
Why fly now? There's no new Troy here in the building,
    No captain to call his old comrades back to arms.
Here's love, here's peace, in which I alone am wounded,
    And this land will enjoy safety beneath your sway.'
But while she yet spoke, Ulysses cast off, left harbour,   285
    And the wind that filled his sails also blew away
Her useless arguments. Poor Circe, burning, resorted
    To her usual tricks – and still couldn't douse *that* fire.
So if you look to my arts for help in trouble, never
    Rely on magic, never trust a spell.   290

If some compelling motive should keep you in the City,
    Here's my special in-the-City advice:
Self-preservation is best achieved by whoever can shatter
    The bonds that cripple his spirit, cast out the pain
From his psyche once and for ever. A man of such rare
        courage   295
    Compels my admiration, but needs no hints
I can give him. No, it's you, who find unlearning passion
    For what you love so painful, who long to do it but can't,

That should follow my precepts. Keep thinking about the
    disfavours
300   Your mistress has done you, the losses you've sustained:
'She has this, she has that, and – not content with her
    plunder –
The greedy bitch has bankrupted me as well!.
She's promised me love, then cheated on her promise –
The times she's left me keeping vigil all night
305 Outside her door! Other men turn her on, for me she's frigid –
    Any travelling salesman can have her, yet I can't.'
Let such thoughts be gall to embitter all your feelings,
    Nurse them, build thence the seedbed of your hate!
Eloquence of expression would also be an advantage –
310   Just *suffer*, though, and you'll find
Fluency comes by itself. Not long ago *my* fancy
    Lit on a girl who didn't suit my tastes:
The doctor was sick – most embarrassing, I admit it –
    But my own prescriptions worked a cure.
315 It helped me to keep dwelling on the flaws in my mistress;
    When I did this, it often brought relief.
'Look at her legs,' I'd say, 'they're just plain awful –'
    (To tell the truth, they were fine);
'And her arms, now, you know, *they're* not exactly pretty –'
320   (To tell the truth, they were);
'How short she is' – she wasn't – 'how much she demands of
    her lover –'
    (Ah, *that* was what put the sharpest edge
On my hatred.) Evil and good are near neighbours; often
    We criticize the virtue, accept the vice.
Whenever you can, run down your girl's attractions,
325   fudge your
    True opinion by a hair's breadth:
If she's plump, then call her 'bloated', 'black' if she's swarthy;
    A svelte girl labelled 'beanpole' doesn't sound good.
She's anything but naïve? Then say she's 'saucy' –
330   Or if she's virtuous, 'naïve' is the word.
What else? Any talent you know your mistress is short on

Keep cajoling her to display:
If she hasn't a voice, then insist on the poor girl singing,
   If she's all arms and legs, make her dance;
Her accent's appalling? Engage her in endless conversation;   335
   She can't strum a chord? Then ask
For a solo lyre recital. She walks awkwardly? Promenade her.
   Her breasts are great udders? Don't let her wear a bra.
If her teeth stick out, get her laughing with funny stories;
   If she's weak-eyed, use pathos, make her cry.   340
You might also try out a brisk early morning visit,
   Unannounced, before she's put on her public face.
We're dazzled by feminine adornment, by the surface,
   All gold and jewels: so little of what we observe
Is the girl herself. And where (you may ask) amid such plenty   345
   Can our object of passion be found? The eye's deceived
By Love's smart camouflage. So arrive without warning,
     catch her
   Defenceless (while *you're* quite safe): her own defects
Will undo her, poor dear. (All the same, too much reliance
   On this rule is a risk: men have often been deceived   350
By artless beauty.) So when she's smearing all that concocted
   Muck on her face is another good time – don't be shy –
To call and inspect her. You'll find pots of make-up in a
     thousand
   Colours, and lanoline grease that's melted and run
Down into her sweaty cleavage: I've often been nauseated   355
   By the putrefying stink of the stuff, a Harpies' feast.

At this point – since Love needs removal from every quarter –
   Some hints on how to conduct yourself during The Act.
There's much on this score that I'd blush to set down:
     just figure
   It out for yourself, read between the lines, augment   360
What I tell you. Some critics, you see, have been attacking
   My poems: in *their* opinion my Muse
Is a scandalous wanton. Yet, so long as I keep my public
   And remain a household name, let the few impugn

365 My work as they please! The envious scholar belittles
    Homer's achievement – but only Homer ensures
That the scholar's name is remembered. Even Virgil's *Aeneid*
    Has been savaged by impious tongues –
Envy attacks the highest, as winds scour mountain summits,
370   And God's flung bolts strike peaks.
So you (whoever you are) who take offence at my licence,
    Learn at least to match metre and theme –
Homer's hexameter goes well with doughty warfare,
    But for erotic trifles it's out of place;
375 Tragic actors declaim: high wrath befits the tragic buskin;
    For commonplaces we put on the comic clog;
When invective's needed, unsheath your sharp iambics
    (Either cursive or last-foot-lame).
Let seductive Elegy celebrate Love and his quiver,
380   Play the frivolous mistress, follow her bent.
To recount the great deeds of Achilles, Callimachean
    Elegiacs won't do; epic verse is out of place
For romance. Who'd accept a soubrette as a tragic leading
      lady?
Andromache played *à la* Thais puts one's teeth
385 On edge. But Thais belongs to my Art, my pleasure's
    Free-roving, not for nice wives: oh yes,
Thais belongs to my Art. If my Muse can match her sportive
    Theme, then I've won, and the charge
Against her is false. So burst, gnawing Envy! I'm famous
390   Already, and if I keep on like this, my fame
Will grow greater yet. You're too quick – if I live, you'll be
      sorry:
I've plenty more poems in my head.
My taste for fame's a delight that grows with adulation;
    My horses still pant and strain
395 On the hill's lowest slopes. What the epic owes to Virgil,
    Elegy likewise owes – and admits it – to me.
So much for rebuttal of Envy. Now rein in more closely,
    Stick to your own poetic track!

*

When you're eager for intercourse, all a young stud's labours,
    And the promised night is close, then to make   400
Quite sure your mistress's charms don't overwhelm you
    If you come to her lusty-fresh, my advice
Is to get in some other girl first, slake your prime voluptuous
    Urges on her: when it's time for round number two
You'll be slow off the mark. Delay most sharpens pleasure:
    winter   405
    Makes us yearn for the sun, in summer we covet shade,
And a drink when we're thirsty. One tip I'm embarrassed to
    tell you,
    But will all the same – choose a position you think
The least effective or suitable. (That's not difficult: women
    seldom
    Admit the truth to themselves, there's nothing they don't   410
Find becoming.) What else? Keep the shutters fully open,
    Let daylight reveal her flaws.
When your passion's spent, when you're past the post and
    lying
    Flat out, exhausted, mind a blank,   415
Revulsion making you wish you'd never had a woman
    And swear you won't touch one again for years,
Then mark and remember every fault in her body,
    Turn a bright light on her defects.
Some may call such things trifling, and so they are: but
    though singly   420
    They amount to nothing, their cumulative aid
Is not to be sneezed at. The bite of a minuscule viper
    Kills the massive ox, and it's often some lightweight dog
That holds the wild boar at bay. So gather all my precepts –
    Safety in numbers: little safeguards soon add up.   425
Still, since there exist as many fashions as postures,
    There's no way (as I see it) I can describe them all.
What could not give the least offence to your own feelings
    In another man's judgement might well
Be a cause for reproach. One lover was stopped
    in mid-performance

430   By a glimpse of the girl's slit as she spread
    Her legs, another by pudendal stains on the bedsheets
       When she got up after the act.
    If such incidents can affect you, you're the merest trifler,
       And the flame that lit your heart was weak indeed.
435 But once let Love draw his strongbow to some purpose
       And wound you – you'll soon be in search
    Of effective first-aid. What about the man whose passion
       Was secretly watching a girl perform that act
    Of discharge which custom makes private? God forbid I
       should offer
440   Such counsel: though it might help, it's not
    Admissible. My advice, then, is to keep *two* mistresses –
       Few men have the stamina for more.
    When the mind's divided, and strays in opposite directions,
       Each desire saps the other's strength.
445 Much channelling reduces the mightiest rivers;
       Rake out the fire, and even the fiercest flame
    Dies down. Your well-caulked ship needs a double anchor,
       One hook will not suffice for those liquid depths.
    The man who's long been equipped with twin consolations
450   Long since emerged as victor in the high
    Citadel: but you – pledged, like a fool, to one mistress –
       Must now go find a new love.
    Minos worked off his hots for Pasiphaë on Procris,
       The second wife of Phineus routed the first,
455 And by making room in bed for Callirrhoë, Alcmaeon
       Drove darling Alphesiboea from his heart.
    Oenone would have kept Prince Paris for ever, had his mistress
       Helen not cut her out. The Odrysian king
    Tereus enjoyed his wife's beauty – but her imprisoned
460   Sister was an even prettier girl.
    Why waste time over all these boring examples? Every
       Old love's eclipsed by a new. The loss
    Of one son among many makes less grief for a mother
       Than when she must wail: 'You, you were my only one!'
    And lest you should think I'm making new rules for you to
465   follow

(Would that the cachet of the idea *were* mine!)
Even Agamemnon saw this – and what should he *not* see,
  With all Greece subject to his rule?
War brought the victor a captive, Chryseis: he loved her –
  Yet her idiot of a father wandered round   470
Shedding big tears. Why cry, you old horror? They're happy;
  This inept concern of yours does nothing but harm.
When Calchas – safe in Achilles' protection – gave orders
  For the girl to be returned, and she was brought
To her father's house, Agamemnon said: 'There's this other   475
  Whose beauty near-matches hers, whose name is the same
Bar one syllable: her, if he's wise, will Achilles freely yield me –
  If not, let him feel my power! And if any of you
Feels tempted to criticize my decision, fellow-Achaeans,
  My strong hand grasps the sceptre: that has to count   480
For something. If I am king, yet sleep with no captive
  Concubine, let Thersites usurp my throne!'
Such were his words. He took her. She proved an ample solace
  For his previous girl. One passion was slaked, replaced
By another. So take the hint from Agamemnon's example,   485
  Acquire new flames, let your love be split two ways
Where two roads meet. How to find them, you ask? Read my
    handbook,
  And your boat will soon be scuppers-deep in girls!

If my precepts have any value, if Apollo delivers
  Useful advice to mortals through the words   490
I utter, now hear this: though your heart be hot as lava,
  Make your mistress believe you all too cold;
Feign indifference; if you're sad, don't let her notice;
  When you feel like crying, laugh.
(I'm not saying you have to jettison your passion   495
  In mid-course: my regimen is not *that* harsh.)
Simulate what you are not, pretend the fit's abated –
  Faking it will lead to the genuine thing.
To avoid social drinking, I've often acted drowsy,
  Then found myself really nodding off;   500
I've laughed at the dupe who made a pretence of loving,

Only to fall, like a fowler, into his own snare.
Love enters the mind through habit, is by habit evicted;
    The man who can counterfeit sanity will prove sane.
505 She's told you to come, so come on the night appointed:
    You arrive, but the house is locked. Just grin
And bear it. Spare the poor door your insults (or endearments),
    Don't lie on that stony sill all night;
The following day, don't indulge in sour recriminations,
510   And keep all telltale signs
Of distress off your face. When she sees your interest waning
    She'll soon swallow her pride. (One more
Pay-off from my advice.) Yet deceive yourself too, don't set up
    Any deadline for tapering off your affair. A horse
515 Will often strain at the bit. Conceal your advantage;
    What you don't proclaim will happen. The bird avoids
A too-obvious net. Don't encourage her self-conceit,
      don't let her
Despise you. Play tough: use toughness to make her yield.
Her door's ajar? Walk past; when she calls you back,
      ignore her.
520 You've a date? Don't show up on the night.
Breaking dates is no great hardship if a lack of endurance
    Can secure instant relief through some easy lay.

Now could anyone call my precepts too tough? Why, I even
    At times play the peacemaker's role:
525 Human variety calls for variety of prescription,
    Disease takes a thousand forms, so must the cure.
Some bodies can scarcely be healed by the keen scalpel,
    Yet many derive relief from drugs and herbs.
Suppose you're too soft, can't break loose, are held in bondage
530   With cruel Love's foot set hard
On your neck: give up the struggle, let the winds rule your
      sailing,
    Follow the run of the waves, let your oar drift.
You have to slake your thirst, you're parched and desperate:
    I admit the need. Drink, then, from midstream –

But drink even more than your heart and passion crave for,   535
    Till your gullet's full, till the water runs down your chin.
Go in there, enjoy your girl with no prohibitions, let her
    Consume your nights and days alike.
Aim for a glut of passion: glutted hearts break off liaisons;
    When you feel you can do without it, still hold on   540
Till you're fed to the back teeth, till love chokes on abundance,
    Till you're sick of the very sight of her house.

That love, too, is tenacious which diffidence nurtures:
    If you want to be rid of it, rid yourself of fear.
Any man who's scared of rivals poaching his women   545
    Will hardly be cured by doctors, even the best.
Which son will any mother love most among her offspring?
    The soldier, who may never (she fears)
Return from the wars. Near the Colline Gate stands an ancient
    Temple of Venus: there dwells Lethaean Love,   550
Who heals hearts with the gift of forgetfulness, douses his
      torches
    In that cool, annealing stream.
Thither come youths who hope to blank out their promises,
    And girls impaled on the charms
Of hard-hearted lovers. This is what Cupid told me   555
    (Was he really there, or a dream? A dream, I think):
'You who induce – and who cure – love's troublesome passions,
    Ovid, add *this* to your precepts. God has assigned
A greater or lesser share of misfortune to each person:
    Let him meditate on his woes, he'll be shot of love.   560
Let the man who's worried by monthly mortgage repayments
    Concentrate in agony on the lump sum
He's borrowed. Suppose your one complaint is a cruel father:
    Then keep that cruel father well in mind.
Here's a husband scraping by on his wife's mean dowry –
      let him   565
    Blame her for blighting his career.
You possess a rich estate, a fruitful vineyard? Worry
    In case the sun scorches your unripe grapes.

A merchant awaiting his ship's return should daily
570   Brood on the cruel sea, our wreck-littered coasts.
X has a drafted son, Y a marriageable daughter –
    Agony! Yet indeed who *isn't* strapped
With a thousand reasons for worry? To whip up hatred
        against his
    Mistress Helen, Paris ought to have dwelt
On his brothers' deaths –' Still speaking, the boyish
575   simulacrum
    Faded out of my dream (if dream it was).
What's to do now? My pilot's gone overboard in mid-passage,
    And I'm driven perforce to explore uncharted seas.

Lonely places, you lovers, are dangerous: shun lonely places,
580   Don't opt out – you'll be safer in a crowd!
You've no need for secrecy (secrecy fosters passion):
    From now on company's what you need.
If you're solitary you'll be sad, your forsaken mistress
    Always there in your mind's eye,
A too-vivid presence. That's why night's grimmer than
585   daytime:
    The friends who might relieve your mood aren't there.
Don't avoid conversation, don't shut the door on callers,
    Don't hide yourself away and cry in the dark.
Always have some Pylades there to back up Orestes:
590   Of friendship's various benefits, this
Is by no means the slightest. What was it destroyed poor Phyllis
    But the secret forest? The cause of her death is clear:
Being alone. Like some Thracian Maenad, all dishevelled
    By the god's triennial rites, hair flying wild,
595 She ran; now paused, where she could, to gaze out seaward,
    Now fell exhausted amid the dunes,
Cried: 'Faithless Demophoön!' to the unhearing breakers
    Till sobs strangled her words.
There was a narrow path, a shady tunnel
600   Which she often walked to the sea:
Nine times the poor girl paced it, upbraiding her lover, deathly

256

Pale, glancing down at her girdle, then up
At the branches: undecided, she shrank from action, fearful
    Fingers trembling towards her throat.
Had you not been alone then, Phyllis (and how I wish it!),
        the mourning   605
    Forest would never have shed its leaves
For your loss. So let Phyllis' fate warn you, avoid excessive
    Seclusion, all mistress-vexed lovers, all man-vexed girls!

There once was a youth who did all that my Muse commanded
    And was almost safe in harbour. But then   610
He relapsed: he'd fallen among some passionate lovers,
    So that Love resumed the weapons he'd laid aside.
If you love, but against your will, then shun contagion:
    Even cattle are often plagued this way. To observe
The lovesick infects the eyes that watch them; through contact   615
    Our bodies are victimized by countless ills.
Water will sometimes seep from a nearby river
    Into hard-parched soil: thus love
Will seep in unseen unless you detach yourself from your lover:
    This is a game at which we all excel.   620
Another young man, though cured, had a neighbourhood
        problem –
    Running into his mistress got him down,
He just couldn't take it. The half-healed scar reopened,
    His old wound was back, my arts
Sustained defeat. When the house next door is blazing,   625
    How fight off the flames? Best to be somewhere else.
Don't stroll down the colonnade which is *her* favourite,
    Avoid the kind of company she keeps.
What's the use of nostalgia? Who wants cold love reheated?
    Live – if you can – in another world. (It's hard,   630
When you're ravenous, to hold back from a laden table;
    Bubbling water puts an edge on your thirst.
Hard, too, to restrain the bull that's glimpsed the heifer;
    A stallion always whinnies at sight of a mare.)
Even then, if you're going to reach shore at length, deserting   635

257

The girl herself isn't enough:
Bid farewell to her sister and mother, to that conniving
  Old nurse, to whoever plays the slightest part
In your mistress's life. Don't accept fake-tearful greetings
640   Brought round by maid or houseboy in her name,
And – though you may ache to know – never ask what she's
      doing:
  Be patient, it'll pay you to hold your tongue.
You too, who keep endlessly bitching about the mistress
  You've left, who insist on telling just why
Your affair broke off – please, quit complaining: the best
645   revenge is
  Silence. Just let her dribble away
From your desires. Keep quiet, don't tell us it's all over:
  The man who protests to the world
'I'm not in love', is. Don't attempt to extinguish your ardour
650   At a stroke, but by slow degrees: phase it out
And you'll be quite safe. Flash floods run deeper than a
      perennial
  River, but soon are gone: the river flows
All year through. Let love wane in slow evanescence,
  Fade on the breeze and die.
655 Yet to hate the girl you once loved is a crime, an end befitting
  None but a savage: indifference will suffice,
And the man whose love breeds hatred either loves still
  Or will find his misery hard to exorcise.
Man and woman so lately one, then enemies – that's ugly,
  Even Venus of the Law-Courts can never condone such
660   strife.
Yet men often prosecute a mistress, and still adore her
  Regardless: where there's no strife, love slips
Away without any urging. Take the case of my young client,
  His wife in a litter, waiting, his every word
665 Abristle with threats against her. Brandishing a summons,
  'Come on out!' he told her. She did. At the sight,
Dumbstruck, he dropped both arms, let fall his petition,
  Went into a clinch, said: 'You win.'

A friendly separation is safer – and more becoming: don't
    hurry
Into court from your bedroom, let her keep   670
The presents you gave her without any litigation –
    Your gain will far outweigh
Any loss you incur. And if, later, some chance should bring
    you
    Together, then keep memory fresh, deploy
All the weapons I've given you. Fight on, courageous soldier,   675
    Now comes your call to arms, now you must slay
Penthesilea herself! Now remember that hard threshold,
    Fond lover-boy, and your rival, and those vain
Oaths that the gods witnessed: don't tidy your hair to meet her,
    Don't drape your gown in a loose   680
Conspicuous style, do *nothing* to impress this discarded mistress,
    Just treat her as one of the crowd.

Though each of us can learn from his own example, let me
    Suggest what it is that most frustrates
All our efforts. We hope to be loved, so postpone the final
    break-off   685
    Too long: while our self-conceit still holds
We're a credulous lot. Don't believe all they tell you (what's
    more deceptive
    Than women's words?), don't credit the vows they swear
To the eternal gods, don't let yourself be softened
    By a girl in tears – they school their eyes to weep   690
On request. They've countless tricks to assault a lover's feelings,
    He's a rock pounded by waves from every side.
Don't explain your reasons for wanting a separation:
    Nurse your grievance, don't spell it out.
Don't mention her faults, she only might correct them –   695
    Why promote her cause at your expense?
Strength lies in silence: the man who heaps reproaches
    On a girl is asking her to prove him wrong.
No Ulysses I, to steal young Cupid's arrows
    Or douse his torch in the stream,   700

Or clip his glimmering wings, or craftily slacken
  The string of his sacred bow.
All my songs offer wise advice, so obey the singer –
  And do you, healing Apollo, come to my aid,
705 Favour this undertaking! The God is come – hear his quiver
  Rattle, the thrum of his lyre: the God is come,
His signs reveal him. Compare the wool that's dyed in
    Amyclae
  With Tyrian purple – it's inferior stuff;
In the same way, compare *your* girls with famous beauties,
710   And who won't begin to find his mistress a bore?
Either one of those goddesses might have attracted Paris
  Till set against Venus: she eclipsed them both.
And don't compare looks alone, match character and talent –
  Just make sure love doesn't warp
Your judgement. My next point's a small one, but
715   notwithstanding
  Helped many, myself amongst them. Beware
Of re-reading those treasured letters from your seductive
  Ex-mistress: such letters, re-read,
Break down the firmest resolve. Grit your teeth and burn the
    packet,
720   Whispering, 'May this prove the pyre of my love!'
Althea consumed the firebrand that spelt life for her absent
  Son: why shrink from committing lies to the flames?
Remove her wax images too, if you can: why let a mute
    portrait
  Torment you? That was the cause
725 Of Laodameia's death. Places, too, can be dangerous:
  Shun scenes of former love, they stir up grief,
Telling you, *Here she lay, that's the bedroom we slept in,*
  Here's where she gave me a good time
All night. Nostalgia will rub love raw, the old wound's opened
730   Afresh: the most trifling error can cripple the weak.
Just as near-extinct embers, when touched with sulphur,
  Spark back into life, blaze up,
So, unless you avoid what's bound to renew your passion,

Its lately quiescent flame
Will burst out anew. Oh, would that those Greek ships had
    avoided
    The headland, the false lights, an old man's revenge!   735
The canny sailor rejoices when Scylla and Charybdis
    Are behind him; what *you* must shun are scenes
Of bygone pleasure. Let these be your perilous cape, your
    quicksands,
    Your maelstrom waters, your destructive reefs.   740

Some things there are that cannot be consciously ordered,
    Yet happening by chance will often help.
Strip Phaedra's riches away, and her stepson's safe from
    Neptune, no grand-daddy's bull from the sea to scare
His horses; Pasiphaë would have loved more wisely minus   745
    Her property. Wealth fosters wanton love.
Why would no man take Hecale, no woman Irus? Simple:
    He was a beggar, she was poor.
Poverty lacks the wherewithal to nourish passion –
    Though that doesn't make it worth while   750
To want to be poor yourself. What *is* worth while's abstention
    From theatres, until you're heartwhole. Flutes,
Zithers and lyres, the singer's voice, the ballerina's
    Gestures in dance: all these can shake your nerve.
Fictitious love's the main theme of the *corps de ballet*,   755
    The actor's art exhibits, in all its allure,
The temptation you must resist. What's more, though I hate
    to say this,
    Love-poems are *out*: the ban extends to my own
Collected works. Don't read Callimachus, he's no stranger
    To passion; Philetas too can do you harm.   760
Sappho, I know, once helped me to soften up my mistress,
    And whatever Anacreon offers, it's certainly not
A strict code of morals. But then, who could leaf through
    Tibullus
    Unscathed, or Propertius, whose single theme was his
    love

For Cynthia? Who can read Gallus, and end in mere
765   indifference?
My poems, too, catch something of this mood.

But unless our patron Apollo's deluded his poets,
    Competition is always the greatest cause
Of our troubles. Yet do not let yourself picture a rival,
770   Believe that she sleeps alone!
Hermione was all the more urgently coveted by Orestes
    Because she had taken up with another man.
Why this grief, Menelaus? You went to Crete sans Helen,
    And took your time there, away from your bride;
775   But when Paris abducted her, *then* you couldn't live wifeless
    One moment longer; it was another's love
Ignited your own. Achilles wept at Briseis' abduction
    To pleasure great Agamemnon: believe you me,
He wept with good reason – the son of Atreus did what
780   None but an impotent sluggard could fail to do.
Certainly *I* would have done it, and I'm no wiser than he was:
    There we touch on their quarrel's core.
He swore that Briseis was still a virgin – by his truncheon:
    But a truncheon (he figured) is no god.
785   May the gods grant you strength to walk past your abandoned
    Mistress's threshold, may your feet hold firm
To their purpose! You'll make it, hang on, now's the time for
    a headlong
    Gallop, spurring your horse
Down the final straight. In that grotto imagine Lotus-Eaters
790   And Sirens: cram on sail, ply oar!
The man whose rivalry once caused you torment I'd have you
    No longer regard as your foe:
At the least, though your hatred linger, try a greeting –
    When you can manage to kiss him, you're cured!

Then there's diet: let me round off the physician's duties,
795   tell you
    What food you should eat, what avoid.

All onions – Italian, or Greek and African imported –
  Are harmful: so too
Is colewort, it sharpens desire, avoid it, and whatever
  Else may impel you sexwards. Instead   800
Try rue, it sharpens the eyesight – and whatever
  Else may negative the sexual urge.
What's my advice about wine, you ask? Much briefer,
  Much more concise than you might
Have expected. Wine promotes sex – unless you take a skinful 805
  And drown your wits in drink.
A fire's blown up by the wind, by the wind extinguished:
  A gentle breeze fans the flame, a harder gust
Puts it out. Either keep off drink, or else hit the bottle
  Till you're riding high: nothing between will serve.   810

My work is concluded: hang wreaths on my seaworn vessel,
  We've made it to the harbour for which I was bound.
Soon, now, you'll discharge your vows to the inspired poet –
  Men and women alike, healed by my spell.

ON FACIAL TREATMENT
FOR LADIES

Girls, learn from me what treatment will embellish
    Your complexions, how beauty is best preserved.
Cultivation forced barren soil to yield rich cereal
    Harvests, killed off the sharp
5 Encroaching briars; cultivation breeds out the bitter
    Flavour of fruit, the grafted stock adopts
Alien bounty. What's cultivated delights: a lofty building
    Is sheathed in gold leaf, black earth
Lies hid under marble, fleeces are dipped and redipped in
      cauldrons
10   Of Tyrian dye, while Indian ivory's carved
Into exquisite *objets d'art*. Those old-time Sabine women,
    Under the early kings, may have chosen to cultivate
Their fathers' fields, not their own persons: when the red-cheeked
    Matron in her high chair was forever spinning yarn
15 With calloused thumb, when the lambs her daughter pastured
    She would pen herself, herself heap twigs and logs
On the family hearth. But your mothers bred delicate daughters,
    You want to be dressed in cloth of gold, you insist
On elaborate scented coiffures, each different from the last one,
20   Your fingers must sparkle with gems,
And two of those Eastern stones from your chunky necklace
    Used as an earbob would pull the lobe out of shape.
No criticism: you need to make yourselves attractive
    These days, when the *men* are so smart –
25 Why, your husbands adorn themselves like regular ladies,
    And a bride's hard put to it to outshine their style.
Girls preen to please themselves; it makes no difference
    With whom they're in love, you can't
Fault them on turn-out. When they're lost in the depths of the
      country

They still fix their hair: set them down on some remote   30
   Mountain-top, they'll start primping. A certain pleasure's
     Bred by self-satisfaction, a girl delights
In her own beauty. The peacock spreads its much-lauded
     Tail-feathers, struts with dumb pride:
That's how to fan up love, don't touch any witch's hand-picked 35
     Urticant roots, steer clear of her horrid craft,
Put no faith in herbals and potions, abjure the deadly
     Stuff distilled by a mare in heat – all this
Is nonsense: Marsians can't burst snakes by incantations,
     And rivers don't flow uphill to their source,   40
Any more than banging away on metal vessels
     Will bring the moon down from the sky.

Your first concern, girls, should be for proper behaviour:
     With a fine personality, features are sure to please.
Love of character's lasting, but age will ravage beauty,   45
     The pretty face wrinkle and line,
Till a time will come when you'll hate to look in the mirror,
     And misery etches those furrows deeper still.
But probity lasts well, will endure for ages, can carry
     Love with its weight of years.   50

*

Let me show you how, when you first wake in the morning,
     Your face can be bright and fresh.
Take imported Libyan barley, strip off its outer
     Husk and chaff, measure two
Pounds of stripped grain, and add an equal measure   55
     Of vetch steeped in ten raw eggs.
Let this mixture dry in the air, then have your donkey grind it
     Slowly, taking the rough quern round; prepare
Two ounces of powdered hartshorn, taken from a vigorous
     Stag's first fallen antlers; stir this well   60
Into the powdery meal, then sift the mixture,
     At once, through fine-meshed sieves.
Take twelve narcissus-bulbs, skin them and pound them
     (Use a marble block); add them in,

65 With two ounces each of gum and Tuscan spelt-seed,
    And a pound and a half of honey. Any girl
Who uses a face-pack according to this prescription
    Will shine brighter than her own
Mirror. Another good recipe: roast pale seeds of lupin,
70   Then fry up beans, the kind that bring flatulence – six
Measured pounds of each precisely – and have this mixture
    Ground small in the black mill.
Make sure you've got white-lead, and essence of red natron,
    And the iris that comes from Illyria: have them ground
75 By energetic young boys, but see that the proper
    Weight is produced – one ounce apiece. The spots
On your face can be banished by means of a preparation
    Extracted from bird's-nests, and known
As halcyon-cream. How much of this is sufficient,
80   You may ask? The answer is half an ounce. To make
This substance cohesive, and easy to rub all over
    The body, add Attic honey from yellow combs.
Incense, though it placates the gods and angered spirits,
    Is not *all* for flaming altars. When you mix
85 Incense with natron (the kind that's good for cleansing
    The skin), measure each at one third
Of a pound in the scales. Add nine ounces of gum (but strip off
    The bark first), plus a moderate-sized cube
Of rich oily myrrh. Then pound these up and sift them
90   Through a fine sieve; you'll need
Honey to settle the powder. Other useful ingredients
    Are fennel – five scruples, to nine of myrrh –
And dried rose-leaves (one full handful), with salt from the
    Libyan
    Desert, and frankincense: the salt
95 And rose-leaves together should equal the weight of the incense;
    Use barley-water to bind them into a paste.
Though you keep this face-pack on for a short while only,
    It will give you a fine complexion. I have known
One girl who moistened poppies in cold water,
100   Then pounded them up, and rubbed them on her cheeks . . .

*

NOTES AND REFERENCES

THE AMORES

Epigram

The first edition of the *Amores*, in five books, is now lost: it may have coexisted for some while with the revised text in our possession. Ovid began to read his earliest poems in public when he was about eighteen (*Trist.* 4.10.57–60): the five original books were probably published (whether together or separately is unknown) by 15 BC, and the three-book second edition by 9 BC, and in any case not earlier than 11 or later than 1 BC. Ovid's main task, clearly, was the pruning of dead wood and juvenilia. What survived will also have been revised, rearranged, and partly rewritten (perhaps with Propertius Bks 1–3 as a conscious model).

BOOK I

1.1

This introductory poem sets the mood for most of what follows. It is witty, charming, ironical and allusive. Yet the common claim that in the *Amores* Ovid begins and ends with love-poetry, not love, with literature rather than life, I find a little specious. What does Ovid in fact say? He was planning a Virgilian-style epic in hexameters, but unaccountably found himself writing elegiacs. Why? Because of Cupid. (The Roman habit of personifying everything from rust to door-hinges can be confusing at times.) Ovid in fact (cf. lines 19–20) was in love with love, a common symptom among sensitive young men, and one all too likely to produce bad and derivative poetry in one with a literary bent.

What he describes here – camouflaging his personal feelings, as so often, behind a smokescreen of mythic witticisms – is the psychological impact of falling in love with an actual person. The symptoms are well described in the following poem (*Am.* 1.2.1–10), and again masked by an elaborate quasi-mythical conceit, this time with political undertones. The girl is not identified yet: indeed, we do not learn her name till 1.5, by which time she has more than made her presence felt – always assuming that the same person is referred to throughout the earlier poems. Ovid is an expert at delayed-action effects: not for him the urgency of Propertius. I suspect that Ovid found his friend's heart-on-the-sleeve approach a trifle vulgar, and more than a trifle ridiculous. It should not be deduced from this, however, that he despised Propertius' poetry (no one could devote so much space to parodying what he did not at heart admire), or that he lacked passionate feelings himself. We shall have ample evidence on both points throughout the *Amores*.

1ff. As most commentators remind us, the first word of this poem, *arma*, 'arms', is also that of Virgil's *Aeneid*. The reference is designed to point up a contrast *ab initio*. Ovid's programme, unlike that of Virgil, is private, *dégagé*, and not above covertly mocking Augustan imperial propaganda (see Introd, pp. 44ff.).

There has been considerable discussion as to how far, if at all, poets such as Virgil, Horace or Propertius were under discreet pressure to produce Augustan propaganda, direct or indirect. The popular current view is that no such pressure existed. This goes hand in hand with the comparable belief that most mistresses and all homosexual relationships in Roman elegy are mere literary conventions derived from Alexandrian models, and that no real-life antecedent for any literary phenomenon should be sought if a plausible *topos* can be found instead. This seems to me (and, I note with relief, to one or two other recent writers) a misleading exaggeration. The pressure may not have been comparable to that applied today in, say, Soviet Russia, but it was real, dangerous, and not to be discounted. Similarly, literary sexual conventions were to a great extent derived from real-life models.

3–4 The hexameter, a primarily dactylic six-foot line, had been the metre of epic since Homer's day. Elegy employed the 'elegiac couplet', hexameter alternating with pentameter, the latter containing five feet only (or, to be more precise, two groups of two-and-a-half feet each). Epic, being lofty, political, military, and thus 'virile', was felt to outweigh erotic verse by far as serious poetry. Ovid, conscious of this, wavers between the defiant, the apologetic and the mocking-ironic in his attitude; his dominant instinct is to deflate what he undoubtedly regarded as pretentious.

9–10 'Our Lady of Wheatfields' is Ceres, the goddess of grain, crops and husbandry; the 'Virgin Huntress' is Diana (parallel to Greek Artemis), whose particular function, apart from professional virginity, was the chase. The 'War-God' (line 12) is Mars (Greek Ares).

*2*ff. The image of Cupid's arrows transfixing the heart with love goes back at least as far as Euripides, and was a commonplace of Hellenistic and Roman elegy: cf. Prop. 2.13.2.

29–30 Sea-myrtle was sacred to Aphrodite (Venus) as Ovid reminds us elsewhere (*Fast.* 4.15, *AA* 3.53, *Am.* 3.1.4). But there is more to this conclusion than meets the eye: we end, as we began, with an allusion to Virgil, an echo of *Georg.* 1.28, the invocation to Octavian – here subtly ridiculed in a new context.

I.2

This seemingly innocuous poem (sometimes taken as a burlesque of Propertius 3.1) should be viewed in its historical context. In 24 BC Augustus had pacified Spain and Gaul. In 22 he had assumed tribunician power, and in 18 BC (see Introd. p. 71) he passed the first stage of his 'moral reform' legislation, which *inter alia* provided the penalty of exile for any man who seduced a freeborn married lady. No intelligent Roman could fail to perceive the essentially authoritarian nature of his rule. Literary men in particular would be sensitive to the policy of propaganda and tacit censorship which he initiated: anyone who chose to attack the official line would need to wear an effective mask. This poem may well be, at one level, a sharp piece of socio-political satire. The mocking description of Cupid's triumph could, all too easily, be transferred to those real celebrations still fresh in everyone's memory; and Cupid, as we are reminded in the final couplet, was related to the Emperor – a bland sideswipe at the deification principle, and perhaps a hint as to how the poem could be read by those who were so inclined. If Augustus, for instance, chose to take lines 28–35 in a political sense, they could be made to look very compromising.

13 A clear echo of Propertius 2.4.3.

23 Myrtle, which was sacred to Venus (see above, *Am.* 1.1.29–30 and note) could also be used to crown the celebrant of a Roman *ovatio*, a minor triumph 'in which the general, *after an easy, bloodless victory, or after a victory over slaves* [my italics], made his public entrance...' (Lewis and Short s.v. *ovatio*). The mocking nature of this passage emerges at once from a comparison with any 'straight' description, e.g. *Trist.* 4.2, esp. lines 19ff., 47ff.

24 Who *was* Cupid's stepfather? *Am.* 2.9b.24 identifies Mars, Venus' lover, in this role.

31 'Conscience', *Mens Bona*, had her, or its, own temple on the Capitol.

51–2 These lines again parody, or echo, Propertius (2.16.41–2). The relationship between Augustus and Cupid was established through Aeneas, Venus' son by Anchises. Propertius' lines were a perfectly serious eulogy of Caesar *qua* magnanimous conqueror. Ovid must have been alluding to the campaign in Spain (26–19 BC). Augustus fell ill during the first year's fighting against the Cantabrian tribes, and took no further part in this 'pacification exercise', which was finally wound up, with brutal efficiency, by Agrippa.

1.3

It is generally supposed that this poem must be taken as a mere erotic *jeu d'esprit*, the mischievous declaration of eternal fidelity by an elsewhere self-confessed Casanova. But Ovid deals in the raw material of passion as unmistakably, and as wittily, as Byron (another great literary *farceur*) did in *Don Juan*. Why should each mood – fidelity and Don Juanism alike – not have been genuine *at the time of writing*? The relationship with Corinna was still fresh: only later would the role of uninvolved rake come to offer psychological protection. Poets and lovers are not notable for academic consistency. Whitman's comment applies: 'Do I contradict myself? Very well, I contradict myself.' Lighthearted love may be this poem's sustaining theme, but Ovid's verse generally turns out 'double-bottomed' – as one scholar puts it – and more often than not, as perhaps here, sexual fun carries undertones of anti-Augustan politics. There had been political *desultores* (see below, note to line 15) both during and after the Civil Wars. Ovid, like other Roman poets, commonly equated Augustus with Jupiter (the deification principle made this almost inevitable); and despite his stern programmes for moral reform at home, already launched, Augustus' own sexual adventures (like those of his daughter and granddaughter) were notorious. Again, oblique criticism of Augustan propaganda, and of the deification principle, comes through clearly.

6ff. Elsewhere in the *Amores* (3.15.5–6), Ovid shows himself carefully snobbish over his 'middle-class' status as an *eques*, emphasizing that his pedigree went back some generations: no post-war *parvenu* he. For his father's thrift see the 'autobiographical elegy', *Trist.* 4.10.21–2, and Introd., p. 26.

11–14 Like Propertius in a similar situation (3.2.7ff.), Ovid has the backing of 'divine inspiration' (Apollo, Bacchus), plus his own genius; he also promises to be faithful, a new gambit.

15 But cf. 2.4.9–10 (with my note, pp. 292–3), where the Don Juan motif is advanced with cheerful impenitence. The 'sexual circus-rider', *desultor amoris*, was a term borrowed from the ring-performer who leapt from one horse to another at full gallop – a trick at least as old as Homer: see *Iliad* 15.679ff.

21–4 Io, daughter of the river-god Inachus, attracted Zeus' favours; but when Hera became angrily jealous, Zeus turned Io into a heifer. Hera tormented the heifer with a gadfly, which drove the poor creature crazy. She finally recovered her sanity in Egypt, where she was worshipped as Isis. Leda, wife of Tyndareus, King of Sparta, was also seduced by Zeus, who took the form of a swan for the occasion (an episode which seems to exert an odd psychological fascination on artists of all periods). Some versions claim that, as a result, Leda hatched Helen from an egg. Europa, daughter of King Agenor of Tyre, also succumbed to Zeus' advances, this time in the guise of a bull, which swam off with her to Crete, where she bore Minos and Rhadamanthus.

1.4

In Book I of the *Ars* (33–4) Ovid was to write: 'Safe love, legitimate liaisons / Will be my theme – this poem breaks no taboos.' In fact the *Ars* is quite clearly aimed at fashionable married ladies, and the disclaimer merely serves the same purpose as the prefatory note to a *roman à clef*, declaring all the characters wholly imaginary and based on no living people. Ovid (unlike his predecessors Catullus, Tibullus and Propertius, all of whom seem to have conducted affairs with technically respectable married ladies) was obliged, at least after 18 BC (see p. 71), to pay lip-service to Augustus' moral legislation. Earlier, in the *Amores*, he had not been nearly so careful. Not only in the present poem, but at 2.2, 2.19, 3.4 and 3.8, it is made quite clear that married women of Ovid's own class, no less than freedwomen and *meretrices* (prostitutes), are fair game for amatory adventure.

1–2 The ambiguous word *vir* – which can mean both 'husband' and 'lover': a godsend for Ovid – here bears the former connotation: at line 64 the *vir* is described as enjoying Ovid's mistress (again unnamed) 'under licence', *iure coacta*, i.e. through the exercise of marital rights. I have, wherever possible or appropriate, translated *vir* by the equally ambiguous (and more approximate) term 'man'.

Once again we have a theme which disregards, if it does not directly attack, Augustan moral legislation. Ambiguity is what we would expect: when the penalty for seducing a married woman was exile to an island, even a poet exploiting a traditional *topos* would be more prone to watch his step. By the time he came to write the *Ars*, Ovid was loudly protesting that his advice was for courtesans only: by then he must have learnt that to impugn the virtue of upper-class Roman matrons was a potentially dangerous sport. Yet even this did not prevent him from turning the dinner-party theme to good use later: see *AA* 1.565–608, with my notes ad loc. (pp. 356ff.).

7 The point of the myth of the centaurs' drunken violence at the wedding-feast of Pirithoüs and Hippodameia is 'to show that the pursuit of Hippodameia by the savage, drunken Centaur meant very little when not even a sober, civilized man could easily refrain from enjoying Corinna's . . . charms' (Ford, *Helikon* 6, 1966, 645–6).

15ff. The various 'clandestine' signals between lovers at dinner-parties and on other such public occasions formed a stock theme for Augustan elegists. It is hard to see how such inherently ludicrous gestures could ever have constituted a secret code: they seem positively to invite attention (if not to suggest some sort of spastic tic or variation on Parkinson's Disease), and Ovid, a poet with a better-developed sense of the ridiculous than most, clearly knew this very well.

35–40 Here Ovid plays, amusingly, with an archaic legal sanction, the *manus iniectio* ('lay hand upon you'). In a process known as *vindicatio*, a claimant would 'lay hand' on property to assert ownership. Ovid thus claims citizen-rights over his mistress's charms and person; the application of a venerable law to this sophisticated and far from respectable situation has its own piquant charm.

45–8 I translate *dulce peregit opus* as 'petted to climax', though with some misgivings; it is hard to visualize a (supposedly unobserved) act of mutual masturbation at dinner, whether the guests were reclining on couches or not.

53   The phrase *somno vinoque*, '[drowned] in sleep and liquor', echoes Virgil, *Aen.* 2.265, but in a calculatedly ridiculous context.

55ff.   Cf. *AA* 1.603ff.

67   Cf. below, *Am.* 3.7, *passim*.

69–70   Ovid here, as in other places (cf. e.g. *Am.* 2.13.6, and in particular 3.14.1–2, 37–40), reveals a very human desire not to acknowledge unwelcome truths about the conduct of his *inamorata*.

1.5

This is among the most charming and direct of Ovid's erotic poems: a visually precise miniature, divided, triptych-like, into three neat and expressive sections (lines 1–8; 9–16; 17–24). The eternal Mediterranean siesta is caught with swift, economic strokes. Political interests are wholly absent, and satirical ones nearly so; but Ovid cannot resist one allusive flick at Corinna. Having compared her to Semiramis, the mythical Queen of Nineveh, Ovid then abruptly adorns this tired cliché by bringing in Lais as a second parallel – Lais having been one of the most famous and highly paid whores of antiquity. This is a straightforward account of a successful act of love. Such a description is, surprisingly, unparalleled in previous Roman love-poetry, and appears to be Ovid's own creation.

3–6   The windows are in fact wooden shutters, with transverse slats, of the sort that are still common throughout the Mediterranean, and have changed little since those depicted in Pompeian wall-paintings. The light filters through the slats; one shutter has been left ajar to catch whatever afternoon breeze may be going.

7–8   This is the first point at which we get a hint that the scene involves something more than a solitary siesta. So far Ovid's camera-eye has simply panned inquisitively round a bedroom empty except for himself. Now he reflects that the setting would be ideal for the seduction of a shy girl.

9–10   Corinna's entry is abrupt, and she is very far – except in the most perfunctory sense – from being a 'modest girl'. It has been suggested, in line with the Corinna-as-fiction theory, that from here on is a dream, or fantasy: that Ovid is simply having an erotic siesta vision, solo.

A potentially more profitable line of approach might be to ask a few pertinent questions about the domestic arrangements which this pleasant seduction scene implies. Where is Ovid? Presumably in his own house, since he is scarcely likely to set up a siesta in his mistress's bedroom without her knowledge. Then where does Corinna appear from? Has she come through the streets alone? Socially improbable to a degree. With a maid, then? If so, where is the maid now? And what about the other occupants of the house? We may assume, if we like, that Ovid, as a habitual Casanova, had a discreet and well-trained hall-porter. But where, we wonder, is his wife? While it is true that, on his own account, Ovid began writing about Corinna in late adolescence (*Tr.* 4.10. 57–60), he also tells us that he was married while still a mere boy (ibid., 69–70), twice in succession. Unless he maintained a discreet *pied-à-terre* (e.g. a friend's house, like Catullus) – this cannot be ruled out, but is unlikely – or alternatively, a theory that will always have takers, made up the whole relationship and incident from a mind well-stocked with Hellenistic poetic cliché, we have to ask ourselves how it came about that Ovid and his *inamorata*, not only here but on various other occasions, had such mysteriously easy access to each other. In this context the theory that the secret of Corinna's identity lay in her being, not Ovid's mistress, but his *first wife*, clearly has a good deal to recommend it.

1.6

This poem embodies the motif of the *paraclausithyron*, the song sung by a lover outside his mistress's front door when (most often because of coquettishness or a disobliging husband) he has failed to win admission. The tradition is both Greek and Roman, though the Augustan elegists made it peculiarly their own.

Generally the lover has been to a party: somewhat tipsy, a torch in one hand and a wreath askew on his head – as here – he serenades his *inamorata* from the street, presumably accompanied by an *obbligato* chorus of angry watchdogs. When his pleas prove ineffectual, he may threaten to batter the door down, or, in more maudlin vein, to commit suicide. Finally he hangs his wreath on the door like a visiting card, scribbles some verses (lovelorn or obscene, according to taste or mood) under it, and either lies down on the step to sleep it off, or else makes his departure, temporarily defeated.

The poem can be compared with Theocritus' Idyll 2, 'The Sorcerer', where a similar symmetrical pattern, complete with repetitive refrain, at once strikes the reader (cf. also Virgil *Ecl.* 8, Ovid *Her.* 9. 143f.). The motif in that case is clearly magical: a woman is casting a spell to bring back her lover, and the poem itself forms the incantatory accompaniment to her actions. I would suggest that Ovid has the same idea in mind here. The whole poem, besides being a *para-clausithyron*, forms a magical – or parody of a magical – incantation (note the *nine* stanzas, a favourite number in spells) designed to sway the will of the janitor, and perhaps to slide free the doorbolts by superhuman means.

The equation of love's campaigning with military service suits the whips-and-suffering mood of the *paraclausithyron* very well. Ovid can present himself, at one level of the image, as a sort of one-man erotic commando-force on a night-exercise. Better still, by using a live porter, chained to the wall, he acquires a ready-made symbol of his own would-be *servitium*. When he says that, if he only had the chance, he would assume the porter's shackles, the reader smiles – because, in a metaphorical sense, Ovid is wearing them already.

53   Boreas, the North Wind, ravished away Oreithyia, daughter of King Erechtheus of Attica, while she was playing by the Ilissus river (near where the Fix brewery now stands), and took her to his 'seven-chambered grotto' in the Rhipaean mountains; there he sired Zetes and Calais on her. Cf. Ovid *Met.* 6.682–721.

1.7

Latin lovers, as we all know, are expert at noisy quarrels and even noisier reconciliations. At least since Terence's day there has been a tradition that 'lovers' quarrels are the renewal of love' (*Andria* 555). In our own time C. Day Lewis (a poet with a good classical education) could write of 'each quarrel that came like a night to blind us / And closer to bind us'. The question, as so often, is to gauge Ovid's mood. The incident certainly stuck in his mind: see below, *AA* 2.169, cf. 3.568–70. Is he in earnest or is the entire poem once more a deadpan put-on, a parody of conventional emotion as well as of the literary genre to which the emotion gave rise?

It is clear that the poem cannot be *wholly* serious: the last couplet, with Ovid telling his girl to go fix her hair and stop him feeling embarrassed, is proof enough of that. The mythological parallels, too, are ludicrously inflated: Ajax, Orestes, Diomede wounding Aphrodite before Troy. Ovid even makes political capital out of this unlikely incident by suggesting, ironically, that he should celebrate a triumph for this victory over a girl (35–40). The jolt in the coda is a characteristically Ovidian trick; but I can't help feeling that what we have here is not so much pure mischievous *nequitia*, but rather an effort to camouflage acute and shamefaced embarrassment. (For an interesting revised version of the scene see *AA* 2.169–76, with my note, p. 368). However one may wrap up the incident with mythic trimmings and parodic exaggeration, the fact remains that to assault a girl is neither funny nor forgivable; and to assault her *in a girlish fashion* – pulling her hair, scratching her cheeks – is even more dubious.

The mood, in fact, is ambivalent. By exaggerating his misdemeanour Ovid hopes to remove it from the realm of serious crime altogether; by indulging in violent self-recrimination he meets the psychological need for confession and repentance (why otherwise write such a poem at all?), while at the same time indicating that the whole business is really a joke. Even if the incident is fictitious, and the narrator simply a *persona* playing variations on a literary *topos*, the same psychological considerations apply.

7–18 Ajax, baulked of Odysseus' armour (which had been adjudicated to Odysseus), determined to slay the Greek leaders whom he held responsible, but Athena took away his wits, so that he slaughtered the army's sheep and cattle instead. Orestes is said to have used Apollo's bow, not very effectively, in self-defence against the Erinyes (Furies). Atalanta, daughter of Iasus and Clymene, was a famous huntress, loved by Meleager, courted and won by Milanion, who beat her in a foot-race by dropping a golden apple in her path. For Theseus' desertion of Ariadne on Naxos see *Her.* 10 *passim.* She either died in childbirth there, or else (less probably) was rescued and wedded by the god Dionysus. Cassandra the seer wore the fillet of a priestess: the reference is half-joking, with an allusion to Ovid's girl and her disarrayed hair, thus effectively undercutting the previous mythical rodomontade. It is more than likely that Ovid – the literary allusions being not over-apt – was in each case thinking of some well-known picture.
31–4 After wounding Aeneas in battle, Diomede also attacked Aphrodite.
35–40 Again, Ovid sets up the image of a triumph in circumstances which make not only the institution but in particular the celebrant look ridiculous. The details are mocked by parody and exaggeration: it is the bombastic self-aggrandizement which Ovid sets out to exploit. We should also remember that Augustus' most famous victory, that of Actium (31 BC) was won over the Egyptian queen Cleopatra: line 38 thus acquires an ambiguous flavour. Cf. *Am.* 2.12.8.

60 Why is it that Ovid only *now* begins to feel culpable? And *how* are the girl's tears his blood? Presumably in the sense that the sight of them wounds him: he bleeds because pierced with remorse, and the tears which caused the wound now become the wound itself. It is a metaphysical conceit worthy of the seventeenth century; and like most such conceits, its emotional impact is stronger than its logic.

1.8

The old bawd with a sideline in magic and the urge to make the poet's mistress better herself through a wealthier alliance is a familiar stage-property of Roman elegy, which probably borrowed her, at one remove, from Greek mime or New Comedy. Her chief function for the elegist was to lecture an innocent Cynthia or Corinna on popular gold-digging techniques. Such persons undoubtedly existed, but our view of them is heavily overlaid with literary fantasy. Ovid's *lena* derives, in essence, from Propertius 4.5, where we similarly find the witch's sales-pitch sandwiched between disobliging comments on the witch herself, delivered *in propria persona* by the poet.

Though Ovid's treatment has a lightness of touch and a blandly sophisticated wit lacking in that of Propertius, both portraits suggest a literary formalization of something once more serious and more frightening. The uninitiated formerly believed in witches; perhaps they still did: but for the sophisticated man of letters in Augustan Rome the bawd–sorceress was no more than a convenient figure of fun. As has often been remarked, there is an odd discrepancy between the horrific magical powers attributed to these crones, and the workaday hints on husband-hunting which we see them actually dispensing. In a poem such as Theocritus' Idyll 2, 'The Sorceress', magic is treated very seriously indeed, and gives every sign of being drawn from actual contemporary practice, as evidenced by the surviving magical papyri. The Roman elegiac poets are equally *au fait* with such activities, but tend to treat them more lightly, as mere literary decoration: Ovid, the apotheosis of intellectual rationalism, finds double pupils, gravity-defying rivers, ghost-raising and similar items of the stock-in-trade no more than a bad superstitious joke. The build-up of the old hag here is in deliberate and anticlimactic contrast to what we actually see her doing.

Extra piquancy is lent to her advice by the fact that it could very well have come from Ovid himself: cf. *AA* 1.417–18, 2.251–72, with my notes, pp. 352 and 370–72. Lines 39ff. in particular sum up the attitude propounded in Bk 3 of the *Art of Love*. *Rusticitas*, the country simplicity of character to which Tibullus at least paid lip-service, has become, in Ovid's book, a regrettable naïvety. His didacticism aims to turn each simple country girl into a sophisticated *demi-mondaine*. Thus the poem becomes, not merely satire, but a kind of double-level self-parody: it is interesting, and revealing, to turn back to it after *The Art of Love* and to study the multi-level literary and social *persona* which Ovid here adopts. Superstition is ridiculed, and elegiac earnestness (in the person of Propertius) mocked by means of elegant pastiche. Behind the bawd's bleary, raddled mask lurks Ovid himself, tempting his own girl with more profitable prospects elsewhere. His shadow (line 109) indeed betrayed him: the poem resembles a receding hall of mirrors.

5–18 The various practices and phenomena mentioned here are all well-known from ancient literature, but vary in kind. One group – the spells, the herbs, the bullroarer, the *hippomanes* – forms, as it were, a witch's *materia magica*. The other represents her various large and miraculous powers: reversing rivers, manipulating weather, bloodying the moon, earth-splitting, ghost-raising, and transformation at will into an owl. Her double pupils serve to identify her as an authentic witch.

19 '*Our* relationship': but what was it? Normally the phrase *thalamos pudicos* would imply marriage, and it is tempting to guess (cf. my note on *Am* 1.5.9–10, pp. 273–4) that this is an early poem involving Ovid's first wife. On the other hand the phrase may be suggestively ironic or ambiguous.

39–44 The rape of the Sabine women (who, respectable if malodorous, held out for monogamy) is described by Livy, 1.9–13, and by Ovid, in greater detail, at *AA* 1.101–34 (cf. my note, pp. 341–2). This delectable passage, with its tongue-in-cheek air and its contemptuous attitude to *rusticitas*, foreshadows the *Art of Love*: see esp. *AA* 1.60, 2.566.

47–8 Both the bow and the horn here carry sexual implications, and were common terms in *sermo amatorius*.

57–8 Ovid deploys a neat ambiguity here: '*read* many thousand [poems]' or *collect* many thousand [coins]'? The Latin ('*milia multa leges*') could mean either: I have tried in my version to preserve something of the double sense.

64 For the practice of marking newly arrived foreign slaves' feet with chalk or gypsum see Juv. 1.111.

73–4 The simulation of a headache to avoid intercourse is frequently mentioned by the elegiac poets; to plead religious abstinence because of an imminent feast of Isis seems also to have been a popular excuse. *85–6* The gods proverbially refrained from taking lovers' oaths seriously: cf. *Am.* 2.1.19f., 3.3.11, 3.11.21; *AA* 1.634.

1.9

To the 'straight' patriotic Roman, love-making as a preferred *occupation* (as opposed to a casual and intermittent activity, with whore or wife) was unmanly, as indeed was the full-time pursuit of poetry; it could be summed up in the word *desidia* (or its adjective *desidiosus*) as 'slackness' or 'an easy option'. Ovid, on the contrary, claims (31–2, 45–6) that love, not war, is the best *cure* for slackness. The elaborate parallel drawn between the soldier's life and the lover's may contain a cover streak of self-justification (perhaps predictable in a young man born too late for the Civil Wars, and never himself subjected to military service in the field); but it is by no means intended as a compliment to patriotic militarism, which Ovid detested and despised.

The notion was to be propounded again in Bk 2 of the *Art of Love* (lines 231–8, 559, 565–6, 674): *militiae species amor est*, 'love is a species of warfare'. But, we note, it emerges as a somewhat specialized branch of the military art, with an emphasis on open-air bivouacking and siege activities: what Ovid once more has in mind as the central feature of courtship is the vigil outside his mistress's closed door. The *obstacles* put in a lover's path form, for him, the essence of the game: as he several times tells us, easy conquests make for boredom. But there is more to it than this: *militia* implies an *adversary*, an object of attack. The parallels drawn in this poem are psychologically suggestive. Soldier and lover both sleep rough out of doors, stand guard before a closed door (7–8). They must be prepared for long journeys and severe weather (15–16, cf. *AA* 2.235–8). They are both on siege operations, determined to break in the gates of a city – or a front door (19–20). Both favour the notion of a surprise attack (21–2, 25–6). All this is highly revealing: seldom can the so-called 'war between the sexes' have been delineated in such graphic terms from a male viewpoint, with phallic predators manoeuvring for an opening against calculating gold-diggers, with both sides simply after sex or money, and bringing an elaborate technique into play to gain their immediate ends.

23–4 Rhesus, King of Thrace, came to Troy as an ally of the Trojans against the Greeks. He was famous for his wind-swift white mares: Diomede and Odysseus, however, made a nocturnal commando raid on his camp, killed Rhesus himself, and got away with the mares.

33–40 To counter the deeply ingrained and primitive belief that love (or, more specifically, the ejaculation of sperm) induces unmanly sloth, Ovid lists various heroic fighters whose prowess in battle was not diminished by their erotic preoccupations; all are chosen from Homer. (We may note one glaring omission: Paris, who in this context would not have suited Ovid's book at all.) Lines 33–6 reveal Ovid's immediate source as Propertius 2.22.27–32, where we find the line *nullus amor vires eripit ipse suas* – 'never does love exhaust its own strength', and the same examples: Achilles and Briseis, Hector's farewell to Andromache. The famous tale of how Ares (Mars) seduced Aphrodite (Venus) and was trapped in bed with her by Hephaestus (Mulciber) is told at length by Homer in the *Odyssey* (*Od.* 8.266–369: cf. Ovid *Met.* 4.169–89, *AA* 2.561–92, with my note, pp. 377–8).

41–2 The picture of the poet as a lazy individual, lying on a day-bed under a shady tree and scribbling verses, was well-established by Ovid's day. This is socially suggestive when we remember that *otium*, leisure, as opposed to *negotium*, business, was an upper-class Roman's ideal. It is clear, however, that, just as only certain occupations (soldiering, government, law, estate management) were socially acceptable, so, equally, one's leisure must be employed in a manner that did not contravene the social norms.

I.10

The shifting tones of this poem have caused some confusion among decent middle-class commentators, perhaps because Ovid is (by any serious standards) so splendidly outrageous in his moral inconsistency. Ovid begins by comparing his *inamorata* to heroines from Greek mythology: Helen, Leda, Europa – all, we note, victims of seduction. Idealism is brought down to earth with a rattle of cash-boxes by her asking for presents. Only the whore should do this: for lovers the pleasure should be mutual (lines 35–6). Even farmyard animals, Ovid claims (25ff.), rut in spontaneous and mutual pleasure, though observation does not always bear this out. This theme, reasonable enough in itself, is now further explored, by means of vivid illustrations from everyday life and mythical *exempla* such as Tarpeia and Eriphyle. Ideal and real are juxtaposed and contrasted through a sketch of the contemporary urban scene, with its pimping, bribes and judicial corruption.

But of course, Ovid can never maintain a moral stance for long, nor is this his object. At lines 53–4 the reader is brought up with a jerk when he hears that it's all right to dun *the rich* for presents, since *they* can afford them. Morality, in fact, has abruptly flown the coop. What has Ovid to offer? Immortality through song. This is the atmosphere of *Am.* 1.3 (with the old bawd of 1.8 muttering disconcertingly off-stage). To complete the moral *peripeteia* the poet's final plea, in the coda, is to let him give presents – which by now he is quite ready to do – but of his own accord, not in answer to demands. The sense of spontaneity must be preserved. Having lurched from mock-idealism to spoof cynicism, the poem closes with a funny-sad (and psychologically acute) comment on the male romantic ego. Ovid considers the various forms Zeus assumed to seduce human maidens – swan, eagle, bull – and hints at another manifestation, most appropriate for what is to follow: the shower of gold in which he penetrated Danaë's defences. Is it possible that once again, as in 1.3 (see above, p. 270), Ovid is hinting indirectly at the Zeus (Jupiter) = Augustus equation? And if so, what does it tell us about his relationship to the girl?

1–6 Leda and Helen need no glossing. Amymone was Danaüs' daughter; while out with a pot on her head to fetch water, during a drought, she succumbed to Poseidon's advances (he having opportunely rescued her from a priapic satyr), and was shown by him the springs of Lerna.

11–12 Ovid's objections to gold-digging girls are repeated in similar terms at *RA* 321–2.

39–40 Under the Lex Cincia of M. Cincius Alimentus (204 BC, reconfirmed by Augustus 18/17 BC), an advocate could not even charge a fee for his services, let alone accept bribes: *ne quis ob causam orandam pecuniam donumve acciperet*. It goes without saying (as Ovid's remarks make clear) that this statute was systematically circumvented; Augustus apparently renewed it, but without noticeable effect.

49–50 Tarpeia, the daughter of Rome's citadel-commander in the quasi-mythical days of Romulus, was bribed by Tatius, the King of the Sabines, to let a commando-group of his soldiers into the fortress. As a price for her services the girl demanded 'what they had on their shield-arms', i.e. their heavy gold bracelets and jewelled rings. Once they were inside, however, the men crushed her to death under their shields.

51–2 Harmonia, daughter of Ares and Aphrodite, received on her wedding-day, from Cadmus, a necklace which proved fatal to all who owned it. Polyneices, son of Oedipus, inherited the necklace and gave it to Eriphyle as a bribe, to persuade her husband Amphiaraus to march with him against Thebes as one of the Seven. This she did (though Amphiaraus had warned her never to accept a gift from Polyneices). Amphiaraus, having promised to abide by Eriphyle's decision, went to Thebes – though as a seer he well knew he would meet his death there. Before leaving he made his sons, including Alcmaeon, swear that, on coming of age, they would kill their mother Eriphyle and themselves assault Thebes.

56–7 Alcinous, King of the Phaeacians on Scheria, was famous for his orchards, which are described at length in the *Odyssey*, 7.112–32.

I.11, I.12

These two poems are naturally taken in conjunction: they form a thematically related diptych (cf. 2.7 and 8; 2.9 and 9B; 2.13 and 14; 3.11A and 11B) which might almost symbolize the two folded leaves of the writing-tablet, their common linking element. Ovid sends a hopeful *billet-doux* – perhaps a love-poem, a forerunner of the published *Amores* – to Corinna by the hand of Napë, her personal maid, who acts as their go-between. Even if Ovid's passion was stimulated by frustration, there is nothing *prima facie* about these poems to prove that Corinna was not modelled on his wife, or that husband and wife were not engaged in private marital games of a type familiar to psychologists. At the close of 1.11 Ovid is strung to high and optimistic expectation, which is swiftly dashed by a curt and negative response from Corinna herself: exactly the kind of communication which annoyed Ovid most (1.11.19–24). The only brief note *he* looks kindly on is a rendezvous. 1.12, after a perfunctory attempt to account for his bad luck by mere superstition (which would, of course, undercut the idea of Corinna's active indifference), devotes itself to a commination service against the wretched writing-tablets, the unwitting instrument of his humiliation.

I.11

1–4 The various uses and advantages of a maid to help one's intrigues are set out at greater length in *AA* 1.351–98. One of the maid's main duties was attending to her mistress's hair (cf. *AA* 3.133–68).

1.12

9–10 For the bitterness of Corsican honey see Virgil, *Ecl.* 9.30. Hemlock, of course, was best known as the poison used to execute criminals in Athens, its most famous victim being Socrates.

13 The purpose of dropping the tablet at a crossroads was not solely to have it crushed by passing traffic, but to prepare the reader for the gibbet image which follows (lines 17–18): criminals were hanged at crossroads, just as, later, vampires were buried there, and crossroads were sacred to Hecate.

19–20 Both Greeks and Romans regarded the night-flying screech-owl, *noctua*, *strix* or *bubo*, with peculiar fear and loathing: partly because of its uncanny whickering cry, but also because of the widespread belief that these creatures were really witches in metamorphosis. The appearance of the vulture, though a scavenger, here is probably due to a slip on Ovid's part, since the vulture is not commonly listed among birds of ill-omen. Nor (as was well known in antiquity) did it normally make its nest in accessible trees.

1.13

The poem is a versified *suasoria*, a rhetorical exercise in persuasion: a witty, subtle, well-argued address to the Dawn with the declared object of delaying her arrival for the benefit of lovers (though not, seemingly, to encourage further coitus so much as to give them a comfortable sleep afterwards). This conceit is neatly articulated to an ironic appraisal of the conventions governing such myths, in particular the portrayal of natural phenomena as persons.

Aurora is, at one level, the dawn as we all know it, complete with dew, glowing sunrise, cool stillness: the prelude (even more strikingly in antiquity) to the day's work, which in Ovid's time began with first light and was ended by darkness. But Aurora is also an all-too-anthropomorphic deity, with an elderly (indeed positively antique) husband, and a well-known penchant for young men. It is this ambiguity in her nature which Ovid explores, with urbane and contrapuntal irony. Three couplets in this poem, including the first and last (lines 1–2, 33–4 and 47–8), are third-person statements concerning Aurora, a frame within which to place the two sections of the *suasoria* addressed to her.

The dawn is the best time for lovers to sleep (or to sleep it off) – a reminder that *inertia* and *otium* are a characteristic ideal for *rentier* writers like Horace and Ovid, to be interpreted in their own peculiar way, which might not be shared by statesmen and conservative patriots (see above, p. 279). Perhaps that is why, in his survey of Roman early risers, Ovid omits the politician. Sailors and soldiers, ploughmen, farmers, schoolboys, housewives – all must obey Aurora's summons (but Horace, we know, was a late riser, and Ovid may well have followed his example). The dawn comes up; public, if not private, life creaks into action; yawning, exhausted lovers must go home. It is at this point that Ovid begins to infiltrate his own argument with comic anthropomorphism. He gets cross with Aurora, as one might with any unpredictable lady. He hopes her axle breaks, or her horses stumble into cloud (as though cloud were solid terrestrial mud). He repeats scandalous stories about her affairs, including the implication that Memnon was sired by some unknown black lover.

Ovid's rhetorical argument now proceeds to its refutation of his adversary's (unspoken) objections. Aurora will argue that delay is physically impossible. But what about the Moon and Endymion, or – even more appropriate – Zeus–Jupiter's extended night of love with Alcmene? The speech ends, and Ovid once more addresses his reader directly. In two lethal lines, one of his most effective and devastating codas, the entire elegant fancy of a living, persuadable Aurora is blown sky-high. The mythopoeic world is flatly undercut by smiling rationalism, and we are left, simply, with a clever, lazy, ironic, over-articulate man making plausible excuses for staying in bed a little longer: the presence or absence of a girl seems almost irrelevant. Dawn – with a last blush, an obliging nod to the pathetic fallacy – comes up on time, as we always knew it would; the rhetoric has been exquisitely and deliberately useless. All that remains at the poem's end is Ovid's mischievous, sexless, disembodied grin, something akin to that of the Cheshire Cat. As usual, he has the last laugh.

1–2 The 'blonde day-bringer' was Aurora or Eos, the personified Dawn. She was also, traditionally, a compulsive fancier of handsome youths, including Cephalus, Cleitus, Astraeus and Orion. One of the most gloriously handsome of all was Tithonus, Priam's brother and son of Laomedon, whom she married. She prayed the gods to bestow immortality on him, which they did; but she forgot at the same time to ask them to give him eternal youth, so that eventually he withered away into a piping ancient husk, like a cicada – hence Ovid's description of him as her 'doddering husband'.

3–4 Memnon, the son of Tithonus and Aurora, was, mysteriously, black, an Ethiopian prince. Hephaestus, at Aurora's request, forged him armour with which to fight against the Greeks at Troy, but he was nevertheless slain by Achilles, and Aurora wept for him every morning: her tears are the dawn dew. His mourning comrades were changed into birds called Memnonides, and Memnon, according to Ovid (*Met.* 13.576–622ff.), became a bird himself.

11–12 The remark about navigation is no mere poetic conceit, but plain fact. Mediterranean sailors, now as in antiquity, navigate solely by the stars, and very well too. During the day Greek sailors were – are – heavily dependent on coastal bearings, and never strayed beyond sight of land if they could help it; it was the Phoenicians who first worked out a system of dead-reckoning.

17–18 Roman schoolchildren began their classes at, or even before, dawn.

19–21 The court referred to was the praetor's tribunal, which handled civil suits. The 'one-word pledge' was the verb *spondeo*, 'I guarantee', and the official formula for going bail was: 'I guarantee to render a like sum' (*ego idem dare spondeo*).

39–40 Line 40 has earned its own immortality by being quoted (slightly wrong) by Marlowe's Faustus, in his last great soliloquy. The son Aurora bore Cephalus was – with a gesture towards marital *pietas* – named Tithonus. Afterwards she obligingly sent Cephalus back to his distraught wife Procris.

43–4 Selene or Luna, the personified Moon, fell in love with a beautiful youth named Endymion. She put him to sleep for all eternity in a glen or cave on Mt Latmos in Caria, so that she could kiss him each evening without his knowledge.

45–6 The occasion was that on which Zeus (doubling for Amphitryon) slept with Alcmene and sired Heracles.

1.14

Whether the incident described in this poem be fact or fiction, it cannot but remind us that Mediterranean humour is, *au fond*, peasant humour – masculine-oriented, at times amazingly cruel: I have seen a small Greek crowd in fits of laughter over a dying donkey – and fundamentally different from our own. The *persona* which Ovid here presents is sophisticated enough, but self-satisfied, cruel, and anti-feminine to a degree. The tone is that of a bitchy homosexual, the teasing far from kind. He mocks the distressed girl, who may have been silly, may have ignored his suggestions, but was obviously trying to make herself look good, presumably for his benefit, and has now suffered one of the worst catastrophes that can befall a woman's natural vanity. After spending over fifty lines telling the poor creature that it's all her own fault, and how could she have been so idiotic, he suddenly (and characteristically) relents in the last couplet and says, in effect: Don't worry, your hair's bound to grow out again.

5–6 Chinese silks were well-known in Rome. Silk was known to the Greeks as early as Aristotle's day, and imported in the wake of Alexander's conquests; but silkworms were not actually cultivated in Europe until the sixth century AD.

33–4 The picture referred to here is the well-known Aphrodite (or Venus) Anadyomene, by the Greek artist Apelles (fourth century BC). This painting had lately been brought by Augustus from Cos to Rome, where it caused something of a sensation; Augustus dedicated it to the deified Caesar, an appropriate enough gesture, since Venus – sometimes, as here, known as Dione, her mother's name: see, e.g., *AA* 2.593 – was Caesar's putative ancestress through her relationship with Aeneas' father Anchises (cf. above, p. 270). Ovid refers to the picture several times (*AA* 3.224, 401–2, *Tr.* 2.526–7, *EP.* 4.1.29), and always emphasizes the fact that the goddess is holding her wet hair in her hands and wringing it out to dry, a gesture he seems to have found particularly attractive (cf. my note on *AA* 3.133–68, p. 387).

39–42 Another glimpse into the sub-world of magic – literary here, and conventionalized, but resting on an all-too-real tradition of spells and, very probably, poisons (no accident that the Greek word *pharmakón* means both, and 'medicine' into the bargain – hence our term 'pharmacy').

45–6 What German conquest was this? The point is important, since it helps substantially in deciding whether the second edition of the *Amores* contained new material, or merely revised earlier existing poems. As we have seen (above, p. 30), the likeliest date for the publication of the first edition was 16/15 BC. Now the Germans in question, as we know from line 49, were the Sygambri. In 17/16 BC they crossed the Rhine and inflicted a severe defeat on the provincial governor, M. Lollius, who was forced to retreat with the loss of the Fifth Legion's eagle. At this Augustus took the field in person, and the Germans retired. This episode is alluded to both by Horace (*Odes* 4.14.51f., 4.2.34f.) and Propertius (4.6.77), the former writing between 16 and 13 BC, the latter not later than 16.

Augustus returned to Rome in 13 BC, and a year later the Sygambri became restive once more. This time their subjugation (along with that of several other German tribes) was undertaken by the Emperor's stepson Drusus, in 12–11 BC. The campaign, though risky, was successful, and Drusus earned an *ovatio*, or lesser triumph, for his part in it. A third campaign (the territory had never been properly pacified) was undertaken in 8/7 BC by Tiberius, Drusus having meanwhile died accidentally after falling from his horse while on reconnaissance near the Elbe (9 BC). The Sygambri were now quiet for a while.

The fact that both Horace and Propertius refer in flattering terms to the shaky settlement of 16 BC – perhaps in immediate anticipation of Augustus' return to Rome – makes it a virtual certainty that Ovid was doing the same, and that the traditional date for the original publication of the *Amores* can stand, without the addition of any known subsequent matter. Rome's shaky record on the German frontier needed all the public boosting it could get.

55–6 'This loss is by no means irreparable' – once again a whole poem's impact is virtually negated in its final couplet, which moves smoothly from a world of mildly hysterical mock-heroics to the everyday commonplace that hair, when cut or destroyed, tends to grow out again – just as dawn comes up on time, whatever poets may say or hope.

1.15

In the first poem of Bk 1 Ovid was casting around for a literary theme, toyed conventionally with the idea of epic, but – impelled by Cupid – settled for erotic elegy instead. By now time has passed; the poetic mining of his affair with Corinna (whether real girl, literary lay-figure, or a fantasy-injected blend of the two) has brought him instant fame – and the unkind attention of sour moral critics. They call him, censoriously, idler and drone, a charge we have already seen him attempting to rebut in 1.9 (cf. esp. note to lines 41–2, p. 280). On the contrary, he protests: he *was* idle, he *was* lazy, but love put an end to all that: pursuing a girl is just as tough an option as military service. Yet by 1.13 he has tacitly reversed his position. For lovers sleep is the sweetest at dawn and after: why should *they* have to get up? There follows (lines 11–24) a list of workaday occupations which compel early rising, and from which Ovid (naturally, as a poet with a private income) by implication dissociates himself. Now, in 1.15 (lines 1–6), he admits that the burden of criticism against him has been that he follows none of the acceptable professions, that he is a mere dilettante. Such human ambitions, he retorts, are ephemeral (and courtroom work is mere literary prostitution). His own hope, his own objective is poetic immortality.

1–6 Ovid, the envious critic asserts, has chosen not to pursue the normal career open to a Roman citizen with his advantages: he is neither a soldier, a lawyer, nor a budding politician. He has abandoned the *cursus honorum*. Both he and his brother had been intended (clearly with Augustus' approval, if not at his instigation) for a senatorial career (*Trist.* 4.10.27–30). Ovid himself actually held some minor official posts, as we have seen (Introd., p. 29), but withdrew from public life before the age of twenty-five in order to practise poetry, remaining for the rest of his life a simple *eques*.

9–30 Ovid's candidates for the literary Hall of Fame have, on the whole, come through pretty well: his judgement compares excellently with that (say) of the Swedish Academy of Sciences in picking the past half-century's literary Nobel prizewinners. Oddly, he is better on Greek poets than Roman: Homer, Hesiod, Sophocles, Menander and Callimachus have indeed won immortality. (cf. *AA* 3.329ff. for another list, which drops several of the names listed here but adds Sappho, Ovid being at pains on that occasion to compile essential reading-matter for smart ladies.) Even Aratus survives: he lived from about 315 to 240/39 BC, dividing his life between Athens and Macedonia, and his best-known work, entitled *Phaenomena*, was several times translated into Latin – e.g. by Varro of Atax, Cicero and Claudius' brother Germanicus (though it is hard, today, to understand the ancient passion for versifying an indigestible *catalogue raisonné* on astronomy). In selecting Roman poets Ovid seems to have stuck to those already dead: hence the absence of Horace and Propertius. Virgil, Lucretius, Gallus and Tibullus were obvious candidates. Yet Lucretius hardly suited the Augustan mood of moral and religious reform, while Gallus was a decidedly risky choice. It may not be true that Virgil removed a panegyric of him from *Georgics* Bk 4 at Augustus' instructions, but for Ovid to ignore the fact that official *damnatio memoriae* had made Gallus something of an 'unperson' (he refers to him by name at least seven times) was, to say the least, tactless.

Ennius and Accius (the latter an early tragedian born *c.* 170 BC) represent a nod to conservative tradition. But who today except scholars remembers Varro of Atax (b. 82 BC), the adaptor, or translator, of Apollonius Rhodius' *Argonautica* (hence the reference to Argo and the Golden Fleece)? The poem is lost, and we know nothing of its author's life. About Gallus, on the other hand, we know a good deal. He seems to have shared with Catullus the original development, as a genre, of Roman love-elegy: not only Ovid himself (besides here at *Am.* 3.9.63–4, *AA* 3.334, *Trist.* 2.445–6, 4.10.53, 5.1.17) but also Propertius (2.34.91–2) and Quintilian (*Inst. Orat.* 10.1.93) mention him in this context. As we have seen, he was also a public careerist, who committed suicide (26 BC) as a result of some ambitious political indiscretion.

34 The Spanish river in question was the Tagus (modern Tajo, or Tejo, in Portugal), and the alluvial gold it washed down was proverbial in antiquity.

BOOK 2

2.1

Like 1.1 (which it in effect duplicates) this poem opens a new book with a programmatic statement of literary intentions. Ovid has – or says he has – been working at an epic, this time what sounds like a very pretentious Gigantomachy (*Tr.* 2.333–8). But during the process of composition his current mistress (presumably Corinna, though Ovid does not name her) stages a lock-out. The *exclusus amator* reacts promptly; his order of priorities is never in doubt. Abandoning the epic, Ovid concentrates on producing a poem (perhaps this one) designed to break down her resistance. What point, he asks, in celebrating heroes, or warfare? Such things will not soften up a potential – or recalcitrant – mistress. Jupiter is unceremoniously relegated to creative limbo: his bolts are no match for the girl's, whereas elegy (as Ovid points out with a punning play on that ambiguous word *carmen*) has magical properties, can reverse the natural order of things – and break down doors. Erotic expertise, unlike spells and cantrips, will produce results, and is therefore worth acquiring; we see here an anticipation of the *Art of Love* as a practical guide. Better, in fact, private magic than public religion; State propaganda has nothing for the dedicated individualist.

How far Ovid's cavalier treatment of Jupiter had (as elsewhere, e.g. *Am.* 1.3.21–4, 1.10.1–8, 1.13.45–6) anti-Augustan overtones it is hard to tell; but the message in general terms is clear. The heroic mode has nothing to offer this poet, and he consciously rejects it. On the other hand, he argues, praise a beauty, and you are likely – as he knows from his own past experience – to enjoy her favours as well as winning literary fame. The attitude is solipsistic, utilitarian. Make love not war: love brings better fringe-benefits, and is, in any case, more congenial to Ovid than military propaganda. He also (never averse to killing two birds with one stone) makes this an opportunity to mock the conventional apologetic of Tibullus and Propertius. We recall the latter explaining to Maecenas why he can't, or won't, write patriotic epic (2.1, esp. 17–26): if he did so, he asserts, it would be no Gigantomachy but the contemporary wars of Maecenas himself and his patron Augustus. Propertius makes this the programme-piece of his own second book, and it is impossible to read Ovid's poem without recalling that of his predecessor. The political implication was there for those who cared to see it.

21–8 Elegy, Ovid argues, is not only his natural medium: within its own sphere it works more effectively than either epic or thunderbolts. The sphere, of course, is that of sexual persuasion. Playing on the multiple meaning of *carmen* ('poem' or 'magical incantation' or 'spell'), and driving his point home with repeated anaphora, he lists the uncanny powers of magical utterance. *Carmina* can 'call down' the moon, a curious skill attributed to witches in antiquity: they were supposed to cull some sort of foam or dew from it, and in general to control the various 'lunar influences' (tidal, menstrual, etc.).

29–32 All the examples chosen are from the *Iliad*. 'Old what's-his-name' is, of course, Odysseus. Atreus' sons were Agamemnon and Menelaus; Achilles, after killing Hector, slit the Trojan's ankles and dragged his body round the walls of Troy at his chariot-tail.

2.2 and 2.3

There has been some discussion as to whether these two pieces, clearly separate in the MSS., may not actually form the *disiecta membra* of a single poem. What we have here is a pair of related and juxtaposed poems – the technique is characteristic: cf. 1.11–1.12, 2.7–2.8, 2.13–2.14 – in which the high speculative hopes of the first are dashed by the second's disappointment in the event. (1.11 and 1.12 form a particularly illuminating analogy.) The first constitutes a rhetorical exercise in persuasion, designed to 'soften up' the eunuch set as watchdog over a girl (not named) who has caught Ovid's fancy. The second reveals failure in this objective, accompanied by some understandable sneers at the eunuch's obduracy and unfortunate physical condition – so apt a symbol of Ovid's own inability (impotence, if you like) to gain his immediate ends. The girl's relationship with her *vir* is left technically ambiguous; but I see no reason to doubt that here, as in 1.4, whatever his later protestations, Ovid was describing the initial approaches in a prospective liaison with a freeborn married lady (see above, pp. 271–2). His exhortation to Bagoas can be compared with his own very similar appeal to the unfeeling janitor in 1.6; it forms part of the traditional literature generated by *servitium amoris*.

2.2

1 'Bagoas' is the name given to several Persian eunuchs by our historical sources, including one who was the minion, successively, of Darius III and Alexander the Great.

3–4 The cloister (or portico) described here was in the temple of Apollo on the Palatine, built by Augustus and formally opened on 9 October 28 BC. It contained between its giallo antico columns statues of the fifty daughters of Danaus, and opposite them their fifty cousins and suitors, the sons of Aegyptus. When forced into marriage, all the brides (with the single exception of Hypermnestra) killed their husbands on their wedding-night – an interesting association of ideas for this erotic elegy on the pursuit-and-rejection theme.

11–12 Once again Ovid uses the ambiguous term *vir* (= 'man' or 'husband') to describe his girl's protector; but the set-up surely implies a socially sanctioned marriage.

15–16 Freedom, *libertas*, has one meaning for Bagoas – that is, manumission – but quite different implications (i.e. sexual licence) for his mistress.

18–27 These lines (enclosed between double asterisks in my translation) are omitted by the oldest surviving MSS. The couplet 23–4 at least must be an intrusion. *Si faciet trade* ('If she's late coming back') is certainly very odd Latin, and the sense marks an unexpected break in an otherwise consistent rhetorical pattern. *Billets-doux*, mysterious stranger, sick girlfriend, visits to temple or theatre, all play some part in the lady's erotic activities – but all, equally, can sustain an innocent explanation. However sceptical Bagoas may be (so Ovid's argument runs), he will be well advised, in his own interests, to accept these excuses at their face value.

25–6 Isis, a Hellenized Egyptian goddess, was very popular in Rome. Octavian, the future Augustus, together with Mark Antony and Lepidus, had in 43 BC built a new temple for Isis and Sarapis, though later his attitude became less favourable to such foreign cults. This temple was located on the Campus Martius, north of the Circus Flaminius and east of the Baths of Agrippa. Ovid himself (*AA* 1.77–8, 3.393, 635–8), Propertius and, later, Juvenal all refer to it as a popular rendezvous for assignations and pick-ups.

44–6 Tantalus betrayed the confidences of Zeus to mortal men, and by way of punishment was placed in a well, so immobilized that he could reach neither the water itself nor the fruit-laden branches overhead, and thus suffered agonies of hunger and thirst. Hence our verb 'tantalize'. On Io cf. my note to *Am.* 1.3.21–4 (above, p. 271). When Hera learnt of her seduction by Zeus, Zeus turned her into a heifer. Since she had been a priestess of Hera, the goddess claimed authority over her, heifer or no, and set Argus the All-Seeing to guard her. Zeus ordered Hermes to steal Io away, which he could only do after killing Argus (Apollod. 2.1.3, cf. schol. Aesch. *Prom.* 561, Ovid *Am.* 3.4.20). It is significant that for Romans Io and Isis were identical: thus while spoilsport Argus died for his pains, Io-Isis survived (in Ovid's Augustan mind) to become the patroness of sexual adventure.

63–4 The verb *coimus* is used by Ovid in a double sense here: not only an assignation, but also the sexual intercourse which followed, is clearly implied. I have tried to reproduce this effect in my translation.

2.3

1–10 Bagoas' refusal is rewarded with a quick change of tone on Ovid's part, an insulting reminder of the eunuch's own defective sexual standing, neither male nor female: slave-boys were usually gelded before puberty – though exceptions were known. Ovid's use, in line 10, of his favourite military metaphor to describe Bagoas' 'harem duties' – emphatically here distinguished, and not as a compliment, from military service (fighting = the proper function of a whole and virile man) – casts an interesting side-light on the poet's concept, elsewhere, of *servitium amoris* as an acceptable alternative to the warrior's career.

2.4

9ff. So wide-ranging a spectrum of types and interests (some, on the face of it, mutually exclusive) suggests, once more, that what turns

Ovid on is sex, with all else ancillary to this one overriding concern –
except literary creativity, which both feeds and feeds off the erotic
preoccupation. A man who finds so many different women attractive
must be drawn, ultimately, by the common factor of their femininity
rather than by the individual traits which distinguish them one from
another. They may be different to begin with, but refracted through
Ovid's gaze they are all alike: all serve the same purpose. Indeed,
throughout the poem what Ovid repeatedly anticipates is getting the
object of his affections into bed (see lines 14, 16, 22, 24, 33, 44–5):
in fact or fantasy makes no difference. The psychology is con-
sistent throughout. And why not? Ovid would ask. Why not, indeed?
Nothing, I suspect, would depress him more, could he return from
the shades, than to see the earnest literary hash posterity has made of
his more casual impulses, the avalanche of solemn exegesis burying his
lightest verse.

19 Callimachus (*c.* 305–*c.* 240 BC) was a North African Greek poet
who emigrated young to Alexandria, and eventually found work in its
great library. His literary quarrel with the epic poet Apollonius of
Rhodes can be summed up in his remark that 'a big book is a big evil';
yet despite this he wrote prolifically (if not at length) himself. Of all
the Hellenistic poets he proved by far the most popular in Roman
times: only Homer is quoted more often, or survives in more papyrus
fragments. Ovid imitated Callimachus' *Aetia* in the *Fasti*, and also
copied the theme of his *Ibis*, besides owing him a generic literary debt
for his elegiac expertise. Callimachus, in fact, is introduced here as the
poet Ovid would regard it as the highest possible compliment to be
told he outshone.

32 Hippolytus, Theseus' chaste and priggish son who dedicated him-
self to the cult of Artemis, the virgin huntress, and was tempted –
unsuccessfully, but with tragic results – by his stepmother Phaedra,
often served as a symbol of male virginity for Greek and Roman poets.
Priapus, similarly, was an obvious symbol of urgent male desire.

44–5 'My sex-life runs the entire mythological gamut' (*omnibus histor-
iis se meus aptat amor*) has been adduced as evidence to show that
Ovid's concern with sex – except, presumably, for decorous marital
encounters – was restricted to his art. The reader may safely be left to
judge the value of such testimony – and of such hypotheses.

2.5

Ovid has been getting a taste of his own capricious medicine, and is
egotist enough to be stung by a woman's infidelities. *His* peccadilloes,

of course, are another matter: presumably here the familiar masculine double standard applies. The self-styled professor of seduction may play the field (he assumes) as he pleases, but when a woman starts cheating on *him* he wants to die and end it. Of course, half the fun lies in watching a repetition of *Am.* 1.4 with Ovid cast as *cocu* rather than gallant – yet invoking the same old-fashioned quasi-legal formula to protect his 'property'. He might, indeed, were this not against every tradition of Roman love-elegy, almost be speaking as an outraged husband.

As *vir*, however, he seems far less inhibited. At a first reading one gets the impression – with mounting incredulity – that he not only breaks up the girl's flirtation, but, to drive home his exclusive rights over her, proceeds to some fairly torrid embraces on his own account, there and then, *coram publico*. Such an interpretation is possible: it was, after all, late in the evening, many guests had left, and those remaining were drunk. But it makes the transition from apostrophe to narrative very strained. Ovid has been going on at Corinna (if it is Corinna) about her infidelities in general: one pictures them in bedroom or boudoir. Then he narrows his attack to one specific occasion: a dinner-party where she flirted, and more than flirted, with someone else. Before we know what has happened, the boudoir scene has been dropped, and Ovid is telling *the reader* what went on between the two of them – still, it would seem, at this ill-fated party. I would suggest that the switch from apostrophe occurs, not at line 33, but four lines earlier, with the narrator's break into *oratio recta*. 1–28 offers a self-contained scene between the lovers. The reader is assumed, but not addressed: Ovid has more immediately important matters on hand. But at line 29 he turns to the reader, as he so often does, in the way a good *raconteur* will address himself to his captive audience in a bar. Now the reader is being brought into the action. It is he who hears *a reported version* of Ovid's complaint to the girl – words that could well have been uttered, originally, in the privacy of their bedroom, as an appendix to the monologue which forms the first part of the poem. If we grant this, then the rest of the poem can be set there too, where it properly belongs, with its purely private emotions of violence and reconciliation. Ovid's problem here was, in fact, one with which all novelists are familiar: how to strike a balance between realism and convention, how to offer the reader–voyeur (and all readers of novels are voyeurs to some degree) an *entrée* on privacy while making the private relations themselves dramatic and immediate.

2.6

As becomes clear when we compare this poem with *Am.* 3.9, the lament for Tibullus, Ovid has here written a detailed parody of the *epicedion*, or commemorative dirge: it includes an introductory address to the mourners (1–16); a *lamentatio*, including the formal outburst against envious fate, the Greek *schetliasmós* (17–42); an account of the deceased parrot's end (43–8); a *consolatio* based on the afterlife (49–58); and, lastly, the funeral (59–62). The notion for honouring a pet with a funeral elegy had good precedents, which went back well beyond the most obvious source, Catullus 3, the hendecasyllables commemorating Lesbia's sparrow.

7–10 King Pandion of Athens had two daughters, Procne and Philomela. According to the Greek version of the myth, Procne was married to Tereus, King of Thrace, who then contracted a violent passion for her sister Philomela, and seduced her, cutting out her tongue to prevent her revealing what had happened. But by weaving characters in a robe she revealed her sorrows to Procne. The two sisters thereupon contrived one of those cannibal revenges in which Greek myth abounds, serving up Tereus' son Itylus, or Itys, to him for dinner. Having done this, they fled, and Tereus, on discovering what they had done, followed after with an axe, bent on revenge. However, the gods turned all three of them into birds: Procne became the nightingale, mourning for Itylus, Philomela the chattering (? presumed tongueless) swallow, and Tereus a hoopoe. Roman tradition, however, as here, reversed the sisters' roles, making Procne the swallow and Philomela the nightingale. It was this botched version that survived into the Renaissance, when 'Philomel[a]' became a synonymous term for 'nightingale'. *cf.* Ovid *Met.* 6.426–674.
34–6 The jackdaw or crow (*graculus*: one American variant is still known as a grackle) and the raven were regarded as weatherwise birds in antiquity, with the gift of predicting rain. The hatred of Minerva (or rather of her Greek analogue Pallas Athena) for the raven had an odd origin. The raven reported to her the disobedience of one or more of her daughters, and their subsequent suicide: Athena turned the raven from white to black, and nursed an undying grudge against it for having been the bearer of bad news.
39–42 The best die young: it has been a favourite belief from Homer's day (see, e.g., *Iliad* 21.34ff.) to that of the survivors from the First World War. Catullus expressed the same sentiment in his lament

for Lesbia's sparrow (3.13), and this may be the passage that Ovid had immediately in mind. Protesilaus, a Thessalian prince, was the first Greek to be slain at Troy; Thersites, ugliest and most cross-grained of the Greeks in this campaign, survived him – but hardly to a ripe old age: he fell victim to Achilles, who killed him for jeering at the grief he, Achilles, showed after slaying the Amazon Penthesilea. Hector's death preceded the fall of Troy, and thus left most, if not all, of his brothers still alive.

48 At last Corinna is named, and we see what this elegant little pastiche is doing in a collection of erotic poems. Here the link with Catullus' *passer, deliciae meae puellae* is closest. The parrot was a lover's gift and the affection between the bird and Corinna is made clear; furthermore, at line 56 Ovid reminds us of the amorous propensities so often attributed to birds themselves.

53–4 The literature on the phoenix, that fabulous bird reputed to live for 500 years and achieve rebirth from its own ashes, is considerable: see esp. Herodotus 2.73, Ovid *Met.* 15.392ff.

2.7 and 2.8

These two poems – like 1.11 and 1.12 a dramatic diptych – are commonly taken as one more demonstration that Ovid in the *Amores* was creating purely fictional situations, exercising his literary talents rather than drawing on experience. But the situation is a perfectly possible one, and Ovid's reactions entirely in character.

It is true that his treatment of the incident shows both rhetorical and literary skill; but does that mean he necessarily invented it? By addressing first Corinna, then Cypassis, Ovid can display his skill at eristics, i.e. arguing opposite viewpoints one after the other, with some aplomb: see esp. 7.19–22, answered by 8.9–14.

2.7

3–6 Women occupied the upper tiers of the auditorium in the theatre: cf. Prop. 4.8.77. The theatre referred to here is that of Pompey, built 55 BC in stone (*marmorei*); previous theatres had been temporary wooden structures. Despite this segregation of the sexes it is clear that the Roman theatre – like Sunday church services during the eighteenth and nineteenth centuries – offered a convenient venue for discreet flirtation: see *AA* 1.89–134 *passim* (cf. 3.394, 633; *RA* 751–2).

17   Ecce, novum crimen! Ovid exclaims: *crimen* is charmingly ambiguous, since it can mean either 'accusation' or 'crime', and thus provides the equivalent of a covert wink to the knowing reader.

2.8

1-2   On the lady's-maid as coiffeuse see above, note to *Am*. 1.11.1-4 (pp. 282-3), and the highly informative section on 'Coiffure' in J. P. V. D. Balsdon's *Roman Women*, pp. 255-60, and pl. 13, opp. p. 240. cf. *AA* 3.135.

3-4   'No country beginner', *non rustica*, with its strong hint of sophistication in matters both social and sexual, is one of Ovid's highest compliments to a woman. For his scornful attitude to *rusticitas*, or naïve provincial respectability, see, e.g., *Am*. 1.8.44, 2.4.13, 3.1.43, 3.4.37, 3.10.18; *AA* 1.607,672; *RA* 329, 330; *EP* 1.77, 4.102, 15.287, 16.13.

10ff.   The parade of mythological precedents for falling in love with a maid (or captive, or some other person outside one's social station) had already been deployed by Horace, *Odes* 2.4.1ff., who also cites, in addition to Achilles/Briseis and Agamemnon/Cassandra, the similar case of Ajax and Tecmessa. See above, *Am*. 1.9.33-44. It is noteworthy that all Ovid's parallels are drawn from cases of women captured in war (as indeed were Horace's); thus with a neat literary echo he reinforces his already close links between the concepts of sexual and military operations: see my introductory note on 1.9 (p. 279).

19-20   For the gods' readiness not to take lovers' oaths seriously, see above, note on *Am*. 1.8.85-6: the belief was widespread and of great antiquity.

22-8   It is not necessary to assume that Cypassis is a coloured girl. At *Am*. 2.4.40 *fusco colore* need mean no more than 'dark' or even 'brunette' in contrast to the blonde, *flava puella*, of line 39, and the same may well be true here.

Ovid's arguments to Cypassis, of course, contain a built-in fallacy. If she refuses to sleep with him, he threatens, he will tell Corinna the whole story of their *affaire*. But this, obviously, would be disastrous for his own relationship with Corinna. The joke, of course, is that Cypassis could well be flustered enough to swallow Ovid's argument, illogicality and all, whereas we, reading the poem at our leisure, do not – surely a deliberate effect?

2.9, 9B

Once again the pros and cons of erotic scalp-hunting are debated, and Ovid uses the occasion to display, as in 2.7 and 8, his eristic skill in putting the *argumentatio* for each side. The poems are notable for several things: their density and concision, their striking imagery, their renewal of a favourite Ovidian motif – sex justified in military terms – and the sharply edged, psychologically acute self-portrait they present: compulsive desire mingled with boredom and self-disgust (9.9–10, 23–4, 9B. 3–10; cf. 1.2.1–12, 2.4 *passim*, 2.10 *passim*, 3.7 *passim*, 3.11B.1–2).

The imagery is hard, sharp, deliberately unromantic: barbed arrows, spears, the gladiator's wooden sword, the runaway horse's bit, the veering yawl, fighting, hunting. But then for Ovid sex *is* (in at least two senses) venery; and for the hunter, as he reminds us here (cf. also *Am.* 2.19.31–16), pursuit is all, while 'girls are such exquisite hell'.

The first half of the diptych, then, calls for a truce in the sex-game, a discharge from service, while the second decides that, after all, life without sex would be as boring as death.

2.9

7–8 During the first, abortive, expedition of the Greek armada to recover Helen, the fleet put in to shore on the Mysian coast, mistaking it for the Troad. The king of Mysia, Telephus, was wounded by Achilles' spear, and afterwards told by an oracle that only the man who wounded him could heal him. He made his way to Argos, and Achilles cured his wound by scraping rust from his spear into it, a clear case of sympathetic magic.

13–14 Ovid at several points in the *Amores* (e.g. 1.6.3–6 and 2.10.23–4, besides the present passage) describes himself as extremely thin, but wiry: he attributes his lack of weight to sexual exercise, and hints that, far from hampering his performance, it actually enhances it – an assertion with which doctors and dieticians would probably not quarrel.

15–24 The idea of a triumph is, once again (cf. 1.2.23ff.) brought in to juxtapose the achievements of love and of Roman imperialism. The veteran's 'State allotment' indicates a period prior to AD 6, when Augustus regularized conditions of discharge for legionaries: ever since the days of Sulla it had been a common practice to settle demobilized troops in new *coloniae*, giving each man a grant of land. A discharged gladiator who had served his time was presented with a wooden sword (*rude donatus*) in token of release from combat.

2.9 B

15–18 Similar sentiments are expressed below (*Am.* 2.10.15), as well as by Tibullus (1.2.75) and Propertius (1.14.15–16).
19–20 These were not the only circumstances in which Ovid welcomed what we might call 'white lies', or discreet silence, from his mistress. See, e.g., *Am.* 1.4.69–70, where he prefers not to be told if she has had intercourse with her husband, but begs for a blanket denial, and *Am.* 3.14 *passim*, where he makes much the same plea apropos her numerous affairs on the side.
23 The inconstancy of Mars (Ares) here referred to is, of course, the famous occasion in Homer (*Od.* 8.262–339) when he and Aphrodite cuckolded the absent Hephaestus, only to be trapped in bed together by the latter's web-like toils – at which sight, not surprisingly, 'laughter unquenchable arose among the deathless gods'.

2.10

As an erotic apologia this cocky poem displays its own innocent charm. Ovid's mood shifts amusingly from the initial irritation with Graecinus to a mood of self-satisfied sexual bravado. How boring, he laments at first, to be stuck between two girls: what a business choosing one or the other! Still, he reflects, better too much sex than none at all – so why not, at a pinch, take them *both* on? After some complacent reflections on his own erotic stamina – as usual, Ovid's notion of 'taking on' a girl looks no further than intercourse – he concludes with the rake's pious prayer down the ages, that he may die while making love.

1 This Graecinus (see Introduction, pp. 36–7) is certainly the addressee of three of the *Black Sea Letters* (1.6, 2.6, 4.9), and in all likelihood C. Pomponius Graecinus, the *consul suffectus* of AD 16.

2.11

This is what was known in antiquity as a *propemptikon*, i.e. a poem addressed to some individual about to make a journey (most often by sea, where the risks were proportionately greater), wishing him or her a safe landfall and a speedy return. The tradition was a long-standing one: not surprisingly, when one reflects on the hazards of Aegean travel ('When you round Cape Malea,' an old proverb ran, 'say good-bye to home.')

All the traditional ingredients of the genre are present: Ovid begins by trying (*schetliasmós*) to dissuade Corinna from making the journey at all (1–32), then wishes her *bon voyage* in two brief lines (33–4), and spends the rest of the poem (35–56) fantasizing about her return. On the surface all is indeed simple delight as Ovid visualizes this latter scene: a magically swift reunion, the innocent, and somewhat un-Ovidian, idea of a beach-picnic, Corinna encouraged, over the wine, to tell her own travellers' tall stories. Yet for those who know – as Ovid's readers most certainly did – their Propertius and Tibullus, an uneasy leitmotiv runs through these final lines. The veiled quotations hint, ominously, at sickness and death: it is as though Ovid were employing them as touchstones for mortality.

1–6 These first six lines contain a cluster of literary allusions that would do credit to *The Waste Land*. The Argo was built, with Thessalian pinewood, from trees felled on Mt Pelion. Corinna, it is made clear, will be exposed in Ovid's mind to all the traditional mythic perils of a sea-voyage: he at once exaggerates and mocks the actual risks with a proem in the high tragic manner. Perhaps by such inflated parallels he hoped to comfort Corinna, if he could not dissuade her, and in so doing to comfort himself as well: 'These fragments have I shored against my ruins.' If Corinna is deserting him (see below) the allusions become even more pointed.

7–8 What Corinna abandons has an ambiguity in Latin that English cannot match: *notumque torum sociosque Penates.* To whom is the bed familiar, and whose joint property are the household gods? My translation catches some, but alas not all, of this suggestive uncertainty. That infidelity and desertion are implied seems certain: note, though, that Ovid carefully omits not only her destination, but also any motive for leaving on Corinna's part.

18–20 The 'African quicksands' mentioned here were the Greater and Lesser Syrtes, two large gulfs in the Libyan Sea between Cyrenaica, Tripolitania and Tunisia, regarded as particularly dangerous for navigation on account of their shallows, sunken reefs and treacherous sand-drifts. They are today the Gulfs of Sidra and Gabès respectively.
29–32 The 'patron gods of sailors' in this context were Leda's

offspring, the twin Dioscuri Castor and Pollux (or Polydeuces in Greek), often referred to by Roman poets.

44 What Ovid says the ship has aboard, in Latin, is *nostros deos*, or 'our gods', at one level the images of the ship's tutelary deities, most often affixed to the vessel's poop or stern. But by poetic licence the plural can be taken as a singular: 'my god', or, in a less specific sense, 'my deity'. Ovid's 'deity', of course, is Corinna herself. I could not find an adequate English equivalent for this associative ambiguity, so came down, with regret, exclusively on Corinna's side of the fence.

2.12

Like Propertius on a similar occasion (2.14), Ovid here celebrates the yielding of his mistress, a night spent triumphantly in her arms. Yet the two poems, despite superficial similarities, are fundamentally distinct. Propertius, full of bitter-sweet joy, senses that the moment will not last. He is involved with Cynthia as a person, and though, like Ovid, he employs the image of a triumph (vv. 23-8), it is for a very different purpose. The spoils of victory which he describes, the captive kings and chariots, the rich offerings to be placed in Venus' shrine, are a metaphor for the night of love he and Cynthia shared: Propertius, in gratitude, is consecrating their common pleasure. Ovid, on the other hand, regards the entire exercise as a military siege-operation, and has congratulations for no one involved but himself. Both poets adduce the mythological parallel of Agamemnon (Prop. vv. 1-2, Ovid vv. 9-10), but while Propertius simply claims greater happiness than the Greek commander at the fall of Troy, Ovid's point is that unlike Agamemnon (who had to share his victory with others), Ovid has scored a one-man triumph: captain, infantry, cavalry and standard-bearer all rolled into one.

7-8 The emphasis on triumphing over a girl gains added political significance when we recall how official propaganda played down Antony's role in the Actium campaign, and emphasized that of Cleopatra.

17-24 Various examples of *cherchez la femme* as the cause of a war: Helen, Hippodameia, Lavinia, the Rape of the Sabines. For the battle of Centaurs and Lapiths at the wedding-feast of Pirithoüs and Hippodameia see *Met.* 12.210-535. Lavinia was the daughter of Latinus and Amata, and originally betrothed to the Rutulian prince Turnus. When Aeneas landed, Latinus remembered an oracle advising him to marry his daughter to a foreign chieftain, and gave Lavinia to the newcomer instead. The result was a war with the Rutulians, in which Turnus was finally killed by Aeneas. The latter married Lavinia, who bore him Ascanius: the town of Lavinium was named after her. On the rape of the Sabine women see *AA* 1.101–34 and note ad loc.

2.13, 2.14

That abortion was common in Rome, particularly among the upper classes, is clear enough not only from literary passages denouncing the practice, or alluding to women's unwillingness to bear children (cf. Juvenal *Sat.* 6.592ff., Ovid *Nux* 24), but perhaps even more from Augustan legislation which penalized the childless while offering bonuses for large families. The *Lex Julia de maritandis ordinibus* of 18 BC and the *Lex Papia Poppaea* of AD 9 both exemplify this trend, and hint eloquently at the state of affairs that Augustus was attempting to remedy. The seniority of the consuls was established by the number of their children, and in the case of a political tied vote the candidate with the larger family was held to have won. It is thus clear that Corinna's act, far from being isolated or extraordinary, was (as 2.14 makes clear) a commonplace occurrence. This does not detract from its dramatic impact, or lessen the shock (and, one fears, the irritation) which Ovid displays.

The first poem is largely taken up with formal prayers to Isis and to Ilithyia, goddess of childbirth: invocation, enumeration of past services, promises of future offerings. However, these prayers are sandwiched between a brief statement of the facts, followed by a somewhat vague admission of paternity (1–6), and a final couplet addressed to Corinna herself (27–8) which suggests, suddenly, that we are to envisage the entire scene, prayers included, as taking place at Corinna's bedside. Once again, Ovid has so loaded his coda as to make us rethink all that preceded it.

2.14, on the other hand, consists – down to the last four lines – of a long general jeremiad against abortion as a practice, backed with numerous mythological (plus two agricultural) *exempla*, and culminating in the reminder, delivered with relish, that women who try to kill their unborn foetus very often end up killing themselves. If we are to regard this as a dramatic continuation of the episode, it seems clear that the narrator has by now recovered both his self-righteousness and his fluent command of literary parallels. The final quatrain, however

(41–4), finds him asking the gods to blow away such ill-omened words, and to overlook Corinna's offence – this once: next time there will be no mercy. Corinna, it would seem, is expected, if the situation recurs, to grin and bear it without complaint (it is typical of Ovid that he leaves us guessing as to whether the abortion was in fact successful or not).

2.14

5ff. What in fact are Ovid's objections to the practice of abortion? Not, we may safely say, moral. If allowed to spread, it could cause the extinction of the human race. If practised by the wrong (i.e. top) people, various VIPs (Achilles, Romulus, Aeneas, Caesar) would not have appeared at moments in history when their services were badly needed. He also applies an agricultural analogy, citing vine and orchard tree for the principle of letting all fruit, and thus each foetus, mature in season (a nod to the Virgil of the *Georgics?*). Revenge on a husband is regarded as a mitigating excuse; the danger of the process to the mother is also considered. What surprises about this is that, for once, Ovid would seem to have embraced the official line. Could he, yet again, be mocking Augustan moral legislation by applying it in a demeaning or subtly ridiculous context – in this case, a lover's obligations towards his mistress?

Contraception, which one might have thought a key topic for any practitioner or *praeceptor amoris*, is ignored both here and throughout the *Ars*. Did Ovid always expect the gentleman to enjoy his fun, while the lady ripened in season? Not if we accept his protestation (*Trist.* 2.351–2) that no husband, *even a lower-class one*, has been saddled with illegitimate offspring as a result of his, Ovid's, sexual adventures.

Another possibility: perhaps Ovid's man-of-the-world pose held up well enough under favourable, i.e. non-demanding, conditions, but the moment something went wrong, or real life intruded on the pose, he was liable to take refuge in an outburst of furious respectability? Or could it be, simply, that here, if nowhere else, his chauvinist attitude happened to coincide with Augustus' moral programme? Unlikely: what Don Juan wants a pregnant love-object? My own, unprovable, suspicion is linked to Ovid's apparent low fertility. We know that this was a common phenomenon in the late Republic and early Empire. This one incident apart, it may well be that Ovid had hitherto been able to ignore the problem altogether, because it never bore any consequences for him. This would explain, *inter alia*, his curious, but significant, uncertainty (2.13.5–6) as to whether he was, in fact, the father of Corinna's unborn child.

11ff. The 'stone-throwing demiurge' was Deucalion, who, with Pyrrha, repeopled the world after a flood by flinging stones over his shoulder. Thetis the sea-nymph bore Achilles to Peleus; Ilia, or Rhea Silvia, was the mother of Romulus and Remus. Augustus, adopted by his great-uncle Julius Caesar, claimed descent from Venus through Aeneas, her son by Anchises: Aeneas' son Iulus was the eponymous ancestor of the *gens Julia*. Medea killed her children because their father Jason had divorced her in Corinth to marry Creon's daughter. For the complex myth of Tereus, Procne, Itys and Philomela, see above, note to *Am.* 2.6.7–10 (p. 295).

2.15

The erotic conceit of a lover who identifies himself with some article in his beloved's possession – especially something that she would wear or carry on her person – dates back at least as far as the Hellenistic period (see, e.g., *Anth. Pal.* 5.83, 84; 12.208), was popular in the Middle Ages, and has seen regular service ever since (e.g. in Tennyson's 'The Miller's Daughter'). It offers splendid scope for various sorts of sexual innuendo: cf. the pseudo-Ovidian *De Pulice*, the ancestor of several similar works, including John Donne's 'The Flea' and a modern calypso known variously as 'Muriel's Treasure' or 'The Bedbug'. Jewellery, a papyrus-roll, a soft breeze, a rose: opportunities are endless. In Ovid's case we also have a double entendre to consider, since the Latin word *anulus*, just as the English word 'ring', can also be used as a synonym for the anus. As so often, Ovid takes a hackneyed literary convention and exploits it *ad absurdum*. We are suddenly faced (lines 25–6) with the mental image of a ring in a shower-bath developing an erection: nothing could more neatly expose the artificiality of this stylized exercise in wishful thinking. To become one's own gift would indeed confer proximity – but *awareness*? The minute we start visualizing a sentient observer somehow concealed, or immanent, in ring, rose, book or what-have-you, the entire conceit collapses into a species of grotesque *adynaton*. After working this deft literary deflation, Ovid winds up with a couplet as commonplace as a Chinese fortune-cookie motto. The ring, having shown off its symbolic paces, reverts to the simple lover's gift of lines 1–6: a nice case, in fact, of ring-composition.

2.16

Ovid's exclusive concentration, throughout the *Amores*, on his main erotic theme can, at times, become a little irritating to the reader, and the description of rural scenery with which this poem opens is a welcome relief. Even so, we have to make the most of very little. Ten lines – and then the ever-interesting topic, by which all else is judged, relentlessly recurs: *at meus ignis abest*, 'but my flame isn't here'. Apart from four more lines (33–6), which again emphasize how dreary the scene is without the presence of his beloved, Ovid wastes no more time on his birthplace for its own sake, and only refers to it perfunctorily elsewhere (*Am.* 3.15.11–14, *Fast.* 4.685–6, *Trist.* 4.10.2–4). It was not that he had no eye for the countryside: several poems exist to disprove such a notion. But he was not, in the last resort, by temperament or life-style, much addicted to the natural habitat of that quality which he can never mention without a sneer – *rusticitas*.

Sulmo, the modern Sulmona, lies in a fertile valley among the wild mountains of the Abruzzi. Its landscape is startling, a pattern of stark contrasts. Ovid, however, only mentions the hills and passes to express a hope that their steep winding roads will become level for his beloved. He compliments the tough Pelignian peasants who fought for independence during the Social War (90–88 BC), but never refers to their living descendants. Highet (p. 196) sums up his urban attitude acutely: 'He liked Sulmo with its surroundings because it was fruitful and well-watered – in fact, a tidy farm, a large garden. As for the inhabitants, he does not seem ever to have noticed them.' Why, on his own terms, should he? To him they were as remote – and brutishly inferior – as the *contadini* of the Abruzzi still remain to any town-dwelling Italian. Ovid proudly acknowledges his Pelignian roots, but has no urge to identify with them: like every small-town boy who has made a successful transfer to the big city, he can only go back for long weekends.

17 The journey to Sulmo must, in fact, have been both difficult and dangerous in Ovid's day. Quite apart from the constant hazard of highwaymen and footpads, the road (then as now) ran through passes which negotiate some of the highest mountains in central Italy, to descend precipitously into the plain below. The forests of the Abruzzi still abound with wild boar, bears and wolves. Ovid's extravagant wish for his girl in the last two lines of the poem is thus no mere literary convention, but based on an all-too-real knowledge of the route she would have to travel.

23–6 Scylla and Charybdis were traditionally located in the Straits of Messina. Scylla's dogs, barking from her womb or groin, were a favourite motif among Roman poets. Cape Malea (the modern Matapan), at the southernmost tip of Laconia, was notoriously dangerous for sailors: cf. introd. note to 2.11, above.

31–2 Hero was a priestess of Aphrodite in Sestos; her lover Leander would swim across the Hellespont from Abydos after dark to visit her, till one stormy night he was drowned.

39–40 The names and places are chosen for their remoteness as well as their barbarian associations. Prometheus' rock in the Caucasus was especially regarded, at least metaphorically, as the 'end of the world'.

41 Italian farmers grafted vines on to elms and used the term 'marry' of the process (*maritare*). This gave rise to a pleasant fantasy about the natural love between them.

2.17

It is probably no accident that whereas in 2.16 Ovid is yearning for Corinna's arrival, his heart made fonder by her protracted absence, both 2.17 and 2.18 emphasize aspects of her character which severely try his patience when she is with him. She puts on airs and treats her cavalier like dirt. Worse, she interrupts his writing and tries to veto any mode of composition, e.g. tragedy, which does not directly refer to her. By 2.19 Ovid (whether in fact or fiction or both) has put two and two together, and is taking the lady's husband to task for not keeping her under stricter surveillance. Too much of her company clearly has its disadvantages – which may go some way to explain why Ovid's appetite, on his own account, is most whetted by frustration and elusiveness. Pursuit, as always, excites him more than possession.

The poem is a neat but at first sight unremarkable exercise: it has interested few commentators. Perhaps its most noteworthy feature is the tantalizing biographical hints it offers us about Corinna. The series of mythological parallels suggests clearly that she not only played the spoilt beauty with Ovid but in some way claimed to be his *social superior*. Ovid promises he will not be a *crimen*, that is an 'accusation', a cause of scandal – or boredom – to her. Their love-affair 'won't ever require disowning'. Ovid agrees to take Corinna on her own terms (line 23). Finally, there is the woman who falsely pretends to be Corinna. In lines 31–2 Ovid, through the image of the two rivers, challenges her assertion. Why the Eurotas and the Po? Surely not just because of the distance between them: the simple answer is because one lady was Greek, the other Italian. Nor, if Corinna put on social airs with Ovid, need we doubt which was which. We shall never, in all likelihood, know Corinna's identity (and many will continue to argue that she was a figment of Ovid's imagination); but this poem, taken in conjunction with our other evidence, suggests strongly that she was a Roman lady of high rank.

3-4 The goddess of Paphos (on Cyprus) and Cythera was, of course, Venus (Aphrodite), who had cults in both places.

15-20 For Calypso and her relations with Odysseus see Homer *Od.* 5 *passim.* The sea-nymph who wed Peleus was Thetis. For Numa and Egeria see Ovid *Fast.* 3.261ff., *Met.* 15.482ff. For Vulcan (Hephaestus) and Venus (Aphrodite) cf. *AA* 2.567-70.

21-2 Ovid compares the short pentameter with Vulcan's lame foot: cf. above, *Am.* 1.1.3ff., 27-8.

32 The Po (Northern Italy) and the Eurotas (Laconia) were, and remain, the two most considerable rivers of Italy and peninsular Greece respectively.

2.18

1-3 The poem's theme suggests that it originally featured as the *envoi* to one of Ovid's five original books, but was displaced on revision. 1.1, 1.15, 2.1, 3.1 and 3.15 all deal with the same topic, Ovid's perennial weakness for being sidetracked by Eros from more weighty themes: only 3.15, as is appropriate, takes a final farewell of love-elegy. The opening lines echo Prop. 1.7.1-5; but whereas Ovid claims to be at least *trying* to write tragedy rather than erotic verse, Propertius proudly nails his colours to the mast (9-10): 'This is the way my life is spent, *this* is my claim to renown, on *this* I want my poetry's spreading reputation to depend.' The reader of Ovid was surely expected to recall those lines. Macer (cf. Introd. pp. 26ff.) was a close friend of Ovid's, with whom as a youth he had travelled in Asia Minor (*EP* 2.10.21ff.); he was also related to Ovid's third wife (ibid., 10). Elsewhere, (*EP* 4.16.6) he is referred to as *Iliacus Macer*, 'Macer of Troy', a title explained by his activities as an epic poet. What he was composing seems to have been a prelude to the *Iliad*, an account of those events that preceded, and led up to, the Wrath of Achilles.

13 The tragic opus in question (see above) was almost certainly

Ovid's lost *Medea*, rated by Tacitus (*Dial.* 12) among the greatest
Roman tragedies, and of which Quintilian (*Inst. Orat.* 10.1.98) wrote
that it just showed what Ovid could do when he chose to discipline his
creative talent rather than indulge it.

21-6 Eight of the first fifteen 'Heroines' Epistles' are mentioned
here: nos. 1 (Penelope to Ulysses), 2 (Phyllis to Demophoön), 5
(Oenone to Paris), 11 (Canace to Macareus), 6 (Hypsipyle to Jason),
10 (Ariadne to Theseus), 4 (Phaedra to Hippolytus), 7 (Dido to
Aeneas) and 15 (Sappho to Phaon). Demophoön was a son of Theseus
who, on his return to Troy, became betrothed to Phyllis, daughter of
King Sithon of Thrace. When Demophoön went off to Cyprus, how-
ever, the girl committed suicide, believing he would never return, and
was turned into an almond-tree. Ovid refers to the story again in *Her.*
2 *passim*, *AA* 2.353-4, 3.37-8, 459-60, and *RA* 55-6, 591-608 (see
my note, pp. 417-18). Oenone was the nymph from Mt Ida (daughter
of a river-god, Cebren) who married Paris and was deserted by him
for Helen. The incestuous passion of Macareus and Canace, both chil-
dren of Aeolus the wind-god, formed the theme of Euripides' lost
Aeolus. When the Argonauts put in to Lemnos (a peculiarly dreary
island) they found it ruled by women, who had murdered their hus-
bands and fathers, under a queen, Hypsipyle. Jason sired two children
on Hypsipyle, but afterwards deserted her. The accounts of Ariadne's
parting from Theseus vary, but Ovid follows the version in which
Theseus deserted her, either on Dia or on Naxos. Theseus (lines 24-
5) was, by the Amazon Antiope, the father of Hippolytus, and the
guilty passion of his wife Phaedra for her stepson was widely treated
by ancient authors. Ovid also treats this theme in *Met.* 15.497ff.,
AA 1.511-12, and *RA* 64. Dido's suicide is described at length by
Virgil in *Aen.* 4.641ff. Ovid picks up the tradition of Sappho's
unhappy heterosexual love-affair with Phaon the ferryman, and her
suicidal leap, after he deserted her and went to Sicily, from the high
cliffs of Leucas.

27-34 Sabinus was a close friend of Ovid's, a poet himself, who died
young (*EP* 4.16.13-16). The fact that he composed replies to these
epistles says little for his literary taste. Only the answer from Ulysses
could have failed to ruin the effect of its counterpart. The order in
which both originals and replies are mentioned here suggests that
Heroides 1-15 already existed much as we have them today.

38 Laodameia was the wife of Protesilaus, the first Greek ashore at
Troy, and the first to be killed there. She continued to pine for him

after his death, even going so far that she 'made an image of him and consorted with it'. Hermes, taking pity on her, brought Protesilaus briefly up from Hades, and Laodameia either expired in his ghostly arms, or else stabbed herself when he was taken back to the underworld.

2.19

This poem is often compared and contrasted with *Am.* 3.4 as an example of how you can never take what Ovid says seriously, how the changing literary *persona* is all. Here, he tells a cuckolded husband to put a stricter guard on his wife, since otherwise he, Ovid, will become bored with her through lack of opposition. There, he informs the same long-suffering gentleman that shutting his wife up is useless, since nothing but natural inclination can produce chastity. When the two poems are juxtaposed, many of the apparent inconsistencies melt away (see my introductory note on 3.4, pp. 315–16), and both propositions are equally valid, from Ovid's viewpoint, in different circumstances. The characteristically masculine notion of rejecting too easy a conquest has a long history. Ovid himself repeats the motif elsewhere, e.g. *Am.* 2.9.9–10, *AA* 3.577–610. On the face of it, though, he is equally resentful of too spirited or stubborn a resistance: *Am.* 1.6, 2.2, 2.3. What suits him best, in fact, is a *show* of elusiveness, a doorkeeper who merely plays tough, caprice that understands the unwritten rules of the game. His real objection, whether to an overindifferent *or* a vulgarly restrictive husband, is that such persons spoil the fun by refusing to take on the roles conceived for them. How can the formal quadrille of civilized seduction survive without their essential cooperation? Ovid is *homo ludens* in person: we do his character less than justice if we reduce its varied literary manifestations to a mere bundle of masks.

19–20 We should note that whoever this girl may be, she is *not* Corinna, with whom in fact Ovid compares her.
21–2 For the theme of the lover-shut-out (*exclusus amator*) and the *paraclausithyron*, the poem written to celebrate such an occasion, see *Am.* 1.6 *passim*, and my introductory note ad loc. (pp. 274–5).
27–8 Danaë was the daughter of Acrisius, king of Argos. An oracle declared that a child born of her would one day kill Acrisius, who therefore kept her shut up in a subterranean chamber, or tower, of

bronze. However, Zeus reached her by transforming himself into a shower of gold, and got her pregnant with Perseus. Mother and child were sent floating out to sea in a chest by Acrisius, but reached Seriphos safely: the oracle, in due course, was fulfilled.

29–30 On Io's vicissitudes as a heifer see *Am.* 2.2.44–6 and my note ad loc. (p. 292).

BOOK 3

3.1

Once again Ovid begins a book with a programmatic poem about his stubborn resistance to the Claims of the Sublime. The allegory is of the lightest. It is possible that the wood may represent the Roman poet or orator's *silva rerum*, that mass of raw material on which he could draw at will. Ovid's predicament much resembles the famous allegorical myth of Prodicus, 'Heracles at the Crossroads' (see Xenophon *Mem.* 2.1.21–34), in which the young hero is similarly confronted with two allegorical yet palpably real ladies, Virtue and Vice, competing for his allegiance. However seriously Ovid took his *Medea*, he simply cannot resist guying Tragedy: 'scarlet buskins/holding her upright against the weight of her hair'. Elegy, on the other hand, cheerfully describes her vicissitudes as a written love-poem, nailed to doors, stuffed in bosoms, or torn up and thrown down the drain (53–9): this incongruous motif recalls Ovid's ring-metamorphosis in *Am.* 2.15 (see my introductory note ad loc., p. 304). We are never in doubt as to which of them, at this point, Ovid will choose – no Bk 3 otherwise – but the plea for postponement is clinched, in wrily mocking self-knowledge, by the prospect of immortalization for his love-affairs. Nearly two millennia later we can relish the irony of that capricious fate which preserved the *Amores*, but condemned the *Medea* to oblivion.

1–4 The description of wood and grotto is deliberately stylized, almost like a Pompeian wall-painting.

9–10 Elegy is symbolically lame to represent the fact that the second line of an elegiac couplet is shorter than the first – and to emphasize the contrast with tragic senarii and epic hexameters.

34–5 Myrtle (cf. *Am.* 1.1.29) was sacred to Venus, and thus an appropriate appurtenance for the allegorical figure of (erotic) Elegy.

3.2

All critics are agreed that this is a delightful and vivid poem, almost unique in ancient literature (perhaps the nearest approach to it, for intimate social realism, is Theocritus' Fifteenth Idyll, the *Adoniazusae*), a monologue addressed to a girl at the races, which not only displays great psychological acumen but offers us an all-too-rare glimpse of Romans enjoying their leisure in a credible and recognizable manner. The scene is as clearly etched as Frith's *Derby Day*. What would seem to have struck nobody, however (and this remains true whether we treat the poem as fiction or as reportage), is the curious ambiguity of the relationship between Ovid and the object of his advances; the girl utters not one word from start to finish. Why not? And how have they come to be where they are in the first place?

It makes a crucial difference how we read the scene. There are the girl and Ovid next to one another in the front row, against the railings (63–4). She has (it would appear from Ovid's complaints) one strange man to her right, and another behind her (20–24), leaving Ovid himself on her left. Thus she must, inevitably it would seem, be either alone, or else Ovid's acknowledged guest. Which is it? If she had come alone – unlikely in any circumstances – she would have, almost by definition, to be a *meretrix*, a prostitute. Who else would haunt the Circus, of all places, unescorted? But if she was a prostitute, the poem would be meaningless, since Ovid employs considerable sympathy and subtlety to make an impression on her, and in the penultimate line (83) merely *thinks* he sees the promise of capitulation in her eye. Whatever this monologue may be, then, it is *not* Ovid's account of how he propositioned a tart.

Such being the case, a natural inference would be that Ovid and his latest girl-of-the-moment are attending the races together – a pleasant excursion with decidedly modern associations. Too modern, indeed, by a long chalk, as we at once realize on reflection. Social difficulties beset this idyllic scene. Under what circumstances, we ask ourselves, could or would a young man legitimately appear in public accompanied by an unchaperoned lady who was not his wife? Again the answer forces itself upon us: only with a *meretrix* or (the next best thing) a *libertina*, a name with unfortunate but hardly accidental associations. But Ovid's companion is clearly neither whore nor freedwoman. He treats her with delicate *social* respect, as an equal: no easy touch there. An unmarried girl of good family, then? Unthinkable. A married lady? Equally unthinkable: discreet private adultery was one thing in

Rome, but (except in very special circumstances) flouting public con-ventions for the whole world to see was quite another. At this point the exasperated reader may well object that if Ovid could not have brought this girl with him, and is not picking her up either, then what in heaven's name *is* supposed to be going on?

Let us compare this poem, for possible illumination, with a related sequence in the *Ars. AA* 1.135–64 (see my note, p. 342) takes the basic material of *Am.* 3.2, but transposes it into didactic advice for others. What Ovid there says, quite clearly, is that the Circus provides admirable conditions for *approaches . . . to a new courtship (aditus . . . novo . . . amori)*. The lady is referred to as *domina* (139), but whether this implies prior acquaintance, or merely hope for the future, is un-certain. What a day at the races can provide, Ovid seems to suggest, is that intimate *physical proximity* essential for the preliminaries of seduc-tion. Now in both these passages (*AA* 1.139–42; *Am.* 3.2.19–20) what rates specific emphasis is *the convenience of the seating-arrangements*. Spectators were packed in close, side by side, irrespec-tive of sex, and a hopeful lover could, by careful manoeuvring, get himself near, or even next to, the lady of his choice. The great advan-tage, clearly, of such contact lay in its apparent fortuitousness: the occasion both gave it social acceptability and robbed it of any overtly scandalous implications.

This suggests a rather different scene from those hitherto proposed. Ovid has fallen in love with a respectable, and almost certainly married lady. He has not yet made love to her (27–36), and does not even know for certain whether she returns his feelings of passion (83). One possible solution is to seat himself next to her at the races. The poem describes this occasion – but what it discreetly omits (partly on grounds of literary economy, but also as a private social joke, and a hint at Ovid's own obsessional state of mind) is all direct mention of the *other people* who must have been participants in the scene: the lady's husband, probably her maid, perhaps even Ovid's own wife. The scene, in its public aspects, now becomes socially innocuous.

On the other hand, Ovid's monologue most certainly does not. No *vir* in the world, however complaisant, is going to sit by while a young poet and gadabout not only flirts outrageously with his wife, but tells him, the husband, to sit a little less close to her (21–2). It is those lines that first give us an inkling of what Ovid is up to. 'Hey, you on the right there, *whoever you are (quicumque es)*', he says: the joke is shared between poet and percipient reader, who will (knowing

Roman social rules) have instantly deduced the husband's unseen and unspoken presence, and chuckle at this cheekily oblique reference to him. But, finally, why *does* the husband keep so obligingly quiet during this elegantly seductive monologue, which subjects his wife to a species of lingering verbal rape? For the same simple reason, I would argue, that the girl herself says never a word either: because *they do not hear what Ovid is saying*. The entire monologue (and not line 83 alone) is conceived as an elaborate fantasy going on in the poet's head, perhaps encouraged by one casual flirtatious glance. Not a word of it – except perhaps Ovid's exhortations to the charioteer, which are legitimate on such an occasion – is to be thought of as being spoken aloud. Of course, if the scene portrays Corinna, and Corinna was in fact here based on Ovid's first wife, then the social proprieties are at once restored, and the joke will lie in Ovid's use of a respectable marital outing to hint at elegant seduction.

11–12 The chariots ran anti-clockwise, past a central barrier known as the *spina*, which they kept on their left. At the turns, a skilful charioteer would edge as close to the end-posts (*metae*) as he could without actually touching them.

15–16 The myth of Pelops and Hippodameia is, to put it mildly, odd. Hippodameia was the daughter of Oenomaus, King of Elis, who nursed an incestuous passion for her, to which she did not respond. To add to his frustration, Oenomaus had been warned by an oracle that his future son-in-law would be responsible for his death. When suitors came seeking Hippodameia's hand, Oenomaus sent them off in their chariot, with his daughter, and himself pursued them. If they got to Corinth ahead of him, they could marry Hippodameia; if Oenomaus caught up with them (which he invariably did) he speared them to death. By the time Pelops came along, there were a dozen suitors' heads nailed to the king's gable. Hippodameia, however, fell in love with Pelops, and bribed Oenomaus' charioteer, Myrtilus, to weaken the linchpins in the wheels of the king's chariot, so that he crashed and was dragged to his death. Even so, Pelops had a narrow escape when he slackened rein at sight of Hippodameia, and just missed being skewered by her urgent father.

19–20 The seating-places in the rows were marked off from each other by a groove (*linea*) carved in the marble.

29–30 Atalanta, daughter of Iasus, was, like Artemis/Diana, a virgin huntress, who took part in the famous hunt for the Calydonian Boar, and wrestled successfully against Peleus. When her father wanted her to marry, she made her suitors race against her, giving them a slight start, and herself running armed. Like Oenomaus in similar circumstances, if she caught the suitor, she killed him. However, if he kept his distance, he married her. Various suitors were neatly dispatched; Atalanta remained a virgin. Milanion, knowing the conditions, brought with him some golden apples he had obtained from Aphrodite. These he dropped at intervals during the race. Atalanta, being both greedy and curious, stopped to pick them up; thus Milanion won both the race and his desired bride.

43-4 The races were preceded by a procession (*pompa*) of ivory images of the gods, borne on wagons or floats, and escorted by officials. The *pompa*, setting out from the Capitol, made its way through the Forum and the Forum Boarium, and so to the Circus by way of the Via Sacra. Once there, it paraded the entire length of the racetrack, with the spectators applauding their patron deities.

54 Castor's reputation as a horseman, and Pollux's as a boxer, go back to Homer's time: see *Iliad* 3.237.

66 The praetor gave the signal for the race to begin by dropping a napkin.

73-4 Races could be stopped and restarted, by public demand among other reasons, in the manner here described.

3.3

Here Ovid offers us what might be described as an elementary essay in eroticized theology. His girl has sworn various oaths, only to break them; yet, like the victims of that famous malediction in 'The Jackdaw of Rheims', she is not one penny the worse as a result. To add insult to injury (lines 13–14), when she generously swore by Ovid's eyes as well as her own, hers remained bright and sparkling, while his promptly became afflicted with one of those numerous ophthalmic complaints to which Romans were apparently so prone. His conclusion from this is simple and predictable. Either the gods do not exist at all, or else they have a partiality for the fair sex which lacks any basis in reason and justice. No such concessions are made where men are concerned: Ovid himself, bleary and smarting, is a nice example (like the lightning-struck temple in line 35) of the gods' ability to hit the wrong target. He begins with an ejaculation of incredulity, but ends, as a good womanizer, by admitting that if he were a god, he would surely act in the same way.

This poem clearly looks forward to a famous passage in the *Ars* (1.631ff.; cf. my note, p. 358), which, after a very similar preamble, advocates a species of cynical unbelieving lip-service to divinity: 'The existence of gods is expedient: let us therefore assume it' (*expedit esse deos, et, ut expedit, esse putemus*).

17–18 Cassiopea, wife of Cepheus, boasted that she was more beautiful than the Nereids – just as Niobe boasted that she was more blessed in her children than Leto, and with equally disastrous results. Poseidon, on the resentful Nereids' behalf, sent a flood and a sea-monster to ravage the land (Ethiopia or Joppa, accounts vary). The Libyan god Ammon, through his oracle, predicted an end of these afflictions if Cassiopea's daughter Andromeda was left bound to a rock as a sacrificial victim for the sea-monster. This was duly done, but Perseus killed the monster and rescued Andromeda.

23–4 This blunt speculation as to the possible non-existence of the gods (cf. below, *Am*. 3.9.35–6) goes one step beyond the Epicurean notion of divine quietism and non-intervention preached by Lucretius in the *De Rerum Natura*, and occasionally postulated by Horace. See *AA* 1.637ff., and my note, pp. 358–9.

33–4 The pragmatic sentiment is akin to Hesiod's: why bother with righteousness if sinners are to flourish?

37–40 Zeus seduced Semele, daughter of Cadmus: Hera discovered the liaison, and persuaded Semele to ask her lover to appear to her in all his glory, as he did when wooing Hera. Since Zeus had promised Semele to do whatever she asked, he could not refuse: he 'came to her bridal chamber in a chariot, with lightnings and thunderings, and launched a thunderbolt'. Semele, not surprisingly, was either burnt to a crisp or else died of fright (accounts differ), but in any case aborted her six- (or seven-) month child, Dionysus. Zeus, ever resourceful, proceeded to sew the baby into his thigh, whence it was born at the proper term.

3.4

It is fashionable nowadays to regard *Am*. 3.4. and 2.19 as expressing directly contrary views, and to use them, on this basis, as evidence for Ovid's 'insincerity', for his adaptation of various literary poses, or *personas*, which bear no direct relation to his own attitudes or beliefs. A careful comparison of the two poems does not bear out this assumption. The contrast is more apparent than real. Lock up your wife, says Ovid in 2.19: if you don't, I'll get bored with chasing her. What's the point of locking her up? he asks in 3.4: you can't forcibly instil the instinct for chastity. Yet in neither case is this proposition the real psychological point of Ovid's discourse. What *both* poems emphasize, repeatedly, is the excitement of deprivation, the boredom of free indulgence.

Far from contradicting one another in essence, 2.19 and 3.4 both emphasize the same central psychological point from different angles. In this context, to lock up or not lock up a wife implies no real inconsistency on Ovid's part. In the first case he is concerned with the wife and her lover, in the second with the husband; but his central thesis remains identical throughout. To put the lady under physical restraint will stimulate both her and her lover: therefore the lover is concerned that all husbands should be coercive. To leave her completely free will remove adultery's major attraction, both for her and for any potential seducer: thus a wise husband will give his wife maximum freedom. Ovid merely reapplies his argument, he does not reverse it. The fundamental premiss still stands. With Penelope available, the wooers held off (4.23–4): Ovid's advice to Odysseus in this matter would, clearly, be the reverse of any hints he might be disposed to hand out to Antinoüs and Co. Are we therefore entitled to accuse him of frivolous literary mask-switching? The answer is self-evident, and only a currently fashionable weakness for addling straightforward human reactions with dubious infusions of rhetoric could ever have led anyone to suppose otherwise.

19–20 For Argus the herdsman, the All-seeing, who had eyes all over his body, cf. my note on *Am.* 2.2.44–6, p. 292.

21–4 For Danäe see my note on *Am.* 2.19.27–8, pp. 309–10.

37–40 This flat statement apropos the *rusticitas* of objecting to adultery, plus the unequivocal use of the word *coniunx* (wife), contrasts strikingly with the formal statement at the beginning of the *Ars* (1.31–4), and the long apologia in the *Black Sea Letters* (3.3.49–64), both of which assert – unconvincingly, but by then he was under political pressure – that Ovid is writing exclusively for, and about, *demimondaines* in the shape of *meretrices* or *libertinae*: see Introd., pp. 71ff. The 'illegitimacy' of Ilia's offspring by Mars was due to her status as a Vestal Virgin: cf. *Am.* 3.6.49.

3.5

2ff. The scene of the dream much resembles that stylized landscape which Ovid so often describes (e.g. at *Am.* 3.1.1ff. when narrating his encounter with Elegy and Tragedy), and which, to judge from Pompeian wall-paintings, formed part of every Roman artist's stock-in-trade.

31-2 Dream-interpretation was a popular skill throughout antiquity, from Homer's day onwards. When such dreams, as here, presented themselves in symbolic form, they required elucidation by an interpreter, or *oneirocrit*.

39-40 The symbolism of crow = bawd is precisely in line with the attributes of the crow in folklore: longevity, loquacity, mischief-making.

3.6

This, with the single exception of 1.8, is the longest poem in the *Amores*, and, perhaps by coincidence, concludes with a very similar imprecation (cf. 3.6.105-6 and 1.8.113-14). It belongs to the category of entreaties directed to one who cannot be assumed to listen to them. Others include 1.6, where Ovid apostrophizes a silent doorkeeper; 1.12 (esp. lines 7-30), in which he addresses his mistress's letter-tablets; 1.13 (Aurora); 2.3 (a guardian eunuch); and 2.9 (Cupid). Only one of these apart from the present poem (1.12) involves an inanimate object. We do not know the location of the river which suggested these lines (if, indeed, it was not pure literary invention): Sulmona is one possibility, but Ovid's travels in Asia Minor and Sicily could well have included just such a *contretemps*. In any case the river becomes an ideal excuse for an equally hyperabundant flow of rhetoric on Ovid's part.

The poem falls naturally into four sections. We have an exordium (1-22), in which Ovid complains to the river about his inability to cross it, and explores (without success) the chances of finding some solution to his problem. There follows (23-44) an appeal: the river should help a lover, because rivers in the past (a catalogue of eight such is given) have been highly susceptible to love themselves. The third section (45-82) gives more extended treatment to the myth of Ilia and the Anio, a theme already treated by Ennius in his *Annals*. Finally (83-106) Ovid, seeing that – despite his display of rhetorical skill – the river is running higher than ever, abandons the whole enterprise with a brisk volley of curses. Why waste literary talent on so unappreciative an audience? Fine words, clearly, are no better for stemming torrents than for buttering proverbial parsnips.

Here, I think, we may detect a significant leitmotiv running through the *Amores*. Proud though Ovid is of his verbal persuasiveness and poetic genius, the world (he well knows) too often remains deaf to such pleas. He is, in fact, habitually unlucky in the objects of his addresses. To consider only those listed above: none of them does what he wants, or even bothers to answer him. The porter's door remains shut, the note from his mistress turns out a put-off, Dawn comes up as usual, the eunuch makes no concessions, and whether Cupid chooses to pierce Ovid's heart or capriciously ignore him is not, clearly, dictated by the poet's own preferences in the matter. His magic, in the last resort, is no more reliable than that of the old bawd in 1.8: less so, perhaps, in the present instance, since Dipsas was at least credited with the ability to make rivers run backwards to their source (1.8.6). Thus the association of the two poems suggested above may not, after all, be wholly fortuitous: both explore the scope and limitations of the magician–artist's ability to transform the world by something more than reason. We are reminded, forcibly, that the same Latin word, *carmen*, does duty for 'poem' and 'spell'. What Ovid sees, with a certain wry realism, is that the magic holds no guarantee, that art can no more be relied upon to conquer than love. It is, I would argue, no coincidence that when he edited *Amores*[2] Ovid placed this poem immediately before one describing a case of sexual impotence.

*13*ff. Perseus, the son of Danaë, was required by King Polydectes of Seriphos to fetch him the head of the Gorgon Medusa. Guided by Hermes and Athena, he found a way to get winged sandals and the cap of Hades (which conferred invisibility) from the Nymphs. Equipped with these, and an adamantine sickle provided by Hermes, he successfully carried out his mission. The airborne chariot from which Triptolemus obtained the first seed-corn (with instructions to sow it world-wide) was Demeter's, and drawn by serpents, which may account for Ovid's association of the two legends.

17–18 This passage is not alone in expressing scepticism as regards the reality of myth: cf. also *Am.* 3.12.21–42; *AA* 1.637ff.; *Trist.* 2.64 (which warns the reader against believing the transformations narrated in the *Metamorphoses*).

20 'So may you flow for ever!': the wish, or prayer, is stylized, part of the *do ut des* pattern inherent in Roman dealings with the gods or other numinous beings.

25-6 Inachus, son of Ocean and Tethys (like numerous other Greek rivers), was both an early king of Argos and a local Argive river-god. Melia, also a daughter of Ocean, bore him Phoroneus and Aegialeus, besides other offspring (including a centaur) sired by various fathers including Silenus, Poseidon and Apollo. Her connection with Bithynia remains obscure.

27-8 According to Homer, the river which flowed in the plain of Troy was called Scamander by mortals, but Xanthus (perhaps because of its yellowish-muddy waters) by the gods. Only Ovid records Xanthus' passion for Neaera. There were (to complicate matters) several mythical nymphs of that name.

29-30 The river Alpheius travelled underground from Elis to Sicily, where its waters mingled with those of the Arethusan spring – still extant – on Ortygia. This fancy lies behind the myth describing how the river-god Alpheius pursued the nymph Arethusa, who fled to Ortygia and was there metamorphosed into a spring. Nothing daunted, Alpheius (in his liquid *persona*) went underground after her.

31-2 Ovid would seem to have conflated two legends here: (i) that in which the nymph Creusa, daughter of Ocean and Earth (Ge), was seduced by the river(-god) Peneius in Thessaly, and bore him Hypseus, later king of the Lapiths, and (ii) that in which another Creusa, daughter of Erechtheus and Praxithea, married Xuthus, son of Hellen, to whom she bore Achaeus and Ion. Only Ovid mentions the ravishment by Peneius of a Creusa previously promised to Xuthus.

33-4 Again, Ovid's version of the myth diverges from other accounts. Asopus, the Boeotian river-god, was generally held to have married Metope (daughter of another river-god), on whom he sired twelve, or perhaps twenty, daughters – including Thebe. While it is not impossible that Asopus was also supposed to have bred children by his own daughter, Thebe's husband is given as Zethus. Yet another tradition makes Thebe a daughter of Prometheus: the one constant factor on which everyone agrees is that she gave Boeotian Thebes its name.

35-8 The river-god Acheloüs fought with Heracles for possession of Deianeira; though he had the power of turning himself into various forms (e.g. a snake and a bull) Acheloüs was nevertheless defeated, and during his bull-metamorphosis Heracles broke off one of the river-

god's horns. Deianeira, the daughter of Oeneus, king of Calydon in
Aetolia, by his wife Althaea, thus had Meleager for a brother.

39–42 Nothing, apart from this reference, is known of Asopus'
daughter Evanthe.

43–4 Salmonis, better known as Tyro, daughter of Salmoneus, fell
in love with the river Enipeus in Thessaly, and often declared her
passion on its banks. Hearing her do so, Poseidon seduced her in the
likeness of the river, and she bore him twin sons, Pelias and Neleus.

45–82 The Anio (now the Teverone) rises in the Sabine hills, and
forms a famous waterfall at Tibur (Tivoli); it finally joins the Tiber as
a tributary. The myth of Ilia (or Rhea Silvia) and her connection with
the Anio had been narrated by Ennius in his *Annals*: as Ovid later
wrote (*Trist* 2.259–60), 'If a lady dips into the *Annals* (and what
could be rougher going?) why, she'll read how Ilia became a mother.'
She was a Vestal Virgin who was seduced by Mars, during a total
eclipse, in a cave whither she had fled to escape a wolf. In due course
she bore twins, Romulus and Remus. Her uncle Amulius condemned
her to be drowned in the Anio for her unchastity; however, the river-
god took pity on her and made her his bride. She is referred to as a
'Trojan lady' and 'daughter of Ilium's royal line' because of her
descent from Aeneas. Again, Ovid's version differs from received
tradition – in particular by making Ilia choose to commit suicide
rather than being forcibly drowned.

91–6 This description, which may strike readers in northern Europe
as somewhat exaggerated, is in fact a clinically accurate picture of
most small rivers in Greece or the more mountainous regions of Italy.

3.7

The explicitness of this poem has led scholars, perhaps unconsciously,
to isolate it from the sequence in which it occurs. This is subtly
misleading. *Amores* 3.5–8, taken together, form a most interesting
overall pattern, psychological no less than thematic. The dream of
desertion which forms the core of 3.5 has become reality (whether
factual or poetic) by 3.8, in which we hear that Ovid's mistress has
left him for a soldier. Why? In 3.8 the reason given is financial gain:
the lady, like most Ovidian ladies, proves a gold-digger at heart. Be-
hind the 'official' reason, however, a second, more embarrassing one
lies imperfectly concealed. The desertion in 3.5 was caused, in part at

least, by a lack of sufficient male ardour, and even in 3.8 Ovid stresses the soldier's crudely attractive virility at least as much as his wealth (cf. Juv. 6.103–13). Ovid's rhetoric fails to impress that all-too-symbolic river in 3.6; his poetic talent cannot compete with 'a bloody oaf who slashed his way to the cash' in 3.8. Just to make sure that no one, even in a pre-Freudian era, misses the point, the poet (licking his own wounds masochistically, but squeezing a good poem out in the process) spends 3.7 describing, in detail, how he first alarmed and finally antagonized his mistress by failing to achieve an erection during love-making. We remember the premonitory dream of 3.5 with a sense of *déjà vu*, and learn of the new lover in 3.8 without surprise.

Psychological impotence is a familiar enough phenomenon today but in antiquity the only explanation anyone could think of for it was that the victim had been 'hexed' by some witch or rival (see below, my note to lines 27–36). The problem was seldom described – Ovid's is the most circumstantial as well as the most detailed case on record.

24–5 Ovid names the three girls: Chlide, Peitho and Libas. All are Greek, and all carry suggestive secondary meanings in their names: wantonness, persuasion and 'anything that drips or trickles' (Liddell and Scott on *libas*).

27–36 For other Ovidian references to magic, see *Am.* 1.8.5–18 and 1.14.39–43, *AA* 2.99–106, 415–26, *RA* 249–90, 719–20, *MF* 35–42, with my notes ad loc. The notion that impotence could be caused by hostile magic is also propounded by Tibullus, 1.5.41, cf. 1.8.17–18. Thessaly was regarded throughout antiquity as the home *par excellence* of witches (cf. the modern reputation of Transylvania for breeding vampires). The particular form of sympathetic magic which involved piercing an image of the victim with pins, and, if the image was of wax, melting it in the fire, was known in Greek as *katadesmós*, and to the Romans as *defixio*. Many such images, most often of lead, have been found with accompanying curse-inscriptions.

39–40 cf. *Am.* 1.5.19–20. The echo, and the contrast of mood, are instructive.

41–2 Nestor of Pylos and Tithonus, the immortal, but far from age-less, husband of Aurora (the Dawn: cf. above, *Am.* 1.13.1–2, with my note ad loc.) were taken as typical representatives of extreme old age.

51–2 For the myth of Tantalus, see my note on *Am.* 2.2.44–6 above (p. 292).

3.8

In Rome there was always an articulate upper (or, later, upper-middle) class eager to proclaim that those further down the social ladder were getting positions and privileges to which their rank – talent being irrelevant – did not entitle them. Senators grumbled about equestrians, old middle-class families poured scorn on *novi homines*, local squires grew apoplectic over jumped-up foreigners. They were money-grubbers (i.e. financially shrewder than those who denigrated them), they were vulgar, they had no proper sense of precedence. In the last resort, such critics would invoke the *Saturnia regna*, the lost Golden Age – pre-agricultural, pre-capitalist, an idyllic top people's fantasy of rural peace and plenty, analogous to the 'ancestral constitution' so popular as a rallying-cry among Athenian ultra-conservatives in the late fifth century BC.

In 3.8 Ovid reveals most of these traits, modified or partially camouflaged to suit his own special circumstances. To begin with, the scale of values he evokes is aesthetic rather than class-based: poetic genius should be (but is not) valued above a high credit rating. The argument is very much *ad hominem*, or, in this case, *ad feminam*, and recalls that of *Am.* 1.10: Ovid's mistress has ditched him for a wealthier man. But he is not only richer, he is a *parvenu*. Ovid, we know, took a conscious pride in his long equestrian pedigree (cf. *Am.* 3.15.5–6, *Trist.* 4.10.7–8), and contrasted it, specifically, with the pretentions of those *equites* whose status had been earned, all too recently, through military service – i.e. who had fought on the right side in the Civil Wars, and earned rich rewards as a result. These men provided the Augustan regime's most solid support and regularly used their army career as a means of entering the equestrian order. Equally, many merchants and traders (often freedmen) who had bought up the lands of the proscribed had no trouble in proving their assets at the figure (400,000 sesterces) required for civilian admission to the ranks of the *equites*.

So Ovid's objections to his successful rival are not only moral-aesthetic and dictated by sexual jealousy, but also based on the crudest sort of class-snobbery. In addition, we have a restatement of the poet's contemptuous revulsion at the whole notion of fighting and militarism together with a bitter reproach for the girls who – whether through avarice or sexual inclination – found soldiers attractive as lovers. Whether it was a covert sense of personal inadequacy that drove him to compensate by describing sexual conquest as *militia* we cannot tell. The argument here leans heavily on the charge of feminine gold-digging. The girl who can bring herself to touch a soldier does so because she is *avara*, rapacious (line 22): the myth of Jupiter (Zeus) and Danaë is couched in terms which reinforce such a hypothesis. The value of Saturn's reign (35–8) was, in the first instance, that precious metals, and thus *a fortiori* coinage and capitalism, remained unknown: beyond this, Ovid does no more than pay traditional lip-service to a kind of dim mesolithic paradise, the nomadic hunter's world, minus all the back-breaking business associated with farming.

This line of thought leads him into somewhat dangerous political speculation. Having poured scorn on the class which constituted the backbone of the Augustan regime, having reiterated his contempt for military virtues as such, Ovid goes on (45–56) to equate the whole process of imperial expansion with greedy financial opportunism (a judgement with which not a few modern historians would concur); to label the Senate, the judiciary and the equestrian order as mere vulgar plutocracies; and to include in this programme of grab-as-grab-can the Caesarian deification principle – overseas acquisitions matched by a take-over bid in heaven. Having delivered himself of his scathing indictment, the poet proceeds (57–66) to wash his hands of public life altogether. This, at least, was no empty rhetorical gesture, but a bold reminder of Ovid's earlier withdrawal from the *cursus honorum*. He had had the offer to a high official career under the regime, and had deliberately rejected it (see Introd., pp. 28ff.) To abstain from politics itself constitutes a political gesture, and Ovid's contempt for the aims, ideals, propaganda and supporters of Augustanism is only too apparent in his work. How seriously, in the last resort, could anyone who believed in poetic divinity take the idea of a deified emperor?

Yet the instinctive repulsion is also, inevitably, laced with envy. Ovid might reject contemporary Roman politics, and withhold himself, in fastidious disdain, from the military–imperial–financial ideal of expansion, conquest and provincial administration; but again and again he reveals his covert envy of the prerogatives (social, sexual or political) enjoyed by highly placed civil or military employees of the regime. From this viewpoint the impotence, whether physical or symbolic, which we find in some poems of Bk 3 is no accident: it extends through every aspect of life in Rome, from politics to love-making. Indeed, as 3.8 makes very clear, the categories tended to overlap. Ovid's physical impotence had its antecedents in the collapse of the Republic.

By leaving him for a *nouveau-riche* military *eques* his mistress was simply acknowledging – and endorsing – the values of the new world in which she lived: she went with the fashion, while Ovid obstinately stood out against it. The bitterness which this poem reveals is rooted in something more subtle than simple jealousy.

1–4 The complaint that girls value cash above poetry is a regular one of Ovid's (cf. e.g. *AA* 2.273–6); it can also be found in Propertius and Tibullus. While a certain contempt for cash values does seem to characterize the landed-aristocratic phase of many societies (cf. the early medieval attitude to money-making and usury), there is little evidence to support Ovid's wishful thinking when he writes: 'Time was when poetic talent/Came dearer than gold'. Homer, surely, could have enlightened him on this topic.

29–34 For the legend of Danaë, impregnated by Zeus in the form of a shower of gold, see my note to *Am.* 2.19.27–8 (above, pp. 309–10).

51–2 The temple of Romulus on the Quirinal dated back as far as 435 BC (Livy 4.21): it was burnt down in 49 BC, and its rebuilding completed by Augustus some thirty-three years later. (This latter date, 16 BC, is probably alluded to by Ovid, and would thus provide some slight corroboration for the publication of *Amores*[1] at a subsequent point: cf. my note on *Am.* 1.14.45–6. Martial (1.71.9) refers to a temple of Bacchus on the Palatine. There were several temples to Hercules within Rome's city-limits, one of them at the Colline Gate, another near the Circus Flaminius. The temple of (Julius) Caesar referred to was the *aedes divi Iuh* adjacent to the Forum, dedicated, again, by Augustus.

55–6 Minimum qualifications of capital were laid down for both senators (800,000 sesterces, later raised to a million) and *equites* (400,000 sesterces). These figures were habitually far exceeded, and even a man such as the Younger Pliny – who was very far from the top of the pile, either socially or financially – astonishes us by the scale of his wealth and munificence.

3.9

Our knowledge of Tibullus' life is comparatively meagre. He was born c. 60–55 BC (cf. the chronological list of poets in Ovid's autobiographical testament, *Trist.* 4.10.51–4), served between 31 and 27 on the staff of M. Valerius Messalla Corvinus, and died, soon after Virgil, in the late autumn of 19. Ovid's poem may thus be presumed to date from 19 or 18. Like *Am.* 2.6, celebrating the death of a pet parrot, it is composed as a formal *epicedion* or funeral lament (cf. above, p. 295), divided into five sections: (i) an introductory address to the mourners (1–16); (ii) the *laudatio* or *lamentatio*, including (a) the 'what avails it...' theme (21–34) and (b) a ritual outburst (Greek *schetliasmós*) against unjust fate (17–20, 35–46); (iii) the deathbed scene (47–58); (iv) a *consolatio* (59–66); and (v) the burial, with a prayer for the repose of the dead (67–8).

The two poems run along strikingly parallel lines, and thus almost insist on joint consideration. Further, it is possible for modern readers (and presumably ancient ones too) to find the *mise en scène* of 2.6, despite its feathered addressee, more attractive than that of the present poem. Ovid seldom produced effects by accident, and I suspect that the correlation 'Tibullus: parrot' was no random juxtaposition either. While his grief was genuine, one unregenerate corner of his mind may well have found the dead poet's private life mildly risible, and his verses not wholly free from excessive (i.e. parrot-like) *imitatio*.

1–2 For the Ethiopian prince Memnon, slain at Troy by Achilles, see my note on *Am.* 1.13.3–4 (p. 285), and cf. *Met.* 13.621–2: his mother the Dawn (Eos, Aurora) wept tears of dew for him each morning. Achilles was killed at the Scaean Gate either by Apollo, or else by Paris under Apollo's direction, and mourned for by his mother Thetis, the sea-nymph.

3–4 Ovid derives the word 'elegy' (*elegeion* or *elegeia*) from *e legei*, '[he] cries Woe!', a fanciful etymology which arose in antiquity from the belief that the elegy was, by origin, a lament. In fact, surviving early elegies are largely unconnected with lamentation, and it is more likely that *elegos* is connected with some foreign word for 'flute', such as survives in Armenian *elegn-*, and that the elegiac was originally a flute-song.

13–14 Iulus, or Ascanius, was the son of Aeneas by either Creusa or Lavinia. Cupid is described as Aeneas' brother since they were both sons of Venus: half-brother would be a more accurate description, Aeneas being sired by Anchises, a mortal, while Cupid (Eros) was the offspring of some god (Hermes, Ares or Zeus: accounts differ).

15–16 The legend of Aphrodite (Venus) and her passion for Adonis exists in at least two different versions, but is based – like the parallel myth of Aphrodite and Anchises, also mentioned here by Ovid – on the archaic Anatolian belief in the Great Mother and her consort, who dies with the year but revivifies in the spring. According to one version, Aphrodite first saw Adonis out hunting, and fell in love with him. Through jealousy, either Ares or Artemis ensured that Adonis was killed by a wild boar. From the dead youth's blood there sprang up flowers – anemones or roses.

17–20 The divine inspiration and numinous nature of poets is referred to elsewhere by Ovid: see esp. *AA* 3.549: 'God is in us, we have dealings with heaven' (cf. 405); *RA* 813; and *Trist.* 4.10.42.

21–4 Orpheus, son of either Oeagrus or (less well documented) Apollo, and the Muse Calliope, was torn to pieces by the Thracian Bassarids (Maenads) in a ritual *sparagmós*: neither his divine parentage nor his fame as a musician (Ovid implies) sufficed to avert this unpleasant demise. Orpheus had a brother, Linus, who was killed by Heracles, and mourned with the ritual cry *ailinon*, explained as 'Woe for Linus!' but in fact perhaps derived from the Phoenician *ai lanu*, meaning simply 'woe to us'. Ovid, as so often, follows an unusual mythical tradition in making Apollo the father of both Orpheus and Linus: his use of the parenthetical phrase 'They say' (*dicitur*) suggests that he was aware of this.

25–8 The dark lake of Aornos or Avernus, 'hell's black waters', now the Lago d'Averno, has a physical location, in Campania, between Cumae and the Bay of Baiae. It lies in the crater of an extinct volcano: this may account for the ancient tradition of mephitic fumes rising from fissures in the adjacent rocks, fumes so strong that no bird (*a*, privative particle, + *ornos*, another typical ancient aetiologizing false derivation) could fly across it. This quality, combined with its gloomy isolation – it lay amid dense woods – may explain how it came to be regarded as an entrance to the underworld.

31–2 Various poems in the first book of Tibullus' elegies mention his mistress Delia (a pseudonym, it would seem, for a lady named Plania). The second book deals with a later mistress, who rejoiced in the mildly disquieting name of Nemesis.

33–4 These lines are a conscious imitation of Tib. 1.3.23–6, where Tibullus, lying sick on Corcyra, asks the absent Delia, rhetorically, what help to him, now, is her observance of the various rites of Isis: the lustrations, the periods of sexual abstinence? Both in Egypt and, later, throughout the Graeco-Roman world, Isis was a renowned healer.

35–6 For Ovid's professed scepticism concerning the gods and their myths cf. *AA* 1.637ff., with my introductory note, pp. 358–90.

45 The hill-town of Eryx (now Monte San Giuliano) in West Sicily was best known in antiquity for its temple of Aphrodite–Astarte, served by *hieroduli*, or sacred prostitutes, and traditionally said to have been founded by Aeneas.

47–8 In Tib. 1.3.3–8 we read how the poet fell ill on the island of Corcyra (Corfu), and was temporarily left behind by his commander and patron Messalla: this must have been in 31/30 BC, shortly after the battle of Actium. The illness does not seem to have lasted long, since both Tibullus himself (1.7.9ff.) and the Tibullan *vita* inform us that he accompanied Messalla on his campaign in Aquitania. On 25 September 27 BC Messalla celebrated a triumph, to which Tibullus devotes a poem (1.7).

61–4 Catullus, Calvus and Gallus are cited here, *honoris causa*, as the best of the early Roman love-elegists. For G. Cornelius Gallus (69–26 BC) see *Am.* 1.15, 29, *AA* 3.334, *RA* 765, and my notes ad loc.: he addressed four books of love-elegies to Mark Antony's ex-mistress Cytheris, whom he called Lycoris, and took his own life rather than face possible treason charges from Augustus while Prefect of Egypt. To single out this unperson for praise was courageous but tactless. G. Valerius Catullus (84–54 BC), best known for his poems to Lesbia (? Clodia), was labelled *doctus* (I translate this epithet as 'poet and scholar') in recognition of his literary Alexandrianism – a taste he shared with his close friend and fellow-poet G. Licinius Calvus (82–? 47 BC), whose oratory was by some critics rated above that of Cicero.

3.10

The last six poems of Bk 3 (even 3.13, which at first sight may not appear relevant to the sequence) chronicle those *odi et amo* vicissitudes, those violent shifts of emotional mood which are virtually inseparable from the break-up of a sexual liaison like that which Ovid describes, in the *Amores*, as existing between himself and Corinna. They also prepare us for the valediction to love-elegy pronounced in the envoi (3.15). The present poem transfers Ovid's reproaches – on the surface – from Corinna herself to the goddess Ceres: at least on this occasion his mistress can produce a legitimate excuse for nine days' sexual abstinence. Yet the undercurrent of personal suspicion remains: such occasions often provided girls with an easy pretext for avoiding intercourse in which they had no wish to indulge, something less obvious than the time-honoured and conventional headache. The paradox of a fertility-goddess imposing chastity is not lost on Ovid; the festival here described makes an interesting – and deliberate – contrast with the feast of Juno in 3.13 (see below, p. 334).

1–2 The festival here described is also mentioned by Ovid in the *Metamorphoses* (10.431ff.). It took place in early August, and should not be confused with the Cerealia of 12–19 April, described by Ovid in the *Fasti* (4.393ff.). The period of abstention, as for the rites of Isis, was nine days and nine nights.

3 Ceres was often depicted, in statues and paintings, as crowned with wheat-ears.

7–14 For primitive life, as a stylized *topos* in Roman literature, and its comparison with the blessings brought by Ceres (or developed agricultural techniques) see esp. Ovid *Fast.* 4.395ff., Virg. *Georg.* 1.147ff. In this tradition the acorn is regularly mentioned as a pre-cereal staple food. Lines 11–14 form a near-parody of the formal hymn in praise of Ceres which we find at *Met.* 5.341ff., and which is familiar from other sources: see, e.g., Virg. *Georg.* 1.147ff.

18 Though Ceres specializes in what Hamlet once referred to as 'country matters', Ovid emphasizes that she is 'no simple rustic', his use of the epithet *rustica* implying that sort of old-fashioned rural prudishness which insists on chastity merely through lack of urban sophistication.

19–24 Cretans were regarded as proverbial liars in antiquity. The Pauline Epistle to Titus (1.12) quotes a line by Epimenides to this effect: 'The Cretans are always liars, evil beasts, slow bellies.' Zeus (here Romanized as 'Jove') was, according to one legend, born to Rhea in a mountain-cave on Crete (whither she had resorted to prevent the child being swallowed at birth by its father, Cronos), and guarded there by the Curetes, while the nymphs provided milk from the horn of Amalthea.

25ff. The union of Ceres (Demeter) with Iasius or Iasion 'in a thrice-ploughed furrow' is clear evidence that the myth embodied a primitive fertility-ritual. The child of their intercourse was Ploutos, Wealth.

41 Minos was the son of Zeus and Europa, and brother of Rhadamanthus: during his life he acquired fame as a lawgiver while king of Crete, and after his death both he and Rhadamanthus became judges in Hades.

45-6 Persephone, daughter of Demeter, was carried off by Pluto, lord of Hades, and became his queen. When Demeter, after searching everywhere for her daughter, finally learnt (from Helios, the Sun) what had become of her, she persuaded Zeus to decree that henceforth Persephone should spend part of the year only (one half or one third: accounts differ) with Pluto, and the rest in the upper world 'with the gods'. This, again, is a classic fertility-myth: Demeter and Persephone are the not-so-remote ancestors of John Barleycorn, with Persephone's spell in Hades corresponding to winter in the agricultural year-cycle.

3.11A–B

Though 3.11 appears in our MSS as one undivided poem, the sharp change of tone and attitude after line 32 has led many editors to print it in separate parts.

Rather more misleading as regards Ovid's fundamental attitude to his chosen theme is the vigorous (and oddly naïve) debate between those who take the poem seriously, and those who treat it as a flippant literary *jeu d'esprit* – a debate which in some quarters extends to the *Amores* as a whole. This simplistic division badly underestimates Ovid's complex irony, his wrily amused self-knowledge, his abundant gift for emotional oxymoron. In particular, the argument that his emotions cannot be taken seriously here *because* of all those literary borrowings and allusions is a complete non-sequitur: to appreciate its shortcomings we need do no more than apply it to *The Waste Land*, Pound's *Cantos* or David Jones's *The Anathemata*. Joking about serious emotions is an unromantic habit; but then Ovid was not, in the modern sense, a romantic poet.

3.11A

1-4 The opening words echo *Am.* 2.19.49 (where Ovid is complaining, ironically enough, about an over-complaisant husband) and also Prop. 2.8.13–14. The image of a slave losing his chains and achieving emancipation (reinforced by lines 10–12, which emphasize the distinction between servile and freeborn actions) evokes, vividly, the conventional (but here all too real) *servitium amoris*.

5-6 For horns as a symbol of strength see Ovid *AA* 1.239; to the best of my knowledge the phrase never in antiquity carried the implication of cuckoldry which it did, say, in Elizabethan times.

9–14 This stock description of the *exclusus amator*, the lover-shut-out (cf. my introductory note to *Am.* 1.6, above, p. 274) gains added force from the image of the lover's successor, stumbling away exhausted – before his ousted rival's eyes – after a hard night's work.

15–16 There is an ironic echo here of an earlier passage by Ovid himself (*Am.* 2.10.15), where the fate he wishes for his enemies is to toss in an empty bed, without company.

17–18 There is an ambiguity here hard to reproduce in English. Two of the roles Ovid claims to have fulfilled are those of *custos* (guardian, as in the case of porter or eunuch, as well as escort) and *vir* (husband as well as lover). This ambiguity extends to lines 25–6, where it is by no means clear *whose* house Ovid is hurrying back to ('*vehi*') – his mistress's or his own. See Introd., p. 23.

23–4 The joke here, of course, is that Ovid's advice to his mistress (*Am.* 1.4.17–20, with my notes, p. 272) has been taken, learnt, and turned neatly against him.

29–30 For the garlanding of a vessel that had reached port safely see, e.g., Virgil *Georg.* 1.303–4; Ovid (cf. *RA* 811–12) uses this image to describe escape from sexual involvement. Ovid, furthermore, contrasts the state of his vessel (*lenta* = 'indifferent', often with a sexual connotation) with the 'swelling' (*tumescentes*) waters outside: the symbolism could hardly be more obvious.

3.11B

1–2 The second line is heavy with literary allusion, recalling not only Catullus' *Odi et amo*, but also a well-known line of Virgil's (embodying a motto that Chaucer put on the Prioress's brooch): *Omnia vincit amor, nos et cedamus amori* (*Ecl.* 10.69): 'Love conquers all: let us too yield to love.'

7 Another famous line, imitated by Martial (12.47, a near-direct quotation), who also picks up line 9 in an earlier epigram (8.53.3–4).

13–16 The touchstone here is Tibullus (1.5.7–8); cf. also *Am.* 3.3.11–12.

19–20 In deliberate contrast to 11A 29–30, where Ovid's 'vessel' is safe from the storm raging outside the harbour, these lines show it running before the wind out at sea.

3.12

This poem has been claimed, without even the benefit of superficial plausibility, as evidence for Corinna's fictitious nature.

If Corinna *was* in fact a real person, one interesting conclusion emerges: Ovid's close acquaintances, at least, must have known, or guessed, her identity. That seems likely enough, and not incompatible with a generally well-kept secret: the girl who falsely claimed to be Corinna (*Am.* 2.17.29–30) must have felt she had a good chance of getting away with such a pose in the circles she frequented – which, clearly, were not Ovid's. The publication of the *Amores* facilitated this kind of imposture. The work acquainted all Rome – and posterity – with just as much as Ovid chose to reveal of his affair, and no more. The rest remained known either to him alone, or else to a close group of discreet friends.

We have here convincing evidence of what we might – given Ovid's temperament – have assumed without proof: that is, a cheerfully sceptical attitude to traditional myth. This trait had its psychologically ambivalent side: no one capable of writing the *Metamorphoses* could be described as a simple rationalist, and in that extraordinary poem he often tends to treat his 'fictional monsters' as though they were real: we may note that a large number of the examples chosen here deal with metamorphosis. The recantation in the *Tristia* (2.64) is not entirely convincing. But in various other passages (*Trist.* 3.8.1–2, 4.7.11–20, and above, *Am.* 3.6.13–18), the scepticism is explicit and detailed. These declarations should be borne in mind when considering his famous passage (*AA* 1.637ff., see below, p. 358) on the existence of the gods.

The general theme continues that of 3.8: poetic talent cannot compete in the social market, and may indeed constitute a positive handicap to the lover. Seen in this context, the attitude to myth becomes openly deprecatory: Ovid treats the whole process as a harmless form of literary escapism.

13–14 In this couplet Ovid brings off an untranslatable, and very effective, double entendre. The phrase *nocuerunt carmina semper* can mean not only 'my poems have brought nothing but trouble', but also 'spells have always been dangerous'. The *praeceptor amoris* suddenly takes on the nervous *persona* of the Sorcerer's Apprentice.

15–16 'Caesar's exploits' are nicely ambiguous in weight here, to be treated as climax or anticlimax according to the reader's bias.

21–2 Ovid conflates what seem originally to have been two quite distinct mythical figures: (i) Scylla, daughter of Nisus, king of Megara, who pulled out the purple lock of hair on which her father's life depended; (ii) the monster Scylla, daughter of Crataeis (or Lamia) and Phorcys, the Old Man of the Sea: supposed to have six heads and twelve feet of dogs 'from the flanks'.

23–40 The catalogue is familiar and traditional. The connection between Perseus, Medusa and Pegasus is close in more ways than one. Perseus killed Medusa, and the winged horse Pegasus was generated from the blood spilt at her decapitation. Perseus acquired winged *sandals* from the daughters of Phorcys, a gift he shared with Hermes. The giant Tityos, offspring of Zeus and Elare, attempted to rape Leto in Delphi. She, however, called her children Apollo and Artemis to her aid, and they shot Tityos to death with their arrows. In Hades he was pegged out for all eternity (rather like Prometheus) while vultures gnawed at his liver. Dragon-tailed Cerberus is known to Homer but there was some dispute in antiquity as to the number of heads this hell-hound possessed. Three, however, was the canonical number. The giant Enceladus was pinned under Sicily by Athena; their combat was sculptured on Apollo's temple at Delphi. Ovid exaggerates his number of arms: according to Hesiod giants had one hundred arms and fifty heads apiece – enough, one might have thought, to be going on with. For the episode of the Sirens see Homer *Od.* 12.39–54, 158–200. Aeolus and his bag of winds are described at length by Homer, *Od.* 10.1–76; cf. Ovid *Met.* 14.223–32. For the myth of Tantalus see above, *Am.* 2.2.44–6, and my note (p. 292). His daughter Niobe boasted that she was blessed with more children than Leto: Leto promptly had all Niobe's offspring slaughtered by her own children, Apollo and Artemis, without even the justification of an attempted rape (see above on Tityos). Niobe went to Mt Sipylos in Asia Minor and was there turned to stone as she wept (this part of the myth is aetiological, designed to explain a striking rock-formation). Callisto was a dedicated virgin and hunting-companion of Artemis. Zeus seduced her forcibly – disguised as either Apollo or, intriguingly, Artemis – and then metamorphosed her into a she-bear to escape Hera's notice. Hera, however, saw all, and had no trouble in persuading Artemis to shoot Callisto for losing her maidenhead, however involuntarily. At this point Zeus, bent on having the last word, transformed the girl-bear into a famous star. For Philomela see above, *Am.* 2.6.7–10 with my note (p. 295). Jupiter's erotic disguises are also listed in *Am*. 1.3.21–4, 1.10.1–6 (see my notes, pp. 271, 286); here Ovid refers to his escapade with Leda, when he became a swan, and perhaps also to the eagle form he adopted when he bore off Ganymede; to his seduction of Danaë by approaching her as a shower of gold (above, *Am*. 2.19.27–8, with my note, pp. 309–10); and to his swimming off to Crete with Europa (the 'hapless virgin') in the semblance of a bull. The various metamorphoses of Proteus are described by Homer (*Od*. 4.417ff., cf. above, *Am*. 2.15.10). The 'sown teeth of the dragon' belong to the legend of Cadmus, who killed a dragon guarding the spring of Ares at Thebes, and on Athena's advice sowed its teeth: there sprang up then from the sown furrows armed men called Spartoi ('Sown') who fought each other. Jason, when at Colchis, similarly sowed some of the dragon's teeth which Athena had given him. This explains Ovid's transition to the fire-breathing bulls which Medea's father Aeëtes ordered Jason to yoke. Phaethon, son of Helios and Clymene, tried to drive the chariot of the Sun, came too near earth, and was struck dead by a thunderbolt from Zeus. He fell into the River Eridanus (Po), where his sisters mourned him in the shape of poplar trees, the amber drops exuding from the tree-trunks forming their tears (Ovid *Met*. 2.349ff.). The 'sea-goddesses conjured from ships' can be traced to a passage in Virgil's *Aeneid* (9.77–122) where, in order to protect Aeneas' fleet against the incendiary activities of Turnus, the ships are metamorphosed into Nereids: cf. Ovid *Met*. 14.527–65. The myth of the sun turning back in the heavens seems originally to have formed part of a competition between Atreus and Thyestes for the kingship over Mycenae: each produced a portent, but that of Atreus (the sun setting in the east) was adjudged clearly superior. However, Ovid prefers a tradition more popular among Roman poets, that the sun turned back *in horror at Atreus*, who first murdered Thyestes' children, then served them up to their unsuspecting father for dinner (Ovid *Trist*. 2.391ff., *AA* 1.327ff.). When Zethus and Amphion, the sons of Zeus by Antiope, fortified Thebes, the stones moved of themselves to the music of Amphion's lyre.

3.13

For any scholar determined to prove structural unity in the *Amores* this poem comes as a considerable embarrassment: perhaps that is why no adequate discussion of it exists. It is not about love; it does not refer to Corinna, or even to some unnamed mistress; and it breaks one cardinal rule of Roman erotic elegy by mentioning the poet's wife. There are no manifest echoes of Propertius. The subject-matter rather looks forward to those antiquarian, folkloric and religious interests which Ovid was soon to explore in the *Fasti* (*Fast.* 6.49 alludes to 'the Juno-worshippers of Falerii'). Just possibly this was an early piece that survived the pruning between *Amores*[1] and *Amores*.[2] Ovid's Faliscan wife cannot be his third, who was Roman-born, and this leaves us hesitating between the two earlier marriages, neither of which lasted long (*Trist.* 4.10.69–72). Both belonged to his early youth. As we saw earlier (*Am.* 2.16 and my introductory note, p. 305), Ovid, despite his urban instincts, retained an observant eye for the countryside; but this is the only instance in the *Amores* of a rural piece unattached to any kind of central erotic motif.

If the placing of 3.13 was deliberate, perhaps it is to be explained through juxtaposition – and contrast – with 3.14, Ovid's agonized yet elegant plea to a mistress (unnamed, but clearly Corinna) whose casual infidelities have all but killed their relationship. Ovid juxtaposes (embarrassingly for literary formalists) erotic convention with the solid background of provincial Roman society, where in-laws are important and feast-days not to be ignored. Reality, in various guises, disrupts the dream and terminates the artifice. Passion, whether literary or erotic (and for Ovid, as for Cavafy, there is no clear dividing-line), cannot, in the end, hold out against society. If there is a 'message', if 3.13 has a functional role in the overall sequence of the *Amores*, it is, surely, to demonstrate this. The merest allusion here to Ovid's wife, the familial implications of this journey to her home-town, have a subtle impact on the agonized and psychologically acute poem (3.14) that follows. If wife and mistress are identical the irony is even more pervasive.

1–2 Falerii was a town in southern Etruria, north of Mt Soracte, near the confluence of the river Treia with the Tiber: its modern name is Cività Castellana. The old town stood on a high plateau about 1 km x 400 m in size, surrounded by steep river-gorges: Ovid's 'exhausting journey over mountain roads' is no exaggeration.

3–4 Epigraphical evidence indicates that the chief festival of Juno Quiritis (the derivation of this epithet remains uncertain) was held on 7 October. It is reasonable to identify the occasion described by Ovid with this celebration.

13–18 Heifers were the most common sacrifice to Hera or Juno. Those of Falerii were of a particularly pure white, which *ipso facto* increased their value for this purpose (Ovid *EP* 4.4.31–2, *Fast.* 1.83.4). Pigs (also calves and rams) are almost equally common sacrificial animals.

18–20 This aetiological myth is not known elsewhere (though it was clearly adduced to explain some kind of scapegoat ritual, as lines 21–2 make clear). Hera's flight from Zeus is presumably to be related to the period before their marriage, when brother and sister became involved without their parents' knowledge, and, according to one odd tradition, Zeus turned himself into a cuckoo – no worse than a swan – to pursue his quarry: which, says Pausanias (2.17.4), is why the statue of Hera has a cuckoo perched on its sceptre.

31–5 Apropos the Argive origin of the Juno-cult at Falerii, Dionysius of Halicarnassus writes (1.21.2): '. . . the manner of the sacrificial ceremonies was similar, holy women served the sacred precinct, and an unmarried girl, called the *canephorus* or 'basket-bearer', performed the initial rites of the sacrifices, and there were choruses of virgins who praised the goddess in the songs of their country'. About Halesus, the founder of Falerii, little is known. He was a companion (some said a bastard son) of Agamemnon. On Agamemnon's murder he fled from the Peloponnese and eventually settled in Etruria.

3.14

The basic message of this poem is simple enough, and can be summed up in two popular adages ('What the eye doesn't see the heart doesn't grieve over' and 'The Eleventh Commandment: Thou shalt not be found out'), the very familiarity of which suggests that Ovid's reaction was by no means as *outré* as critics seem to imply: cf. *AA* 2.387–408, with my note, p. 374. I'm a reasonable, broad-minded man, he says in effect. I can't control your private life – but must you flaunt it quite so openly under my nose? There is a certain social decorum in these matters. Be more discreet about your *billets-doux*. Make your bed when your previous lover has gone. Don't let me see the love-bites on your neck. I have no desire to probe your activities like a private detective; I'm more than ready to believe your cover-stories. But please at least take the trouble to make them convincing.

Humankind, as Eliot reminded us, cannot bear very much reality.

This is Ovid at his most human. The affair with Corinna is clearly almost finished, but should we on that account regard 3.14 as a symbolic rejection of love-elegy as such?

Catullus, Propertius, Ovid: all three were hurt in love, each one adopts a different *persona* to deal with the raw truth of infidelity. Catullus (76.23–6) abandons any hope of Lesbia returning his passion, much less of her remaining faithful; all he prays for is a chance to exorcise his own desire, which he stigmatizes as 'this filthy disease' (*taetrum hunc . . . morbum*). Propertius, with greater sophistication, protects himself by downgrading the importance of the relationship, and emphasizing the social *cachet* of smart promiscuity. Ovid, while equally alert to the claims of society – he seems at least as much worried by Corinna's vulgar public exhibitionism as by her indifference to *him* – nevertheless shows his feelings in a way that comes rather closer to Catullus – and more than once echoes him: with lines 1ff. cf. Cat. 76.23–4, and with lines 25–6, Cat. 6.7–11. Nothing will ever tempt this poet into displays of raw emotionalism: yet 3.14 is, in its way, a *cri de cœur*. A short envoi apart, 3.14 is the final poem of the *Amores*. Ovid could forgive, but Corinna, all too clearly, forgot. A phase in his life, and his poetry, was over: the two were more closely interwoven than modern criticism will allow. No accident that in this poem he figures simultaneously as judge, prosecutor and defender (again, with a sprinkling of quasi-legal terminology): nothing could better highlight the ambivalence of his attitude.

3.15

With a flurry of conventional periphrastic imagery, Ovid announces his final decision (hinted at on several earlier occasions, e.g. *Am.* 2.18. 1–4, 13–14, and 3.1 *passim*) to abandon elegiac love-poetry in favour of the tragic Muse (cf. my note on *Am.* 2.18.1–3, p. 307). The tragedy in question, on which he had begun work earlier, but laid aside (*Am.* 2.18.13–14), was his *Medea*: the only tragedy he ever wrote, praised to the skies by Tacitus and Quintilian, and now, ironically enough, lost. Despite Ovid's talk about a new start, his subject was once more love and jealousy, though now on a heroic scale; and his renunciation of elegy looks a little specious when we recall how soon he was to begin work on the *Art of Love* (see above, pp. 38–9). However, for the moment at least he believed in his own new programme; and it is arguable (though not susceptible of proof) that what finally drove him into tragedy, and dictated his choice of theme, was his break with Corinna. When the elegist reappears, moreover, his literary *persona* has changed. He is no longer the poet-lover, but *praeceptor amoris*, a professor of seduction. The practitioner has turned to teaching.

This envoi also contains a brief but intriguing autobiographical section, which emphasizes Ovid's respectable provincial pedigree (in sharp contrast to those new equestrians who had done well out of the Civil Wars: see *Am.* 3.8 *passim*, and my introductory note, pp. 322ff.), praises the rugged independence of his Paelignian ancestors, and uses Paelignian *libertas* to excuse or justify his rather daring erotic poems. Conventional poetic self-advertisement here goes hand-in-hand with a somewhat unexpected local pride. Where, now, is Ovid's *urbanitas?* 'Freedom with honour' can apply to poetry and politics alike: Ovid clearly means the two concepts to merge in the image he presents. For further biographical details see Introd., pp. 15ff.

4 'A man whose delights have never let him down': I have attempted here to catch the studied ambiguity of the original (*nec me deliciae dedecuere meae*), an ambiguity unnoticed, as far as I can tell, by all commentators. *Deliciae* can mean (i) sensuality, (ii) light verse, and (iii) darling. The meaning everyone attaches to the line is something like, 'My poems may be erotic, but I'm respectable.' This is certainly one possible interpretation. But the verb *dedecet* can convey the notion of 'unbecomingness' as well as 'dishonour', and the range of possible meanings for the line is startling: 'My girlfriend was quite smart enough for me,' 'my elegies lived up to my reputation,' 'my sensuality never let me down,' and so on. Surely Ovid, with mischievous skill, went for this ambiguous effect deliberately?

THE ART OF LOVE

BOOK I

1–40 These introductory lines, the so called 'proem' and *partitio*, are rightly recognized as an important statement of Ovid's intentions for the whole work. Finesse, technique – *ars*, Greek *téchnē* – this is what Ovid, as *praeceptor amoris*, has to teach (1–2). Love-making is a sport open to all, but its transformation into an art requires special knowledge. The didactic stance Ovid adopts links this skill to the honest arts of human society: navigation, chariot-racing, sailing (3–4) and, later, hunting or farming. The first three in particular – besides having appropriate erotic connotations in their metaphorical use – call for *expert control*; by analogy with those mythical embodiments of specialized expertise, Tiphys and Automedon, Ovid proclaims himself uniquely qualified to control love (5–8), and suggests that the passions are amenable to such control.

Indeed, the first thing that strikes one is his self-confidence, and, linked with this, the absence of a formal divine invocation to open the poem – in sharp contrast to Virgil's *Georgics*, or even to the anti-religious *De Rerum Natura* of Lucretius. This attitude is reinforced by Ovid's careful disclaimer (25–30): his work is based on experience, not on divine inspiration, and the appeal to Venus is perfunctory rather than climactic. The images of Chiron moulding Achilles (11–16) and of bulls or horses being broken in for domestic use (19–20) stress the fact that Ovid is presenting himself, Chiron-like, as a purveyor of *cultus*, of civilized instruction. They also hint at the attitude he will take to love, and by extension to women, as something wild, unpredictable, immature, yet ultimately malleable: a case of civilization v. nature, well expressed in terms of those agricultural metaphors which abound throughout the poems.

At lines 31–40 (the *partitio*) Ovid outlines his general plan. It is noteworthy that – in contrast to what we might have been led to suppose by parts of the *Amores* – the affairs resulting from these pick-ups and seductions *are meant to last* (38), though briefer liaisons also rate a mention (92). Book 2, in fact, is devoted (cf. lines 11–14) to techniques for keeping a girl once you have won her. Book 1, meanwhile, is divided into two main sections after the proem and general proposal: (a) a description of the best places – almost all in Rome – to acquire a mistress (41–262): the colonnades, foreign temples, the theatres and Circus, triumphal processions, dinner-parties, coastal spas and, oddly, the secluded woodland shrine of Diana near Aricia; (b) after a short bridging passage (263–8), the remainder of Bk 1, apart from a postscript and envoi (755–72), is devoted to various ploys and techniques – some naïve, some subtle – for gaining a lady's favours. All women, ultimately, can be won, Ovid says (a theme to which he recurs several times). Their maids must be cultivated – but not, for preference, seduced. Don't let them con you into giving them expensive presents. Soften them up with love-letters, use words persuasively. Be clean in your toilet, but not effeminate. Don't drink too much at dinner – in fact, pretend you've drunk more than you have, it makes a good cover and excuse. Promise anything: lovers' oaths don't count. Use tears; if necessary, use violence. Look pale and thin to prove your sincerity.

5–6 Tiphys was the helmsman of Argo on the voyage in search of the Golden Fleece. The choice of imagery is suggestive: both charioteer and helmsman evoke the picture of *skilled mastery* – over the elements in one case, and horses in the other. 'Control' and 'technique' are Ovid's watchwords, and the approach (besides highlighting its author's spoof-didactic structure) is suggestive as regards his fundamental attitude to women in this poem.

19–20 We meet here a metaphor, that drawn from the breaking-in of horses and cattle, which is central to Ovid's purpose and recurs throughout this poem: e.g. in Bk I alone at lines 43–50, 93–6, 277–82, 360, 471–2, 755–72.

25–30 Ovid's credibility as expert (*artifex*) is rooted in personal experience: he does not rely on supernatural enlightenment, whether from Apollo, or prophetic birds or an epiphany of the Muses as described by Hesiod. This deliberate rejection of divine guidance in favour of experience underwrites his credibility.

35–40 Ovid's descriptive programme of contents, or *partitio* – a regular feature of serious Roman didactic poetry – refers only to the contents of Bks I (finding and wooing a mistress) and 2 (keeping her once won): this lends some support to the theory – cf. my note on *AA* 2.733–46, p. 381 – which sees Bk 3 as an afterthought or later addition to the original scheme. The pursuit of love as *militia* (36–7) is an image already familiar to us from the *Amores* (see esp. 1.9, with my introductory note p.279), and Ovid develops it further in Bk 2 of the *Ars* (233ff., with my note, p. 370; 559, 565–6, 674). The charioteer image (39–40) is, similarly, not unknown in the *Amores* (e.g. at 3.15.2), and has strong erotic associations (3.2), but achieves its maximum effect in the *Ars* as a symbol of technical skill and control (above, lines 5–6 with my note ad loc., cf. *AA* 2.425ff., 727ff., etc.). Line 39 is adapted from the Roman custom of driving a plough round the site of a future city, so that Ovid is marking out the bounds of his subject-matter.

43–50 The use of hunting, fowling or fishing metaphors – conventional for erotic purposes, but just why deserves some scrutiny – also serves to point up a presumptive contrast between male 'rational' initiative and female 'instinctual' reactions: the lover as hunter deploys a range of suitable techniques to bring down his quarry. See, e.g., *AA* 1.89, 253, 269–70, 391–3, 763–6; 2.185–92; 3.425–8, 591–2, 669–70.

53–4 For the rescue of Andromeda by Perseus from the prospective attentions of a sea-monster, see my note to *Am.* 3.3.17–18 (p. 315). The 'coloured Indies' here probably refers to Ethiopia. What, we may wonder, has the victim chained to her rock in common with Helen, the all-too-willing adulteress? The answer would seem to be, nothing: Ovid's only concern with these two episodes, apart from incidental decoration, is the fact that Perseus and Paris both went far out of their way – in the most literal sense – to get what they could have found at Rome simply by crossing the street.

55–60 This survey employs a favourite rhetorical device of Ovid's, *variatio*, the ornamental decorative accumulation of detail. There is also a sly attack on the clichés of official patriotism then current. At one stroke patriotism is subverted by Ovid's private erotic fancy. Worse still, we are reminded (line 60) that Augustus' mythical ancestor, pious Aeneas, was traditionally not only the son of Venus, by Anchises, but also Cupid's half-brother (a joke Ovid had previously deployed at *Am.* 1.2.51–2, again in a political context: see my note, p. 270.

57 Gargara was a high spur of Mt Ida in the Troad, haunted by wild beasts, famous for the richness of its crops, and the scene of that famous cloud-covered passage of love between Zeus and Hera (Homer *Il.* 14.292ff.). The wine of Methymna, a delightful town on the north-west coast of Lesbos, was much praised in antiquity. Today – *experto crede* – it is something of an acquired taste.

67–74 Among all the Roman locales which Ovid recommends as profitable hunting-grounds for young men after an easy pick-up, the porticoes and colonnades, mostly of recent construction, take pride of place. The list given here is repeated (with the addition of Agrippa's Porticus Argonautarum and the Theatre of Marcellus) at *AA* 3.389–96, in a passage addressed to the women themselves (see my note, p. 392). The Danaids' Portico is twice alluded to in the *Amores* (2.2.3–4; 3.1.60–62), while colonnades in general recur later in the present book of the *Ars* (491ff.: either the Danaids' or Pompey's portico may be meant here. To a Roman reader these landmarks, as depicted by Ovid, must have conveyed a sense not only of familiarity – the urban milieu of Rome is crucial to the *Ars* – but also of shock, offset for some by irreverent delight.

Augustus, as we know from his *Res Gestae* (4.19–21, cf. Suet. *Div. Aug.* 28.2), took great pride in the fact that he had 'found Rome brick and left it marble'. Yet for Ovid all this pomp and circumstance, these colonnades, theatres and temples have one function and one only: to serve as a stage on which the pursuit of women may be conveniently conducted.

75–6 Meetings at religious festivals were popular, both in Greece and in Rome, these being among the few occasions on which young unmarried girls were allowed out in public.

77–8 For the cult of Isis in Rome see my notes to *Am.* 1.8.73–4, and esp. 2.2.25–6 (p. 292). The identification of Zeus' ex-mistress Io with Isis was due to her presence in Egypt while metamorphosed into a heifer. See my notes to *Am.* 1.3.21–4 (p. 271) and 2.2.44–6 (p. 292).

79–88 Ovid never passes up a chance (cf. lines 585–8 below) to ridicule the pretensions of lawyers and legal terminology: cf. also *Am.* 1.4.35–40 (with my note, p. 272), 1.15.5–6 and 2.5.29–32. The double meanings in this passage, based on nuances of legal jargon, are almost impossible to convey in translation.

89–92 Ovid frequently refers to the theatre as a promising venue for pick-ups and assignations: see, beside the present passage, *Am.* 2.2.26, 2.7.3–4; *AA* 1.497–502; 3.329–32, 394, 633; *RA* 751–6, where it is suggested that music and dancing act as an aphrodisiac.

101–34 In a delectable parody of the aetiological-type poem designed to explain some traditional myth, Ovid produces his own idiosyncratic reason for the theatre's popularity as a seducers' hunting-ground: it all started with Romulus and the rape of the Sabine women! This not only mocks the Romans' fondness for *mos maiorum* (ancestral tradition) and the tendency to seek historical precedent for their actions; it is also, in more ways than one, a dig at Augustus. Romulus was much touted by the Princeps as the founder of Roman greatness; at one point he had even considered taking Romulus' name. Ovid bluntly presents this revered, if misty, ancestral figure as the instigator of civil war (*Fast.* 3.202) and mass rape. He is also making fun of that censorious puritanism which regarded the theatre as a hotbed of vice – and thus, again, mocking Augustus, who in 18 BC had legislated to keep men and women separate in the auditorium.

At 129–32 Ovid both dramatizes, and subtly mocks, the traditional reassurances made to the girls by Romulus that the rape was with a view to marriage – a popular seducer's gambit – and that their new husbands would, *inter alia*, replace home and parents. The notion of the girl as spoil or booty of course fits in very well with the general pattern, not only of the *Ars* (cf. 2.406,743–4; 3.759f.), but of love-elegy as *militia amoris* (cf. *Am.* 1.2.19ff., 1.7.35–40 and elsewhere).

135–62 This whole passage, as has often been noted, represents a mock-didactic reworking of *Am.* 3.2, with which it merits close comparison. Ovid, far more than his elegiac predecessors, developed and repeated material – ideas, words, phrases, motifs – not only from other poets, but also from his own earlier work. Repetition on the present scale, however (like the revamping at lines 565ff. – see below, p. 356 – of *Am.* 1.4.1–58), is more properly regarded as *variatio*: the differences are at least as important as the similarities. *Am.* 3.2 (see my introductory note, pp. 311ff.) is a self-contained dramatic monologue, whereas the present, much shorter sequence forms one item only in a list of the various preserves where women, like big game, may be found and hunted down. Ovid's colourful first-person narrative is replaced by a series of brisk protreptic injunctions.

163–70 From the races Ovid turns his attention to gladiatorial combats. These were not *ludi* but *munera*, i.e., originally, funerary rites in honour of the dead; and not Roman, but an Etruscan import that found its way to the Urbs by way of Campania. Such *munera* are recorded as early as 264 BC; by the end of the Republic they had become wholly secularized, and immensely popular. Observe with what skill Ovid uses the bloody image of the arena to intensify a tired conventional metaphor – Cupid's darts (cf. *Am.* 1.2.7ff. and elsewhere) piercing the susceptible male heart. The carefree seducer is instantly metamorphosed into a dying Gaul.

171–6 The 'naval mock-battle' took place on 1 August 2 BC – a *terminus post quem* for the poem's final draft – in what afterwards became the 'grove of the Caesars' below the Janiculum. It was a re-enactment of the Battle of Salamis, in which no less than 3,000 combatants took part, exclusive of rowers. The occasion – which Ovid ignores – was the dedication by Augustus of the temple of Mars the Avenger (*Ultor*) in the new Forum Augusti, in fulfilment of a vow made at Philippi. The Princeps took great pride in this spectacle; yet Ovid dismisses it in a single couplet (171–2), and only regards it as noteworthy because of the huge crowds – girls in particular – that it drew from the entire Roman world. Nor, alas, was it, in his view, the spectacle that attracted them, but the matchless opportunities for sexual adventure.

177–228 Gaius Caesar (b. 20 BC) was the eldest son of Agrippa and

THE ART OF LOVE: BOOK I

Julia, the daughter of Augustus – who, when the boy was three, adopted him with a view to securing the succession. In 1 BC he married, and, as consul-designate, with proconsular powers, was sent out East. His ostensible mission was to settle local problems in Parthia and Armenia, whence (with the encouragement and assistance of the Parthians) a pro-Roman client-king had been expelled. He was also meant to 'display the heir apparent' in regions which had seen neither Augustus nor his nominees for over a decade.

Just over a year later Gaius was wounded during a minor skirmish in Armenia. His health broke down, and on 21 February AD 4 he died at Limyra in Lycia, during the voyage back to Italy. With his death Augustus' last hopes for a planned succession were destroyed, and he was forced – wholly against his will – to adopt the embittered Tiberius as his heir-designate.

In retrospect (that is, after AD 4) the entire passage must have been acutely embarrassing to anyone with even a moderately 'official' outlook. Gaius, far from basking in the glory of a well-earned triumph, was dead. Nor (*pace RA* 155–6) had he been killed at the climax of a glorious campaign. He succumbed to a lingering wound inflicted in dubious circumstances, and possibly not even on the battlefield, but during some highly unromantic shuttle-diplomacy. The poetic prophecies had been proved false, the hyperbolic flattery had turned sour. The whole passage stood as an unforgettable – and surely unforgotten – testament to the hollowness of Augustan literary propaganda (cf. below, my note on 199ff., p. 345), a permanent reminder to the Princeps himself of the bright hopes that had finally been laid to rest in Gaius' grave. The most significant fact about these lines is, surely, that Ovid let them stand unmodified, even after time had made a mockery of their message.

179–80 M. Licinius Crassus, a member (with Caesar and Pompey) of the First Triumvirate, whose immense wealth was only matched by his ambition, in 53 BC undertook a Parthian expedition – mainly to improve his military reputation *vis-à-vis* those of his two more famous colleagues. At Carrhae, beyond the Euphrates, his force was wiped out, he himself (together with his son Publius, one of Caesar's best lieutenants in Gaul) was killed – according to one account, by having molten gold poured down his throat – and the legions' standards were captured. Not until 20 BC were these spoils of war recovered, when Augustus, by putting effective diplomatic pressure on King Phraates, got back not only Crassus' lost standards, but those of Mark Antony as well.

*181*ff. Gaius was sent to the East as soon as he had celebrated his twentieth birthday. We should remember that Augustus (or Octavian, as he then was) had himself held a command when he was even younger: the compliment was two-edged in more ways than one, since Octavian had the reputation of falling sick whenever a major battle had to be fought.

187–90 That true heroism and *savoir-faire* are not incompatible with extreme youth (at least in certain rare cases) Ovid affects to demonstrate by two mythical *exempla*. (i) After Hercules' birth (eight or ten months later: accounts differ) Hera, in jealousy, sent a pair of snakes to kill the child in its cradle, whereupon Hercules strangled them both with his bare hands. (ii) The youthful Bacchus (Dionysus) traversed the whole of India with his followers, overcoming all opposition and teaching the inhabitants the cultivation of the vine. These parallels are suggestive, in that the two examples selected were (a) demi-gods (b) precocious and (c) achieved divinity through their benefits to mankind. Both were great conquerors, and Bacchus, furthermore, had triumphed in the East.

191–2 This is a singularly ambivalent couplet. Whose years, and luck, does Ovid have in mind? We are forcibly reminded that the boy's true – as opposed to adoptive – father was the great Agrippa, who not only far eclipsed Augustus as a general, but on occasion had to finish off the younger man's work for him (e.g. in Spain: see my note to *Am.* 1.2.51–2, p. 270). Even at Actium it was Agrippa who did all the real work.

193–4 'So great a name': that of Caesar, in this instance as embodied by his adopted great-nephew Augustus. 'Prince of the youths' (*princeps iuventutis*) was a title bestowed by Augustus on both Gaius and his brother Lucius when each assumed the *toga virilis* of manhood. In Gaius' case this was in 5 BC; Lucius' turn came three years later. Both were also admitted to the Senate, and Gaius was designated consul for AD 1. Lucius, like Gaius, died young, succumbing in AD 2 while on his way to Spain: many believed that Livia, Augustus' wife, had had them both poisoned to clear the way to the succession for her own son Tiberius. 'Tomorrow of their seniors' is a clear hint at the title of 'Leader of the Senate' (*princeps senatus*) which Augustus himself held, and suggests, tactfully, eventual succession to Augustus' position.

195–6 This is a difficult couplet to interpret. Phraates IV of Parthia had a son, Phraataces, by an Italian slave-girl. This woman intrigued to win her son the throne, and persuaded the king to send his four legitimate sons to Rome as hostages. Since Gaius has brothers (Lucius and Agrippa Postumus), Ovid argues, he will appreciate the wrong done to these Parthian hostage-princes, now supplanted by their scheming half-brother. Since he has a father (Augustus) he will appreciate the rights of *their* father (Phraates IV) to choose which of his sons should succeed him – even though, *bien entendu*, that son reached the throne prematurely, by parricide. There is an uncomfortable similarity between this story and the rumours circulating about Livia – or, indeed, the ambiguity implicit in the reference to Gaius' father (see above, my note on 191–2). Ovid was a subtle and sophisticated man: he is more likely, here as elsewhere, to have been guilty of sly political malice than of naïvety. The digression on Gaius, ironically enough, despite its fulsome flattery, must have caused more irritation in the Imperial household – for one reason and another – than almost anything else Ovid wrote.

198 The enemy who won his throne by parricide was Phraataces (see above), subsequently Phraates V, of Parthia, who murdered his father, Phraates IV, in April 2 BC, being impatient to succeed.

199–202 Echoes of Propertius' reference to the Parthian campaign (4.6.79–84) alert us – if such warning were needed – to the fact that Ovid here is laying on the clichés with a parodic trowel. The Roman javelin is pitted, symbolically, against the Parthian arrow.

*203*ff. What we have here is a partial *propemptikon* (prayer for the traveller's safety; offering promised for his return; anticipation of festivities when that return is accomplished). For a fuller discussion of the genre see my introductory note to *Am.* 2.11, pp. 299–300.

*213*ff. It is interesting to compare this triumphal procession with that of Love in *Am.* 1.2.23–52, and indeed with official Roman practice generally. The use of four white horses to draw the victor's chariot seems to have been initiated by Caesar, but soon became customary. The captives that adorned the procession were normally led off to prison and execution before it reached the Capitol. Floats drew representations of conquered mountains and rivers, or battle-scenes.

229–52 The generic notion of a dinner-party or banquet, where men and women reclined together, as a suitable venue for seduction is familiar to us from the *Amores* (1.4 and 2.5, *passim*), and recurs at *AA* 1.565ff., 3.749ff. We may note, however, that each of these passages in the *Ars* also contains a highly specific warning against the incidental risks of inebriation. Ovid, like the Porter in *Macbeth*, was well aware that while heavy drinking may provoke desire, it also seriously diminishes performance (*AA* 1.233), not to mention impairing judgement (*AA* 1.243ff., 507–8, 3.753–4), causing quarrels (*AA* 1.591ff.), and making the drinker unattractive (*AA* 3.765–6). At the same time, drunkenness *in others* can be exploited to some advantage, by both men and women (*AA* 1.241–4, 3.753–4, cf. *Am.* 1.4.51–2), while to feign intoxication oneself (*AA* 1.597ff., cf. *Am.* 2.5.13ff.) often disarms opposition. Wine is thus an ambiguous element in the game.

237–48 The tribute to wine (especially in an erotic context) is conventional. So, in a sense, is the contrast between lamplight (fallacious) and daylight (revealing). It is, however, worth recalling in this context that though the Judgement of Paris (247–8) was conducted in broad daylight, all three goddesses offered Paris a bribe, and that the inducement put up by Venus (Aphrodite) was the seduction of Helen.

249–52 It is instructive to compare these warning lines with *AA* 3.753–4, where women are told exactly the same thing – but there as a useful device for helping Plain Jane to catch a lover. Once again it is significant that women are placed, almost by definition, in the same category (251–2) as luxury merchandise.

255–8 Baiae lay on the coast in the sheltered Bay of Puteoli, near Misenum, and due west of Neapolis (Naples). Its original attraction lay in its climate, its thermal springs, and its delightful scenery. Many wealthy persons built villas here, including Marius, Lucullus, Pompey and Caesar. Like many luxury seaside spas, it very soon became a byword for dissipation and immorality. The joke at 257–8 depends on the fact that some sulphur-springs were thought to be therapeutic for wounds, but here the man who came for a cure leaves with a different sort of trauma.

259–62 The 'woodland shrine' sacred to Diana was situated by a small lake, the modern Lago di Nemi, on the forest-clad lower slopes of the Alban Hills, about three miles from Aricia. (Aricia itself was the first way-station from Rome towards Brindisi, some sixteen miles down the Via Appia.) It was most famous, or notorious, for its slave-priest, the so-called 'King of the Grove' (*Rex Nemorensis*), who took office by killing his predecessor, after challenging him by plucking a bough from the sacred precinct. However, Ovid may well be referring to another ceremony, the torch-race run by women to the shrine from the city. This ritual offered ample opportunity for casual dalliance to those who ignored Diana's example of virginity: Ovid suggests that if they 'got hurt' in consequence, this was due to the goddess's anger.

263–8 These lines form a bridge between the first main topic of Bk I (where to find girls) and the second (how to catch them when found): the recapitulation, coupled with Ovid's use here of his favourite hunting metaphor, once again suggests that he is parodying serious didactic poetry as a genre.

269ff. The ultimate seducibility of all women is a point to which Ovid recurs several times in Bk I: see, e.g., lines 343–8, 471–8, 485–6. This general proposition, especially if considered in a didactic context, has to be universally valid: we cannot – nor, despite his earlier disclaimers (in particular, at 31–4), did Ovid intend that we should – assume that upper-class Roman wives, by definition, are to be excluded from what follows. Indeed, the mythological *exempla* chosen almost all dwell, to a striking degree, on *adultery*: see esp. vv. 295, 301–2, 304, 309, 311, 327, 333–8, 341–4 (cf. 2.543–6, 3.643–4). Lines 271–4, besides repeating the imagery of the chase, offer a good instance of the rhetorical *adynaton*, or argument from comparative impossibility: sooner will X (generally something against the natural order) happen than Y (the immediate matter in hand).

277–82 Ovid's concept of the female nature as wild, uncontrollable, and passionate in an animal sense is repeated later (*AA* 2.372–86); this helps to dramatize the dominant image of her male pursuer (but see lines 704ff. and my note pp. 360–61). He is not only a hunter, but also an agriculturalist and stockman. Whereas the male sexual instinct is controlled, that of women (281) is 'rabid'. To drive this point home, there follow no less than ten mythological illustrations (283–340) of excessive, and illicit, feminine passion. If women are like *that*, Ovid implies, how can a man, any man, fail to get his way with them?

283–8 Various versions of the myth of Byblis are known, but one constant feature in them all is the incestuous passion she nursed for her brother Caunus – or *vice versa*. When Caunus fled to Lycia, Byblis either hanged herself from grief, or was metamorphosed into a stream or fountain. Ovid tells the story in much greater detail in his *Metamorphoses* (9.446–664). Myrrha, or Smyrna, was the daughter of Thias, king of Assyria, with whom she was doomed by Aphrodite to have an incestuous relationship: he did not recognize her until it was too late (Ovid *Met.* 10.298ff.). He then pursued her with a drawn sword; but she prayed to be made invisible, and the gods turned her into a myrrh-tree. The oozing drops of gum from the tree's bark were thought to be her tears. In due course Myrrha-the-tree burst open and gave birth to Adonis.

289ff. Why is so much space – no less than 38 lines – devoted to the story of Minos' aberrant wife Pasiphaë in Ovid's catalogue? Ovid may be genuinely fascinated by the myth, which he treats as an Alexandrian motif, a working out in psychopathic terms of 'the feminine libido gone beyond all bounds'. The fascination is undoubtedly there, since Ovid later returns to the act, and its various consequences, in extended *mythoi* dealing not only with Ariadne (*AA* 1.525ff.) but also with Daedalus (*AA* 2.21ff.), whose ingenious wooden cow facilitated Pasiphaë's miscegenation. It is also worth noting how close the imagery is to that of *Am.* 3.5; if the earlier poem is in fact Ovidian, this could suggest another, more personal reason for treating Pasiphaë's story at length in a context discussing uncontrollable female sexuality. The fruit of this contrived miscegenation was, of course, the Minotaur. Mt Ida (289) is the central massif of the long Cretan range, snow-capped for much of the year, and associated with various legends concerning Zeus.

297–8 For the tradition concerning Cretans as congenital liars, see my note on *Am.* 3.10.19–24, p. 328.

299–336 We have here a classic example of Ovid's penchant for exploiting the potentially ludicrous elements in a myth; yet his treatment is, at the same time, undeniably horrific, in a style that recalls Bosch or Goya, since Pasiphaë, with her gown and mirror in the meadow, may be a figure of fun, but is nevertheless quite capable of murdering her 'rivals' and ripping out their entrails with her bare hands (319–20). Despite this, Ovid contrives to mock the whole notion of her taurine *mésalliance* by means of sly visual juxtapositions, so that the overall effect is one of harmless grotesquerie – like the 'Dance of the Hours' in Disney's *Fantasia* – with disturbing undertones. An extra dimension is created by the fact that Pasiphaë's disposal of the herd's more attractive cows can be parallelled, in human terms, from Greek tragedy.

327–30 Aerope, the wife of Atreus, committed adultery with his brother Thyestes. When Atreus discovered Aerope's infidelity, he killed three of Thyestes' children, invited him to a banquet, and served them up to him for dinner. According to one tradition, which became very popular with the Roman poets – Ovid alludes to it again at *Tr.* 2.391ff. – it was in horror at this act of murder and cannibalism that the Sun reversed his course over Mycenae, setting in the east rather than the west.

331–40 Ovid's list of mythological crimes 'prompted by woman's lust' (341) continues with Scylla, daughter of Nisus, King of Megara. Having fallen in love with Minos, who was besieging Megara with his fleet, Scylla pulled out the purple lock, or hair, on which her father's life (according to an oracle) depended. Nisus duly died, and Scylla betrayed Megara to Minos. This did her little good: when Minos had secured Megara, he slung Scylla by the heels down from the stern of his ship, and drowned her. Agamemnon's murder at the hands of Clytemnestra and her lover Aegisthus is familiar from Homer and many other sources. After Jason and Medea (335–6) had lived in Corinth for some while, Creon, the King of Corinth, persuaded Jason to divorce Medea in order to marry Creon's own daughter, Creüsa (she is more commonly referred to as Glauce). Medea first sent her prospective replacement a poisoned robe, which burnt her up when put on, and then murdered her own two children by Jason. Phoenix (337) was accused by his father Amyntor's mistress, Phthia, of having seduced her; according to Homer the charge was true, and Phoenix had been urged into the act by his jealous mother; there is no mention of Amyntor blinding his son in punishment. When Theseus, mistakenly, believed his son Hippolytus guilty of adultery with the boy's stepmother, Phaedra, he cursed him, and Poseidon sent a bull from the sea that scared the horses of Hippolytus' chariot, so that they stampeded, the chariot was smashed up, and Hippolytus, tangled in the reins, was dragged to death. A similar false accusation of seduction was made to Phineus (339–40) concerning his two sons, again by their stepmother, Idaea or Idothea. Phineus, like Amyntor in similar circumstances, apparently blinded them both.

341–50 The cumulative impact of Ovid's cautionary tales leaves us with no more than a secondary impression of the lust involved; what really sticks in the mind is that lethal parade of malice, perversion, perjury, jealousy and revengeful violence, up to and including murder. Hell, in fact, hath no fury like a woman scorned: let any would-be seducer take warning (cf. *AA* 2.387ff., and, in a quieter vein, below, lines 365ff.). Yet, in the passage that follows, our *praeceptor amoris* makes a quite different point. Observe, he says the intensity of the female sexual urge. No woman can resist a man's advances – or even if she does, she will find the attention *per se* enjoyable. Besides, novelty has its own built-in attractions, and our neighbour's fields and flocks always look more enticing than our own – a thought as seductive in antiquity as today. Here we discern a re-statement of Ovid's much-emphasized claim (*Am.* 2.19 and 3.4, with my introd. note to the latter, pp. 315–16) that 'what's allowed is a bore, it's what isn't / That turns me on'. If sex can drive women to murder, no man equipped with the appropriate *ars*, or technique, should have any trouble getting them into bed.

*351*ff. The various advantages and disadvantages of having one's mistress's personal maid – generally her coiffeuse – privy to the intrigue are examined (from a more involved standpoint) in the *Amores*: see esp. *Am.* 1.11, 1.12, 2.7 and 2.8. Her obvious function is as go-between, a bearer of messages (*Am.* 1.11.3–8) and interpreter of moods (ibid. 17–18). She can also – for whatever ulterior purpose – become sexually involved herself with her lady's lover, or would-be lover (*Am.* 2.7.17ff., 2.8 *passim*; cf. my notes ad loc.). The dangers of this practice are set out in the present passage (375ff.) in a cool and rational manner – though by *AA* 2.251ff. Ovid has quite forgotten them, and is recommending the cultivation of madam's personal servants with unqualified enthusiasm. Readers of the *Amores* will also recall, with amusement, Ovid's anxious protestations, *qua* lover, to Corinna (2.7.19ff.) on the awkward occasion that so clearly influenced his ultra-cautious line (375ff.) as *praeceptor amoris* thereafter. Indeed, in Bk 3 (663–6), while discussing the problem of jealousy between women, he openly admits his personal involvement.

360 Note the characteristic agricultural image, designed to enhance Ovid's concept of women as fundamentally akin to cows or wheatfields: a natural phenomenon to be tamed, cultivated, ploughed in season and, ultimately, harvested: see below, 755–8, and frequently in Bk 2 (e.g. 322, 513, 667–8). At 391–4 the image of hunting (or fishing, or fowling) is used to describe a seducer's dealings with the maid if he decides to claim her favours as well as those of her mistress.

363–4 The image here is abruptly changed to one which Ovid often employs elsewhere: that of a beleaguered town, with its easily interchangeable military and sexual symbolism. See, e.g., *Am.* 1.9.19–20, where an explicit parallel is drawn between the 'gates' and 'threshold' of girl and city. While the cliché of the *exclusus amator* can render this image officially innocuous, its sexual implications remain clear.

*399*ff. The notion of ordering life and nature through traditional social, practical and religious rules – doing the right thing at the right time – was central to the didactic tradition. The very title of Hesiod's *Works and Days* embodied it, and it recurs throughout the *Georgics* of Virgil. Several scholars have pointed out that these lines, with their allusions to farming, sailing, and star-lore, are fundamentally parodic.

There are echoes of Hesiod, Virgil, even Aratus. But the real joke – to which the reader has been alerted by these touchstones – is the frivolous application of a serious didactic formula to the tactics of seduction. Just as sowing or sailing are best avoided at certain seasons, Ovid argues (339–402), so there are ill-omened days for the pursuit of women. The motif is already familiar from the *Amores* (see esp. 1.10 *passim*, and 1.8.87–100). Ovidian women go to great lengths to wheedle expensive gifts out of their lovers, and this *quid pro quo* attitude comes in for heavy criticism. Since the lover-poet's own presents offer cachet rather than cash (*Am.* 1.3.25–6, 1.8.61–2, 1.10.59–62, 2.17.27, 2.17.27, 3.8.1–8) he is more vulnerable than most to gold-digging in a woman, attacks it resentfully, and here – as *praeceptor amoris* – offers hints on how best to side-step the various most obvious pitfalls. We may note, wrily, that things clearly have not changed all that much in two millennia. Then as now, birthdays and Christmas (or the equivalent) formed the major hazards: new taboo days to add to the old Hesiodic calendar or the rich Roman assortment of *dies nefasti*.

405–6 The 'feast of Venus' mentioned here, celebrated on 1 April, seems to have been a joint festival associated with Venus Verticordia (as 'Changer of Hearts') and Fortuna Virilis. In honour of the latter women attended the men's baths; the celebration was also open to courtesans, and clearly originated as a fertility-cult. Venus Verticordia was given her first temple in 114 BC (as the result of an injunction taken from the Sibylline Books) after three Vestal Virgins had been found guilty of incest: she was worshipped by upper-class women. However, no other source suggests that this was a day for giving presents; and the suspicion that Ovid may, once again, be poking fun at respectable ladies gains considerable support from the phrase 'in conjunction with Mars'. On 1 March was celebrated the Matronalia, a feast linked with Juno Lucina (as goddess of childbirth) and the birth of Mars: a notable feature of this festival was the giving of presents to *wives by their husbands*. Clearly Ovid is hinting at both dates: adulterers, no less than the fancy-free, are to beware of exploitation.

407–8 The reference here is to the midwinter festival of the Saturnalia, which began on 17 December and continued for between three and seven days of public holiday. The most famous feature of this festival was the reversal of roles between masters and slaves; but equally traditional – a tradition that still survives today –

was the giving of presents, known as *apophoreta*. Martial, in Bk 14 of his *Epigrams*, provides a fascinating survey of such gifts, for which he wrote accompanying verses. Medicine chests, backscratchers, socks, comforters, woolly slippers, table-games, gold-inlaid dishes – the list recalls every popular Christmas catalogue. Originally such gifts had consisted only of *sigillaria*, small images made from earthenware or pastry; but little by little the occasion became more commercialized, the presents increasingly expensive: a familiar story.

409–12 The seven stars of the Pleiads had their heliacal rising in May, while their cosmical setting in November (between the 8th and 11th of the month) heralded not only the sowing season, but also the end of sailing for the year and the onset of winter storms. Bad weather, similarly, is associated with the Kid's setting: it was, in general, regarded as a stormy constellation. At line 412 Ovid's use of the phrase 'dismembered vessel' (*naufraga membra ratis*) strongly suggests erotic no less than maritime failure. *Membrum*, like various other words in Ovid's vocabulary (e.g. *testis, nervus, latus, coire, miscere, surgere, cadere, iacere*) is commonly exploited for suggestive double entendre: see my notes on lines 631–6, p. 358 and *AA* 3.398, p. 394.

413–6 The best days on which to pursue the business of seduction, says Ovid, with exemplary logic, are those on which the shops are shut, and presents therefore unobtainable. His first example might have been deliberately chosen to annoy officialdom: 18 July, a day of national mourning, a *dies ater*, the anniversary of Rome's crushing defeat by the Gauls under Brennus (390 BC) on the banks of the Allia, which led to the city's sack and capture. No public business could ever be transacted on this day, so a lover was reasonably safe from financial demands then. The same applied to the Jewish Sabbath, which – at least as far as doing business went – was now observed by many Gentiles in Rome.

417–8 These lines, together with 429–30, remind us of the old bawd's advice in *Am.* 1.8.93–4, recommending a birthday as a good occasion for dunning prospective lovers. Presents, a party, a cake – all were obligatory.

419–24 Not only Ovid (*Am.* 1.10) but also Tibullus emphasizes the persistent and ingenious rapacity displayed by the gold-diggers of his day. Propertius, too, bitterly taunts Cynthia with her insatiable greed for gifts. The door-to-door pedlar (*institor*) not only supplied these demands; he was also, like the modern commercial traveller, popularly supposed to enjoy his customers' sexual favours. To be 'loose-garbed' (*discinctus*) was thought to indicate a corresponding sexual laxity.

433–6 Again, the request for a loan without intention of repayment recalls the advice given by Dipsas at *Am* 1.8.101–2. The word used here (435) to describe these gold-diggers is *meretricum*, literally 'prostitutes'; but I suspect that what Ovid has in mind is their mercenary, *quid pro quo* attitude, and that the term is used as a conscious insult rather than as an accurate social description.

437ff. Ovid's would-be lover is in the business of persuasion: specialized, but amenable to a traditional set of rules formulated by the rhetoricians. As we have already seen (*Am.* 1.15.1–6, with my note p. 288), Ovid's professed aim is to adapt this talent to erotic and literary ends, while at the same time rejecting those activities – law, soldiering, statesmanship – with which it was more commonly associated. He now, *qua* instructor, outlines the potential of the written word as an initial approach to seduction.

440–44 There is deliberate cynicism in the choice of examples here, well suited to the complaints Ovid makes elsewhere (*Am.* 3.8.1ff.; *AA* 2.272ff.; etc.) that gold is now the only potent persuader – a social objection regularly raised by angry conservative poets in antiquity (most notably, Theognis and Pindar). It was not only, or even primarily, Priam's *entreaties* that overcame Achilles' refusal to surrender Hector's body, but the king's ransom that the old man brought him: Homer *Il.* 24.228–35. Similarly, wrathful gods are more likely, in Ovid's view, to be appeased by offerings than by prayers – or at least by prayers when suitable offerings accompany them.

451–3 The italicized words are a direct quotation from Virgil (*Aen.* 6.129) and thus provide something rare in Ovid: specific parody. Aeneas has just made his heartfelt appeal to the Sibyl to show him the way to the underworld, where, we remember, a climactic vision of Rome's future greatness awaits him (6.756–853): cf. my note on *AA* 2.79–82 (p. 366). The way down, the Sibyl replies, is simple, but 'to retrace your steps, and get out into the upper air once more – this is the task, this the labour'. For Ovid, of course, the task and labour are to get your girl into bed without laying out expensive gifts on her first.

457–8 Acontius, a young man from the island of Ceos (modern Kea), off the Attica coast, saw Cydippe, chaperoned by her nurse, at the annual festival on Delos, and fell in love with her at first sight. He followed the pair to Artemis' shrine, where he threw in front of the nurse an apple on which he had written the words: 'I swear by Artemis I will marry Acontius.' The nurse handed the apple to Cydippe – apples were frequently given as a declaration of love – and the girl, without thinking, read the message inscribed on it: aloud, as was the custom in antiquity. Though she threw the apple away, she still felt herself bound by this unintentional oath. Three times her father tried to marry her off to some other suitor: on each occasion Cydippe contracted a mysterious (and presumably psychosomatic) illness. Prior to their fourth attempt, the family consulted the Delphic Oracle, all became clear, and Cydippe duly married Acontius (a cynic might be forgiven for deducing that she in fact had wanted him from the start).

459–86 Once again Ovid attacks official values, by changing the motive for acquiring the technique of eloquence from success in court or forum to success in bed. His opening words are a mockery of old-fashioned rhetoric and virtue; they also recall Virgil's advice to farmers (*Georg.* 2.35–6) to learn the arts of *cultus*, a term that echoes ambiguously in this context. 'Young men of Rome' (*Romana iuventus*) was a favourite phrase of Ennius, and the 'noble arts' associated with the orator and advocate sound a trifle hollow when exercised, not on senator or judge, but against the defences of a girl.

From line 469 onwards another didactic precept, similarly adduced from the agricultural world, is introduced: patience. With patience, horses and oxen are broken for domestic use. Ploughing wears down the coulter, water dissolves stone. Persistence is all.

487–504 With a decidedly awkward break in the flow of his argument, Ovid now turns to advice on how to approach one's mistress in public. That it is a mistress he is describing seems clear from the use of the term *domina* in lines 488 and 504. Yet most of the advice, apart from the cryptic exchanges he envisages by the lady's litter (487–90), seems designed to achieve a pick-up (491–6) or attract attention (497–504). The kind of behaviour he advocates in colonnade and theatre (cf. 67ff.) is meaningless if directed towards a prize already won, and I suspect that here (as often) his weakness for the associative erotic cliché has led him to compose a thematically loose sequence.

For the theatre (497–504) as an ideal setting for pick-ups and feminine exhibitionism see 89–92 above, with my note p. 341. If the use of eyebrows and sign-language was no more subtle than that in fashion at dinner-parties (*Am.* 1.4.15ff. and my note p. 272), a Roman auditorium must have offered a fascinating spectacle during the intermission. While it is true that the mime, with its eternally cuckolded husbands, must have encouraged an atmosphere conducive to adultery, Ovid's advice here could not, by any stretch of the imagination, be thought sophisticated. The heavily significant behaviour he advocates – applauding lovers' roles, sitting on till the girl of your choice leaves, then leaving too, hint, hint – is in line with his earlier prescriptions for action at a dinner-party (*Am.* 1.4) or the races (*Am.* 3.2, cf. 135–64 above), and suggests, to put it mildly, a certain naïvety. Ovid's flippant advice to 'waste time at your mistress's whim' would not have gone down at all well with serious-minded Romans, who structured their day like any American executive.

505–24 This rather unexpected mini-lecture on masculine toiletry and hygiene fits very well into the didactic tradition that Ovid is exploiting. It also sheds some interesting light on the conventional standards of the day, not least as regards the emphasis – essentially Greek-derived – that smart Romans placed on hair-styling. Ovid's general line is one still familiar today, and carefully taken into account by advertisers of, e.g., men's colognes and after-shave lotions: i.e. that while a man should keep himself reasonably clean, well-groomed, free from body-odour and pure of breath, to go much beyond this smacks of effeminacy (505ff., 523–4, and cf. *AA* 3.433ff.). 'Cybele's votaries' (507) were the eunuch temple-attendants of the great Anatolian mother-goddess, conventionally regarded as homosexual, and thus liable to curl their hair and depilate themselves. Their cult had been introduced into Rome in the late 3rd cent. BC, but clearly still aroused hostile feelings among conservative Romans.

Ovid's general attitude to adult homosexuality is casual, pragmatic and dismissive (*AA* 2.683–4 with my note, p. 380, cf. *Am.* 1.1.20). This seems odd when we recall his otherwise enlightened and considerate sexual preferences, but is probably attributable to that stereotyped distinction made in antiquity between paederasty of a formalized sort and homosexual relationships among grown men. Exercise taken in the Campus Martius is also described at *AA* 3.383–6. For the abduction of Ariadne by Theseus see 527ff. below, and my note p. 356; for Phaedra's infatuation with her stepson Hippolytus, my note to *Am.* 2.18.21–6 (p. 308); for Adonis and Aphrodite (Venus), my note to *Am.* 3.9.15–16 (pp. 325–6). Neither Hippolytus nor Adonis – though both outdoor characters – could be said to typify the normal masculine ideal: their use here in such a context is suggestive.

525ff. The rescue of Ariadne from Naxos by Dionysus (Bacchus) was a famous myth that had attracted many writers and painters before Ovid.

Bacchus (Dionysus), like Apollo, was, *inter alia*, a patron of poets, perhaps because of the conventional view – not moribund yet: consider the Dylan Thomas myth – that strong drink and poetic inspiration were indissoluble. Being susceptible to love (525–6) he also favours lovers: the link with what comes before and after may be tenuous, but it is there. What Ovid says here, viewed in non-anthropomorphic terms, is that drink (provided you do not take too much of it) can give you Dutch courage for seducing women. That is the meaning of 231–6 (see my note, pp. 345–6); the same point recurs, in slightly different terms, at 569ff. Wine removes inhibitions, stimulates courage. Wine gives a shy man the strength to approach and, with luck, carry off, his own dinner-table Ariadne.

558 The more common version of this heavenly translation, in which Dionysus (Bacchus, Liber) merely set Ariadne's crown, and not the lady herself, in the heavens, can be found told by Ovid at *Met.* 8.178ff. The 'Cretan Crown' is what we know today as the Aurora Borealis.

565ff. Once again we find – with significant didactic variations – the restatement of a theme which Ovid had used in the *Amores* as background to some personal experience: see above, lines 229–52, and my note, pp. 345–6. That dinner-parties and banquets did offer real opportunities, and correspondingly real dangers, in the sphere of adulterous seduction is no mere literary fiction: see my note to *Am.* 1.4.53. That Ovid's anxiety about intoxication was due to something more than natural abstemiousness is clear enough (see, e.g., 567–8, 589ff.). There was also the quarrelsomeness associated with such occasions. It would be to any seducer's advantage to keep his head clear and his wits about him in such circumstances. The 'Lord of Darkness and Nocturnal Orgies' (567) is, of course, Dionysus or Bacchus, whose rites (*orgia*) were held at night.

569–78 The devices here recommended all appear in the *Amores*, thus once again offering at least literary confirmation of Ovid's claim (29–30) to be writing from personal experience. Double-talk: 569–70 = *Am.* 2.5.19–20, 3.11.23–4 (cf. *AA* 2.543, 3.514). Writing in wine: 571–2 = *Am.* 1.4.20, 2.5.17–18 (with my note, p. 272). Meaningful glances: 573–4 = *Am.* 1.4.17–19, 2.5.15–16, cf. *Her.* 17.77. Symbolic use of drinking-cup or food: 575–8 = *Am.* 1.4.29–34. On the other hand, the various 'secret' signs listed at *Am.* 1.4.21–8 do not – perhaps understandably – figure in Ovid's didactic presentation.

579–84 The notion of *cultivating* a lady's husband or other official escort, even if (601–2) you curse him under your breath at the same time, is something new on Ovid's part. Previously, perhaps for dramatic purposes, the *vir* has elicited little from him on such occasions but curses: *Am.* 1.4.1–6, 29–30, 33–40. The only 'cultivation' involved on these occasions is the plan to get the man hopelessly drunk (ibid. 51–4) so that he passes out. The idea that husbands are more useful to the would-be seducer as friends, and therefore deserve special consideration, may be tactically advantageous, but is not advice that Ovid ever portrays himself as having taken.

585–8 Prior to this quatrain, Ovid has been passing out cheerfully cynical instructions on what tactics best serve the would-be seducer at a dinner-party. After it he resumes in the same vein – brisk, pragmatic, protreptic. The nearest we come to morality is the vexation of Juno and Pallas (625–6) at being outsmarted by Venus during the Judgement of Paris. Yet the text as it stands requires us to believe that for four lines Ovid solemnly moralizes at his audience about the evils of abusing friendship, and how such conduct leads the collector (*procurator*: it could also mean 'agent' or 'bailiff') to collect more than his proper charge, i.e. to take over his master's wife along with his accounts. Such lines are clearly out of place here. Flabby language, inappropriateness of sentiment, and quite striking irrelevance to the matter in hand all stamp these lines as 'a moralizer's feebly composed insertion' (Goold, p. 92).

589–94 The mythological example of the fight between Centaurs (of whom Eurytion, killed during the brawl, was one) and Lapiths is well chosen in this context, since at the wedding of Hippodameia the Centaurs became violent-drunk, and tried to rape the bride.

601 The toast is, of course, ambiguous: while the company may take 'the man she sleeps with' to be her 'present partner' (*viro*), the proposer – and the girl – will know better.

603–6 Once again Ovid is adapting earlier material to didactic ends. Two passages from the *Amores* describe the end of a party. (i) At 2.5.21ff. Ovid's rival takes advantage of Ovid's apparent (but in fact feigned: cf. 597–600, which acquire an ironic flavour in this context) drunkenness to snatch some heavy kisses from his girl. (ii) At 1.4.53ff., a near-parallel situation to that posited here, Ovid proposes to meet his girl in the crowd when the guests are departing, and her husband will, hopefully, be unconscious-drunk under the table. As he well knows, such a set-up has only limited potential. Even a drunk husband comes home eventually, more often than not sooner rather than later, and proceeds to lock his wife away. All the pair can hope for, realistically – like Ovid's girl and her new lover in (i) above – are a few hurried kisses; or, here, where a pick-up rather than a reunion is assumed, some fast and persuasive talking on the man's part to lay the foundations for a future affair (607–30).

607–10 What I have translated as 'clodhopping bashfulness' (*rustice ...Pudor*) was a favourite target of Ovid's: for his attitude to *rusticitas* cf. below, 659–72, and *AA* 3.127–8, with my notes, pp. 359–60 and 385–6.

611–30 The erotic axioms propounded here are familiar and perennial. Flattery will get you anywhere; every woman, whether virtuous or not, not only loves to be flattered, but takes it for granted, whatever her appearance, that she is well worth flattering. Even if you hand out compliments in a mood of cynical indifference, you may well end up in love anyway.

631–6 The idea that lovers' oaths were not binding had a long history, going back at least to Hesiod, who made the remark apropos Zeus (Jupiter) when the god, having turned Io into a white heifer, denied on oath to Hera (Juno) that he had had intercourse with her. It seems possible that Ovid had this occasion in mind when writing lines 635–6. Line 632, *pollicito testes quoslibet adde deos*, contains a classic sexual double entendre impossible to render adequately in translation. It can mean either 'Call any gods you please to witness your promises', or 'Promise any sexual performance you like, and throw the gods in too'. By no accident, a similar joke turns up, in an identical context, at *Am.* 3.3.19, where the gods whom Ovid's mistress has falsely invoked are described as *sine pondere testes* – 'worthless witnesses' or 'half-cock performers': my rendering 'puffball witnesses' at least tries to catch some of the ambiguity.

637–42 This famous passage (with which cf. Plin. *HN* 2.26) has been quoted more often than properly understood. The existence of gods was indeed expedient for Augustus (who doubtless *believed* in them no more than did Ovid) and for his policy of social regeneration. The old religion was an instrument by which the Princeps hoped to achieve order, revive tradition, idealize the past, control the present. Its ritual patterns formed a cohesive agent with which the fragmented society of the Republic might, hopefully, be glued together again. Most important of all, it offered some kind of ultimate moral sanction in an age which singularly lacked such things.

It is from this programme that Ovid, in six packed lines, strips away the highfalutin pretensions of Augustan moral reform to reveal the political realities beneath. Religious utilitarianism was nothing new in Roman thought: it had been prefigured by Varro. But Ovid exposes the rationale behind the system with acid clarity. Gods are politically useful: so let us assume their existence and observe their festivals (637-8). The injunction not to 'embezzle deposits' may sound a little odd to a modern reader; but when no such thing as a bank safety vault existed, valuables or cash were often left in trust with a friend, who was under a religious obligation to return them on demand (cf. Juv. 13.15-16).

643-58 The argument proceeds smoothly from premiss to conclusion. (i) the gods, by imperial decree if for no other reason, are to be taken seriously, not least in the matter of keeping one's sworn oath; (ii) however, lovers' oaths are traditionally inoperative; therefore (iii) reserve your lying promises for the girls you aim to seduce. A fourth argument is added by way of rider: Since women themselves are congenital cheats (cf. *Am.* 3.3, *passim*), they can be deceived with impunity, and, indeed, with a good semblance of moral justification: let perjury earn perjury in return. This proposition Ovid then illustrates, not over aptly, with two popular just-so stories often linked by ancient rhetoricians, the common element being an adviser or inventor hoist with his own petard.

The first theme (647-52) concerns Busiris, a mythical king of Egypt, who at the instigation of a Cypriot seer, Thrasias (or Phrasias) attempted to end a nine-year drought by sacrificing a stranger annually – the first victim being Thrasias himself. Ovid's second motif (653-4, expanded at *Tr.* 3.11.40ff.) commemorates a 6th cent. BC inventor, one Perillus or Perilaos, who designed a brazen bull in which victims could be roasted, and offered this device to Phalaris, the tyrant of Acragas in Sicily. Phalaris – a historical, and highly unpleasant, character datable to the mid-sixth cent. BC – accepted the gift, but is said to have made Perillus himself the bull's first victim. The irony of line 655, of course, is that these are the only recorded occasions on which either Busiris or Phalaris displayed any feeling for justice at all. Clearly in all ages the psychological urge to 'make the punishment fit the crime' (even when no crime has been committed) far exceeds any concern for historical accuracy.

659-72 Observe the skill with which Ovid moves into his most morally questionable gambit. Tears and kisses, he says, make potent emotional inroads on a girl's resistance. The atmosphere thus conjured up is one of pleading, of gentle blandishment: such kisses, Ovid remarks parenthetically (667-8), must not be too violent. Yet the key phrase here is 'she wants to be overcome' (666), with its echoes of that charming seduction scene in the *Amores* (1.5.15–16). The axiom that a woman never means it when she says no – familiar to all students of rape and its mythology – offers a perfect lead-in to the advocacy of erotic violence that immediately follows (673–704), and automatically justifies it. The man who fails to press home his advantage after stealing kisses can now be described, without embarrassment, as guilty of the worst solecism Ovid knows – *rusticitas*, here translated as 'gaucheness', and broadly identified in the poet's mind with either a conscience or else provincial naïvety (the two being interdependent) as regards illicit love-making (cf. *Am.* 3.4.37–40, 3.10.18; *AA* 2.565–6).

673–704 The proposition that all women either welcome rape or are converted to it by their ravishers – thus justifying the use of violence to break down their resistance (673–4) – is illustrated by two interesting mythical examples. The first, which Ovid mentions only in passing (679–80), is the carrying off of Leucippus' daughters, Phoebe and Hilaira, by the Dioscuri (Castor and Polydeuces, or Pollux). The latter had been invited to the girls' double wedding at Messene, being cousins not only of the brides, but also of the brothers they were to marry. Instead, the Dioscuri eloped with Phoebe and Hilaira themselves. This incident was a popular theme in ancient art. So indeed was Ovid's second example, the rape of Deidameia, daughter of Lycomedes, king of Scyros, by the youthful Achilles, when disguised as a girl. When Achilles was nine, Calchas the prophet foretold that Troy could not be taken without him. The boy's mother, Thetis, therefore disguised him as a girl and sent him to Scyros, where he was raised among the maidens of Lycomedes' court. The background (683–8), beginning with the Judgement of Paris (see my note on 247–8, p. 346) and Helen's removal to Troy, assumes familiarity with the myth in the reader.

704–22 Having made his point, Ovid now quickly backs off. The caveman axiom of irresistible (and secretly coveted) violence is replaced by a watered-down, socially more acceptable version of male domination: man leads, woman follows. Despite his claim (above, lines 277–82, with my note, p. 347) that women would in fact make the running did men not order things otherwise, he here suggests – with more than a hint of self-contradiction – that these sexually voracious creatures might nevertheless feel social embarrassment (*pudor*) in the leading role. They are – a favourite leitmotiv – dying to be asked (above, line 666; cf. *Am.* 1.5.15–16, and, equally apposite here, *Am.* 1.8.43–4, where the old bawd suggests that what prevents girls pursuing the matter themselves is not *pudor* but rather *rusticitas*, a revealing change). The clinching argument comes at 713-14: no girl ever seduced Jupiter, *he* always went after *them* – a pleasantly irreverent conceit, especially when we remember the Jupiter:Augustus equation and Augustus' known partiality to young girls.

723-38 With allusions to sailors (723), husbandmen (725) and athletes (727), Ovid recaptures the didactic motif: a weatherbeaten complexion may suit such professions, but the lover – also, for Ovid, a professional – should be pale and wan, a traditional convention. Unfortunately, the poet is so pleased with this stock *topos* that he forgets his own earlier recommendation, i.e. that lovers should acquire a good healthy suntan from outdoor exercise (513). Two mythological instances of pallor in the lover follow: (i) Orion in the woods, lamenting his bride Side, whom Hera sent down to Hades because she rivalled Hera in beauty, and (ii) Daphnis, the Sicilian poet-shepherd, also apparently pining for a Naiad, though her name, and circumstances, remain obscure. Another stock symptom of the lover was thinness (733-6), several times asserted by Ovid to be one of his own physical characteristics (*Am.* 1.6.3-6, 2.9B.13-14, 2.10.23-4, with my note, p. 298).

739-54 Right and wrong, friendship and honour (*fas, nefas, amicitia, fides*), the core-elements of Roman morality, are here re-defined in simplistic and far from elevated terms, based on the central criterion of not stealing your friend's mistress. For the professional lover this is an understandable moral code. Few, however, if we are to believe Ovid, maintain even these standards. There follows (743-6) a list of mythical relationships marked by honourable restraint. Patroclus presumably refrained from cuckolding Achilles with 'fair-cheeked Diomede'; their friendship, like that between Theseus and Pirithous, was proverbial. Pirithous did not seduce Phaedra, Theseus' wife; and Pylades, similarly, refrained from making advances to Helen's daughter Hermione, despite her famed beauty, because she was married to his close companion Orestes. The isolation of these shining exceptions vividly illustrates what was regarded as the norm. The last two instances of pure love both involve brother and sister: Apollo and Athena, Castor and Helen. However, at 747-8 Ovid makes it clear that anyone who still believes in such honourable restraint is living in a fantasy world: the argument from impossibility (*adynaton*: cf. lines 271-2 above, with my note, p. 347) is invoked with telling effect.

755-72 At the close of Bk I Ovid reverts to a didactic theory he has expressed earlier (see, e.g., lines 360 and 459ff., with my notes, pp. 350 and 354): the comparison of women to fields, crops and harvest. Their cultivation (*cultus*) then becomes the business of the lover in Bk 2, and their own concern in Bk 3. The echoes of Virgil are explicit (757–8 recalls *Georg.* 1.54–6, 2.109–11), and hunting metaphors recur to reinforce the point. Proteus (761–2), the Old Man of the Sea, was a symbol of metamorphosis as early as Homer's day: Ovid *Met.*8.732ff. The nautical image of the concluding lines (771–2) picks up the reference to Jason's steersman Tiphys in the proem (above, 5–8): Ovid as *praeceptor amoris* is reminding us of the boast with which he embarked on his task.

BOOK 2

1–10 Ovid's actual exclamation (line 1), odd to non-Roman ears, was 'Io Paean': in English 'hurrah' is a tame parallel, but will have to do. 'Paean' was originally a title of Apollo in his function as healer, then a processional chant (often, as here, a victory-song) addressed to the god. It is interesting that Ovid should, after his declaration at *AA* 1.25, begin *AA* 2 with an indirect acknowledgement of Apollo's aid. But then, as we have already seen (my note to *AA* 1.25–30, p. 339) Ovid was perfectly willing to use Apollo as a symbol of inspiration or godhead when it suited him. Why here? Because his poetic art, as exercised in Bk 1, has demonstrably triumphed. Like all good didactic verse, it has a practical end in view, it is *opus utile*: endorsement by readers provides the best proof of its success. Thus the opening distich operates at two levels: (i) the reader (as Ovid hoped) has applied the precepts and caught his girl (with a repetition of the by now familiar hunting metaphor); and (ii) Ovid himself has attained his own objective, the composition of a successful work of art, which not only eclipses Homer but also beats the old arch-didacticist Hesiod at his own game. For the curious myth of Pelops and Hippodameia (7–8) see my note to *Am.* 3.2.15–16, p. 313.

Just as in *AA* 1.30, so Ovid here (15) slips across his appeal to Venus more or less out of the corner of his mouth. At the same time the reference to Erato (16) is, from a literary viewpoint, loaded. Erato was the Muse of love-poetry, and thus appropriate enough in this context. Ovid, however, means the reader to recall two other passages, both from well-known epic poems, where Erato was similarly invoked at a critical moment: the *Argonautica* of Apollonius Rhodius (3.1–5), and Virgil's *Aeneid* (7.37–44). Apollonius is introducing the great love-story of Jason and Medea; but the invocation in the *Aeneid* solemnly commemorates Aeneas' landing on the shores of Latium, the onset of great wars and heroic deeds. Once again Ovid is undercutting Augustan propaganda by evoking it in an emphatically non-heroic context: even the 'too-ambitious project' (*magna paro*) of line 17 echoes a similar claim by Virgil (7.45: *maius opus moveo*).

19ff. The device with which Ovid both introduces (19–20) and rounds off (97–8) his lengthy narration of the Daedalus–Icarus myth is, at first sight, both contrived and hyperbolic. He claims that his task, as *praeceptor amoris*, is to clip the wings of a god (for this double sense of Amor cf. *AA* 1.7) – a control that Minos could not even exercise over mortals. What is the point of this *mythos*?

The basic notions that Ovid may have been trying to get across are: (i) The difficulty of controlling a god (since Minos could not even restrain a man); (ii) *Per contra*, the ability of *ars*, here personified in Daedalus, to master any difficulty *en principe*; and (iii) Bearing in mind how his particular adventure turned out for Icarus, an illustration (*paradeigma*) of the dangers attendant upon *ars* incorrectly applied or wilfully ignored. But it is, surely, the third that most fully explains the *mythos*.

If Ovid, like Daedalus, personifies the true *artifex*, then the wing-clipping, the control of flight at which he aims has as its object not merely Love (*Amor*) *qua* anthropomorphized deity, but also unruly passion as manifested in the unwise student. Icarus, in fact, is the symbol of the rash, headstrong, uncontrolled lover, an awful example of what may happen when passion throws off the prudent guidance of *ars*, of rational technique. The parental bond linking Daedalus and Icarus is analogous to the teacher–student relationship between Ovid and the young gallant he is addressing: it also recalls Chiron and Achilles in the proem to Bk 1. The moral is simple, almost Horatian: follow reason and avoid extremes; otherwise you are liable to wind up like Icarus.

25–8 Daedalus was an Athenian, of the Erechtheid royal clan, and cousin to Theseus; he also figured as the prototype of the versatile creative artist – architect, sculptor, metalworker, inventor, and much else besides. He is said to have murdered his nephew and pupil Talus by throwing him off the Acropolis out of jealousy at the younger man's inventive skills; as a result he was tried by the Areopagus, and left Athens as an exile, winding up at Minos' court in Crete, where his skills found him profitable employment.

45ff. Ovid gives a more detailed description of the way Daedalus created his flying gear at *Met.* 8.189ff.

55-6 The constellations mentioned here are chosen specifically as navigators' aids: Icarus is *not* to steer by the stars, but simply to follow his father. For ancient legends about the Great Bear (today more commonly known as the Dipper) see my note on *Am.* 3.12.23-40, p. 332. Orion the hunter tried to rape Artemis, who, ever-resourceful, had him bitten to death by a scorpion: both the scorpion and Orion were then turned into constellations. That is why, in the heavens, Orion always flees westward round the sky from Scorpio – a nice just-so story or aetiological myth.

77-8 This vivid detail (expanded at *Met.* 8.217-20) cannot but call to mind Pieter Brueghel's 'The Fall of Icarus', so tellingly interpreted by Auden in his famous anthology poem 'Musée des Beaux Arts'. It makes us ask ourselves, not only whether Brueghel consciously used Ovid (which he may well have done), but also what may be the relationship between Ovid's descriptions and various Pompeian wall-paintings depicting the same scene. Did Ovid inspire the paintings? Or are both he and they dependent on a well-known and well-articulated Hellenistic tradition? The second of these possibilities is intrinsically more probable; at least ten Pompeian paintings of the Fall of Icarus survive.

79-98 Ovid's presentation of Daedalus' flight-plan, both here and in the *Metamorphoses*, has aroused surprisingly little critical comment. Daedalus has expressed a wish (25-8, cf. *Met.* 8.183-4) at least to lay his weary bones to rest in his native soil, i.e. in Attica (cf. above): very reasonably, since to be buried – or, worse, *not* buried – in a foreign land was regarded as the worst sort of fate that could befall a man. When Minos proves obdurate, Daedalus fabricates wings for himself and Icarus, and they set off – presumably for Athens, or perhaps, bearing Daedalus' ancient exile in mind, for some destination on, or just beyond, the frontiers of Attica. Daedalus tells his son not to navigate by the stars (55-8, cf. *Met.* 8.206-8), but simply to follow him. This, arguably, was a mistake.

From Cnossos to Delos (79) their route lay due north: Virgil (*Aen.* 6.16) confirms the direction. This, if not the most direct flight-route to Athens (which would have taken them north-west from Thera, now Santorini, by way of Siphnos, Seriphos, Cythnos and Ceos, the modern Kea), was – so far – a perfectly reasonable way of getting there. It used the major islands (Thera, Naxos, Paros) as landmarks, and from Delos onward could follow the long coastlines of Andros and southern Euboea. But at Delos, against all probability, Ovid makes Daedalus turn, not north-west but due east. This is why, when the pair reached the island of Icaria, Samos lay ahead of them, a little to port, while the islands of Lebynthos, Calymne (now Kalymnos, renowned for its sponge-fishers) and Astypalaea were well away to the south, on their right hand, just as Ovid describes the scene (a traveller on the Olympic Airways Athens–Samos flight gets a perfect bird's-eye gloss on this passage). Icarus now flew too near the sun, fell in the sea, and was drowned. Hence the name Icaria. Daedalus, nothing daunted, now revised – indeed, reversed – his itinerary, and proceeded to fly due west for something like 500 miles non-stop, finally touching down in Sicily (*Met.* 8.260–61). Ovid describes him at this point as 'exhausted': we may well believe it.

Clearly, something is very badly amiss with Ovid's account – and, *a fortiori*, with the whole popular tradition on which he drew. Why, after reaching Delos, does Daedalus turn east instead of north-west? Further, if his original route to Icaria and the eastern Aegean was planned, and not accidental, what was he meaning to do there in the first place, and why did he change his mind? And why, after the death of Icarus, did he then fly, not to Attica (as might rationally have been expected) but clear out of the Aegean to Sicily (or Campania: Virgil's account, *Aen.* 6.14–17, has him touch down at Cumae)?

Ovid will have been well aware of the alternative tradition, according to which Daedalus *did* fly to Athens or Attica, just as we might expect. But, we ask at this point, if the flight-plan was logical, and Attica was indeed Daedalus's destination, how does Icaria come to form so integral an element in the tradition? The key to the whole story, in almost every source, is the eponymous association of Icaria, or the Icarian Sea (line 96), or both, with the fall of Icarus. Icarus gave Icaria its name. In the face of this consensus we can only conclude that tradition, very early on, settled for the wrong Icaria. Once that assumption is made, the solution to the problem becomes simple and obvious.

There is only one Icaria which offers a serious alternative to the eastern Aegean island of that name: the famous Attic deme of Icaria or Icarion, which belonged to the Aegeid tribe. It lay three or four miles south-west of Marathon and east of the modern village of Ekali, on an elevated plateau between the main massif of Pendéli and the smaller

Dionysovouni, within easy reach of Marathon Bay. Its connection with Dionysus reminds us that one of its better-known demesmen was Thespis, the early exponent of Attic tragedy. If Daedalus was making for the Marathon region from Delos, his flight would take him directly over Andros and south Euboea: the latter, as we shall see in a moment, may be significant.

If Icarus, in the original version of the legend, was associated with Icaria in Attica, where did Daedalus himself land? Can we explain or adjust the final stage of his uniformly paradoxical flight-plan? Granted that he may well, in the course of time, have taken himself off to Sicily or Magna Graecia, what was his original immediate destination? The tradition followed by Virgil is helpful here. The old Greek name for Cumae was Cyme; and we know two cities of that name in the Aegean world. One, the most familiar, lay on the coast of the mainland opposite Lesbos: it was from here that Hesiod's father sailed to Boeotia. But the other lay on the Euboean coast, a high citadel looking out towards Scyros, a natural landfall for the aerial traveller, and Daedalus could well have ended his journey there, safe from a renewed charge of blood-guilt, but still close enough to Attica. If one strong tradition made him go to Sicily after Icarus' death, whether by air or sea, it would be only too easy to claim him, as does Virgil, for Cumae – or, indeed, for the Icarian Sea.

Though Ovid does not mention Cumae, his entire sequence dealing with Daedalus could not fail to recall the dramatic opening of Virgil's *Aeneid* Bk 6 (lines 14ff., and in particular 23ff., where the whole myth of Pasiphaë, the Minotaur, the Labyrinth, the ball of twine and the death of Icarus is outlined). Daedalus, Aeneas and Augustus are all symbolically linked by Virgil. The great artificer is 'indeed a mythological prototype of the brilliant Augustus', to whose imperial achievements the latter part of Bk 6 looks forward. Just as Ovid earlier mocked Virgil's pretensions by applying the older poet's phraseology in a frivolous erotic context (see *AA* 1.453, with my note, p. 353) so here Daedalus as a symbol of creative achievement is transerred from the Virgilian context of Rome's future greatness to Ovid's equation with the *praeceptor amoris*. This, in effect, Ovid says, was what it all led to, its culminating point – the art of picking up pretty girls in a sophisticated metropolis.

99–106 Ovid's attitude to magic is somewhat ambivalent. As an aphrodisiac it earns his condemnation on two counts: drugs can be dangerous, while spells are ineffectual. In addition to the present passage see lines 415–26, where he sanctions the use of mildly aphrodisiac foods; *RA* 249–90; *MF* 35–42 (a very brisk dismissal); and *Her.* 6.83–94, where he is again discussing Medea. The argument is neat and compelling: a famous sorceress who cannot keep her own lover no more inspires confidence than a bald promoter of hair-restoratives. Elsewhere, particularly in the *Amores*, he shows himself well aware of the links, verbal and affective, e.g. in the double sense of the word *carmen*, 'spell' and 'song' or 'poem', between magic and poetry (cf. Hor. *Sat.* 2.1.82). One poem (*Am.* 1.6, cf. my note, p. 275) is actually built round a magical refrain, the purpose of which is to soften the obdurate heart of the poet's mistress. There is also a hint of sympathetic love-magic at *RA* 719–20. Thus Ovid, we see, only objects to the use of magic in its pharmacopoeic sense (which can be physically harmful), and as vulgar hocus-pocus (a corruption of true verbal magic, i.e. the poet's art, as he makes clear at *RA* 251–2).

107–44 Looks fade, but a glib tongue lasts for ever: thus, invest in persuasiveness as an insurance against middle-aged physical depreciation. No accident, either, that the example Ovid picks is Ulysses (Odysseus), who to a Roman reader would be primarily associated with smooth trickery and deceit. If we further weigh in the hero's striking ability to charm women – whether goddesses, nymphs, virgins, or indeed his own wife – then his value to Ovid as a symbol of the blarneying lover becomes obvious.

Nireus (109) was the handsomest man at Troy after Achilles: this led later writers to use him as the conventional type-figure of male beauty. Hylas (110), a pretty young boy, accompanied his lover Heracles on the first stage of the voyage of the Argonauts. While drawing water from a spring on the Mysian coast he was stolen away by nymphs who fell in love with his good looks. The passage describing the decay of beauty with age (113–20, cf. *MF* 45–50) is, as we might expect from a sensitive hedonist, both serious and poignant. The episode from the Trojan War which Odysseus is represented as describing here can be found in Bk 10 of the *Iliad*. He and Diomede made a night-sortie to kill the recently arrived King Rhesus of Thrace and steal his famous white horses. During this expedition they also caught and killed a Trojan spy, Dolon, who (with over-nice parallelism) was himself hoping to spirit away the horses of Achilles. Note the symbolism of that intrusive wave (139–40): reality will keep breaking in on the teller of tales.

145–76 After eloquence, tolerance. The lover may in fact be a persistent wolf but must on occasion don sheep's clothing to gain his desired end. The tart broadside against marriage as an institution (153–8), with its emphasis on 'law' and 'legal fiat', cannot have much pleased Augustus, so anxious to promote the state of matrimony, so fierce against those who abused it; there may even be a covert allusion here to the Leges Iuliae (see Introd., p. 71). And would Livia, who offered her consort a shrine dedicated to Concord (Ovid *Fast.* 6.637–8), have cared for the reference to wrangling wives? The financial side of love-making, too (161ff.), is never absent from Ovid's mind for long. The pattern is established as early as *Am.* 1.3.7ff.: on the one hand crass rivals whose strength lies in their bank-balance; on the other the poet–narrator who offers genius in lieu of cash (cf. *Am.* 1.8.57ff., 1.10.11ff., 3.8 *passim*). The autobiographical motif (once again confirming *AA* 1.29, his claim to teach from experience) is reintroduced at 165–6 with the candid admission, never before made in plain terms, that he 'couldn't afford gifts, so spun words' – a characteristic ambiguity, since the phrase 'spun words' (*verba dabam*) carries in Latin the secondary meaning of 'cheat' or 'deceive'.

Retrospective allusions in Ovid often, as here (169–76), demonstrate an interesting ability on the poet's part to reinterpret, revise or openly manipulate past experience (whether real or fictional). The reader will recall the original version of this hair-pulling episode in *Am.* 1.7 (cf. my introductory note, pp. 275–6), where the girl was terrified, Ovid showed himself abjectly repentant, and the dress-tearing never occurred at all, but was merely an *arrière-pensée*. In the new presentation the girl is a mercenary bitch who knows exactly how to cash in on Ovid's remorse, and the worst that Ovid has to say about himself, by implication, is that such outbursts of emotion come expensive and are fit only for raw adolescents (cf. *AA* 3.568–71). The *praeceptor amoris* now knows better, and is ready to use his younger self as an object-lesson – though even here he cannot resist a feline cut at imperial policy, in the shape of the boy Gaius' disastrous Parthian expedition (175, cf. *AA* 1.177ff., and my note on 181ff., p. 344): disastrous, he clearly implies, *because* of Gaius' youth.

177–232 We know (*AA* 1.755ff.) that women's characters vary; but we have come a long way, here, from the tough seducer of Ovid's original programme. Diplomacy and charm imperceptibly merge into stubborn persistence, a gambit we have met before (cf. *AA* 1.470ff.), but in the lines that follow, this obduracy, *per contra*, melts away and leaves our gallant doing, again and again, whatever his girl may dictate, however unreasonable. Adoption of all her enthusiasms (199ff., cf. *AA* 1.503–4, and my note, p. 355) is followed by deliberately losing to her at games; before we know where we are the lover is performing (209ff.) all those menial tasks that were normally a slave's responsibility, but formed the traditional self-imposed burden of the Roman elegiac lover, the so-called 'servitude of love'. How far Ovid in this passage is slily mocking the absurdities of such a convention can scarcely be determined with any objectivity; but I suspect a certain ironic ambiguity, not least because of the way in which *servitium amoris* is here juxtaposed, somewhat bizarrely, with Ovid's familiar agricultural–didactic motif (e.g. *AA* 1.43–50, and my note, pp. 339–40). The woman before whom a lover must abase himself is variously described as a stubborn branch (177–9), a newly grafted green bough (647ff.), a fallow (351ff.) or fertile (667–8) or barren (513) field; this vegetable passivity is not entirely offset by allusions to the ferocity or jealousy of a provoked mistress (372ff.), the erotically aggressive urges of the sex in a more primitive society (477ff.).

For the image (184) of the bull and the yoke cf. *Am.* 3.10.13, 3.11.36, and esp. *AA* 1.19, where it gains added programmatic emphasis as part of the procm. For the story of how Milanion won Atalanta as his bride (185ff.) see my note on *Am.* 3.2.29–30, pp. 313–14. Apparently he had earlier dogged her footsteps, love-smitten, while she was out hunting in the Arcadian hills: Prop. 1.1.9–14 tells a similar story. This devotion had its hazards. On one such trip two centaurs, Rhoecus and Hylaeus, tried to rape Atalanta, and Milanion was either shot or clubbed by Hylaeus while rescuing her

Unfortunately we know little in detail about Greek or Roman board-games: the general sense of these lines (230–8) is clear enough, but the detailed rationale behind them eludes us. Lines 203–4 look as though they describe something akin to draughts or backgammon, perhaps the 'twelve-point game' (*ludus duodecim scriptorum*), while 205–6 would seem to be the standard dice-game (cf. Cic. *De Div.* 1.13). What I have loosely paraphrased as 'halma' was the game known as 'robbery' (*latrocinium*) or 'the robbers' game' (*ludus latrunculorum*).

When Hercules (215–22) had completed his twelve Labours he went off to Oechalia and won an archery contest given to decide who should obtain Eurytus' daughter Iole in marriage. Eurytus, however, refused him as a son-in-law on the grounds that he might once more go mad and kill his children. Subsequently, in somewhat obscure circumstances, Hercules killed Eurytus' son Iphitus, and was afflicted with some kind of disease as a result. To cure himself, the Delphic Oracle told him, he must serve as a slave for three years, and the sum obtained from his sale must be paid as compensation to the sons of Iphitus. His purchaser was Omphale, queen of Lydia, who according to some accounts made Hercules work as a tirewoman, spinning and weaving. Later, to revenge himself on Eurytus, he captured Oechalia, slew the king, and carried off Iole by force.

233–54 In this passage Ovid, with some ingenuity, manages to draw together three conventional themes: (i) Love as military service, (ii) Love as servitude, and (iii), a corollary of (ii), the lover-shut-out (*exclusus amator*). It might be thought that (i), with its connotations of pursuit and conquest, was incompatible with the other two; but by stressing the hardships of the soldier's lot, Ovid contrives to avoid overt inconsistency. His paradoxical fusion of predatory action and masochistic passivity is, to say the least, psychologically suggestive. There are, of course, obvious parallels between a love-affair and a military campaign, which must have dictated the *topos* to begin with, and Ovid exploits these most fully in *Am.* 1.9 (see my introductory note, p. 279). But the features he stresses, as here (note the bad-weather cross-country lead-in of 231–2) are route-marches, bivouacks and sieges, with their obvious symbolism (cf. my note on *AA* 1.363–4, p. 350. This enables him, in the present passage, to combine the roles of erotic commando, passion's slave and *exclusus amator* in eighteen short lines – a remarkable piece of manipulation. The hardships of a soldier must be accepted with a slave's humility; and the ·reference to 'slack troopers' recalls Ovid's definition (*Am.* 1.9.41ff.) of lovemaking as a *cure* for sloth or idleness. On Hero and Leander see my note on *Am.* 2.16.31–2, p. 306.

The 'enslaved god' motif was used by Greek writers, the two most popular examples being (i) Heracles–Omphale, already . discussed above, and (ii) Apollo–Admetus, briefly alluded to here in lines 241–2, the argument in each case being 'Why should a mere mortal object to suffering what a god was forced to undergo?' When Zeus slew Asclepius with a thunderbolt for raising the dead, Apollo in anger killed the Cyclopes who had forged the bolt. Zeus wanted to hurl Apollo down to Tartarus, but at Leto's intercession he commuted this punishment to a nine-year's thraldom under Admetus, king of Pherae.

254–72 Earlier, at lines 161ff., Ovid showed himself ultra-cautious, not to say parsimonious, in the matter of gift-giving (cf. *AA* 1.413ff., and my note, p. 352). The circumstances, however, are significantly different. There, as in *Am.* 1.10, what Ovid objects to is being dunned for presents by a gold-digger. Here he is rather laying out ground-bait in the hope of future successes. Linking the two attitudes we find conscious echoes of the plausible old bawd in *Am.* 1.8 (cf. my introductory note, pp. 277–8): see, e.g., the lines describing the slave who asks for presents (265–6 = 89–90), or the notion of buying something in a city shop under false pretences (265–6 = 99–100). Later, we may note that empty-handed Homer (279–80) is the precise analogue of the penniless but blue-blooded suitor (65–6) who gets an equally brisk *congé* – and for the same reason – from the object of his affections. As so often, Ovid shows himself ambivalent in attitude. For the most part he is advocating that hopefully conspiratorial approach to servants portrayed in *Am.* 1.6, 2.2, 2.3 (doorkeeper) or 1.11, 1.12 (maid as go-between). Regarding the seduction of maids, however (see *Am.* 2.7, 2.8, and *AA* 1.351ff., with my note, p. 350) he remains – for reasons based on experience – ultra-cautious.

'Good Luck Day' (255–6) was 24 June, the day on which Servius Tullius, one of the early kings of Rome, dedicated a temple outside the city, on the right bank of the Tiber, to Fors Fortuna. Ovid gives a fuller account of Fors Fortuna at *Fast.* 6.773–86. The festival took place at the midsummer solstice, on what is now St John the Baptist's day. Lines 257ff. allude, obliquely, to the so-called 'Maids' Festival' (*Ancillarum Feriae*) held on 7 July. According to legend, when the Gauls had been driven from Rome by Camillus and the city was still in a weakened state, many of the Latin tribes besieged Rome, and, as the price of peace, demanded that the Romans surrender their wives and daughters. At this, a certain maidservant (Philotis or Tutula, accounts differ) advised sending herself, and other servant-girls, dressed up as freeborn women: during the night they would light a fire-signal from a fig-tree, and the Romans could then kill their enemies while they were asleep. The ruse was successful, and the girls were rewarded. That this myth was aetiological is clear enough. It offered to explain (a) why the festival of 7 July was also called 'the fig-tree Nones' (*Nonae Caprotinae*) and (b) why on it slave-girls dressed up as matrons received presents, were feasted in booths made of fig-branches, and took part in mock battles – all of which suggests a primitive fertility ritual akin to that of the Saturnalia.

Ovid's ambivalent exploitation of pastoral motifs and allusions in lines 261–72 repays careful attention. As against the expensive gifts demanded by an urban lady, he calls for a return to the traditional love-tokens consecrated by bucolic tradition: fruit, apples in particular, fulfilled this function from an early period. The counter-point is driven home by Ovid's reference to Amaryllis and her chestnuts, a verbal parody of Virgil *Ecl.*2.52 (from a passage where Corydon, lovestruck, is promising the beautiful boy Alexis a regular cornucopia of flowers and fruit). Amaryllis is no country shepherdess these days; she disdains such simple offerings. On the other hand her citified lover is no more rural than she is: his basket of fruit is bought in the Via Sacra. So much for Augustus' back-to-the-land movement, and the Virgilian poems that promoted it.

273-86 Once again we catch, suitably transmuted, the cynical advice of Dipsas in the *Amores* (1.8.57-66). What is the value, Ovid asks, of a poem? What is the true criterion of desirability? Here the *praeceptor amoris* is forced, regretfully but with pragmatic insight, to agree with the old bawd (and to repeat his own lament from *Am.* 3.8). Cash is the quickest way to any woman's heart. This is the Age of Gold indeed, but not, alas, the ideal Saturnian revival envisaged in Virgil's Fourth Eclogue (esp. lines 4ff.), with its scarcely veiled allusions to Augustus' beneficent New Order. No writer except Plato refers to the Golden Age so often as Ovid – yet he never once (in sharp contrast to his Augustan contemporaries) envisages its possible return. Homer, he claims, the very embodiment of poetic genius, would get nowhere now without wealth (61 = 279-80); as Dipsas saw (65-6), blue blood is equally powerless. Ovid's poetic spells (*carmina*) are, in the last resort, no more effective than the cantrips of a common witch.

287-94 A nice instance of making generosity to inferiors provide a psychological bonus in erotic terms.

295-314 Again Ovid adduces the dubious ploy of indiscriminate compliments (cf. *AA* 1.503-4, 2.199ff.), but here (309-10) also hints at the allied technique of what we may term cosmetic euphemism, i.e. converting a vice or blemish into its mirror-virtue, a device of long standing and even with some magical or apotropaic overtones – as when Greek sailors hopefully referred to the Black Sea, a notoriously treacherous stretch of water, as the Euxine (i.e. 'kindly to strangers'), or to the Furies as the Eumenides ('Benevolent Ones'). The *topos* in relation to women had a long literary history: see below, lines 641-62, and my note, p. 379. That Medusa (309) should have been chosen as the type of the 'fierce' female lover (Ovid clearly preferred his girls passive) is significant when we recall her chief power – that of petrification. We should perhaps refer this allusion to the situation in *Am*. 3.7, where a girl takes the initiative, briskly, with Ovid, but (as Mistress Quickly said of Falstaff in a different context) 'all was cold as any stone'. See my note, pp. 320–21. The familiar maxim *ars est celare artem* (cf. 313–14) has obvious practical application in Ovid's case, and not only as a precept for the cosmetician (*AA* 3.151–8). The compliments, it is clear from this whole passage, are insincere, though their recipient must believe them genuine.

315–36 Autumnal fevers (probably increased by the breeding of the anopheles mosquito) were a recurrent plague in Rome, and often referred to by poets. It may be noted that the most common reaction of an elegiac poet whose *inamorata* fell ill was to offer up prayers for her – at a safe distance. Even Ovid's own poems on Corinna's abortions (*Am*. 2.13, 2.14) could be construed in this light. Thus his present advice, while offered primarily as a device for advancing a lover's chances, does also involve the lover himself in considerable personal risk while (for whatever motive) doing his lady an unsolicited kindness. On the other hand, the familiar agricultural metaphor at line 322 not only relegates her to the status of a cultivable field (cf. *AA* 1.360, 755ff., with my notes, pp. 350 and 361–2; it also reinforces the image by recalling Virgil's description of cattle-diseases that are, likewise, most common in autumn (Virg. *Georg*. 3.440ff.).

337–52 The use of metaphors drawn from ships and sailing to describe sexual progress recurs throughout the amatory poems: see, e.g., *Am*. 2.9B.7–8, 3.6 *passim* (esp. 23ff.); *AA* 1.5–8, 771–2 (with my notes, pp. 339 and 362); 2.181–2, 514; 3.99–100, 500, 584; *RA* 447–8, 811–12. The notion of skilled steering, controlling the seas of passion, etc., all emphasize seduction as a skilled art, the woman (whether active or passive) as a natural phenomenon. So, of course, do the agricultural images: in particular, that of the fallow field soaking up rain (351–2) reminds us of Ovid's equation between women and crops. The human psychology of the advice given here (345ff.) may be trite ('absence makes the heart grow fonder') but is, unlike so many of Ovid's *obiter dicta*, at least *prima facie* credible.

353–6 As usual, the aphorism is illustrated by mythical *exempla*. For Demophoön and Phyllis see *Am*. 2.18.22 and *RA* 591ff., with my notes, pp. 308 and 417–18. Penelope's frustrated desires during Odysseus's long absence are given extra point by the interpretation put on her 'testing' of the wooers at *Am*. 1.8.47–8 (cf. however *Am*. 3.4.23–4). Laodameia's passion for Protesilaus, the first Greek ashore –

and the first casualty – at Troy is well-attested (cf. my note on *Am.* 2.18.38, pp. 308–9), especially after his death; but she had been married to him before his departure, and it is nowhere suggested that his presence around the house bored her: to that extent the example is somewhat inappropriate. We may note that though Penelope, like Phyllis, is given her epistle in the *Heroides* (§ 1), Ovid avoids the notion of having Laodameia dispatch hopeful *outre-tombe* messages to Hades.

357–72 After the general proposition, a limiting rider. Absence, yes, but not too long an absence, otherwise the counter-proverb applies: Out of sight, out of mind. Again, this piece of psychological common sense is illustrated from myth: the seduction of Helen by Paris. When Paris came to Sparta Helen had already been married to Menelaus for a decade: her daughter Hermione was nine years old. Menelaus entertained Paris for just over a week, but then had to leave for Crete to attend the funeral of his maternal grandfather Catreus. Profiting by his absence, Paris made off with Helen. The choice of illustration is interesting, since Ovid does not criticize Helen for adultery, merely blames her husband for not keeping better watch over her (and on the motives for even this concern cf. *Am.* 2.19 *passim*, with my introductory note, p. 309).

373–86 With elegant aplomb Ovid continues to hand out his (perhaps deliberately) trite pieces of proverbial wisdom. Hell, he says in effect, hath no fury like a woman scorned. The examples of Medea and Procne are equally well-worn in such a context. For Medea's murder of her children see my note on *AA* 1.331–40, p. 349, and for Procne, that on *Am.* 2.6.7–10, p. 295.

387–408 However, Ovid continues, still relentlessly plying his readers with the apt aphoristic cliché, what the eye doesn't see, the heart doesn't grieve over (the theme echoes that of *Am.* 3.14: see my introductory note, p. 335). Play the field – but make sure you cover your tracks adequately. For the dangers of ill-erased tablets cf. *Am.*2.5.5–6, *AA* 3.495. To illustrate his proposition, Ovid manipulates the story of Clytemnestra, Aegisthus and Agamemnon in a most remarkable way. We hear nothing about the sacrifice of Iphigeneia, which in Aeschylus' *Oresteia* provided Clytemnestra with her main motive for revenge. Nor, here, is Aegisthus established in Mycenae as the queen's consort long before Agamemnon's return. Instead, Clytemnestra remains chaste even after hearing rumours of Agamemnon's supposed wartime concubines, Chryseis and Briseis, only committing herself to

Aegisthus when Agamemnon actually appears with Cassandra in tow! Surely this cleaned-up version of an all too well-known legend shows Ovid at his most ironical, tongue demurely in cheek?

409–24 The advice to 'deny all' echoes – in a different context – *Am.* 3.14.15ff. That only successful performance in bed can dissipate suspicions of infidelity is strongly suggested by *Am.* 3.7.75ff. On the use, and avoidance, of aphrodisiacs, magic or otherwise, see above, 105–6, and my note, pp. 366–7. Pepper and nettleseed were, for obvious reasons, regular ingredients in urticant aphrodisiacs: nettle, indeed, was regarded as a general panacea for anything from nose-bleeds and dog-bites to a prolapsed anus. Ovid seems to be alone in attributing aphrodisiac qualities to yellow camomile (pyrethrum), and his advice to eat honey and pine-nuts sounds uncommonly like an ordinary high-calory, energy-producing diet formula. The goddess worshipped on Mt Eryx was Venus: see *Am.* 3.9.45, and my note, p. 327.

425–34 The sailing and chariot-racing metaphors of the original proem (cf. *AA* 1.1–40, with my note, p. 339) are deployed at intervals throughout the *Ars*, as here, to mark the poem's several stages of development, to re-emphasize the need for technical skill and control, and to provide structural links in the overall pattern.

435–54 The use of competitive rivalry, or the threat of it (427–8), to stimulate flagging passion is a constant factor in Ovidian psychology: cf. below, lines 547ff., *AA* 3.579ff., 675ff., and especially *Am.* 2.5, 2.19 and 3.4 *passim*, with my introductory notes, pp. 309 and 315–16. Ovid admits (*AA* 3.597–8) that his own desires are only kindled by 'wrongs' (*iniuria*): both in that passage and this (439–40) he uses the tell-tale image of embers to make his point.

455–92 The whole passage describing reconciliation in bed (459–66) is not only brilliant – and psychologically sound – but also, with characteristic mischievousness, contrives at the same time to parody the Virgilian glorification of Roman imperial rule. At 467ff. one wonders, to begin with, why Ovid should suddenly launch into a short account of the creation of the universe (cf. *Met.* 1.5–88 for a more extended version). The answer comes at 477ff. Sex, we learn, was a great civilizing influence on primitive and brutal mankind: even in a more sophisticated age it can (489–92) still heal anger and resentment. As usual with Ovid, there is more in this digression than meets the eye. The passage contains powerful echoes of Lucretius, a poet whom Ovid, as we know (*Am* 1.15.23, cf. my note on 9–30 p. 288), much admired.

The passage of the *De Rerum Natura* most commonly adduced as the inspiration for Ovid's lines is 5.925–1027, Lucretius' description of primitive life on earth, and in particular 1011–18 for the softening effect of sex on wild men of the woods. This is a very curious misapprehension, since what Lucretius actually portrays here as an instrument of civilization is *the institution of marriage*, or at least of monogamous cohabitation. If Ovid means the reader to recall this passage, he surely has his tongue, as so often, in his cheek, since what *he* is describing (489–92) is sex as a device to soften up your mistress when she suspects you of infidelity.

Machaon, son of Asclepius, with his brother Podalirius, was surgeon to the Greeks at Troy.

493–508 The epiphany of Apollo to poets is a literary device with a long ancestry. Though Ovid is quite capable of inconsistency in his attitude to the god (see *AA* 1.25–30, and my note, p. 339), here, clearly, as at *RA* 75–8, he introduces Apollo both as the god of healing – thus providing a link with the previous section through his reference to Apollo's nephew Machaon – and as the patron of poets. The god endorses his *praeceptor amoris* by repeating two pieces of advice that Ovid had already himself handed out in Bk 1 (2.505–6 = 1.595–6; 2.507–8 = 1.463–8); but he also reminds Ovid, *qua* poet, that a high-flown digression such as 467–92 is not appropriate to the matter in hand, that he should stick to his erotic last. It is not only the lover (cf. *AA* 1.463ff.) who must remember to suit style to audience. While Bk 1 is mostly concerned with overcoming external obstacles, Bk 2 has as its central aim self-knowledge, self-control, and humility. Hence a third reason for introducing Apollo at this point: the application of the Delphic precept (500). Yet even here, as the sequence makes plain, 'Know yourself' is only prescribed in the adoption of favourable, self-flattering positions. Cf. *AA* 3.771, where the same principle is recommended to women.

509–38 Though Ovid allows the god to terminate his digression and put him back on track, Apollo gets no more of the credit for the poem's actual content than he did at *AA* 1.25; it is 'my techniques' (512) that will bring a lover success. The guarantee is accompanied by a familiar warning. Seduction is not a matter of unbroken successes: the setbacks outnumber the triumphs, a suitor must work by trial and error. As the metaphor of the furrow (513) reinforces Ovid's concept of woman as a field ripe for ploughing, so both it and the sailing image that follows (cf. above) emphasize the virtues of intelligent control.

This control in turn involves hardship: our old friend *servitium amoris* (see my introductory note to *Am.* 1.6, p. 274), the notion of 'passion's slave' (515ff.). The cluster of allusive comparisons (517–20) at once recalls a similar passage in Bk 1 (57–60) – except that there it is the number of girls in Rome that Ovid is touting, whereas what he emphasizes here are the troubles a lover will perforce go through in getting them. The contrast is significant: cf. also *AA* 3.149–52.

539–600 With a portentous mock-epic build-up Ovid announces his key precept, to be regarded with the respect normally accorded an oracle (541–2): a lover should tolerate, and where possible ignore, any rivals. This is 'hard and exacting' (538, cf. *RA* 768), as Ovid is well aware: at 547ff. he admits his own imperfections in this respect, with a plain reference to the incident described in *Am.* 2.5.13ff. (cf. my introductory note, pp. 293–4). At the same time both the advice itself and the myth employed to illustrate it (561–92) are presented in highly ambiguous terms. Ovid is addressing a hypothetical lover (contrasted, at 597–8, with a legitimate husband), and in his 'autobiographical' confession (547ff.) himself assumes the lover's role. A lover, he says, must wink at his mistress's infidelities, just as (545–6) a husband (*maritus*) will allow such latitude to his lawful wife (*uxor*) – a situation with which we are familiar from *Am.* 2.19. Why? Because detection simply encourages flagrant and persistent adultery (559–60): the guilty parties have nothing further to lose, and might as well get their money's-worth of fun. This thesis Ovid then illustrates by retelling the story of Hephaestus (Vulcan), Ares (Mars) and Aphrodite (Venus). In conclusion, and apparently with a straight face, Ovid asserts (599–600) that he is not discussing, or addressing, respectable married ladies.

What are we to make of this contradictory hodge-podge? If Ovid is concerned solely with lovers (the only way in which he could justify his final disclaimer), why does he (a) emphasize, in unequivocal language, the complaisance of *husbands*, and (b) tell, at great length, a myth in which the husband is the spoilsport, and adultery gets no criticism at all – indeed, even Homer's statement that Ares had to pay a fine for his sexual poaching is suppressed (cf. 357–72, 399–408, with my notes, pp. 374–5)? If, on the other hand, he is concerned with both husbands and lovers, what is the point of the disclaimer? Is his paradoxical conclusion – that the revelation of adultery encourages its continued enjoyment – one that bears much, if any, resemblance to observable facts? To take only the most notorious instance, still a fresh scandal when the *Ars* was published, would the elder Julia, Augustus' daughter, and her five known lovers (there were others) have been inclined to endorse Ovid's theory? Iullus Antonius was executed, and the rest, including Julia herself, banished (Syme (1), p. 426, with reff.). Even granted that adultery in the ancient world did thrive on exposure, like a cultured broth, can the myth of Ares and Aphrodite in fact be employed to support such a notion? Certainly not in Homer's version (*Od.* 8.266–366), on which Ovid has mainly drawn: Ares retreats to Thrace, Aphrodite to Paphos, and there is no hint of a reunion.

The truth of the matter surely is that Ovid's disclaimer here, like that at *AA* 1.31–4, was tacked on, with careless indifference, to a text which belied it throughout. The advice is ostensibly for lovers alone, but applies *a fortiori* to Roman husbands, whose wives – whatever Ovid may say for the record – clearly played the adultery game with expertise and enthusiasm. Yet if Ovid is merely trying to warn off any marital busybody who might try to spoil the fun (and that would seem, on the face of it, the obvious explanation), he has chosen a singularly inept way of doing so. The *cause célèbre* of Julia's exposure was so fresh when Bk 2 of the *Ars* appeared that it is hard not to suspect Ovid of alluding to it; but Julia on her island was in no position to carry on with anyone, let alone with her previous lovers. If the advice is ironic, the irony can only be described as heavy-handed. Perhaps Ovid's implication is that while Augustus' harsh measures might work in special cases, such as that of Julia, to apply them generally would – like modern laws on drugs and homosexuality – create a gross public nuisance without being in the slightest degree effective. Hence, arguably, the advice (555–6) to know nothing, leave guilty secrets hidden and force no confessions from the lady. There is extra piquancy in the fact that Augustus prided himself on his own descent from Venus.

601–40 The train of thought here is intriguing. Religious mysteries should not be divulged: sex is one such mystery, under the auspices of Venus. The act, like those parts of the body associated with it, should be kept hidden. Even primitive man observed this kind of privacy, in contrast to animals, that copulate without shame or concealment. But today, though men may not actually perform *coram publico*, they nevertheless boast of their conquests indiscriminately, naming names. Worse, they claim, falsely, to have seduced girls whom they never in fact touched, so that 'though the flesh escape defilement, repute is tarnished' (634–5). About his own affairs Ovid maintains – or so he says – a discreet reticence: just how should we relate this assertion to the *Amores*? And after getting used to a poet who continually exploits religion in terms of sex, how seriously are we to take him when he announces sex as a species of religion? Since he totally ignores its procreative aspects (except as an unwanted calamity in *Am.* 2.13 and 2.14, with the rider that indiscriminate abortion might have deprived Rome of its most famous leaders) he cannot share Lucretius' celebration of Venus as *élan vital*. I suspect that what his advice boils down to, stripped of its fine verbiage, is simply 'Be discreet – and don't ruin reputations by loose talk, especially if the scandal happens not to be true.'

The rites of Ceres (Demeter), being associated with the Eleusinian Mysteries, were proverbially secret, and restricted to initiates. The island of Samothrace in the northern Aegean was the cult-centre of mysterious chthonian deities known as the Cabiri (Kabeiroi), probably Phrygian in origin. For Tantalus (605) see my note to *Am.* 2.2.44–6, p. 292.

641–62 Besides repeating clichés to emphasize their triteness, Ovid will sometimes take a well-worn commonplace and give it a completely new twist for his own purposes. Here he borrows two such rhetorical-psychological propositions, and combines them: (i) that a lover is, in his blindness, attracted by the actual faults of the person he worships, and (ii) that by giving a fault a euphemistic label it can be turned into a virtue.

What is original about Ovid's treatment is this: he assumes, not that the lover is infatuated by the defects in his beloved – far from it. Rather he finds them repulsive, while at the same time being smart enough, in his own interests (642), to conceal his disgust, and to produce a commendatory euphemism for the feature that turns him off. Ovid, with some psychological shrewdness, notes that patience and tolerance of this sort will, after a while, acclimatize their practitioner to the fault they accommodate, so that he barely notices it. Once again *ars*, conscious technique, has triumphed over irrational impulse; once again the sillier manifestations of passion are demurely mocked. For Andromeda see my notes on *Am.* 3.3.17–18, p. 315, and *AA* 1.53, p. 340. Ovid again refers to Hector's wife Andromache as a tall woman at *AA* 3.777 (cf. *Am.* 2.4.33).

663–702 Ovid's sexual preferences are clear: he favours mutual passion and preferably simultaneous orgasms (cf. 725–9, and *Am.* 1.10.36–7). This does not necessarily indicate altruistic consideration on his part: it is what he needs to give *him* pleasure, and possibly to arouse his own desires. Conversely, he dislikes, and presumably is sexually put off by, the mercenary element in prostitution (or gold-digging, its amateur analogue), which he equates with *absence of desire* (*Am.* 1.10 *passim*, esp. 21–4). The somewhat cryptic remark about homosexuality (684) is presumably to be explained by an assumption on Ovid's part that boys submitted to sodomization, or indeed any sexual approaches, not out of desire, but for profit. Ovid seems to have held – as indeed did Aristophanes, Horace, Catullus and Juvenal: the assumption was widespread and perennial – that while paederasty in the strict sense, i.e. love of adolescent boys, was permissible, if not over-rewarding, effeminacy in adult men could not be socially condoned (cf. *AA* 1.523–4).

All this helps to explain the present passage, a lively recommendation of older women as lovers: not for Ovid the pursuit of bashful virgins. Not only are such women uninhibited, not only have they reached their full sexual potential, but – best of all – they are expert as well as experienced (675ff.). Thus Ovid can, somewhat unexpectedly, introduce yet another argument in favour of *ars*, rational technique, this time from the women's viewpoint – even while still describing her, in sexual terms, as 'a field worth sowing' (668, cf. 697–8).

703–32, 669–74   It is a paradoxical commonplace that, in a poem entitled the *Art of Love*, Ovid should spend so little time – especially considering his preoccupation with technique – on the actual business of love-making. His Muse is formally bidden (704) to remain outside the bedroom door: ostensibly as a token of civilized modesty (cf. 615–24), but in fact, one suspects, in accordance with the popular belief that people have always known by instinct (*Am.* 1.5.25) just what to do when they find themselves in bed and in love.

The imagery, as one might expect at this point, picks up, in a final recapitulation, several of Ovid's most dominant motifs: the control of boat (725, 732) or horse (732) – cf. 425–34, with my note, p. 375 – and in particular the association of love and warfare (709–16). Most interesting of all are the mythological illustrations. Both Andromache and Briseis, by no accident, are portrayed as women who enjoy the advances of a military lover hot from the battlefield. The original purpose of these two *exempla* emerges far more clearly at *Am.* 1.9.33–40 (cf. my note, p. 280): Achilles and Hector were no less fierce in battle *after they had made love* to Briseis or Andromache. Surely the reader would be expected to remember that fact here? In addition to his other encouragement, the *praeceptor amoris*, despite the fact that he presents seduction (673-4) as an act virtually calling for Churchillian 'blood, toil, tears and sweat', is nevertheless reassuring each hopeful gallant that a fine performance in bed will not unfit him for those other occupations – sailing, farming, fighting – which Roman society accepted and valued.

733-46 My task is ended, Ovid says (733), and indeed his closing lines (all save the final couplet, which looks very much like a later addition) do read very much as though they were planned to form a coda for the whole poem. There are confirmatory hints of this original two-book *Ars* in the body of the text; and the coda itself, with its extravagant boasts of prowess – setting Ovid in the company of various great mythical masters, repeating the comparison with Automedon, the pointed references to Achilles – forms a neat and satisfactory counterpart to the original proem of Bk 1. We have to imagine a two-book poem which later acquired Bk 3 and the *Cures* more or less piecemeal. For myrtle as sacred to Venus see *Am.* 1.1.29-30, 1.2.23, with my notes, p. 269. For Machaon's brother Podalirius cf. my note on 467-92, *ad fin.*, p. 376, and for Nestor, that on *Am.* 3.7.41-2, p. 321. Calchas, the chief Greek soothsayer during the Trojan War, was also responsible for Iphigeneia's sacrifice at Aulis. The mention of Automedon the charioteer links this passage structurally with *AA* 1.5-8, an extension of that compositional pattern we have already noted in Bk 1 (cf. pp. 77-8). Ovid as Chiron the teacher (*AA* 1.11-18) has been replaced by Ovid as Vulcan the armourer (741-2): precepts are now weapons, to be used in the chase, the war-game, of seduction. The cycle is complete.

BOOK 3

1-40 Bk 3 opens with that familiar rhetorical device, the *captatio benevolentiae*, or bid for sympathy. There is a subtle piece of parodic self-flattery in the opening couplet. As so often, Ovid is expressing his theme in mock-epic terms, this time with a broad allusion to Homer's *Iliad*. The events immediately following the end of the *Iliad* were described by Arctinus of Miletus in his lost *Aethiopis*, and some texts actually alter the closing line of Bk 24 to provide a smooth transition: 'Such was the funeral for Hector: then came the Amazon, daughter of great-hearted Ares, the man-slayer.' The Amazon was Penthesilea, whom Achilles slew in battle; he is said to have fallen in love with her as he transfixed her (one for the Freudians), or with her corpse, and to have killed Thersites for jeering at his grief. Ovid is thus playfully comparing himself, not only to Calchas, Nestor, Ajax and Automedon (2.737–40), but also to Homer *qua* poet (cf. line 415). After the picture of women he painted in Bks 1 and 2, the objections he foresees to his volte-face (7–8) are understandable, and not really settled by his barrage of mythological examples. Helen and Clytemnestra (11–12) were both daughters of Tyndareus – just as their respective husbands, Menelaus and Agamemnon, were Atreus' sons. For Eriphyle and Amphiaraus see my note to *Am.* 1.10.51–2, p. 282, and for Protesilaus and Laodameia those to *Am.* 2.18.38, pp. 308–9, and *AA* 2.353–6, pp. 373–4.

Admetus, king of Pherae in Thessaly, who was once served by no less a herdsman than Apollo (see *AA* 2.239, and my note, p. 370), married Alcestis, daughter of Pelias. Apollo, in gratitude for Admetus' kindly treatment, persuaded the Fates to agree that, when the king was due to die, his life would be spared if he could find a substitute. Neither of Admetus' parents would die for him; finally his own wife, Alcestis, volunteered to do so. She was afterwards restored to him from Hades, either by the generosity of Persephone or through Heracles' wrestling her away from Death. During the battle between Argives and Cadmeans for Thebes, Capaneus, one of the Seven Champions, was blasted by Zeus with a thunderbolt while scaling the walls on a ladder. His wife Evadne committed suttee by immolating herself on his pyre. Not only were these mythical heroines noble and virtuous, Ovid triumphantly concludes; Virtue (23) is traditionally *personified* as a woman. The mention of Virtue in this context betrays Ovid's mischievous sense of irony – though he at once concedes that his own role as instructor calls for less exalted principles.

There is, as usual, a reason for this careful coyness. The examples Ovid has been giving are all drawn from what we might call the mythological *grand monde*: no pert little freedwomen here, not even elegant courtesans, but famous wives and even more famous adulteresses. Later (57–8) we get a belated reminder of just who is entitled to benefit from Ovid's instruction; here, however, we may reflect that his 'little craft', one way and another, is sailing very close to the wind. (The sailing image as a metaphor for the creative process is used more often in Bk 3 than that of the chariot: cf. 99–100, 499–500, 747–8.)

Perhaps through embarrassment, perhaps once more with mischievous intent, Ovid's arguments here are something less than logical. The claim that women seldom deceive will deceive no one, least of all a reader of the *Amores*; and men are no more likely to shoot flaming arrows (metaphorical or actual) at women than women are at men. The only archer given to this sport, impartially, is Cupid. Further, most people, if asked what Phyllis, Dido, Ariadne and Medea had in common – apart from all figuring in the *Heroides* – would probably agree that their relationships with men were something less than successful. But Ovid's corollary – that in each case this could be blamed on lack of feminine finesse – takes us straight into the world of *The Ladies' Home Journal*, where all marriages can be saved by a few elementary seductive gambits on the woman's part. Once again, it would seem, Ovid's tongue is firmly in his cheek; also, the suspicion arises that, whatever he may say to the contrary, he still, *au fond*, is aiming at a masculine readership.

For Medea and Jason see my note to *AA* 1.331–40, p. 349; for Ariadne and Theseus, ibid., 525–64, p. 355. Demophoön was Theseus' son: desertion seems to have run in the family. For his abandonment of Phyllis see my notes on *Am.* 2.18.21–6, p. 308, and the fuller version at *RA* 591–608, pp. 417–18. Nine Ways (Ennea Hodoi) was near Eion, on the river Strymon, and the site of the Athenian colony of Amphipolis. Phyllis, a Bisaltian Thracian, accompanied Demophoön as far as Nine Ways when he sailed away to Cyprus. The true origin of the place-name was clearly as a road-junction, but Ovid (*RA* 601–2) attributes it to Phyllis pacing a certain lane to the sea nine times before committing suicide. His final instance is Virgil's 'pious Aeneas', whose departure from Carthage for Italy drove the deserted Dido to kill herself: in this context Aeneas is scarcely presented as a sympathetic, let alone a patriotic figure.

41–56 While ironically advancing his own claims, at an epic level, Ovid also loses no opportunity to deflate the epic world itself. First, he presents a group of renowned mythical heroines as mere cases of erotic disappointment. Now he compounds the insult by suggesting (41ff.) that all they lacked was feminine sophistication – which he, of course, as *praeceptor amoris*, can readily supply. Later (517–24) he goes on to assert, in much the same vein, that many of the famous women of antiquity – a Tecmessa, an Andromache – were dreary bores. It is worth noting the number of times he reverts, in this context, to the Trojan War: and sure enough, after a while, he announces proudly (*RA* 65–6) that if only *he* had been there, with sound professional advice, the war – along with various other tragedies – could have been avoided altogether.

The epiphany of Apollo in Bk 2 (493ff., cf. my note, p. 376) is matched here by the appearance of Venus, urging equal treatment for women, and reinforcing her demands with a thinly veiled threat. The Greek poet Stesichorus (?630–?555 BC), who wrote a work entitled *Helen*, telling the usual version of that heroine's story, was traditionally supposed to have been struck blind for his presumption: he then wrote a palinode or recantation, containing the lines: 'This legend is not true; / you never went in the benched ships, / you never came to Troy's citadel' – and at once miraculously regained his sight.

57–100 This passage urging women to take lovers wittily parodies the rhetorical exercise known as the *suasoria*, or formal persuasive address. At the same time it contrives, with its reflections on the transience of human beauty, to be unexpectedly moving. The *carpe diem* motif was, of course, a commonplace in Roman literature, perhaps best known from Horace. Its corollary is the brutally realistic picture of feminine old age (lines 69ff.), which, again, forms a favourite theme in Hellenistic and Roman poetry. The cruel mockery of perished loveliness, in an era with a brief and hazardous life-expectation, could not but render the enskyment of youth even more intense and poignant. To an extent that we today can only imagine, every moment – this is also strikingly true of the Elizabethan period – must indeed be enjoyed to the full, since the pleasures it brought were so fleeting. The ominous word 'tomorrow' (*cras*) recurs again and again in this context; the horrific proximity of decay and death was a fact that each individual had to live with from childhood.

Note (57–58) Ovid's formal claim, once again (cf. *AA* 1.31–4 and 2.599–600), *not* to be offering his erotic instruction to respectable Roman ladies, but solely to the *demi-mondaine*. The ability of the snake (77–8) to shed its skin – and with it, as some thought, its age – made a great impression on Greek and Roman poets. One argument in favour of seduction – that women should not drift into physical degeneration through lack of use – Ovid repeats from the *Amores* (2.3.14). The fact that a plucked flower withers faster than an unplucked one is perhaps unfortunate for his image and argument. Lines 80–81 contain one of his very few allusions to childbirth (cf. below, 785, and *Am.* 2.13, 2.14, *passim*). In the two poems about Corinna's abortion he argues *in favour* of large families, for all the world as though he were a PR man for Augustus; here, however, he puts forward what must have been the standard view among his upper-class clientele, that child-bearing ruined the figure, produced unsightly striations and led to premature ageing. For Endymion and the Moon (83) see my note to *Am*. 1.13.44, p. 285. This poem was certainly in Ovid's mind, since his second example here – that of Cephalus and Aurora, the Dawn (84) – also figures in the earlier work (see my note, p. 284), and is obliquely alluded to later in two full-scale versions of the death of Procris (*AA* 3.685–746, with my note, pp. 399–401; cf. *Met*. 7.701ff.). Venus' passion for Adonis is discussed in my note to *Am*. 3.9.15–16, pp. 325–6. To answer Ovid's question (86), Harmonia was the daughter of Aphrodite (Venus) by Ares, presumably conceived during their notorious (and ultimately much-publicized) adultery: cf. *AA* 2.561ff., with my note, p. 377. Anchises' affair with Aphrodite is mentioned by both Homer and Hesiod. The child of their union was Aeneas.

At line 87 we learn the reason for these *exempla*: mere mortal women should not blush to follow the lead of a goddess. There follows what must surely rank as Ovid's most *outré* argument: a reassurance that the human vagina, unlike stone and metal, is infinitely elastic and does not wear out as a result of heavy use! Not encouraging promiscuous conduct (97)? Surely this line carries a stage-wink for male readers? And when he gaily asks (89) 'Why worry?' he, like jesting Pilate, does not wait for the answers, some of which (unwanted pregnancies being the most obvious) he was well aware of himself. At moments such as this the eristic dexterity cannot mask a fundamental hollowness of purpose. For the use of douche-water cf. *Am*. 3.7.84. The nautical image (99–100) acts as a marker to indicate the end of the proem or introduction, a clearly defined stage in the creative pattern. These two lines also identify the first half of this book as elementary instruction, in contrast to the more advanced advice given later (see 499ff., with my note, p. 395).

101–32 As Hesiod (*Theog.* 1) began with the Muses, or Aratus (*Phaen.* 1) with Zeus, so Ovid here sets up as his own prime divinity *cultus*, cultivation or culture, equally applicable to girls, agriculture and urban life. At one stroke the gods, the didactic genre, and the female sex are all put firmly in their place. Though Bk 3 is dedicated to women, they are still being compared to grapes or wheat; whereas the men are urged to develop their *ingenium*, their natural skills (*AA* 2.112), women should look to their *cultus*, their physical appearance. We have switched from the intellectual to the cosmetic. A similar prescription opens the fragment *On Facial Treatment For Ladies* (*MF*): see lines 1–7 and my note, p. 403. From the advocacy of *cultus* for women – 'care of the person' would be a fair equivalent – Ovid's train of thought moves, by easy degrees, to another aspect of *cultus*, the sophisticated refinement achieved by contemporary society. This he much prefers to the crude artlessness it supplanted: indeed, lines 121–8 form a kind of personal credo. Once again we see Ovid actively rejecting, in his own terms, the whole Augustan programme of religious, moral and agricultural reform. Perhaps 'rejecting' is too strong a word when Ovid clearly regards this official line as something both vulgar and risible. The deflation of imperial pseudo-primitivism is done with conviction as well as irony. It recurs elsewhere (e.g. *Fast.* 2.133ff., *AA* 2.268ff.), and always with the same edge of amused contempt. Ovid had no more time than did Gibbon for the triumph of barbarism and religion; the homespun rural virtues of Augustus' ideal godfearing farmer he can scarcely mention without a sneer (cf. *AA* 1.241ff., 607ff., 672). The contrast with a passage such as Virg. *Georg.* 2.458–532, that memorable encomium of country life, is both striking and pointed. At the same time Ovid is careful to emphasize that what he enjoys is not so much luxury as good taste; we are reminded that *cultus* could be used in a pejorative sense, and that Horace anticipated Ovid's distaste for extravagant building schemes. The picture of excessive and tasteless luxury in house-construction leads neatly into an analogous (129–32) warning against personal ostentation (hung ear-bobs, heavy gold brocade).

The far from complimentary allusions (109–12) to Hector's wife Andromache, and Ajax with his vast shield, bring the archaic world of the Trojan War into sharp juxtaposition with Ovid's own society. The Capitol here designates not the whole hill but, specifically, the temple of Jupiter, first built by the Etruscan rulers Tarquinius Priscus and Tarquinius Superbus (6th cent. BC), burnt to the ground in July 83, and rebuilt fourteen years later. It was this second, more ornate temple (Platner–Ashby, pp. 299–300) that Ovid knew. The Palatine (Mons Palatinus) was the centremost of Rome's seven hills, and traditionally the earliest to be occupied by a settlement: archaeology tends to confirm this belief. The reference to 'Apollo and our princes' glances not only at the great temple of Apollo dedicated by Augustus in 28 BC, and the Emperor's own private residence, but also at the fact that various other distinguished persons (including Livia and Tiberius) built their homes on the Palatine.

133-68 Ovid, as we have had leisure to observe in these poems, was fascinated by women's hair – and not merely because careful hairdressing, in Hellenistic style, was a popular Augustan affectation. The 'fallen city' (155) was Oechalia: for Heracles and Iole see my note on *AA* 2.215-22, pp. 269-70. The rescue of Ariadne by Bacchus is described at length in Bk I (lines 525-64). The boutiques (167-8) were located in the Porticus Philippi, an arcade built round the temple of Hercules and the Muses, close to the south-west side of the Circus Flaminius. Here there stood a statue of Hercules playing the lyre and representations of the Nine Muses. Close by was that popular site for assignations, the Portico of Octavia: the boutiques were thus assured of customers.

169-92 The materials for clothing and cosmetics can be subsumed to Ovid's overall schema of *ars* and *cultus*, since they come from nature as raw material and must, like their users, be refined. The primary emphasis on colour is significant. Sculptural tradition would suggest a remarkable absence of change in women's fashions at Rome over three centuries; but if the *cut and shape* of the robe (*stola*) remained standard, its *texture or colour* both reveal immense variety. Purple, a dye obtained from the murex shellfish, was the most expensive (line 170); because of this, and its exclusive associations with high rank, it always found a ready clientele.

It is interesting to note that the caution against luxurious clothes and ostentatious jewellery (cf. lines 129-133) does not apply in *MF* (cf. below, lines 205-8). In that fragment (17-26) both are taken for granted. Ovid is simply acknowledging the situation as it already existed in his day: advice does not come into the matter.

The rescuer of King Athamas' children Phrixus and Helle was their mother Nephele in her function as dark rain-cloud. Nephele was Athamas' first wife: he subsequently married Ino, who – in typical wicked stepmother fashion – both brought about an artificial crop-failure, and suborned Athamas' messengers to Delphi to claim that an oracle had foretold relief from dearth if Phrixus was sacrificed to Zeus. Nephele, hearing of this, gave them a ram with a golden fleece on which to make their escape.

193-208 This passage should be compared with *AA* 1.505-24, where similar hints on elementary hygiene are given to the men (cf. my note, p. 355). However, while both sexes are advised to wash, clean their teeth and avoid unpleasant armpit odour, the girls (194, 199ff.) receive directives on depilation and make-up, activities which the men, *per contra*, are warned to avoid (505-12) as effeminate affectation. Mysia, a province in north-west Asia Minor, and the Caucasus are taken as symbolic of areas to which culture has never penetrated. For the surviving fragments of Ovid's short didactic poem *On Facial Treatment for Ladies* (*Medicamina Faciei Femineae*: *MF*), referred to here at lines 205–8, see pp. 264ff., and my notes ad loc. (below, pp. 426ff.). The reference provides a *terminus ante quem* for the composition of this little *jeu d'esprit* at least prior to *AA* 3.

209–35 *Ars est* – in every sense – *celare artem*. The process of making up one's face is compared (219–24) to the sculptor's, goldsmith's or couturier's creative skills, and thus, at one level, equated with both the poet's and the lover's *ars*; but this implied compliment is savagely undercut by the almost Swiftian repulsion with which the details of the dressing-table are described. The passage thus has a double significance. Art, Ovid says, of whatever sort, is artifice, a process not only of refinement but also of illusion, where nothing prior to the end-product should be revealed, lest the *trompe-l'œil* effect be lost (cf. the wooden statues covered with gold foil, lines 231ff.). But in the case of a woman producing her public image, this artistic process, if observed, gives away rather more than the details of a *grande illusion*. It betrays the fact – something Ovid, at least, regards as axiomatic (cf. *RA* 341–56) – that women in their natural, unmasked state are, fundamentally, not just uncivilized but actively disgusting (cf. in particular lines 229–30).

The Greek sculptor Myron of Eleutherae was an earlier contemporary of Pheidias (mid-fifth cent. BC). The representation of Venus here described is the famous Aphrodite Anadyomene by Apelles: see my note on *Am.* 1.14.33–4 (p. 286).

235–50 It is characteristic of Ovid (see above) that the one boudoir activity he is prepared to let girls carry out while their lovers watch is combing and dressing their hair. Even so, savagery and ugliness lurk in the background: the moral is that it takes more than cosmetics to create an acceptable façade. *Private* unpleasantness Ovid takes as axiomatic: his first hypothetical example is a filthy-tempered virago (cf. also lines 369–76, 499–504), his second a bald prima donna: lines 250ff. merely confirm the general picture. The 'ladies-only temple' was that of the so-called 'Good Goddess' (*Bona Dea*), worshipped exclusively by women: it stood at the north-east end of the Aventine, and was restored by Augustus' wife Livia. The reference to 'Parthian girls' (248) is apropos the Parthian archer's habit of turning backwards in the saddle to shoot at a pursuing foe: the girl who did this with her wig reversed would then have it facing the right way.

251-80 Ovid's female readers, he assumes, are for the most part not only personally unpleasant, but also physically ill-favoured. Just as his advice for men (*AA* 2.160–68) was not planned to suit a wealthy clientele, so here he is not catering for great or legendary beauties: beauty and wealth (255–8) are their own most persuasive arguments. Good wine needs no bush: what use would Helen or Semele have for a *praeceptor amoris*? There is a certain psychological acuity about these claims insofar as they can be related to their author's ostensible function *qua* instructor: the clientele of a marriage bureau or lonelyhearts column is not drawn, by and large, from the well-heeled, the well-favoured or the well-adjusted. At the same time Ovid clearly used this as an excuse to exercise a carefully controlled vein of genial contempt for the whole female sex. The short, pallid, scrawny, flat-chested composite figure, with buck teeth and bad breath, that emerges from these lines is both plausible and drawn with a kind of lingering and venomous passion. A concentration on such physical defects is later recommended to the lover (*RA* 417) as an effective antaphrodisiac, just as he is also told to make a girl with bad teeth laugh (279–80; *RA* 339).

280-310 Ovid is here making two separate but related points concerning conscious technical skills as they apply to women. First, they are needed in every sphere of activity, however improbable: laughing or crying, walking and talking. The key phrase here is at line 291: 'Where does art not enter?' At the same time Ovid sees that too zealous a pursuit of anti-rustic urban smartness can very soon degenerate into the worst sort of modish affectation: here lines 305–7 apply, with their counsel to avoid both extremes. The examples are chosen to illustrate pitfalls at either end of the scale: don't walk or laugh like a peasant (another calculated jab at the simple rustic virtues promoted by Augustan policy), but, equally, don't mince along like a city *cocotte*. Moderation in all things. The example of conscious mispronunciation (293ff.) is a nice borderline case, where a very thin line, clearly, divides charm from mere tiresomeness. The moral, though not overstressed, is unmistakable.

311-28 We now embark on a series of pointers to socially advantageous accomplishments: each requires skill, most (but not all: cf. 353ff.) have some artistic content. They form an instructive analogue to the parallel advice (*AA* 2.121–44) bestowed upon men, where the prime emphasis is placed upon cultivation of the intellect. From each according to her ability, to each according to her needs. First, then, music: a girl must be able to sing and to play some stringed instrument. However, as the mythical *exempla* chosen make all too clear, the object is not art for art's sake. Like the geisha, Ovid's girls must learn what will attract, and hold, a male audience. They will perform the latest, most exotic hits (no suggestion, note, that they should acquire, much less observe, any standards of musical appreciation); and the men, like Cerberus, like Arion's dolphin, like Odysseus' crew or the very stones of Troy, will be held spellbound. By the Augustan period singing and dancing, once thought an improper activity for respectable persons of either sex, had become socially acceptable if performed privately and with decent restraint. Alexandria on the Nile was a great centre of musical activity. Alexandrian melodies, and the *virtuosi* who performed them, were much sought after. The Phoenician instrument mentioned here (327–8) was the *nablium*, or *nablus*, a large upright instrument with 10–12 strings, somewhat resembling a Welsh harp, and played two-handed, in the same manner.

For Cerberus, Amphion, and Odysseus' encounter with the Sirens, see my note on *Am.* 3.12.23–40, p. 332. Orpheus' descent to Hades and bewitchment of Cerberus: my note to *Am.* 3.9.21–24, p. 326. The famous story of Arion – who on his way back to Periander's court at Corinth (? *c.* 680 BC), after a successful concert tour in Magna Graecia, was robbed and thrown overboard by the ship's crew but rescued by dolphins entranced with his musical talent – is told at length by Herodotus (1.24) and Plutarch (*Moral.* 161B–162B).

329–48 The reading-list given here serves a less exalted purpose than the roll-call of classics that Ovid reels off at *Am.* 1.15.9–30 (cf. my note, p. 288). He is no longer predicting literary immortality – except, hopefully and characteristically, for his own works; he is enumerating a smart girl's minimal social accomplishments. If she is to catch, and hold, an intelligent (*AA* 2.121–44) man's attention, she must not only sing, dance and play table-games without losing her temper; she should be familiar with the poetry – in particular the love-poetry – now fashionable, and have the ability to recite it (with or without musical accompaniment) on demand. Six of the names recommended – Callimachus, Menander, Tibullus, Gallus, Varro of Atax, and Virgil – are repeated from the earlier catalogue. Homer, Hesiod, Sophocles, Aratus, Ennius – but see 409–10 – and Accius are dropped (presumably as 'heavies' lacking in romantic appeal) and replaced by Philetas, Anacreon, Sappho and Propertius, all of whose works displayed a strong personal and erotic content. For similar reasons there is no tragedy here (not even Ovid's own *Medea*), and no prose.

It is characteristic of Ovid that he should devote as much space (339–

48) to the promotional puffing of his own works as he does to those of all other poets combined. He elsewhere prophesies, in general terms, immortality for his creative *œuvre*: *Am.* 1.15.7ff., esp. 41–2; 3.15.7ff., *Met.* 15.871ff. Here he goes further, and identifies individual poems: the *Art of Love* (341–2), the *Amores* (343–4) and the *Heroides*, or *Letters of Legendary Women* (345–6).

349–52 Ovid's susceptibility to singing and dancing girls has already been made clear: see *Am.* 2.4.25–30. While the reference to public performers (351–2, the ballerinas of the *pantomimus*: cf. *RA* 753ff., with my note, pp. 422–4) might at first sight suggest that he is here addressing only freedwomen or *meretrices*, the passage, if carefully scrutinized, makes it clear that in fact the ballerinas are merely brought in as models for enthusiastic amateurs to imitate.

353–68 With two omissions, the list of board games given here by Ovid (353–66) is repeated later in the *Poems of Lamentation* (*Tristia*): see 2.473–82 and cf. above, *AA* 2.203–8, with my note, p. 369. Of the various games described, 'rolling the bones', a simple dice-game, is the least controversial. These knucklebones, or dice made to resemble knucklebones (ἀστράγαλος, *talus*) were marked only on their four long sides, unlike the six-sided dice (κύβος, *tessera*) used for board-games, and with which we are still familiar today. Lines 355–6 do not refer to a specific game or situation, but form 'a prefatory couplet describing the application of dice to board-games in general' (Austin, p. 33 n.1). However, since the game I have loosely equated with halma, the *ludus latrunculorum*, 357–60, was played without dice, Ovid may here be alluding to backgammon (*xii scripta*, 363ff., now known in the Near East as *tavli* or *tric-trac*), or to some other game resembling draughts. The *ludus latrunculorum* itself was a 'soldier-game' or 'war-game'. It should not, however, be equated – as is still too often the case – with chess. The twelve-point game was an ancestor of backgammon, played with six-sided dice and thirty pieces (fifteen a side) on a board consisting of three rows of twelve 'points', or spaces, each row being divided into two groups of six, separated by a wheel, circle or other symbol.

Another comparatively simple game was that alluded to in lines 365–6, for which no Roman namé survives. In essence it resembled that generic group of games including Gobang, Fox and Geese, Merels (from the French *marelle*), and, most familiar to us, Noughts and Crosses. It was played on an eight-line board: the object of the game was to get three pieces in a row, diagonally.

This leaves the game mentioned at 361–2, which is so out of place in this sequence of dice-and-board games that one suspects textual transposition or interpolation. What it describes – something nowhere else referred to in ancient literature – is a number of 'smooth balls' being emptied into a net, the object being to move one without disturbing the rest. How this was done is not at all clear. It suggests that popular, and far more comprehensible, children's game known as spillikins.

It is no accident (cf. my note on 235–50, p. 388) that Ovid's chief concern with a woman games-player (369–80) is to prevent her losing her temper and revealing her *true nature*. Art (see 209–34) must mask both itself and nature: nature, insofar as the female sex is concerned, gives good grounds for such concealment, being savage, violent, aggressive and uncivilized.

381–96 Ovid's implicit distinction between masculine and feminine talents, in both scope and opportunity, is here confirmed by social observation. Rome offered a whole range of public activities to men from which women were traditionally debarred. While men take public exercise (cf. *AA* 1.513), women should make the rounds of the various sites where (as the poet has already told his masculine readers, especially in Bk 1, lines 67–262) they can be most conveniently approached: the colonnades and porticoes, the theatres, the temple of Isis, the Circus and the racecourse. Nowhere is the double sexual standard more explicitly stated.

Lines 387–92 are more openly derisive of Augustan pretensions than most allusions of this sort in the *AA*. Pompey's colonnade had been restored by the Princeps, at great expense, in 32 BC. The Palatine temple of Apollo was Augustus' most magnificent building: cf. *Am.* 2.2.3–4 and my note, p. 291. He dedicated it in 28 BC as a thank-offering for his victory at Actium three years earlier, over Antony and Cleopatra. Thus Ovid mockingly ascribes that victory (390) to Apollo's direct intervention. The Princeps' wife and sister (391) were, respectively, Livia and Octavia. His son-in-law (392) was M. Vipsanius Agrippa, who (at a somewhat advanced age) married Julia and was honoured with two successive consulships (28 and 27 BC). Agrippa had played a crucial part in the victories at Actium (31 BC) and over Sextus Pompeius off Sicily (36 BC), on which occasion he won the 'naval crown' (*corona navalis*) for valour. In thanksgiving for his victories Agrippa, too, dedicated a colonnade. The 'Memphian cow' is a derisive periphrasis for Isis: see my note on *AA* 1.77–8, p. 341.

397–432 Ovid here interweaves two of his favourite themes. First and foremost, there is the poet's overriding concern, his pursuit of fame (403ff.). We have already examined his views on this at length (my introductory note to *Am.* 1.15, pp. 277–8). As a bait to the girls he is pursuing, he frequently emphasizes the fame *they* will acquire from being written about by him, but this always remains a secondary consideration: *his* immortality will, as it were, rub off on *them*. Good examples of this phenomenon occur at *Am.* 1.3.19–26, 1.10.61–2 and 2.17.27–30. In the present passage (413–16) the stitches, amusingly, show: this may even have been a deliberate effect. Without the *Iliad*, Ovid asks, who would have heard of – well, of whom? Andromache? Helen? Even Achilles? No, of *Homer*: what really lies close to his heart is the *poet*'s reputation, not that of his subject. But then he remembers, or affects to remember, that what he originally set out to discuss in this section, before getting sidetracked by his favourite obsession, was essential publicity *for women*. He therefore hastily follows this (strictly speaking, irrelevant) example with that of Danaë, rescued from eternal obscurity in her tower by timely poetical PR work. There follows the admonition that girls (417ff.) should seek maximum exposure on the party circuit.

The pursuit of immortality, however, also leads Ovid into another favourite obsession: what he regards as a contemporary decline in the poet's public status (cf. *Am.* 3.8, *passim*, 3.9.17–18, *AA* 2.273ff., with my note, p. 372). The Roman example he chooses, interestingly enough, is (409–10) Q. Ennius (239–169 BC), the Romanized Calabrian who was patronized by Scipio Nasica, Scipio Africanus, and M. and Q. Fulvius Nobilior. It is ironic that his belief that Ennius was buried in the Scipionic family vault is almost certainly false; even the tradition of the poet's statue having been set up there is suspect.

His argument, in fact, is totally specious. His frequently reiterated assertion that the elegist's art demands respect as hard work, and is not in any sense an idler's soft option, was not calculated to make any impression at all (except as a smart but suspect paradox) on Roman upper-class society at large – and that would have been even more true, *a fortiori*, of the crusty Republican society in which Ennius was privileged to move. There is, furthermore, a good deal which might lead us to suppose that Augustus' patronage of Horace and Virgil – poets whom Ovid, again and again, mocks for their patriotic attitudinizing – was considerably more flexible and enlightened than anything we know of the Scipionic Circle. Yet Ovid carefully avoids mentioning Horace and Virgil in this context, though they would have served his argument very well: his anti-Augustanism was too deeply engrained to allow any hint that the status of poets had been actually enhanced by the new regime. Better a dishonest argument from the Republic than any furtive trucking with Maecenism.

Line 398 offers yet another neat – and unmistakable – instance of sexual double entendre (cf. *AA* 1.409–12, 631–6, with my notes, pp. 352 and 358). The Latin (*fructus abest, facies cum bona teste caret*) can mean either (i) 'A pretty face, unseen, gets no results', or (ii) 'A pretty girl, if never balled, won't get pregnant'. The pun on *testis* ('witness' or 'testicle') is repeated elsewhere (e.g. *Am.* 3.3.19, *AA* 1.632). I have tried to bring out at least a hint of this double meaning in my translation.

'Music unheard gives little joy' (399–400) was a proverbial phrase. On Danaë see my note (pp. 309–10) to *Am.* 2.19.27–28, and on Andromeda those to *Am.* 3.3.17–18, p. 315, and *AA* 1.53–4, p. 340: cf. Apollod. 2.4.3–5.

433–66 Ovid is warning the girls what kind of man they should avoid: the over-elegant exquisite, the compulsive rake, the habitual oath-breaker. From a pragmatic feminine viewpoint – and Ovid's view of human relationships is nothing if not pragmatic, cf. lines 461–6 – these offer what can only be termed high-risk investments. In literary terms there is ironic satisfaction to be got from watching the *praeceptor amoris* adapt his ploys to a new audience with such bland eristic dexterity. The mythical reference-points gain piquancy from familiarity. Both Theseus' desertion of Ariadne, and his son Demophoön's abandonment of Phyllis, are favourite Ovidian themes: see, e.g., *AA* 1.525–64, *Am.* 2.18.21–6, *AA* 2.353ff., *RA* 591–608, *Her.* 2 and 10, *passim*.

Lines 461–6 reveal – against much of his protestations elsewhere – Ovid's highly Roman, and legalistic, sense of the fundamentals governing human relationships: *amicitia* – our word 'friendship' does less than justice to this elusive concept – with its carefully graded mutual benefits, is here envisaged as operating also in the sexual sphere: cf. my *Essays in Antiquity* (London, 1960) pp. 143–5, and further literature there cited.

What is the point of lines 439–40? In the context it is clear enough. Ovid wants an *exemplum* to prove the danger of having anything to do with a dandified lover; and Paris is the epitome of the sexually irresistible, subtly effeminate charmer. When Paris sailed for Sparta, Cassandra prophesied the disaster his venture would bring upon Troy. The couplet 441-2 contains a characteristic sexual pun on the word *pudenda*, which I have attempted to convey in my translation (cf. notes on 397-432, p. 394, and 768, p. 401); there is a similar innuendo in the 'door' of 456.

467-8 For Ovid's practice, in this poem, of using imagery drawn from chariot-driving or sailing to indicate functional and thematic divisions, see above, my note on *AA* 2.425-34, p. 375: there, as here, the apostrophe is introduced to terminate a digression.

469-98 Ovid's advocacy of the written approach is by now familiar to us: familiar enough for the reader to appreciate his present variations on the basic theme. We have seen it demonstrated in the *Amores* (1.11 and 1.12, *passim*, cf. 2.2.5-6, 2.19.41), and recommended to ambitious gallants in Bk 1 of the *AA* (lines 437-86, cf.2.395ff.). In all these cases the lady's-maid (470) formed the crucial go-between (cf. also Am.1.11, 1.12; *AA* 1.351ff., with my note, p. 350, 2.251ff.). The present passage is clearly meant to be read with *AA* 1.437ff. in mind.

499-524 At this point Ovid marks a formal break between elementary and advanced instruction (cf. lines 99-100, with my note, p. 385; and for the image, my note on 467-8, above), although the theme on which he now embarks – control of one's temper – has already been touched on in connection with games-playing (above, lines 369-80, with my note, pp. 391-2). There, as here, the natural savagery of women is emphasized (see also lines 235-50, and my note, p. 388), which makes the need for controlling artifice all the more essential: a woman's public image, whether achieved by cosmetics or psychological discipline, masks something both unpleasant and feral. At the same time, he is fair enough to acknowledge that men, too, are well advised to keep a tight rein on their temper: the present passage forms a diptych with *AA* 2.145-76, which conveys a very similar message.

For the Gorgon Medusa (504) as a symbol of petrifying female anger or contempt cf. *AA* 2.700; a nice modern parallel is supplied by Tennyson's famous phrase from 'Maud', 'Gorgonized me from head to foot with a stony British stare'. When Athena (505-6) was playing the flute (or pan-pipes), and saw her puffed and swollen cheeks reflected in the river, she flung the instrument away in disgust (it was later retrieved by Marsyas).

Why are Tecmessa and Andromache type-cast by Ovid as symbols of dreary and anti-sexual depression? Why are they mentioned together, not only here, but at lines 109–12? Surely because both were classic instances of sexual war-victims. Andromache – the epitome of the faithful and loving wife – was, after Hector's death, taken prisoner and allotted as booty to Neoptolemus, the son of her husband's killer; while Tecmessa, the daughter of a Phrygian chieftain, was captured during a Greek raid, and made the slave-wife of Ajax (who had killed her father). Ovid's rejection of both Andromache and Tecmessa as desirable mistresses (519–20) is based, in part at least, on covert compassion; Tecmessa may, as he says, have been a 'dreary woman' (523), but she had every good reason to refuse Ajax a lover's endearments, and the same is true *a fortiori* of Andromache.

525–52 Ovid here returns to one of his pet obsessions, the justification of the poet's life, art, and *mores*, in particular as these affect the women with whom he has to do. He begins with a bold, not to say an impudent comparison: girls should dispose of their admirers in the same spirit as Augustus makes his military appointments (525–30) – a logical extension of the lover-as-soldier motif (cf. *Am.* 1.9, *AA* 2.233ff., with my notes, pp. 279 and 370). At the same time he is careful to stress, as so often, that poets (i) lack wealth, so cannot be looked to for expensive presents (cf. my notes on *AA* 2.161ff., p. 368, and 2.273–86, p. 372, with further reff.); (ii) are not 'professional men' as Rome normally understood that term (cf. *Am.* 1.9.41–2, with my note, p. 280); but (iii) should be cultivated in their own right, since they can bestow fame on those whom they celebrate (e.g. *Am.* 1.3.19ff., 1.10.59ff., cf. my note on lines 397–432 above, pp. 393–4); and (iv) are expert in matters of love (*AA* 1.1ff., and *passim*). For Nemesis, the mistress of Tibullus, see *Am.* 3.9.31–2, and my note, p. 326. Cynthia fulfilled a similar role for Propertius: see Introd., pp. 32–3. For Gallus and Lycoris see my note to *Am.* 3.9.61–4, p. 327. This identity of Corinna is discussed in my Introduction (pp. 22ff.) and frequently referred to.

Lines 539ff. work further variations on this basic theme. Ovid reiterates his belief that poets are not suited to the occupations of businessman, politician (541), orator (542) or – metaphorical erotic conceits notwithstanding – soldier (539, with a backward glance at 525ff.). We remember, not for the first time, that Augustus had offered Ovid and his brother the chance to enter on a career of public service, which Ovid had tried but, after a short time, firmly and finally rejected (see Introd., pp. 28–30).

553–76 Just as a man is advised, on occasion, to find his way into a

woman's bed by an initial display of (non-sexual) friendship
(*AA* 1.719–22), so a woman, too, must avoid appearing too openly
rapacious, lest she scare off her potential quarry (553f.): we remem-
ber, here, Ovid's remarks concerning the supposed violence of female
lust (*AA* 1.269–350) – and his recommendation to men to press on
with a seduction regardless (ibid., 667ff.). Once again the double stan-
dard applies. The same techniques are not appropriate for dealing
with callow youths and mature men (555ff.): as a long-term proposition
the older lover, male as well as female, has many advantages. It is not
often that Ovid so clearly stresses his own age; but in this passage the
contrast between the young, inexperienced lover of the *Amores* and the
wordly-wise teacher of the *Ars* is pointed up with great care.

577–610 Since I have betrayed the male citadel, Ovid argues, I
might as well go on and complete the job. We expect novel revela-
tions. But though the idea of betrayal, in a military context, is new to
elegy, what follows is all too familiar: the much-touted proposition
that deprival and competition stimulate jaded appetites. The shut-out
lover or *exclusus amator* (581–2, 587–8), Ovid's best-known image of
erotic deprivation, recurs throughout his work, and is a standard
property of love-elegy.

Ovid, then, has simply rehashed old material in a new context:
there is not even a change of emphasis. What we detect here is the
axe-grinding of an obsessional *idée fixe*. Psychologically, as we have
had ample occasion to note, this love-poet thrives on frustration, and
the conventions of elegy provide him with ample scope in this area.
What more natural (and more egotistical) advice could he give women
than to do everything that would most effectively pander to his own
mildly masochistic instincts? This also, of course, gives him the
opportunity to recapitulate, briefly and *da capo*, a number of domi-
nant literary motifs from his earlier work: the technique is deliberately
evocative, hauntingly effective.

Line 578 is interesting as the source of a much-quoted (and even
more exuberantly oxymoronic) couplet in Tennyson's *Idylls of the
King*, where the poet observes, apropos Lancelot's passion for
Guinevere, 'His honour rooted in dishonour stood, / And faith
unfaithful kept him falsely true' ('Lancelot and Elaine', 871–2).

611–66 It is a curious fact (and one, so far as I know, not remarked
on by commentators) that, for all his ambivalent preoccupation with
the social frustrations attendant upon a would-be seducer, Ovid no-
where in the first two books of the *AA* offers men any formal guidance

on how to circumvent such permanent obstacles as husband, lover or guardian. Certainly there exists no sequence comparable to the present list of smart dodges designed for the ladies. This striking omission, when juxtaposed with Ovid's obvious masochistic pleasure in love's servitude, confirms one's suspicion that – whatever we may feel about his professed Don Juanism – in some ways he very much expected his women to make the running.

The disclaimer of 611–16 is, of course, pure eyewash (cf. *AA* 1.25–30). Ovid may once more pretend, as a safeguard, that his instructions are not designed for respectable married ladies: the context, as always, suggests otherwise. The presence of that intrusive husband-rival recalls the swinging upper-class love-affairs of the late Republic, so accurately reflected in the poems of Catullus, and still all-too-prevalent thirty or forty years later. Nor, of course, would Ovid's warning discourage a lady reader bent on adultery: quite the reverse. On top of that, how safe was it, in fact, at the time of writing, to suggest that freedwomen (615) were fair game? Augustus had, as part of his moral legislation, sanctioned marriage with freedwomen for all Roman citizens except senators. He clearly did not stipulate that such wives would 'be at liberty to deceive their husbands and would be exempt from the penalties of adultery' (Rudd, p. 6). In other words, while making his perfunctory genuflexion to the official line on adultery, Ovid cannot resist negating the gesture by the derisive irony of its context.

For Argus the many-eyed herdsman cf. my notes on *Am.* 3.4.19–20, p. 316, and 2.2.44–6, p. 292. The matter of writing letters has already been discussed from both the man's and the woman's viewpoint: see *AA* 1.437ff. with my note, p. 353, and above, lines 469ff., with my note, p. 395. Now Ovid lists all the tricks that can be employed by the go-between – generally the lady's personal maid (*Am.* 1.11.3–4, Tib. 2.6.45–6) – to keep such illicit correspondence moving without detection.

Ovid sees Danaë (631) as a mythical symbol for the locked-up girl reached – and indeed impregnated – against all predictable odds: see, e.g., *Am.* 2.19.27–8, with my note, pp. 309–10. Her father was Acrisius, King of Argos. In lines 633ff. we have a list, again, of the best places of assignation in Rome: theatres, race-track, and certain temples (cf. *AA* 1.75–162), especially those of Isis (635, cf. *Am.* 2.13.7ff.) and the Good Goddess (*Bona Dea*: 637, cf. above, line 244, with my note, p. 388), to which males, including over-sedulous guardians, were forbidden access.

667–86 It goes without saying that Ovid's claim to be crazy or out of control in the exposition of his subject-matter should not be taken seriously. However, just as the *praeceptor amoris* must demonstrate mastery of his subject, so the poet, to show himself truly inspired, must on occasion be carried away – this being the conventional guarantee, in antiquity, of bardic status. The poet may be inspired, but Love's old soldier and shikaree has things well under control. In fact, while apparently showing the girls, with caustic concision, how to manipulate male stupidity and male egotism, Ovid is also quietly setting them up to do just what will suit men best. 'Lemnian swords' (672) were proverbial. The women of Lemnos, in mythical times, did not worship Aphrodite. The goddess, in pique, afflicted them all with such disgusting body-odour or halitosis that their husbands refused to sleep with them any longer, but took Thracian concubines instead. Thus dishonoured, the Lemnian wives murdered not only their husbands, but also their fathers – an intriguing detail that should appeal to Freudians. Hypsipyle alone saved her father; she afterwards became queen. For the sequel to this myth, involving the Argonauts, see my note on *Am.* 2.18.33, p. 308.

687–746 We cannot complain that Ovid does not warn us what he is about when introducing the myth of Cephalus and Procris at this juncture. It is to be a cautionary tale designed to discourage over-suspicious girls; and the clear implication of all that has gone before is that the girls have, indeed, something to be suspicious about. We would therefore expect Ovid to choose an *exemplum* in which the mythical lover had been – *and was traditionally known to have been* – guilty of infidelity, but to manipulate it in such a way that he should, on this occasion, appear convincingly innocent – at least to Ovid's hypothetical girl-students, if not to those more cynical and sophisticated male readers who were well up in the by-ways of mythology, and knew by heart (like Tiberius' professors) just what songs the Sirens sang. When we scrutinize the myth in its totality – as handled by Ovid himself, among other writers – it becomes only too clear that this is precisely what he has done, with subtle skill and the most calculated allusiveness.

Cephalus has been twice mentioned already in the amatory poems (*Am.* 1.13.39–40, *AA* 3.84, with my notes, pp. 285 and 385), on each occasion as the lover of Aurora, the Dawn. The verbal similarity Aura–Aurora will at once strike the reader, all the more so since Ovid went for it deliberately: in the Greek version of the myth the breeze is not in question at all. What Cephalus there addresses is *nephéle*, 'cloud'. The innocence and pathos at once become a little suspect; and by the time we have reminded ourselves of the myth as a whole, they evaporate altogether.*

Procris was the daughter of Erechtheus, king of Athens. Her sister was Oreithyia, who acquired notoriety after getting herself raped by Boreas: winds with sexual characteristics seem endemic to this story. She married Cephalus, son of Deion or Deioneus, who as a husband behaved a little oddly, even by mythical criteria. He left his bride shortly after their marriage, and went abroad for eight years. He then returned, in disguise, determined to test his wife's fidelity. Both the disguise and the idea of the test had been put into his head by Aurora, the Dawn. Why was this? Because, it transpires, the reason for his disappearance was that Aurora – a notorious man-eater – had met him on Hymettus, only a month or so after his wedding, and seduced him, subsequently bearing him a son, Phaethon. Aurora gave him a magically swift hound, and a spear that never missed its mark (this was the spear with which Cephalus afterwards killed his wife). In the *Metamorphoses* it is Procris who, after her reconciliation with Cephalus (7.750ff.) demurely presents both gifts to him – leaving the acute reader to recall how she had acquired them in the first place.

At all events, when Cephalus returned home from this adventure to his putatively faithful wife, he decided to test her fidelity by attempting her seduction in disguise. Cephalus revealed his identity *post coitum*, upbraided his wife severely, and from then on – having thus got himself a splendid psychological advantage – spent most of his time out hunting. Procris, not surprisingly when we recall her spouse's earlier activities on Hymettus, suspected him in turn of having a mistress.

A Roman audience, certainly the well-read audience at which Ovid directed his work, would not, in any case, forget that in the early Greek tradition not only did Procris *accompany* Cephalus, as a fellow-hunter, on the expedition during which she met her death – note Ovid's emphasis on her partiality for *solitary* hunting – but Cephalus actually saw her *before* he threw his spear, and ran her through, not by accident, but in a fit of sudden anger, an act for which he was after-

---

* For a more detailed investigation of the Cephalus–Procris myth and its literary evolution, see now my article 'The innocence of Procris: Ovid *AA* 3.687–746', *CJ* 75 (1979–80) 15–24.

wards condemned to exile by the Areopagus. No changeable breezes there. Their mutual adulteries were equally well known. Ovid, in fact, would have been hard put to it to find a more squalid myth in the corpus when going in search of innocence and pathos; it is reasonable to assume that he knew what he was doing.

Silly girls were expected to take their cue from this silly Procris and to swallow Cephalus' *ad hoc* excuses; Ovid's literate male audience would know better. Educated men would read the whole episode with sharply malicious literary pleasure, and their faith in double standards considerably enhanced. When we reflect on the prominent position this narrative *mythos* occupies, it surely tells us a great deal about the underlying temper and tone of the *AA* as a whole. Ovid in his own way adored women; but no one who so consistently likened them to crops, cows and other such farmyard phenomena really, in his heart of hearts, believed in the equality of the sexes. Women, like a well-run estate, required *cultus*; but *ars* – and possibly *ingenium* too – was, in the last resort, a male prerogative.

The spring on Hymettus forms the source of the Ilissos, famous from Plato's description (*Phaedr.* 229A–230C). Today its outflow gushes from a marble ram's head on the monastery wall at Kaisariani; before the building of the Marathon Dam it supplied Athens with drinking water. As Ovid will have been well aware, its waters were supposed to cure sterility, and a shrine of Aphrodite stood nearby. Though Hymettus as a whole has suffered severe deforestation, Kaisariani itself is still thickly overgrown with pine, cypress, plane and (a tree Ovid never knew) eucalyptus. Aromatic shrubs – thyme, sage, bay, mint, rosemary, lavender – cluster thickly over the hillside; the area of the spring forms a cool and delightful oasis that exactly matches Ovid's description.

'Mercurial Cephalus' (725): 'mercurial' as the son of Hermes (Roman Mercury).

747–68 Once again, as at several key points in this book (e.g. lines 25–6, 99–100, 499–500) Ovid uses the sailing image (747–8) to mark a completed stage in his instruction: cf. my note on 467–8, p. 395, where the chariot metaphor serves a similar function. Here, not surprisingly – since it forms a prelude to specifically sexual instruction, 769ff. – we find an obvious double entendre. The 'bare facts of the case' (*nudis rebus*) are, in every sense, 'naked matters': indeed at this stage we may, if we will, see the entire recurrent metaphor in sexual terms (boat = penis, harbour = vagina).

It has often been implied that in this section women receive more or less the same advice, *mutatis mutandis*, as men (*AA* 1.229–52, 565–602) on the subject of dinner-parties: i.e. that liquor can help get things going, but should only be used in moderation. This is true as far as it goes, but completely ignores the striking contrast in Ovid's approach to the female sex. Lines 751–4 offer a neat and amusing reversal of *AA* 1.245–50. While men are warned against deceptive half-light, women are urged to cultivate it. Then we recall that there were good reasons for such advice: cf. lines 251–80, with my note, p. 346, on Ovid's distaste for their physical attributes. What follows amply confirms this impression. Ovid may warn men against drinking too much, but he does not expect them to become dead drunk; nor does he anywhere feel called upon to remind them that gross gorging of food in public is unattractive. On the other hand, he spends a good deal of time instructing them on how to be the (seductive) life and soul of the party: 1.569–88, 595–610. Women get no such hints on how to attract or amuse; instead they are told, briefly, (i) not to slurp and gobble (755–60), and (ii) not to pass out in a stupor at the table (761–8). In both cases (759–60, 765) the unattractiveness of such habits is stressed; in the second, the danger of sexual advances which the girl is in no state to resist.

769–808 This passage should be considered in conjunction with *AA* 2.703–32, 669–74, where sexual advice, of an equally stylized and perfunctory sort, is offered to men (cf. my note, pp. 380–81). Unlike the men, who are merely told, in passing (*AA* 2.679), that positions for intercourse are numerous, women are advised which ones to choose, in accordance with their individual endowments or flaws.

809–12 These lines form a shorter, more perfunctory echo of the valedictory coda at the end of Bk 2 (see lines 733–44, with my note, p. 381), topped and tailed with identical, or near-identical, phrases ('My task/sport is ended', 'Ovid was my guide'). They are also mischievously allusive, with verbal echoes of the coda to Bk 2 of Virgil's *Georgics* (541–2), where the poet declares: '*High time* to *turn loose* our steaming horses'. What is more, the *praeceptor amoris*, having used this image at regular intervals to emphasize (a) his control and (b) the progress of the work (see my notes on *AA* 2.425ff., p. 375, and 3.467–8, p. 395), now, at the very last moment, reveals that his imposing chariot is drawn, not by horses but by *swans*, as was that of Venus. Propertius made a similar claim (3.3.39); but it took Ovid to introduce swans where his readers had been conditioned to expect

Virgilian horses, and thus to end on a note of subtle, but absolutely characteristic, literary deflation. The grandiose claims expressed in the earlier coda are here cut down to size, and the Automedon of Love makes his exit, grinning, behind a gaggle of long-necked birds.

CURES FOR LOVE

1–10 The proem to the *Remedia Amoris* closely parallels that to Bk 3 of the *AA*: in both Ovid offers to provide a new class of person with rational weapons for the love-game. The poem's title is implicit in the opening couplet (which otherwise would be meaningless to the reader), and the by now familiar military metaphor (love = warfare) at once picks up a whole range of earlier references. Diomede son of Tydeus (5–6), in the fighting before Troy, wounded Aphrodite (Venus), who was carried out of the fighting to Olympus by Ares (Mars) in his chariot; she was, of course, the mother of Eros (Cupid) whom Ovid is here addressing. He is also consciously echoing his own previous reference at *Am.* 1.7.31.

The contrast between instinct (*impetus*) and rule (*ratio*) expressed in line 10 lies at the heart of Ovid's erotic-didactic poetry, as we have seen throughout the *AA*. Uncontrolled – and uncontrollable – passion is the motif that distinguishes his elegiac predecessors. This attitude Ovid consistently attacks and ridicules, most often by skilful use of agricultural, hunting or, in the *RA*, medical metaphor. Love, for him, is most often only regarded as a kind of intellectual game subject to specific ground-rules; but it also, significantly, implies a fundamental lack of *ratio* in women.

11–22 Ovid's claim *not* to be writing a recantation or palinode (11–12) is a perfectly legitimate assertion. He is not attacking Love as such, but rather those unfortunate or inappropriate passions, dictated by *impetus* without benefit of *ratio*, that tend to get Eros a bad name among the uninformed. (That he expected hostile critics to tag him with the 'palinode theory', however, is clear not only from this passage but also from 379–96 below.) In other words, just as the two books of advice to men were followed by one offering counter-precepts for women, so the *AA* as a whole, with its instructions to both sexes on achieving, and maintaining, successful relationships is balanced by the *RA*, which offers, similarly, counter-precepts on how both men and women (49–52) can avoid a bad (i.e. uncontrolled)

403

involvement, or get out of one that has gone wrong. Ovid's careful exculpation of Eros (20ff.) in cases of tragedy, most often suicide, induced by unruly passions is thus, on his own terms, perfectly logical. Love cannot be held responsible for irrational excesses in the individual.

By entering the sphere of cures and antidotes Ovid was able to add a fresh dimension to his didactic parody – that of medicine. Throughout the *RA* the narrator's *persona* is, more often than not, that of a doctor: see, e.g., 43–4, 76, 109, 115, 313, 525–8, 546, 795. Nor is he restricted simply to reversing advice previously given in the *AA*: no more than 16 out of a total of 42 precepts fall into this category. For Eros as 'peace-lover' cf. *Am.* 1.10.15, *AA* 1.10. The paradox of consistently expressing pacific habits in terms of bellicose imagery perhaps hints at an unresolved conflict in Ovid's emotional attitude to his subject.

23–40 Ovid is still defending Cupid and seeking his approval for the present undertaking. He has raised the charge of indirect murder only to dispose of it here: 'You *could* have used your arrows to kill – but they remain clean of bloodshed.' Some people, Ovid concedes, do die as a result of star-crossed passions, but Cupid is not responsible: he could, had he so wished, have used his arrows for this purpose, but chose otherwise.

Cupid's stepfather is Mars: see *Am.* 1.2.24, with my note, p. 270. To claim that no mother was ever bereaved as a result of Venus' wiles (29–30) suggests a sly tongue-in-cheek piece of flattery, since the most notorious evidence to the contrary was provided by Ovid's own favourite mythical *exemplum*, the Trojan War, in the person of Helen.

41–8 Ovid is here employing a traditional mode of exposition that goes back as far as Hesiod: the lessons imparted to the poet by a god in epiphany are then passed on, as vatic utterance, to the public. For the Telephus myth and its magical implications see *Am.* 2.9.7, with my note, p. 298.

49–52 These lines look like an afterthought, or aside, and I have bracketed them in my translation, since though Ovid goes on to discuss, among others, Phyllis and Medea, nevertheless his main interest throughout the book (as in the rest of his erotic poems) is with the sexual problems and aspirations of men. The claim (50) to be 'giving arms to both sides' reminds us that the battle of the sexes is just that (cf. *AA* 2.741, 3.1ff., 667f., and below, 675f.), but there can be no doubt, despite his professions of impartiality, where Ovid's true sympathies lay.

55–68 All the *exempla* chosen by Ovid in this section are familiar from earlier use, including Phyllis, Dido and Paris (for a very similar catalogue see *Am.* 2.18.21–38), and form part of that carefully orchestrated *da capo* effect with which Ovid linked the thematic and illustrative material in his erotic corpus. Phyllis' desertion by Demophoön is treated at length in *Her.* 2; we have already encountered the episode at *Am.* 2.18.22 (cf. my note, p. 308, for details of the myth), and Ovid reworks it yet again below, at 591–608, where the reference – mysterious unless one knows the story – to her ninth retreading of that fatal path is elucidated (see pp. 256–7). Not only Phyllis, but also Dido and Medea are treated at *AA* 3.33–40, while Myrrha (referred to below, 99–100), Pasiphaë, Scylla and Phaedra all figure in *AA* 1.283–340. The story of Tereus and Philomela ('so rudely forc'd') appears in the *Amores* (2.6.7–10: see my note, p. 295), while Paris and Helen get two epistles between them (*Her.* 16 and 17). For Dido's unfortunate relationship with Aeneas see Virg. *Aen.* Bk 4, esp. lines 410–11 (verbally echoed here) and 641ff. on her suicide. Medea: *Am.* 2.14.32 (verbally echoed at line 60), *AA* 1.336, and my note, p. 349. Pasiphaë is analysed at length in *AA* 1.289ff. (see my note, p. 348, for the myth and further reff.); for Phaedra see *Am.* 2.18.30, and *AA* 1.338, with my notes, p. 308 and 349.

69–74 The self-advertisement of the *praeceptor amoris*, the emphasis on rational control, the nautical image – all these are characteristic, and, we find, equally applicable to remedy as to promotion in the love-game. The legal phraseology ('public deliverer', 'rod that proclaims your freedom') that Ovid, uniquely among Augustan poets, exploits as a metaphor, refers to the process known as *vindicatio in libertatem*, that normally accompanied the freeing of slaves. The deliverer (*assertor*) would touch the person to be freed with the rod (*vindicta*) as a symbol of manumission.

75–8 For similar invocations at the beginning of earlier books cf. *AA* 1.30 and 2.15: the appeal to Apollo also picks up the god's earlier epiphany at *AA* 2.493–510: cf. my note, p. 376.

93–106 The didactic is always in danger of sliding into the pit of aphoristic sententiousness, a hazard Ovid does not always manage to avoid. 'Don't put off till tomorrow what you can do now' – the advice is perennial. For Myrrha's incest with her father, and subsequent metamorphosis into a myrrh-tree (99–100) see *AA* 1.283–8 and my note, p. 347. Ovid visualizes a still-human Myrrha somehow hidden, in shame, behind the tree's bark, through which her gummy tears ooze – a fundamentally comic (and typically Ovidian) visual conceit for which there are numerous typological parallels.

107–34 If the disease cannot be nipped in the bud, then wait till its fury has subsided. True to his role as metaphorical doctor, Ovid is here borrowing a commonplace from ancient medical theory, that of the 'opportune moment' (*kairós, occasio*): with lines 131–4 compare the parenthetical reference to this practice at *AA* 1.357, where we read of doctors awaiting the propitious time to apply their medicines.

Philoctetes (111–14), one of Helen's original suitors and leader of the Olizonians against Troy, was bitten on the foot by a snake while at sacrifice on an Aegean island (Tenedos, Chryse or Lemnos: accounts differ); the wound suppurated, and emitted so unpleasant a smell that Philoctetes was marooned on Lemnos, where he spent the ten years of the Trojan War. After this time, however, Calchas (or Helenus) prophesied that the war could not be won without Philoctetes and his bow (a gift from Heracles). Odysseus and Diomede thereupon fetched Philoctetes from Lemnos; either Machaon or Podalirius at last cured his wound, and he shot Paris. The capture of Troy soon followed. Lines 121–2 recall *AA* 2.181–2, where the same image is used, in almost identical words, to make the same point about swimming across a river.

135–50 Ovid was neither the first nor (most certainly) the last writer to deprecate leisure (*otium*) as a promoter of loose morals. As he says, eliminate leisure, and the love-game tends to get squeezed out (or at the very least severely restricted) by that simple fact (139–40). The argument here is that of the traditional Roman conservative for whom 'leisure' and 'idleness' are terms of abuse; the reader will recall, as he was meant to, that elsewhere Ovid had argued a precisely opposite case: see *Am.* 1.15, with my introductory note and further reff. Much of the pleasure – and force – of the *RA* derives from this rational, quasi-behaviourist and, above all, *reversible* manipulation of the human psyche.

Why does the plane-tree (141) rejoice in wine? According to Pliny (*HN* 12.8), 'their growth is encouraged by having wine poured on them'. Since plane-trees, then as now, were regularly grown outside inns to provide cool shade for al fresco drinkers, and, in addition, often had trailing vines trained over their branches, it is not hard to see how the association arose.

151–68 The 'respectable' professions – lawyer, politician, soldier and (below, 169ff.) gentleman farmer – are all, predictably, trotted out here as handy diversions for the love-lorn, in Ovid's eyes their only legitimate function. The allusion to Gaius' recent Parthian expedition (for a detailed account see *AA* 1.177–228, and my note, pp. 342ff.) is particularly sardonic. Gaius, the Imperial protégé notable mainly for his untried youth (*pueritia*), did not fight a successful campaign: with the help of experienced advisers he merely negotiated a far-from-romantic concordat. The 'glorious triumph' (155) is thus set in its true perspective: Gaius' death (AD 4) merely gave an added twist to the passage, which Ovid, at the time of composition, could not have anticipated. This, of course, helps to date the *RA*: if Ovid is not being overtly cynical in 155–8, news of the concordat (signed 1 May AD 2, on the Euphrates) had not yet reached Rome when he wrote these lines. Even so, his conclusion is cool enough: the best, clearly, that this Parthian settlement can achieve is parity of value with a lover's victory over his own unruly passions. The idea of a 'trophy' in the imagery of erotic warfare seems to be Ovid's own. For the wounding of Aphrodite (Venus) by Diomede see above, line 5, and my note, p. 403. The Roman anachronistic touches in Ovid's account of Aegisthus' seduction of Clytemnestra add their own flavour: Argos is seen as a kind of mini-Rome, complete with Forum.

169–98 The farmer's life offered Ovid an ideal diversion from affairs of the heart. It was an all-seasons occupation (187ff.) that made constant, and heavy, demands on anyone who took it up; it also had its own stylized pastoral charm, well brought out in this passage, and reinforced by the influential encomia of Virgil and Tibullus. Unlike the latter poet, Ovid had not been in the habit of picturing the country as an ideal place to make love; his attitude was rather that of Browning's smart Italian in 'Up in the City, Down at the Villa', who preferred to admire the countryside from the vantage-point of a populous city-square. Thus there was nothing to stop him using rural life as an *antidote* to passion, rather than as a backdrop, in the Tibullan manner, for a kind of non-stop erotic *fête champêtre*.

199–212 Pity the poor rentier, whose mind obstinately keeps running on sex: without a hard day's work to drain his energies and divert his mind, substitute activities become all the more essential. Hunting is as good an occupation as any: no worse than the Victorian cult of team-sports and cold baths, and, from a Roman viewpoint, preferable to farming, since the latter was under the patronage of Ceres (Demeter), an ultra-fecund deity, while the hunter – like Hippolytus, hopefully chaste – could invoke the aid of that professional virgin

Diana (Artemis). The phrase for 'sound sleep' in 206, *pingui quiete*, has slightly ironic associations, since at *Am.* 1.13.7 the same epithet is used to describe post-coital dawn slumbers, and this is not likely, in Ovid's case, to be coincidental. It is also worth remembering that Ovid in the *AA*, as we have seen, regularly employs hunting imagery to describe the pursuit of women, and that a passage immediately before that recalled in the next section (*AA* 1.391–4) refers successively to fowling, boar-hunting and fishing. Note that the student is required to 'unlearn' (*dediscis*) his passion, in a converse process clearly regarded as analogous to that of acquiring the seductive techniques outlined in the *AA*.

213–24 Cicero recommends a change of scene as beneficial for the love-sick, as for any other convalescent invalid. Ovid is more specific: let the victim put as many miles as he can, as quickly as possible, between himself and the object of his affections. What we have here, in fact, is the reversal of the situation in *Am.* 2.16 or 3.16, when Ovid is parted from his mistress, and pondering ways and means to get to her or have her come to him. There is a deliberate allusion to earlier advice at 219–20, when Ovid's half-unwilling student is shown offering various excuses for not leaving Rome: days of ill-omen, foreign sabbaths. The alert reader will at once recall that passage in *AA* Bk 1 where our prospective suitor is being taught on which days to advance his cause (399ff., esp. 413–16), on which to avoid committing himself. Two occasions regarded as propitious were, precisely, the Jewish Sabbath and that same 'black day' mentioned here, 18 July, the anniversary of Rome's defeat on the banks of the river Allia by the Gauls in 390 BC (cf. my note, p. 352). One advantage such *dies atri* had for the suitor was that on them the shops were shut, and presents therefore unobtainable. Now they are being used as an excuse for not travelling. At 155 (cf. my note, p. 407) the fugitive Parthian was, however ironically, treated as cause for a Roman triumph; here he is made the synonym ('so far') for safe escape from an enemy. The reader is also left with a mildly ridiculous second image in mind, since 'Parthian flight' automatically evokes the trick (cf. *AA* 1.211, 3.786 – the latter in a sexual context) of shooting backwards at pursuers, and we cannot but picture Ovid's retreating lover stopping, every now and then, to loose off an antaphrodisiac arrow in the general direction of some hotfoot deserted mistress, hell-bent on his recapture. This effect, too, I am certain, was not accidental.

225–48 The clichés of the doctor ('to recover health demands much suffering', etc.) are neatly articulated to evocative phrases used earlier in a very different, and most often erotic, context (cf. lines 523ff. below, where the theme is repeated *da capo*). As a guarantee of experience Ovid here (227–8), as later (313–14), admits to having himself endured the sickness he describes, and to having employed his own remedies (311–12, 356, 715–16, 768). Note that the reader to whom Ovid addresses himself is assumed to possess the kind of private income that will facilitate extended travel abroad (237ff.). A plug for the pleasures of travel (241–2) is, incidentally, very rare in the ancient world – and with good reason. The image of passion as a fire, which can die away to mere embers (244), is repeated from *AA* 2.439ff., and had traditional antecedents in Hellenistic poetry; cf. lines 731ff. below.

249–90 Ovid's advice against employing magic, for whatever purpose, is a recurrent theme: we first encountered it at *AA* 2.99–106 (see my note, pp. 366–7), and shall meet it again at *MF* 35–42. As before, he makes a sharp distinction here between the illegitimate magic of spells and drugs, and the true magic of inspired poetry (251–2), with a conscious metaphorical play on the ambiguous semantics of the word *carmen*. He also, interestingly, repeats, with variations, his two mythical *exempla*, i.e. Circe and Medea (on whom cf. *AA* 2.101–4). These two ladies fit far less well into the present context than the earlier one. It is true that in both instances Ovid's main point is identical, i.e. that their magic simply failed to work, that the witch-physician could not heal herself. But whereas in the *Ars* Medea and Circe are depicted, quite naturally, as exerting all their wiles (with whatever success) to retain the affections of Jason and Ulysses respectively, here – since *cures* for love are now the order of the day – Medea must perform spells to stop Jason taking her away from Colchis (261–2), while Circe is made to deploy somewhat perfunctory charms and potions against the onset of passion (267–8, 287 –8) at a time when that passion has, clearly, long been a *fait accompli*. The belief that magic could be used to extinguish as well as to induce desire was widespread in antiquity. It is hard to resist the conclusion that here Ovid simply adapted, out of strict context, some ready-to-hand material from working stock.

291–310 If withdrawal techniques are out of the question (after all, *some* people have to stay in Rome), then try, Ovid suggests, a little home-made aversion therapy. The imagined monologue of his model student (301–6) is revealing: we are back in the familiar world of presents begrudged and sexual favours denied (cf. *Am.* 1.10 *passim*, and *AA* 3.461–6, with my notes, pp. 280–81 and 394), and at once recall a very similar earlier passage (*AA* 1.419ff., with my note, p. 352), which even repeats that perennial figure of sexual experiment and fantasy, the travelling pedlar or door-to-door salesman (*institor*). It is equally suggestive that 309–10, a couplet promoting the notion that suffering makes for spontaneous eloquence, should be so close a verbal echo of *AA* 1.609–10, where precisely the same result is attributed to brisk courtship. Passion of whatever sort, Ovid seems to be saying, promotes fluency, and can thus be used impartially either to make or unmake a sexual liaison.

311–30 The process of reversal is both detailed and neat. 'Habit breeds tolerance', the student is told at *AA* 2.647: 'time heals each physical blemish' (653), 'labels minimize feelings' (657). However, he is now reminded (*RA* 323), 'evil and good are near neighbours', a proposition repeated, with reversed emphasis, from *AA* 2.662, and a familiar *topos*. Precisely. Euphemisms (*AA* 2.657) must now be turned inside-out (*RA* 325–6). The lover should think of his girl as ugly even if she isn't, a dumpy creature with bad arms and legs (317–20). He should reflect on how much she costs him (321–2) – a charge, significantly, which gets no factual rebuttal (see above, my note on 291–310, and cf. *Am.* 1.10.63). Ovid then gets down to naming names, and the straight reversals come thick and fast: 327 = 661 + 657–8 (plumpness, swarthiness); 328 = 660 (thinness); 329–30 = *Am.* 2.4.13 (*rusticitas v.* sophistication). The latter passage reminds us of another twist to the joke. Several of the qualities described by Ovid in the *RA* as antipathetic figure in the *Amores* as erotic attractions, e.g. diminutive stature (*RA* 321: *Am.* 2.14.35) or a swarthy complexion (*RA* 327: *Am.* 2.14.40). For the connotations of *rusticitas*, equated by Ovid with prudishness or naïvety, see my note on *AA* 1.659–72, pp. 359–60. Beauty, as we know, lies in the eye of the beholder; Ovid is simply rationalizing this proposition into an all-purpose instrument for self-advancement or self-protection. As so often, he is, in effect, talking exclusively to men: Ovid's girl-students are not encouraged to analyse their male lovers' physical charms.

331–56 The utilization of various earlier precepts, culled from the *AA* and then switched round for a reverse effect, here reaches its climax. The examples chosen fall into two closely correlated categories: (a) forcing the girl to expose her worst physical traits and most conspicuous areas of incompetence; (b) invading her privacy before she has, in every sense, put on her 'public face'.

The 'Harpies' feast' (356) refers to the blinding by the gods of Phineus, King of Salmydessos in Thrace, for the circumstances of which see my note (p. 349) on *AA* 1.339. As an additional punishment he was afflicted with insatiable hunger. Whenever he sat down to eat, however, Harpies would swoop from the sky and snatch his meal. By way of adding insult to injury, they would foul the table with their droppings as they flew off, and any food left behind stank so revoltingly – either because of the droppings, or else through divine fiat – that it was quite inedible.

357–98 Ovid now proposes to offer his reader one or two antaphrodisiac tips applicable during sexual intercourse: it is, I think, significant that his cures for love tend to involve, not less sex, but a good deal more, ranging from voyeurism (437–8) to a second mistress (441ff.). But at this point he recalls (361ff.) that sexually explicit or morally questionable passages in the *AA* have lately earned him a good deal of criticism. After the Julian scandal of 2 BC this is not surprising. Women were, in fact, being prosecuted for adultery about this time. In a brief digression (361–95) Ovid sets about countering his critics' arguments. First, he claims not to care about such attacks, since he enjoys universal fame and popularity (363–4). Second, he attributes any hostility to envy on the part of unsuccessful literary rivals (365–70: another classic line of defence). Thirdly, he argues (371–88) that if his form and style are appropriate to his subject-matter, the charge against him fails by definition – a presumption that might appeal to art-for-art's-sakers, but would hardly satisfy a Catonian moralist. He concludes (389–96) with a triumphant and self-confident snub to his enemies: they have, he claims, mistimed their attack, since he is only now getting into his stride, more and better poems are on the way, and in the end elegy's debt to him will be acknowledged to rival that of epic to Virgil.

This defence is outrageous, not least because it so gratuitously begs a moral question in literary terms. Granted that a wanton (*proterva*) Muse calls for wanton expression, what obligation has Ovid to choose such a subject in the first place? The implication is that a poet can turn his hand to any genre, and his *protervitas* is simply a manner adopted for the moment because of literary considerations. Even the familiar claim (383–6, cf. *AA* 1.31, 2.599ff., 3.27, with my note, pp. 599–600) that the audience for the *AA* and the *RA* is restricted to freedwomen and courtesans rings speciously hollow; while the piling up of examples to illustrate the suitability of different metres and genres for different themes (371ff.) flattens a minor argument with rhetorical overkill. Ovid, in short, is very much on the defensive, and as a result protesting too much, in the wrong way.

The promise of 357–8 is picked up at 399ff. With 359–60 cf. *Am.* 1.5.25–6: it is ironic that Ovid should have been criticized for indecorousness, since the mechanics of intercourse (and to a great extent the act *per se*) clearly bore him. Pursuit is all.

'Some critics' (361) are later, it seems, reduced to one individual (371, *tu*; 391, *properas*): we do not know who this person was. The 'envious scholar' (365) was Zoilus, a 4th cent. BC Cynic philosopher from Amphipolis, known as Homeromastix ('the scourge of Homer') for his vigorous critical attacks on the poet, whom he faulted chiefly for introducing fabulous or otherwise incredible matter into his work. The 'impious tongues' that attacked the *Aeneid* (367–8) did not wait until Virgil was dead. A *vita* preserved by Donatus, and probably from the *De Viris Illustribus* (*On Famous Men*) of Suetonius, ends with a brief but intriguing account of various charges brought against Virgil – the chief ones being affectation of language and literary plagiarism.

With the introduction of Thais (383–6) Ovid gives his argument a fresh self-exculpatory twist. A famous courtesan of the 4th cent. BC, and the reputed companion of Alexander the Great, Thais passed into literature as the stylized *meretrix* of New Comedy, and thence was taken up at Rome by Terence (e.g. in *The Eunuch*) and Plautus. When Ovid claims that 'Thais belongs to my Art' (385) he is, not over-subtly, justifying his earlier erotic-didactic poetry. Just as the various genres have their own metres, so they also are restricted in the characters they present. For the *libertinae* and *meretrices* who (supposedly) form his audience, Ovid claims, and bearing in mind the nature of his poetry, Thais is a proper and legitimate subject for study. In other words, the only criterion is to be one of *literary* propriety (387–8).

As we have seen (Introd. pp. 70ff., and *AA* 3.611–16, pp. 397–8), all this is specious eyewash. Whatever he may have claimed, Ovid was in fact aiming at a readership of upper-class Roman matrons (cf. *Am.* 1.4, with my introductory note, pp. 271–2); and in any case the social availability of married freedwomen was not quite what he would have us believe. The whole passage is tinged with that bright unreality, at once sophisticated and naïve, which cannot properly distinguish between literature and life, a failure liable (in Ovid's case as in Oscar Wilde's) to have tragic consequences.

399–440 After this digression, Ovid returns to the study of aversion techniques. Four specific recommendations are offered. While they conform, in general terms, to his advice (made on the basis of personal experience) at 315 – that is, 'concentrate on your mistress's bad points' – they are all associated with the sexual act. Ovid clearly believed in the paradoxical principle of *sauter pour mieux reculer*. The student anxious to rid himself of an unwelcome passion should (i) make love to another girl first: this will take the edge off his desire (401–4); (ii) choose an uncomfortable and indecorous position for intercourse (women, he adds, are so conceited that they think *any* posture flatters them: 407–10); (ii) open the windows and perform in broad daylight (411–12); (iv) immediately after orgasm, when a lover's mood is, or should be, one of satiated disgust, scrutinize all his mistress's physical blemishes with particular care (413–18). Other things, he adds, can turn some men off – the sight of the girl's private parts prior to climax (429–30), or tell-tale stains on the bedsheet afterwards (431–2) – but no one affected by such trifles can count himself seriously in love (433–6). It is also possible to try shock-aversion, e.g. by secretly watching your mistress defecate (437–8), a notion that would have appealed to Swift; Ovid concedes that such tactics may work, but blushes to recommend them (439–40).

441–88 Ovid now turns to his main recommendation for getting an overmastering passion out of one's system – the acquisition of a second mistress to dilute the impact of the first, redemption from fire by fire. In the *Amores* (2.10) Ovid himself claimed at one point to be enamoured of two girls simultaneously, and to find it an enjoyable, if exhausting, experience: there are deliberate echoes of this poem in the present passage.

The image of fishing (448) as a metaphor for the pursuit of love is perennial ('as many good fish in the sea as ever came out of it', etc.), and picked up at the end of this section with the charming conceit (488) of a boat loaded down with hooked girls: cf. also *AA* 1.48, 393, 763; 3.425. At 449–50, as at *AA* 2.539–40, Ovid applies the image of a triumphant consul on the Capitol to a lover; there, to one who puts up with a rival, here, to one who takes two mistresses. Whether either reference has political colouring is hard to determine: perhaps it is merely an example of a metaphor appropriate to 'erotic warfare' (*militia amoris*: cf. *Am.* 1.7.35ff.).

We have already met Cephalus' eccentric wife Procris (see *AA* 3.687ff. and my note, pp. 399ff): her affair with Minos was, to say the least, *outré*. She fled to him in Crete after being caught by her husband in an adulterous relationship. Minos, eager to seduce her (and clearly convinced that on her track-record she would be an easy conquest), gave her a hunting-dog, Laelaps, that caught whatever it pursued, and a magical javelin that never missed its mark. Procris, presumably, was left to infer that the donor himself would prove equally irresistible.

On Phineus (454) see *AA* 1.339 and *RA* 355, with my notes, pp. 349 and 411. His first wife, Cleopatra, bore him two sons, Plexippus and Pandion: his second, Idaea, the traditional wicked stepmother, accused the boys of attempting her seduction. For the family background of Alcmaeon (455–6) see *Am.* 1.10.51–2, and my note, p. 282. After the capture of Thebes, Alcmaeon killed his mother Eriphyle for her treachery, went temporarily mad (being hounded, like Orestes in similar circumstances, by the Furies), was purified by Phegeus at Psophis, and married Phegeus' daughter Alphesiboea or Arsinoë. After a further purification by the river-god Acheloüs, Alcmaeon transferred his affections to the god's daughter Callirhoë ('Beautiful Stream'), and was subsequently murdered by his first father-in-law's servants. Ovid's account suggests, without quite saying so, that Alcmaeon had both girls in the same bed at once: I have tried to catch this innuendo in my translation. Oenone, the nymph of Mt Ida (today perhaps best known from Tennyson's poem of that name) was married to Paris, who deserted her for Helen. She also had the gift of prophecy, and not only warned Paris against Helen, but also knew that if he was ever wounded only she herself could heal him. When Paris was shot by Philoctetes he appealed to Oenone for help; in her bitterness she refused. He died, and Oenone then hanged herself out of remorse. For the story of Tereus, Procne and Philomela see my note on *Am.* 2.6.7–10, p. 295.

The final and longest example admirably demonstrates Ovid's penchant for trivializing and ridiculing myth. It is also, strictly considered, irrelevant to the main point being made, since Agamemnon hardly demanded Achilles' prize in order to cure his own hopeless passion for Chryses' daughter, but rather to satisfy his own touchy pride, what a modern Greek would call his *philótimo*. Ovid uses the incident to justify his erotic strategy (if Agamemnon can legitimately steal another man's girl, a mythic precedent has been established), and also exploits it, with some skill, for its inherent low comedy: the *mise-en-scène*, as he presents it, resembles something by Menander.

Ovid's attitude to the distress of Chryses (Hom. *Il.* 1.12.ff.) is pragmatic and derisive: if his daughter was lucky enough to catch the eye of the C-in-C, so much the better for both of them (469–72). For Thersites (482) see my note on *Am.* 2.6.39–42, p. 296. The paradoxical quality of Ovid's advice, in a poem supposedly devoted to *curing* passion, is crystallized at 487–8, where – anxious to help students seeking substitute mistresses – the *praeceptor amoris* not only slips in a plug for the *Ars*, but visualizes his reader sailing harbourwards with a whole trawl of girls as a result of reading it.

489–522 From this point forward, Ovid's dependence upon the reversal or re-interpretation of his own earlier *praecepta* increases (cf. below, 577–8), while the influence of external sources such as Lucretius is less evident. With a polite nod to Apollo (whose support and inspiration he had evoked at 75–8, and whose own *praecepta* immediately precede a passage, *AA* 2.515ff., that Ovid is about to stand on its head), our erotic deprogrammer offers his next piece of practical psychological advice. Feign indifference even if indifferent is the last thing you feel; play it cool, be elusive (491ff.). This has at least two advantages: (i) if you fake an emotion persistently enough, it will very often become genuine (497ff.); (ii) such tactics (511–12) will very soon make your mistress abandon her own high-and-mighty ways. The basic notion promoted here is adapted from *AA* 1.611ff., where a suitor is advised to affect passion even though he may not feel it, with the parallel assurance (615–16) that he will probably end up genuinely in love as a result.

But it has a further calculated effect: it undercuts the whole artificial structure of *servitium amoris*, the lover as abject and devoted slave. At *AA* 2.515–34 Ovid advised the desperate lover to suffer all insults, blows included, with patience, to spend uncomfortable nights outside his loved one's door, to go through each demeaning hoop traditionally required of the *exclusus amator*. Here, however, he not only takes a diametrically opposite line (505ff.) but makes it very clear (511–12) that by calling the lady's bluff and ignoring her gambits (517–22) a prospective lover can in fact make her a great deal more malleable. *Don't* lie outside her door, he says now; ignore her, break dates, look incorrigibly cheerful, play hard to get. By modern standards (and I find it hard to believe that the same notion had not occurred to Ovid) these are far more effective techniques for taming a mistress than for alienating or discarding her. Ovid would probably argue that, by applying such techniques, the lover saddled with an obdurate mistress had a double option. If they did not soften up the lady (which they well might) at least they would help to get her victims off the hook.

For Ovid's careful avoidance of excessive social drinking (499) and its possible motivation, cf. *AA* 1.565ff. and 3.761ff., with my notes, pp. 356 and 402. There may well be a subtle, and typically Ovidian, joke implied here. One good reason not to drink too much at a dinner-party was, clearly, to keep an eye on your partner's behaviour: at *Am.* 1.4.51–4 Ovid instructs his mistress to ply her husband with wine in the hope of making him pass out over the fruit and nuts. Better still, at *Am.* 2.5.13–32 he describes what he saw going on between his girl and another man while he was *pretending to be asleep*. Surely we are meant to recall that scene here, and laugh at the thought of Ovid setting up a trap – only to nod off in the middle of it? 'I've laughed at the dupe –' he goes on (*deceptum risi*), and so does his audience.

523–42 'Could anyone', Ovid inquires, 'call my precepts too tough?' (523): clearly a rhetorical question, since at line 225 he had already predicted that indeed some people would do just that. For them, he offers another solution: aversion through systematic over-indulgence, killing the cat by drowning it in cream (531ff.). The notion of every pleasure having its point of satiety (*taedium*, κόρος), beyond which it aroused only disgust, was as old as Homer, who instanced sleep and love-making. The immediate sources (both strongly indicative of Ovid's attitude to amatory pursuits in general) are *Am.* 2.19 (see esp. lines 3–4, 25ff.) and 3.4 (esp. 17–18, 25–6: for a detailed analysis see my introductory note to 3.4, pp. 315–16), where the thesis is maintained that erotic interest gains edge from frustration, is dissipated by satiety.

543–78 The love nurtured by diffidence (543–6) refers back to several earlier passages: *AA* 2.445, where the lover is advised to keep his mistress fearful and uncertain; *AA* 3.593ff., where similar advice is given, *mutatis mutandis*, to a mistress; and *AA* 3.579–80, which illuminates the connection between this passage and Ovid's previous argument by suggesting that such uncertainty is desirable in order to avoid boredom in a lover. Ovid once again reverses his own earlier precept: anxiety and jealousy, he reminds us, are not the best instruments for the exorcism of passion. Just as a loving mother worries most (547–8) over a son on active service, so an anxious lover will fret obsessionally over possible infidelities (cf. *Am.* 3.14). Ovid's advice, therefore (543), is: 'Rid yourself of fear.' But how? The introduction of Lethaean Love in a dream-epiphany suggests healing oblivion; but this oblivion is not achieved by a miraculous drink. Instead, Ovid (preferring, as always, psychology to magic) recommends keeping the mind busy with other worries in order to crowd out any thought of love.

The temple of Venus Erycina near the Colline Gate (549–50) was a copy of the famous shrine on Mt Eryx in Sicily (for which cf. my note on *Am.* 3.9.45, p. 327): though it did not offer the latter's notorious temple-prostitutes (*hierodouloi*), it seems to have been, like so many foreign shrines (cf. *AA* 1.75–8, and my note, p. 341), an unofficial rendezvous for street-walkers, amateur tarts and young men on the make. Built as early as 181 BC, it was the scene of annual festivals on 23 April (the Vinalia, Ovid *Fast.* 4.871) and 24 October. The 'Lethaean Love' was a statue of Eros. The text makes clear that this figure was attached to a fountain, probably in the large temple-portico, and spouted water, with symbolic appropriateness, on to its own torch. It seems safe to apply a modern, though traditional, analogy, and infer that young people were in the habit of throwing a coin in the fountain-basin, and praying for relief from troubles of the heart (553–4).

579–608 If leisure (*otium*) is to be avoided, then so, *a fortiori*, is solitude. Our modern assumptions on this topic differ radically from those of the ancient world. In certain circumstances we value solitude highly, whereas Mediterranean man did – and does – both fear and detest it. Thus we may have trouble in realizing that Ovid is here simply polishing up a familiar social cliché. An ancient lover, however, *was* thought of as being prone – among other lunacies – to solitary moping, of a noisy and complaining sort, especially at night. This, of course, reinforced the widespread belief that love was a form of insanity, since anyone who shunned human contact in this way had by definition to be off his head, and might well do himself, if not his neighbours, serious mischief. Hence, in this context, the cautionary tale of Phyllis and Demophöon.

As we have already had occasion to note (*Am.* 2.18.22, *AA* 2.353–4, 3.37–8, 459–60, *Her.* 2, *passim*, with my notes ad loc.), Ovid had an obsessional concern with this story of desertion and transformation. The myth was popular in antiquity. It is curious that Ovid did *not* use it where we might have expected him to, i.e. in the *Metamorphoses*. After Phyllis hanged herself she was turned into a leafless almond-tree, and when the remorseful Demophöon returned and embraced its trunk, it promptly burst into leaf. After her suicide, trees took root in her grave, and when their leaves withered and fell they were said to be mourning her: the myth clearly looks back to some sort of primitive vegetation ceremony. For the friendship between Orestes and Pylades (589) cf. my note on *AA* 1.745, p. 361. Ovid's use of this example in such a context is, of course, a deadpan black joke. He is discussing cures for love: what, we ask ourselves, did Pylades do to help Orestes in this respect? That famous isolated outburst in Aeschylus' *Choephori* (900–903) gives the answer: he rallied his friend's faltering determination to kill Clytemnestra. Thus, in the example chosen, what we are considering is *mother*-love, and the cure turns out to be matricide! Such friends we should all have. It may well be that Phyllis would not have committed suicide with a faithful attendant there to dissuade her; but where was Pylades when Orestes fled from the Furies?

609–42 At this point Ovid begins the third, and last, main section of his 'Cures for Love', that dealing with the various dangers of relapse after an initial separation.

The medical analogy of contagion offers him considerable scope for metaphorical precept: if love is a disease, then contact with lovers must be avoided, and the 'patient' placed in a species of erotic quarantine. (Ovid enhances realism by giving what purport to be two 'case-histories' at this point.)

643–82 Ovid now offers four pieces of purely psychological or situational advice, of which the first, strictly considered, does not fall in the category of 'cures for love' at all: (i) Avoid over-protestation; better to keep quiet, since the man who insists he is not in love generally is (643–8); (ii) Phase out your passion gradually: dramatic ruptures are undesirable (649–54); (iii) Don't part in hatred: this is not only personally obnoxious, but implies (*exemplum* attached) that you are still really in love (655–72); (iv) If circumstances beyond your control bring you into her company, *then* is the time to use all the lessons you have been taught, and treat her as merely another casual acquaintance (673–82). In so far as the medical analogy still applies, Ovid is dealing with a rather shaky convalescent in danger of relapse. We may note, too, the increasing prevalence of psychological analysis at the expense of concrete illustration. Much of the psychology is sound: in particular, Ovid was well aware of the dangers inherent in what we have learnt to describe as a love–hate relationship, the Catullan *odi et amo* (85): cf. *Am.* 3.11B *passim*, which exemplifies, very strikingly, the

close interrelationship between violence and passion. Studied indiffer-
ence, in other words, offers a far better guarantee of erotic immunity
than does fierce rejection, itself too often no more than passion-in-
reverse; and whereas such rejection normally represents a sudden
change of front, indifference must be worked for, calmly and un-
emotionally, over a long period.

'Venus of the Law-Courts' (660) was, appropriately enough in this
context, Venus Genetrix, whose temple, with the Appian Fountain in
front of it, faced the Forum Iulii, where public litigation took place:
see *AA* 1.81. The reference to Penthesilea, slain by Achilles at Troy
(676), reminds us that Ovid had earlier (*AA* 2.743-4, 3.1-2) used the
Amazons and their queen – revealingly – to represent women generally
in the battle of the sexes. There are ironic undertones here, since in the
act of spearing Penthesilea to death Achilles conceived a violent passion
for her.

683-98 What, Ovid asks, are the main hazards working against
speedy emotional disentanglement? First, hopeful self-conceit on the
part of the men (685-6): they, like their female counterparts
(*AA* 1.613-14), cannot believe themselves unattractive. The psych-
ology, if simple, is shrewd. Second, the range of devious and deceitful
tricks women can deploy to win back reluctant lovers (687ff.), against
which silence, rather than counter-argument (which can often, 697-8,
prove counter-productive), is at times the only effective weapon.
Ovid's remarks about separation (693ff.) should be read with his pre-
vious example of the young husband bent on prosecuting his wife
(663ff.) closely in mind. We should note that though the term *divor-
tium* (693) can sometimes be used to indicate a separation in the general
sense, more often it carries the specific connotation of legal divorce,
and it looks very much as though this is what Ovid has in mind here.
The advice contained in lines 693-8 is shrewd: it could well be given
by any worldly-wise solicitor today. If you want to avoid a relapse into
infatuation, Ovid says in effect, you must not only ignore the lady's
persuasive attempts at reconciliation but also avoid spelling out your
own attitude, since she will simply use your arguments to improve her
own (revised) case – and then convert you to it.

707-24 After a brief digression, Ovid returns to his list of do's and
don't's for the man who has managed an initial break with his mis-
tress, but remains emotionally vulnerable. Make detailed compari-
sons, he advises, between your ex-lover and a few really stunning
fashion-plate models (707-14: once again we note the assumption –

cf. *AA* 3.261ff. – that Ovid's readers do not, by definition, pick really attractive women), and you will soon find her an embarrassment – unless, of course (714, a typically Ovidian touch), you allow love to warp your judgement. Don't read her old letters: better to burn them (715–22). Get rid of all portraits (723–4). The advice, if commonplace, is sound. Amyclae (707) was a village near Sparta, on the banks of the Eurotas, where the festival of the Hyacinthia took place, and widely celebrated for its purple-dye industry: the murex shellfish, from which the dye was extracted, flourished (then as now) off the shores of Laconia.

The letters that Ovid tells his reader to burn (715–22) are, of course, those that he earlier advised the ladies to write (*AA* 3.469ff., with my note, p. 395). Despite his strictures against magic (*AA* 2.99ff., with my note, pp. 366–7), Ovid seems here (719–20) to hint at a recognizable spell (ritual accompanied by formulaic phrase), operating on the sympathetic principle of *similia pro similibus*, and designed to burn away passion, as though it were a corpse on the funeral pyre, by consigning to the flames the love-letters in which that passion had been expressed. Althaea, daughter of Thestius, King of Aetolia, had, by Oeneus, a son, Meleager. When the boy was seven days old the Fates declared that as soon as the log burning on Althaea's hearth was finally consumed Meleager would die. Althaea at once removed the log from the fire and put it away for safety in a chest. Later, when Meleager was a grown man, he quarrelled with his mother's brothers after the hunting of the Caledonian boar (they resented his giving the skin to Atalanta), and slew them in a rage, at which Althaea put the log back in the fire, and Meleager in due course died. The myth is based on sympathetic magic of an unmistakable sort, and is precisely analogous to the recommendation that Ovid has just made. For Laodameia's marriage cf. my note on *Am*. 2.18.38, pp. 308–9, and also Ovid *Her*. 13.149ff. After the death of her husband Protesilaus at Troy, she had intercourse with a waxen effigy of him, till her father, discovering what she was about, had the image burnt, whereupon Laodameia, in a rather *outré* form of suttee, cast herself upon the bonfire, and so perished.

725–40   The unusually dense and varied imagery in this sequence – some of the best poetry Ovid ever wrote – conveys a sense of strong emotional pressure. Ovid knows, all too well, how delicate the scar-tissue on a cicatrized love-affair is liable to be, and just what nostalgic associations can reopen the wound (725–30). Besides this major metaphor he employs two others: the smouldering fire (731–4) and the perilous sea-journey (734–40). No other Roman poet, not even Propertius, dwells in quite this way on the psychological effect of background memories, the touchstones of recollected happiness. For earlier instances in Ovid himself see, e.g., *Her.* 10.51–8, 13.137–46. (We may note, incidentally, that each example concentrates, to the exclusion of all else, whether in boudoir or forest glade, on sexual intercourse: Ovid's sense of place is highly selective, and picks appropriate objects to express its associations: an unmade bed, a heap of dried leaves.)

The obscure allusion at 735–6 refers to the revenge taken by Nauplius for the rigged execution of his son Palamedes at Troy. Palamedes was the man who exposed Odysseus' feigned madness, and forced him to join the Trojan Expedition; by way of revenge Odysseus later fabricated evidence that got Palamedes condemned to death as a traitor. Nauplius, after failing to obtain satisfaction from Agamemnon, not only encouraged all the Greek leaders' wives to cuckold their absent husbands (just how, we are not told), but set false lights on Mt Caphareus, a dangerous rocky promontory in south-east Euboea, so that the returning Greek fleet stood in for the shore at night, supposing the lights to mark a harbour, and suffered heavy losses through shipwreck. For Scylla and Charybdis see my note on *Am.* 3.12.21, p. 332. It is symbolically appropriate that the sailing metaphor which throughout the *AA* and the *RA* has designated the lover's progress (or regress) – see, e.g., *AA* 2.9–10, 427–34, 3.99–100; *RA* 119–22, 577–8 – should here be closely linked to the voyages of Odysseus, great lover as well as great wanderer, who not only took on nymphs and goddesses (Calypso, Circe), but successfully ditched them when they became over-importunate or he had other calls on his time (cf. also 789–90 below). The quicksands of 739 are the Syrtes, for which see my note on *Am.* 2.11.18–20, p. 300; the 'perilous headland' is the proverbially storm-ridden Acroceraunian promontory in north Epirus, a by-word for dangerous navigation.

741–50 What Ovid has in mind is upper-class adultery, a notoriously expensive occupation. The gold-digging habits of the kept mistress form a recurrent leitmotiv in these poems, as we have seen (*Am.* 1.10, *AA* 1.419ff., 2.275ff., etc.): 'wealth', Ovid says, 'fosters wanton love' (746). Here he also returns, by implication, to another favourite theme of his: leisure (*otium*), that essential ingredient of cultivated seduction (see above, 135ff., with my note, p. 406). Promiscuity, in fact, requires both time and money. There is also a clear hint, conveyed in the choice of Phaedra and Pasiphaë as *exempla* (743-6), that the gratification of *outré* or perverse passions likewise tends to be the prerogative of the wealthy and leisured – a thesis for which some support could be found today in the jet-set world of Rome or California. To complete his sociological digression, Ovid picks (747-8) two contrasting mythological figures – the virtuous Hecale, the loud-mouthed beggar Irus – who have nothing in common save poverty, but, because of this, fail to attract willing partners in either love or (Ovid clearly implies) marriage. The paradoxical conclusion is clear: though lack of money remains *per se* a dismal condition, and one which no sane man could advocate (750), it does nevertheless constitute a remarkable amatory prophylactic.

Phaedra, the wife of Theseus, conceived a disastrous and unrequited passion for her aggressively chaste stepson Hippolytus: cf. my notes on *Am.* 2.4.32, p. 293, and *AA* 1.338, p. 349. On being rejected by him, she told Theseus that he had attempted to rape her. Theseus, believing her, prayed to Poseidon (Neptune), who, according to some sources, was his father, to destroy Hippolytus. Poseidon sent a bull from the sea that panicked the boy's horses, overturned his chariot and thus caused him injuries from which he afterwards died. Ovid's emphasis on the idea of Neptune as Hippolytus' 'grand-daddy' exactly epitomizes his trivializing and ridiculing of myth. At 744 Ovid does not name Pasiphaë; he merely refers to the 'woman of Cnossos' (*Cnosida*) – who, of course, could equally well be Ariadne: the term undoubtedly refers to Ariadne at *AA* 1.527 (cf. 556) and *Her.* 15.25. But what is being described here are cases of *perverse* rather than merely unfortunate passion; and though Ariadne was deserted by Theseus, her affection for him seems to have been all too conventional. It is Pasiphaë, with her dark taurine appetites, who fits the present context to perfection (for Ovid's obsession with this myth see *AA* 1.289ff. and my note, p. 348); in fact we have already found her bracketed with Phaedra, as a joint illustration of unruly and exotic passion, earlier in the *RA* (lines 63-4). For the Homeric beggar Irus see *Od.* 18.1-116. Hecale (747) was an old woman who lived alone in a hut near Marathon, where she gave Theseus shelter.

751-66 Entertainments recommended in the *AA* as conducive to seduction or generally erotic in atmosphere are here listed, conversely, as danger-areas to avoid: (a) the theatre; (b) singing, dancing and the playing of musical instruments; (c) love-poetry. It is clear from the context that what Ovid has in mind at lines 753–6 is the immensely popular Roman ballet (*pantomimus*). 'Flutes, zithers and lyres' (752–3) formed the normal accompaniment to such performances. Like an Indian dancer such as Ram Gopal, performers in a Roman *pantomimus* would 'talk with their hands' and eloquently mime anything from the intercourse of Venus and Mars to Cronos eating his children. Ovid's own amatory poems were thus presented in the guise of ballets, and Augustus himself attended their performance (*Tr.* 2.519–20). There is a sexual double-entendre in 'shake your nerve' (*enervant*): *nervus* frequently = 'penis'.

The list of proscribed love-poets (757–66) coincides almost exactly with that recommended at *AA* 3.329–46 as suitable reading material for young ladies who aim to charm. Common to both, and in much the same order, are (a) Callimachus (759 = 329), (b) Philetas (760 = 329), (c) Sappho (761 = 331), (d) Anacreon (762 = 330), (e) Tibullus (763 = 334), (f) Propertius (764 = 333), (g) Gallus (765 = 334), (h) Ovid himself (776 = 339). The casual, almost throwaway, reference to his own work (766) is in striking contrast to Ovid's sedulous self-promotion at *AA* 3.339–48 (cf. my note, pp. 390–91) and elsewhere.

767–84 The point made here, that very often passion is only aroused by another man setting about one's present wife or prospective mistress, has already been hammered home to Ovid's readers a dozen times. Indeed, such associative references increase in density as the narrative develops. There is a structural and thematic neatness about these numerous echoes-in-reverse towards the close of the poem: in my end is my beginning. The effect is subtly enhanced by the mythical illustrations chosen, since these all look back to Ovid's earlier *Letters of Heroines* (*Heroides*): in *Her.* 8 Hermione writes to Orestes, Helen and Paris exchange letters in *Her.* 16–17, while Briseis makes her appeal to Achilles (sounding exactly like a ditched foreign *au pair* girl) in *Her.* 3. The closing mood is nostalgic and retrospective – appropriately enough, since after so many half-hearted attempts to change his poetic genre, Ovid was now, at last, on the point of breaking away from love-elegy for ever.

Hermione (771–2) was the daughter of Helen and Menelaus. While Menelaus was at Troy, her grandfather Tyndareus betrothed and married her to Agamemnon's son Orestes. Menelaus, in ignorance of this, meanwhile promised her to Achilles' son Neoptolemus. After the war Neoptolemus therefore took her from Orestes by force, though she was pregnant at the time. Neoptolemus was afterwards slain at Delphi either by Orestes himself or else by a Delphian accomplice of his. Menelaus (773–4), after entertaining Paris at Sparta, had to leave for Crete to attend a funeral (cf. my note on *AA* 2.357ff., p. 374).

Ovid picks up Agamemnon's quarrel with Achilles over Briseis from lines 467–86 above: besides being familiar from Homer, the story was popular with Roman elegists and a favourite of Ovid's (*Am.* 1.9.33, 2.8.11, *Her.* 3 *passim*, *AA* 2.403, 713, 3.189). Because of this, the variations on it here are intriguing. Everyone knew that Agamemnon swore he had left the girl *virgo intacta*; Ovid, however, cheerfully assumes, judging by his own credo concerning lovers' oaths (see *AA* 1.631ff., with my note, p. 358), that on this occasion Agamemnon perjured himself (779–84), and would, indeed, have been something less than a man (780) had he failed to seduce Briseis once he had her at his disposal.

Besides offering a nice instance of that trivialization of mythic dignity which we have already more than once noted, not to mention securing a rare personal assertion from the narrator that this is how *he* would have behaved in similar circumstances (781), the passage shows us just how far Ovid would go to work in a sexual double entendre. In Homer Agamemnon does *not* swear by his 'truncheon' or sceptre (783–4), but by Zeus, Earth, the Sun and the Furies (*Il.* 19.26off.). The person who *does* so swear is Achilles, in Bk 1 (233–44), when withdrawing his services from the Achaean army.

785–94 The desire for an enjoyable double entendre likewise explains the reintroduction of the rival at this point. The whole passage, in fact, is riddled with similar sexual teasing. The mistress's 'threshold' (786) refers to more than her house-door, while the 'grotto' (*antro*, 789) where her ex-lover is invited to picture the temptations besetting Odysseus bears, at one level, a close resemblance to Scylla's womb with its chorus of yelping hounds. To make sure we do not miss the point, Ovid's imagery, of spurred horse and well-plied oar, deployed here when instructing his pupils to *hurry past* these danger-areas, is directly borrowed from a context (*AA* 2.725–6, 731–2) in which it refers to techniques for achieving satisfactory simultaneous orgasm. The irony of reversal here reaches its anticlimactic climax.

795–810 Ancient medical theory placed great emphasis on dietetics (see, e.g., the four books *On Regimen* in the Hippocratic Corpus), and

Ovid perhaps felt obliged, when discussing cures for love, to make at least a gesture in this direction (795–6).

The advantages and hazards of intoxicating liquor are frequently mentioned in the amatory poems. With exemplary logic, Ovid therefore recommends, to those shunning renewed erotic entanglement, either total abstinence, or else getting blind drunk (809–10): anything between these two extremes is dangerous. Again, we find conscious verbal echoes (*AA* 1.237; *RA* 805) of earlier positive precepts, but there is no hint of a formal climax to the poem. As has often been remarked, there is a logically disjunctive quality to the presentation of ideas from line 642 onwards: themes are stated (750ff.), dropped (766), then resumed (795ff.) after an apparent digression (767–94). How far this is due to deliberate retrospective evocation, and how far to Ovid utilizing surplus material left over from earlier sections, cannot now be determined with any confidence. But one does get the impression (as with Juvenal's huge sixth satire) that Ovid at this point was out of fuel, knew he had, quantitatively speaking, written enough, and therefore simply stopped.

811–14 The envoi or coda to the *RA* (811–14) is generically akin to those concluding *AA* 2 (741–4) and *AA* 3 (809–12): perhaps, *inter alia*, an indication that Ovid originally planned the *AA* in two books only (cf. my note on *AA* 2.733ff., p. 381), since *AA* 1 ends with a two-line link-passage (771–2). Both *AA* 3 and the *RA* will then have been added successively, the poet being convinced on each occasion – but only the second time with justification – that this was positively his last word on the subject. As befits a valediction, not only to the present group of poems, but to the whole erotic genre, each phrase carries its full weight. 'My work is concluded' (811) he announces (as he had already done, prematurely, but with less significance, at *AA* 2.733 and 3.810). The image of the poem as a voyage of erotic-didactic exploration – for the *praeceptor* as for his audience – reaches its conclusion here with the poet's vessel safely entering harbour. Grateful readers will make their ex-voto offerings (could this be a polite bid for a *pourboire*?) to 'the inspired poet' (813). The fruit of that divine inspiration is the spell, the *carmen* (814), the poetry in which true magic (as opposed to false hocus-pocus) resides. Finally, the word 'healed' (*sanati*) recalls the extended metaphor in this poem of Ovid-as-physician, whose gifts are available to men and women alike (814).

ON FACIAL TREATMENT FOR LADIES

1–50   At *AA* 3.205–8 (see p. 220) we find a clear reference to the prior existence of this little pseudo-didactic poem, which Ovid mined to some purpose when composing the *AA*. What we have here is certainly not the whole poem. Indeed, the size of the extant sequence – one hundred lines precisely, with a sharp break in sense and style after line 50 – strongly suggests two loose non-consecutive double leaves, each with twenty-five lines to the page, from a MS. that once contained substantially more – though just how much more it is now impossible to determine. In several MSS. the fragment is reproduced among the minor poems (*Nux, Ibis* or *Somnium* [=*Am.* 3.5]), which seems a fair judgement. Its main interest today lies in its sketching of several themes that recur, more fully developed, as integral elements of the *AA*, most notably in Bk 3. This applies more particularly to lines 1–50.

For Ovid's promotion of *cultus*, cultivation – and his deliberate playing on the word's double meaning when applying it to women – see my note on *AA* 3.101–32, pp. 385–6. The specific recommendation to care for facial beauty is picked up from 105–6, cf. 199ff., and the metaphorical reinforcement of the image from orchard-farming and tree-grafts (*MF* 5–6) recalls *AA* 2.649ff. and *RA* 195ff. The superior sneer at rude female simplicity in the early Republic (*MF* 11–16) is familiar not only from the *AA* (3.107ff.) but also from the *Amores* (1.8.39ff.). Yet here we become aware of a different attitude. At *AA* 3.123–8 Ovid emphasizes that his preference for the contemporary world over those simple far-off days does *not* stem from the vast increase in affluence and luxury, but rather from the advent of *cultus* – elegance and sophistication. Here, however (*MF* 17ff.), no such distinction is made: Ovid positively revels in the jewellery, rich dresses and elaborate coiffures (something he was afterwards to condemn in no uncertain terms, *AA* 3.129ff., 169–72), and justifies them (23–6) by the curious excuse that nowadays husbands are more elegantly turned out than their wives, a joke with distinctly homosexual overtones (cf. *Am.* 1.8.66–7, *AA* 1.505–8, 3.433ff., with my note, p. 394). He begins, as so often, from a popular truism: girls are narcissists all, whose main aim is to please themselves rather than other people (31ff.), so that both their natural beauty and their artificial adornment are judged, finally, in the mirror. From this follow two obvious corollaries: (a) delight in one's own beauty will thrive only on extravagant compliments, just as the peacock (33–4) refuses to spread its plumage unless praised (for this belief see *AA* 1.627–8, cf. *Am.* 2.6.55–6), and (b) such natural methods of attracting courtship are far more effective, and desirable, than messing around with spells or aphrodisiacs (35–42). This flat statement by Ovid of disbelief in magic (37ff.), reinforced with a string of negatives (*nec ... nec ... nec ... nec ... nunquam*), is stronger and more uncompromising than any of his other pronouncements on the subject.

51–100 The second surviving fragment of *MF* is devoted to five detailed recipes for facial beauty-treatment, of which the last remains incomplete: (i) 53–66, a face-pack guaranteed to produce a bright complexion – the ingredients are face-cleaners; (ii) 69–76, not a face-pack but a cleansing aid designed for general application to the body, and containing mineral ingredients; (iii) 77–82, one ingredient, *alcyaneum*, plus honey as a binder, designed to remove spots or freckles; (iv) another face-pack, but of different type, designed to cleanse the complexion and remove blemishes or wrinkles; (v) 99–100, the final, incomplete formula, which is equally therapeutic, poppy being used as a cure for skin eruptions.

It is impossible to conclude an investigation of these recipes without feeling considerable admiration for Ovid's practical knowledge and discrimination.* His judgement in such matters is anything but that of a mere *littérateur*. This is all the more striking when we reflect on the temptations involved. Just how perversely fantastic such formulas could be – and how credulous the literary mind that collected them – we know, all too well, from Pliny. The old polymath devoted one section of his *Natural History* (*HN* 30.28–30) to facial remedies and

---

* See Green (3) *passim*. Pliny's own claim (*HN* 30.33) that Ovid was his source for a prescription against quinsy that included goose-gall, owls' brains and ashes of burnt swallow is intrinsically implausible: where would Ovid have written up such a thing? It does not figure anywhere in the surviving works (which account for by far the greater part of Ovid's output), and, since it has nothing to do with the complexion, clearly would be out of place in the *MF*. Nor is it easy to imagine it finding a place in any of the known lost works, such as the poem on Tiberius' victories in Pannonia (*EP* 3.4, cf. 2.5.7) or any of the other commemorative minor verses listed by Owen at the end of his OCT text of the *Tristia* and *Epistulae ex Ponto*. The *Medea*. perhaps, as part of the eponymous heroine's *pharmacopoeia magica*? Hardly, when we recall that this was a tragody, which won high praise from both Quintilian (*Inst. Orat.* 10.1.98) and Tacitus (*Dial.* 12).

skin-cures. Among other substances he recommends for this purpose we find mouse-droppings, macerated ants, vulture's blood, and locusts' legs beaten up with goat-suet. Elsewhere (*HN* 28.185–6) he similarly recommends bull's dung, and a formula involving ass's urine taken at the rising of the Dog Star. He also states, as though it were the result of personal experiment, 'I find that a heavy cold clears up if the sufferer kisses a mule's muzzle' (*HN* 30.31). But Ovid will have no truck with this kind of hocus-pocus, and the implications are both intriguing and significant. It is not Ovid, but Pliny, who is revealed as the literary scholar incapable of looking beyond, or indeed evaluating, his source-material. Ovid, on the other hand, delivers the goods. At the beginning of the *Art of Love* (1.29) he was to write: *Usus opus movet hoc: vati parete perito* ('This work is based on experience: what I write, believe me, I have practised'). The *MF* formulas reinforce this claim in a solidly practical way, and should make us very cautious indeed about underestimating Ovid's respect, in literature, especially didactic literature (whether parodied or not), for the basic facts of life. The *praeceptor amoris* turns out to be well acquainted with the technicalities of the beauty-parlour; and this familiarity dates back to the period of the *Amores*. Ovid's anguish over Corinna's maltreatment of her hair (*Am.* 1.14, *passim*) clearly stems from a very modern knowledge of the damage that could be done by a harsh lye bleach. Our attitude to his didactic pose must be adjusted in the light of this expert knowledge. Why should a mere literary *jeu d'esprit* practise such nice cosmetic discrimination? And – a corollary that should give us much food for thought – if the *MF* was intended as serious practical advice, is it not possible that we have, similarly, underestimated the practical purpose of the *Art of Love*? The two causes of Ovid's exile, *carmen et error*, the poem and the blunder (*Tr.* 2.207) may, after all, be more closely linked than it is nowadays fashionable to assume.

SELECT READING LIST

Austin, R. G., 'Roman board games': I, *Greece and Rome* 4 (1934) 24
–34; II, ibid. (1935) 76–82

Balsdon, J.P.V.D. (1) *Life and Leisure in Ancient Rome*, London, 1969
(2) *Roman Women: Their History and Habits*, London, 1962; 4th
impr. rev. ed. 1974

Barsby, J. (ed.), *Ovid: Amores Book 1*, edited with translation and
running commentary, Oxford, 1973

Binns, J. W. (ed.), *Ovid*, London, 1973

Bornecque, H. (1) *Ovide: L'Art d'aimer*, ed. Budé, 2nd ed., Paris,
1960
(2) *Ovide: Les Remèdes à l'amour; Les Produits de beauté pour le visage
de la femme*, ed. Budé, 2nd ed., Paris, 1961
(3) *Ovide: Les Amours*, ed. Budé, 3rd ed., Paris, 1960

Carcopino, J., *Daily Life in Ancient Rome*, trs. E. O. Lorimer, New
Haven, 1940

Brandt, P. (1) *P. Ovidi Nasonis Amorum Libri Tres*, Leipzig, 1911.
(2) *P. Ovidi Nasonis de Arte Amatoria Libri Tres*, Leipzig, 1902

Fraenkel, H., *Ovid: A Poet between Two Worlds* (Sather Classical Lec-
tures, Vol. 18), Berkeley, 1945

Goold, G. P. 'Amatoria critica', *HSCPh* 69 (1965) 1–107

Green, P. (1) *Essays in Antiquity*, London, 1960, esp. Chs. vi and viii
(2) 'The flight-plan of Daedalus', *Echos du monde classique/Classical
News and Views* 23 (1979) 30–35
(3) '*Ars gratia cultus*: Ovid as beautician', *AJPh* 100 (1979) 381–92
(4) 'The innocence of Procris: Ovid *AA* 3.687–746', *CJ* 75 (1979/
80) 15–24

Henderson, A.A.R. (ed.), *P. Ovidi Nasonis Remedia Amoris*, edited
with introduction and commentary, Edinburgh, 1979

Higham, T. F. (1) 'Ovid and rhetoric', *Ovidiana*, pp. 32–48
(2) 'Ovid: Some aspects of his character and aims', *CR* 48 (1934)
105–16

SELECT READING LIST

Highet, G., *Poets in a Landscape*, London, 1957, esp. Ch. vi

Hollis, A. S., *Ovid: Ars Amatoria Book I*, edited with an introduction and commentary, Oxford, 1974

Kenney, E. J., *Amores, Medicamina Faciei Femineae, Ars Amatoria, Remedia Amoris*, Oxford, 1961, repr. with corrections 1965

Leach, E. W., 'Georgic imagery in the *Ars Amatoria*', TAPhA 95 (1964) 142–54

Lee, A. G. (1) '*Tenerorum lusor amorum*', *Critical Essays on Roman Literature: Elegy and Lyric*, London, 1962, pp. 149–79
(2) *Ovid's Amores*, London, 1968

Luck, G., *The Latin Love Elegy*, 2nd ed., London, 1969

Mozley, J. H., *Ovid: The Art of Love and Other Poems* (Loeb ed.), 2nd ed. rev. G. P. Goold, London, 1979

Otis, B., *Ovid as an Epic Poet*, Cambridge, 1966

Owen, S. G. (ed.) (1) *Ovid: Tristia Book I*, Oxford, 1890
(2) *P. Ovidi Nasonis Tristium Liber Secundus*, Oxford, 1924

Platner, S. B., and Ashby, T., *A Topological Dictionary of Ancient Rome*, Oxford, 1929

Quinn, K., *Latin Explorations*, London, 1963, esp. Ch. ix

Rand, E. K., *Ovid and His Influence*, New York, 1928

Rudd, N., 'Ovid and the Augustan myth', *Lines of Enquiry*, Cambridge, 1976, pp. 1–31

Showerman, G., *Ovid: Heroides and Amores* (Loet ed.), 2nd ed. rev. G. P. Goold, London, 1977

Syme, R. (1) *The Roman Revolution*, Oxford, 1939
(2) *History in Ovid*, Oxford, 1978

Tavenner, E., *Studies in Magic from Latin Literature*, New York, 1916

Thibault, J. C., *The Mystery of Ovid's Exile*, Berkeley, 1964

Wheeler, A. L., *Ovid: Tristia, Ex Ponto* (Loeb ed.), London, 1924

Wilkinson, L. P., *Ovid Recalled*, Cambridge, 1955

Williams, G., *Tradition and Originality in Roman Poetry*, Oxford, 1968

INDEX

Abortion, in Rome: 23–4, 127–9, 302–4

Abruzzi: 16, 305

Abydos: 306

Accius: 110, 288, 390

Achaeans: 213, 253

Achaemenids: 173

Achaeus: 319

Acheloüs, R.: 147, 149, 319–20, 414

Achilles: 102, 112, 121, 122, 133, 154, 166, 180, 187–8, 189, 195, 212, 213, 240, 250, 262, 280, 285, 290, 296, 297, 298, 303, 304, 307, 325, 338, 353, 360, 361, 363, 367, 380, 381, 393, 414, 419, 423–4

Acontius: 353–4

Acragas: 359

Acrisius: 309–10, 398

Acroceraunian Promontory: 421

Actium: 18, 35, 276, 301, 327, 344, 392

Admetus: 199, 214, 370, 382

Adonis: 155, 168, 182, 216, 325–6, 347, 355, 385

Adriatic: 48

Adultery, in Rome: 32, 33, 40, 70–71, 72, 98, 113–14, 143, 144, 146, 166–263 passim, 311–12, 337–403 passim, 421–2

Aeëtes: 333

Aegean: 300, 365

Aegialeus: 319

Aegisthus: 203, 243, 349, 374–5, 407

Aegyptus: 291

Aemilius Paulus, L.: 57, 58

Aeneas: 98, 129, 134, 155, 168, 215, 216, 276, 286, 301–2, 303, 304, 308, 320, 325, 327, 333, 340, 353, 363, 366, 383, 385, 405

Aeolus: 161, 308, 332

Aerope: 176, 348

Aeschylus: 374, 418

Aetolia: 147, 320, 420

Africa, African: 125, 127, 262, 293, 300

Agamemnon: 102, 121, 162, 176, 203, 253, 262, 290, 297, 301, 335, 349, 374–5, 382, 414, 421, 423–4

Agenor: 271

Agrippa, M. Vipsanius: 226, 270, 292, 340, 342, 344, 392

Agrippa Postumus, M. Vipsanius: 52, 55–6, 57, 345

Ajax: 95, 213, 217, 229, 275, 276, 297, 382, 386, 396

Alban Hills: 346

Alcestis: 214, 382

Alcinoüs: 104, 282

FOR THE BEST IN PAPERBACKS, LOOK FOR THE 🐧

In every corner of the world, on every subject under the sun, Penguin represents quality and variety – the very best in publishing today.

For complete information about books available from Penguin – including Puffins, Penguin Classics and Arkana – and how to order them, write to us at the appropriate address below. Please note that for copyright reasons the selection of books varies from country to country.

In the United Kingdom: Please write to *Dept JC, Penguin Books Ltd, FREEPOST, West Drayton, Middlesex, UB7 0BR.*

If you have any difficulty in obtaining a title, please send your order with the correct money, plus ten per cent for postage and packaging, to *PO Box No 11, West Drayton, Middlesex*

In the United States: Please write to *Dept BA, Penguin, 299 Murray Hill Parkway, East Rutherford, New Jersey 07073*

In Canada: Please write to *Penguin Books Canada Ltd, 2801 John Street, Markham, Ontario L3R 1B4*

In Australia: Please write to the *Marketing Department, Penguin Books Australia Ltd, P.O. Box 257, Ringwood, Victoria 3134*

In New Zealand: Please write to the *Marketing Department, Penguin Books (NZ) Ltd, Private Bag, Takapuna, Auckland 9*

In India: Please write to *Penguin Overseas Ltd, 706 Eros Apartments, 56 Nehru Place, New Delhi, 110019*

In the Netherlands: Please write to *Penguin Books Netherlands B.V., Postbus 3507, NL–1001 AH, Amsterdam*

In West Germany: Please write to *Penguin Books Ltd, Friedrichstrasse 10–12, D–6000 Frankfurt/Main 1*

In Spain: Please write to *Alhambra Longman S.A., Fernandez de la Hoz 9, E–28010 Madrid*

In Italy: Please write to *Penguin Italia s.r.l., Via Como 4, I-20096 Pioltello (Milano)*

In France: Please write to *Penguin France S.A., 17 rue Lejeune, F-31000 Toulouse*

In Japan: Please write to *Longman Penguin Japan Co Ltd, Yamaguchi Building, 2–12–9 Kanda Jimbocho, Chiyoda-Ku, Tokyo 101*

FOR THE BEST IN PAPERBACKS, LOOK FOR THE

With over 350 titles in print, Penguin is the leader in authoritative classics texts. From literature to philosophy, from poetry to plays and essays, all contain lucid, scholarly introductions, and many include notes and index material for easy reference.

If you would like a catalogue of the Penguin Classics library, please write to:

Penguin Marketing, 27 Wrights Lane, London W8 5TZ

(Available while stocks last)

Aeschylus	**The Oresteian Trilogy**
	(Agamemnon/The Choephori/The Eumenides)
	Prometheus Bound/The Suppliants/Seven
	Against Thebes/The Persians
Aesop	**Fables**
Ammianus Marcellinus	**The Later Roman Empire (AD 353–378)**
Apollonius of Rhodes	**The Voyage of Argo**
Apuleius	**The Golden Ass**
Aristophanes	**The Knights/Peace/The Birds/The Assembly**
	Women/Wealth
	Lysistrata/The Acharnians/The Clouds/
	The Wasps/The Poet and the Women/The Frogs
Aristotle	**The Athenian Constitution**
	The Ethics
	The Politics
	De Anima
Arrian	**The Campaigns of Alexander**
Saint Augustine	**City of God**
	Confessions
Boethius	**The Consolation of Philosophy**
Caesar	**The Civil War**
	The Conquest of Gaul
Catullus	**Poems**
Cicero	**The Murder Trials**
	The Nature of the Gods
	On the Good Life
	Selected Letters
	Selected Political Speeches
	Selected Works
Euripides	**Alcestis/Iphigenia in Tauris/Hippolytus**
	The Bacchae/Ion/The Women of Troy/Helen
	Medea/Hecabe/Electra/Heracles
	Orestes/The Children of Heracles/
	Andromache/The Suppliant Women/
	The Phoenician Women/Iphigenia in Aulis

FOR THE BEST IN PAPERBACKS, LOOK FOR THE 🐧

PENGUIN CLASSICS

Hesiod/Theognis	**Theogony** and **Works and Days/Elegies**
Hippocrates	**Hippocratic Writings**
Homer	**The Iliad**
	The Odyssey
Horace	**Complete Odes and Epodes**
Horace/Persius	**Satires** and **Epistles**
Juvenal	**Sixteen Satires**
Livy	**The Early History of Rome**
	Rome and Italy
	Rome and the Mediterranean
	The War with Hannibal
Lucretius	**On the Nature of the Universe**
Marcus Aurelius	**Meditations**
Martial	**Epigrams**
Ovid	**The Erotic Poems**
	Heroides
	The Metamorphoses
Pausanias	**Guide to Greece** (in two volumes)
Petronius/Seneca	**The Satyricon/The Apocolocyntosis**
Pindar	**The Odes**
Plato	**Early Socratic Dialogues**
	Gorgias
	The Last Days of Socrates (Euthyphro/ The Apology/Crito/Phaedo)
	The Laws
	Phaedrus and **Letters VII and VIII**
	Philebus
	Protagoras and **Meno**
	The Republic
	The Symposium
	Theaetetus
	Timaeus and Critias

FOR THE BEST IN PAPERBACKS, LOOK FOR THE 🐧

PENGUIN CLASSICS

FOR THE BEST IN PAPERBACKS, LOOK FOR THE 🐧

PENGUIN CLASSICS

ANTHOLOGIES AND ANONYMOUS WORKS

The Age of Bede
Alfred the Great
Beowulf
A Celtic Miscellany
The Cloud of Unknowing and Other Works
The Death of King Arthur
The Earliest English Poems
Early Christian Writings
Early Irish Myths and Sagas
Egil's Saga
King Arthur's Death
The Letters of Abelard and Heloise
Medieval English Verse
Njal's Saga
Seven Viking Romances
Sir Gawain and the Green Knight
The Song of Roland

FOR THE BEST IN PAPERBACKS, LOOK FOR THE

PENGUIN CLASSICS

The House of Ulloa Emilia Pardo Bazán

The finest achievement of one of European literature's most dynamic and controversial figures – ardent feminist, traveller, intellectual – and one of the great 19th century Spanish novels, *The House of Ulloa* traces the decline of the old aristocracy at the time of the Glorious Revolution of 1868, while exposing the moral vacuum of the new democracy.

The Republic Plato

The best-known of Plato's dialogues, *The Republic* is also one of the supreme masterpieces of Western philosophy whose influence cannot be overestimated.

The Life of Johnson James Boswell

Perhaps the finest 'life' ever written, Boswell's *Johnson* captures for all time one of the most colourful and talented figures in English literary history.

The Metamorphoses Ovid

A golden treasury of myths and legends which has proved a major influence on Western literature.

A Nietzsche Reader Friedrich Nietzsche

A superb selection from all the major works of one of the greatest thinkers and writers in world literature, translated into clear, modern English.

Madame Bovary Gustave Flaubert

With *Madame Bovary* Flaubert established the realistic novel in France; while his central character of Emma Bovary, the bored wife of a provincial doctor, remains one of the great creations of modern literature.

Netochka Nezvanova Fyodor Dostoyevsky

Dostoyevsky's first book tells the story of 'Nameless Nobody' and introduces many of the themes and issues which dominate his great masterpieces.

Selections from the Carmina Burana A verse translation by David Parlett

The famous songs from the *Carmina Burana* (made into an oratorio by Carl Orff) tell of lecherous monks and corrupt clerics, drinkers and gamblers, and the fleeting pleasures of youth.

Fear and Trembling Søren Kierkegaard

A profound meditation on the nature of faith and submission to God's will which examines with startling originality the story of Abraham and Isaac.

Selected Prose Charles Lamb

Lamb's famous essays (under the strange pseudonym of Elia) on anything and everything have long been celebrated for their apparently innocent charm; this major new edition allows readers to discover the darker and more interesting aspects of Lamb.

The Picture of Dorian Gray Oscar Wilde

Wilde's superb and macabre novella, one of his supreme works, is reprinted here with a masterly Introduction and valuable notes by Peter Ackroyd.

A Treatise of Human Nature David Hume

A universally acknowledged masterpiece by 'the greatest of all British Philosophers' – A. J. Ayer

FOR THE BEST IN PAPERBACKS, LOOK FOR THE 🐧

PENGUIN CLASSICS

Bashō	**The Narrow Road to the Deep North**
	On Love and Barley
Cao Xueqin	**The Story of the Stone** *also known as* **The**
	Dream of the Red Chamber (in five volumes)
Confucius	**The Analects**
Khayyam	**The Ruba'iyat of Omar Khayyam**
Lao Tzu	**Tao Te Ching**
Li Po/Tu Fu	**Li Po and Tu Fu**
Sei Shōnagon	**The Pillow Book of Sei Shōnagon**

ANTHOLOGIES AND ANONYMOUS WORKS

The Bhagavad Gita
Buddhist Scriptures
The Dhammapada
Hindu Myths
The Koran
New Songs from a Jade Terrace
The Rig Veda
Speaking of Śiva
Tales from the Thousand and One Nights
The Upanishads